[~THE IMPOSSIBLE MAN~]

Henry-Michael Brown

Published by Henry–Michael Brown in 2019

ISBN: 978-0-578-51650-9 (paperback)

Cover image: Original Artwork by Henry–Michael Brown © 2019

Para mis abuelas, Gloria y Olga…
Para mis abuelos, Raul y Miguel…
…con cariño, salud!

Henry–Michael Brown, 2019

First a shout out to the funniest comedy writers and actors I ever saw on film and read in books & manga: Masaki Kajishima & Hiroki Hayashi (*Tenchi Muyo!*), Rumiko Takahashi (*Ranma ½*), Ken Akamatsu (*Love Hina, Negima!*), Benny Hill (*The Benny Hill Show*), Douglas Adams (*Hitchhiker's Guide to the Galaxy*), the Zucker Bros. (*Airplane!, Top Secret!*). Finally, a very special shout out to Kōshi Rikudō (*Excel Saga*). Your show *Excel Saga* and the character Pedro were an inspiration to me.

Henry–Michael Brown, 2019

All is illogical...

...expect the impossible.

Episode 1

[~ The Employee, the Package, and the Oddity ~]

Anime...I love it. Collecting anime series on DVD is one of my favorite hobbies, next to collecting Japanese comics, or manga, and video games. I have a sizable collection of anime, in genres ranging from Romantic Comedy to Martial Arts to Magical Girl to Mecha and more. I guess that's why I started my own anime and manga shop on Grove Street in Little Edo, a simple Japanese district in the middle of Denfair City, New Jersey.

A new package is arriving today. The latest DVD release of *Endless Heart* is coming, and I have a lot of pre-orders to fulfill. It's going to be a great Monday. I can't wait to get started.

April 8, 2002

A sunny spring afternoon brought out all the citizens of Denfair City. Families on their day off strolled towards the parks, while tourists explored the wonders of the city, and all the stores starting from the intersections of Grove Street and Main Street—State Highway 51 outward opened for business as usual, including The Impossible Man's Anime and Manga Shop, or I-Man's for short, where an "Open for Business" sign, in English, Spanish, and Japanese, hung on the front door.

As a group of teenagers entered the shop, a nineteen-year-old woman stood outside the door, waiting for them to finish shopping. She had long, straight, jet-black hair, and was dressed in a long-sleeve shirt with the store's logo on it, featuring a green perched frog with its tongue sticking out and a navy blue colored letter 'I' tattoo on the side of its head, just like the shop's emblem sticker on the storefront window.

After the customers left, she entered the store and stood before a twenty one-year-old man at the register, with short green hair, jeans, and a grey t-shirt with the store logo on it. The young woman had a piercing look in her eyes and a wooden sword in her hand, but she received an uninterested stare in return; the young man just rolled his eyes.

"What is it now, Kaori?" he said. "I thought you were promoting the store at the fundraiser today."

"It was a bachelor party, Jamal!"

"Oh." His eyes widened.

"Where is Michael?!" she said.

A crashing noise was heard from the storage room in the back. Boxes fell over at the door. There was a scream. A hand landed on the ground, the arm rolled over, and the fingers tapped the ground as though it were searching for something. It caressed the floor, curled into a fist, and pounded it. Jamal sighed.

"Dying as usual," he said. He picked up a magazine as Kaori raised her wooden sword and stomped to the storage room.

"Michael!" she yelled.

"Jamal!" called a man's voice from the storage room, and another box rolled over the pile onto the floor. Suddenly, his voice was somehow heard from the store's front entrance. "Watch the store!"

Jamal and Kaori turned around and saw the twenty-year-old man with short, dark brown hair, dressed in a black shirt and jeans, standing at the store entrance.

"Now, Michael," said Kaori, raising her wooden sword at him with a growl. "The blade of Seizon would like a word with you!"

✻ ✻ ✻

Seizon. In English, it means existence. In feudal Japan, the master swordsman Miyamoto Musashi whittled a very powerful wooden sword from a dead tree limb for his most famous battle. Then he discarded it due to its flimsiness, and instead whittled an oar into his most famous wooden sword, the one that dispatched his final opponent. That first discarded sword found its way into the hands of a wanderer, who sold it to a young boy who wanted to be a samurai for 765 Ryo. He purchased it. Upon his return home to the fishing village, people asked the boy how he was sure that the sword was from Musashi himself. He said:

"You see, I asked the same question, and the wanderer told me that Musashi's very soul possesses it. His spirit flows within."

"He's still alive!" yelled a man in the crowd.

"What?" said the boy, and as the crowd began to laugh, he fell silent.

After that, the sword never left the young boy's possession. Becoming a samurai, he passed it down from generation to generation of samurai, right into the hands of the Saito's family youngest daughter, Kaori. It is indeed a powerful sword. For its very name alone has made Buddha himself re-seek the path to enlightenment, so they say. The very cut of the wooden edge would slice existence itself, in ways that would make God ask, "How can that be possible?"

"Slice the heavens into eternal enlightenment!" cried the boy that fateful day, and that remains the Saito family's creed.

✳ ✳ ✳

Michael pushed the front door open violently, running over a young woman dressed in a blue-and-white school uniform who'd been standing outside the door, and knocking over her suitcase.

"Sorry!" he called back to her. As he ran off into the city, his voice faded in the distance. Kaori jumped over the woman.

"Michael!" she yelled. "Don't you run away from me!"

Michael ran through the crowd, dodging people. Kaori was right behind him with Seizon over her head, each swing missing him. He passed by a garbage can and grabbed a lid. He tossed it behind him, hoping to slow Kaori down. He watched her sword slice through it, and the lid burst into sparkles of light; erased from existence. She caught up to Michael and grabbed him, her fingers wrapped around his collar, and with a firm grip she pulled him to a stop. The point of the wooden blade poked Michael's back, and he smiled.

"That tickles."

"Don't play with me! Those perverts wanted me to give them lap dances. They didn't care about what I had to promote for the store." Michael opened his mouth to talk, but Kaori interrupted him. "Shut up! Prepare to die."

She lifted the sword over her head, ready to bash Michael, when she felt his foot crush her toe. As she jumped up and down in pain, Michael ran toward a nearby corner. She followed him, but when she rounded the corner, he was gone. All she saw was an empty alley, with a car passing by the other end. She screamed, then left the area, searching for her victim.

✳ ✳ ✳

When Michael returned to the store after losing Kaori, he saw Jamal waiting outside, waving him to hurry over, but when Jamal turned to the door, Michael was standing inside. "What is it?"

Jamal stood still. "I wish you'd stop that. You were only a few feet away."

Michael said in a deadpan tone, "But it's fun."

"Focus. We have a slight problem. That woman you ran over is out cold."

"Great, that means a lawsuit. Blast that Kaori."

"Kaori, eh?" Jamal's eyes shifted towards Michael, who looked innocent.

"Where is she, Jamal?" he said.

"In your apartment."

"Idiot! Why did you put her in my apartment?"

"Well, where do you want *me* to put her? Out in the middle of the street?"

"Or maybe a dumpster."

Jamal tapped Michael on the back of the head, grabbed his shirt, and dragged him to the back of the store. There was a door marked 'Private' next to the employee counter, and Jamal opened it. Inside was a messy apartment: a living room with a couch, a table, and a television. Visible from the right of the living room was the kitchen, and to the left of the living room were the bedroom and shower. Jamal stood Michael before the couch, and laying there was a young, silver-haired woman with her eyes closed. Her suitcase lay on the floor beside her. Michael noticed her school uniform. He turned and growled at Jamal. "Really?"

"You ran her over. We could get sued if people saw her outside."

Michael sighed and knelt down by the couch. At first he noticed a layer of black hair underneath her silver hair, with no indication of hair dye. Attached to her blouse was a blue and pink brooch, shaped like a ribbon with a red gem in the center. For a second, he thought he saw a gleam of light slide over the surface. He pressed two fingers to her neck, felt the softness of her skin and the pulsing of her veins.

"She's alive, Michael," said Jamal.

"One can never tell."

The young woman groaned, and her eyes opened. Michael breathed a sigh of relief, and as he did, she punched him in the face. He flew over the table and landed on his back; Jamal just stood there with his arms crossed, shaking his head. The woman got up quickly and slouched over in pain, holding her head. She patted her uniform and breathed a sigh of relief when she felt her brooch.

"Aey," Michael said to her, lifting himself up. "I'm sorry about that, but Kaori doesn't know how to leave me alone."

"Kaori, eh?" Jamal said again, as Michael walked past him to the woman.

"Stay out of this," Michael replied with a glare. He turned his attention back to the young woman. "So are you okay?"

"Yes," she said, looking around at the living room. "Where am I?"

"You're in my apartment."

"Oh no." She jumped off the couch, grabbing her suitcase, and started to run around, trying to find the nearest door. "I've been kidnapped!"

She ran back and forth in a panic as Michael and Jamal stood by with one sweatdrop over each of their heads, watching her. She opened the back door and stepped into the store, and when she saw it, her eyes grew wide. It was a remarkable sight. She walked along the aisles, looking at the merchandise, turning her head at the posters hanging on the walls, the DVDs and VHS tapes on the shelves and the plushy dolls in the baskets. Manga books were lined up like a library, and TVs were mounted at each corner of the ceiling. After taking a deep breath, the woman turned to Michael and Jamal, who were standing by the cash register.

"We're not bad guys," Jamal said.

"I own this place," Michael said, pointing to his chest with his thumb.

"*We* own this place," Jamal said. As Michael opened his mouth, Jamal's stare silenced him.

"You own 'The Impossible Man's Anime and Manga Shop'?" she said.

"Yep."

"Liar!" She grabbed a rare videocassette tape from the shelf and threw it at Michael, but just as she threw the tape, it appeared in his hand. She stood, frozen, and looked at her hand where the tape had been. She watched Michael set the merchandise on the counter.

"Your name, please," Michael said.

"Yuki Shimizu. I'm looking for the one called Michael Garcia."

"I see. So what do you want with me?"

"You're Michael Garcia?" Yuki placed her hands on her hips.

"Last time I checked."

She jerked her head back. At first, she hesitated, but then she opened the side pocket of her suitcase and pulled out a manila envelope. She presented it to Michael, and he opened it.

Inside was an employment application. He read the paperwork and saw a woman's signature, "Garcia" on the documents and the stamp marked underneath, "Human Resources Department."

"My mother hired you?" he said. "As store security?"

"Yes. She did."

"Why?" Michael switched pages. "She didn't say anything to me about a new hire. Jamal?"

"No," Jamal replied.

Yuki tapped her fingers on the application. "You see, I came from—"

She was interrupted by a loud roar from outside, which rattled the windows. Everyone looked outside, and there was Kaori, marching through the door. When Yuki turned to Michael, he was no longer there. She saw him peeking out from the storage room.

Kaori stomped up close to her and Jamal, waving Seizon. Yuki stepped aside and had a view of both Kaori and the storage room.

"Kaori," said Jamal, presenting Yuki, "I'd like you to meet our new—"

"Where's Michael?"

"Excuse me," Yuki said.

"What?!" Kaori turned to Yuki.

"I'm afraid the person you are looking for hasn't arrived yet."

"And how would you know?" Kaori replied, staring Yuki down.

"I've been here for a while now, and I didn't see the man you were chasing."

"Damn." Kaori turned to Jamal. "I'll be back."

Yuki and Jamal watched Kaori stomp out of the store. Once she disappeared from their sight, Michael appeared outside the front window and entered the store. Yuki's eyes blinked, and she turned to the storage room; he was gone.

"How?" She shifted her gaze back to Michael. "Probably a back door."

"Jamal Jones," said Michael, pointing to Jamal. "I'm Michael Garcia. Yuki Shimizu, welcome to our store. Show her the basics, Jamal. I'll be in my room passing out."

With the documents in hand, Michael walked past Yuki. Her eyes followed as he headed back into his apartment. "Excuse me. Garcia-san."

"Please, call me Michael," he said.

"Oh." Yuki was shocked until she remembered that Michael's mother said it was okay to address co-workers by their first name in America, even dropping the honorific suffix-*san*. "Michael. Uh…Yuki."

"Yuki."

"Thank you very much. I'll do my best." Yuki bowed and Michael returned the gesture with a bow himself.

As Michael went to his apartment, Jamal led Yuki behind the counter. When she passed the storage room, she noticed how small it was: just boxes, a sink, a rooster costume, and shelves hugging the wall. "Wait," she said, hurried over to the room, and entered. There was no other door except the one she stood at. She had the storage room in her sight while talking to Kaori.

"How did he do that? It's not possible."

"Michael will explain later," Jamal said from behind, and Yuki turned around. "You got lucky fooling Kaori. Her temper blinded her from going to the storage room. She's our public relations representative. She'll be back tomorrow. Come, let me teach you how to work the register so you can understand what needs to be secured...and you may call me Jamal."

"Jamal. Uh...Yuki."

Michael, meanwhile, sat on his couch, dropping the employment documents on the table. He leaned back and took a deep breath. Such a stressful morning—he never could get a break with Kaori when weird things happened, and that his mother had hired someone without his knowledge or permission was irritating.

Now there was a loud banging on the door from the kitchen. It would not stop. Michael got to his feet and walked over, but when he peeked out the peephole, he saw no one there. Then the loud banging happened once more.

When he cracked the door open, a small, old man stood in the hallway: Kensuke Tanaka, Michael's landlord. He wore a blue business suit and leather shoes, and carried a cane with a diamond head on it. When the old man lifted his head up, Michael unleashed a false smile.

"Mr. Tanaka, my favorite landlord. Now's not the time."

Michael tried to close the door, but Mr. Tanaka pushed the door open with his cane. "Don't brush me off, gaijin. Today's rent day, and I want my rent money." Mr. Tanaka took out his gold watch from his pocket. "Twenty seconds ago, actually."

"First thing in the morning."

"No! I want my money."

Michael closed the door in Mr. Tanaka's face, went into the kitchen, and stood before the refrigerator. "Damn Tanaka, piling on more problems today. It's a Monday. Can't I breathe? The rent doesn't need to be cashed until Friday anyway. He's got plenty of time. My poor cookie jar."

There was a cookie jar on top marked *Sweet*. Michael opened the lid, reached inside, and pulled out a checkbook. After writing out the check, he returned and opened the front door.

"Here's your money," he said.

When Mr. Tanaka reached for the check, Michael jerked it up into the air. Michael then lowered the check for the landlord to take, but then yanked it back out of reach. They repeated this two more times until the landlord growled and kicked Michael in the leg, freeing the check. It landed in his hands like a falling leaf, and he walked away.

"Idiot!" Mr. Tanaka said in Japanese, over his shoulder.

"Idiot!" Michael replied in Spanish.

He closed the door and made his way back to the fridge.

When he opened it, he saw only a jar of mustard staring back at him. He slammed the fridge, already reaching his boiling point. He reached into the cookie jar, took out a wad of cash, and marched back outside to the shop, standing before Yuki and Jamal with a cracked smile. His stomach rumbled, and Yuki giggled.

"I see," said Jamal, grabbing the phone. "I'll order some pizza."

"Thank you," Michael said.

"I've never had pizza before," Yuki said to Michael.

"Blasphemy!" Michael turned to Yuki.

"What?" Yuki stepped back.

"He's just joking, Yuki," said Jamal.

"Oh. Well, no. I always wanted to try American pizza." As Jamal ordered over the phone, she said, "Your mother called you the Impossible Man. Why?"

"With a capital 'T'?" The corner of his eyes towered over her, while his fingers twiddled at her as if he was trying to mind control her.

As Jamal slapped Michael's hands down, Yuki stepped back. "Uh…yes. Why?"

Michael abruptly walked away. Jamal cleared his throat, and she turned to him. He leaned in close and whispered, "It would be best if you didn't ask Michael that question."

"I was just curious."

"I know, but he doesn't like to reveal himself so easily to people."

"Why?"

"Because it requires a lot of thought to understand

why he calls himself The Impossible Man. You keep asking him that question, and all you'll get is that dramatic scene over there." Jamal pointed to the storefront window, where Michael was looking outside, with his left arm held behind his back in a serious and dramatic posture. To Yuki, he looked ridiculous.

As Michael stood there, watching people walk back and forth, a large brown van stopped in front of the store. A courier climbed out the back of the truck, carrying a large package, and approached. With a smile, Michael read *Anime Club Video* on the box. He opened the door and signed for the package, then carried it to the center aisle.

"It's finally here," Jamal said.

"Slow as usual," Michael replied, planting the box on the floor.

"What is it?" Yuki said, as all three stood over the box.

"It's the newest volume of the Endless Heart anime, Yuki."

"Endless Heart? Wow!"

"You both sound like kids in a '90s commercial," Jamal said.

"Radical," said Michael, taking out a box cutter from behind the counter. He appeared again next to Yuki from out of nowhere, startling her, and kneeling down before the box. As she leaned her body closer to Michael, he sliced the tape off and removed the Styrofoam pieces. Michael and Jamal both turned to Yuki, and she straightened herself.

"Since you're new here," Michael said, "you have the honors."

"Honors?" Yuki turned to Jamal, and he nodded.

"You get to take out the first DVD." Jamal slid the box before Yuki, and the young woman knelt down. With a smile, she pulled out a DVD titled *Endless Heart Volume Two*. On the front cover was a picture of a teenage girl with white and light blue hair, and teal-tipped white wings made of light. She wore a skirted costume, holding a large red staff with wings attached.

Yuki handed Jamal the disc, which was marked "store sample," and he walked behind the counter. When he turned it on, Yuki stood up. She spun in a circle when each TV turned on, one by one. When she stopped spinning, Michael spoke.

"Whimsy!"

"What?"

"You were whimsy," said Michael, watching the show. "Like, ahhh…"

Yuki shook her head at what he'd just said. She turned to Jamal, who was cleaning up the Styrofoam, paying no attention to Michael.

When the first episode ended, the pizza arrived, but everyone was focused on unpacking the rest of the merchandise. Michael read the inventory list, checking off all the orders, while Jamal taught Yuki where to place the new DVDs in the New Release shelf and shifted the week-old releases to another section. Jamal then sat at the computer and taught her how to place new orders for the next week.

It was a busy workday, and over time, they were all tired out. As Yuki and Jamal stood around the pizza, ready to eat,

Michael opened the pizza box. A silver spoon, with a lion's head on the handle, lay in the center of the pie. Michael picked it up, examined it.

"The restaurant must have accidentally put this in here," he said.

"Strange," Jamal replied. "It looks like real silver."

"Just like your hair, Yuki." Michael reached over to Yuki with the spoon and saw that the colors matched. He tossed it to the register without care. "Well, let's eat."

"Thank you for the meal," everyone said in Japanese, and Michael took a slice. They ate the pizza, and Yuki smiled in delight.

"Delicious!" she said in Japanese, and Michael spoke.

"Just don't turn into a turtle. We have no ninja weapons here."

Yuki turned to Michael. "That's … a joke."

As Michael nodded, a message became visible in the box within the greasy stain. Michael moved the remaining slices to the side, revealing the note: *Hide the Spoon.*

"Okay," said Michael, scratching his head. He picked up the spoon. "Someone has issues."

"Hide the spoon," Yuki read. "Why?"

She turned to Jamal, who shrugged his shoulders.

A red glow surrounded the spoon in Michael's hand, catching his attention, and the glow stopped.

"Did you see that?" Michael said, leaning closely at the spoon.

"See what?" Jamal replied.

"The spoon glowed."

"I didn't see any glow," Yuki said.

The trio stared at the spoon, and Yuki noticed an inscription on it, written in Japanese.

"Spoon," she said.

"How original," said Michael.

"I think we should stop now," said Jamal, crossing his arms and looking away.

"Why, Jamal?" Michael turned to where Jamal was looking, and saw a couple of teenage customers standing at the entrance blinking at them. "Sorry, welcome to I-Man's."

The rest of the day went on without incident; they ignored the spoon that sat on the counter. Yuki's training on the register continued, and she took care of each customer that arrived. Her greetings brought them smiles, and they left with their items, feeling happy. Michael noticed this and nodded with a smile.

The clock struck seven. The sun set at the end of the day, and it was time to close up the store. Wishing the last customers goodbye, Michael flipped a welcome sign over that read "Store Closed" in English, Spanish, and Japanese.

He turned around. "Jamal, you up for a round or two at the Gaming Sector?"

"Sorry," said Jamal, "but I have to get home and take care of the bills."

"How about you, Yuki? I can show you around."

"Thank you, but I have to go to my hotel room," said Yuki, who was carrying her suitcase out.

"Okay. Well, I open the store at eleven. Also, you don't have to wear your school clothes when you work here."

Michael took a second look at Yuki's clothing. "Why are you wearing school clothes, anyway? I thought your application said you were eighteen and had completed high school."

Yuki stood there with innocent eyes as Michael and Jamal waited for an answer. "Well, I have to go now," she finally said. "Thank you very much for hiring me. You're weird, but great to work with." She stepped back toward the entrance. "I'm looking forward to doing my best and making this store a great place to shop. Well, good night."

She turned around and bumped her face right into the front door. Yuki fell back and found herself caught in Michael's arms. It happened fast. With a little blush, she stood to her feet and turned around.

"Are you okay?" he asked.

"Yes." Yuki cleared her throat.

Michael unlocked the door, opened it for Yuki, and watched her walk outside.

"Aey, Yuki," he said, and she turned around. "You did good on your first day. You just have to dress normal, okay?"

"Okay." Yuki bowed politely. "Thank you again."

"No problem, and just … be careful with the doors."

"I will. Good night."

"Good night," Michael and Jamal said together, closing the door.

Yuki looked back inside the store as she walked by, and smiled.

After Michael locked the door, he walked over to the counter to read the day's receipts. He noticed the spoon was gone, and turned to Jamal.

"Where's the spoon?"

"The spoon?" Jamal faced Michael. "Who cares?"

"Because it was right here." Michael felt something in his pocket. He reached inside, pulled out the silver spoon, and jerked his head back.

Jamal shrugged and walked away. "Focus, Michael. We have to clean up and work on the budget."

Michael placed the spoon back on the counter, turning his attention to helping Jamal clean up the store.

After Michael and Jamal closed up for the night, bidding each other farewell, Michael went into his apartment. Ignoring the letter from his mother attached to Yuki's application, he walked over to the fridge and stared at the jar of mustard. With a sigh, he reached for the cookie jar instead, taking out a wad of cash. He left the building through the main apartment entrance, heading for the grocery store. For a moment, he stared at the full moon, and a shadow leapt across the rooftops.

"Michael?" A young woman's voice got his attention.

Michael's forehead turned blue. He turned around, and saw Kaori raise Seizon over her head. He ran off, and she chased after him with a banshee-like scream. Michael screamed, running past garbage cans, knocking them over on his way to slow her down. He saw her jump over them with ease, even gain speed. Michael turned the corner into an alley, and Kaori kept pace, but she stopped when she saw Michael behind a tall chain-link fence, smiling at her. Michael stuck out his tongue, then turned around, slapping his butt to taunt her.

The sound of her growl silenced Michael. Kaori sliced the metal fence in half with the wooden sword, nearly creating a hole in the air itself, and a portion of the fence vanished. Michael screamed like a girl and ran out into the next street. He accidentally tripped over a crack in the sidewalk, landing on his face. When he turned around, lying on his back, Kaori held the tip of the wooden blade to his neck.

"Don't you ever give up, Kaori?"

"After humiliating me?" Kaori flipped the sword to its blunt side. "Not as long as you're walking on two feet."

"I really didn't know. I'm sorry."

"You didn't do your research. You should have known better."

Eye to eye, they were preparing for their next move when suddenly Michael saw the shadow jumping from one rooftop to the next. A bright star fell towards him and Kaori from high in the air, and exploded, surrounding them with a plume of smoke. When it dissipated, Michael was gone.

"Michael?" Kaori took a few steps forward and pounded the wall with her fist. "Damn it, why can't you be more like him?"

Michael peeked out from behind a car a few blocks away. He looked up to the sky and wondered what the star had been. With a sigh, he felt something in his pockets, reached in, and pulled out the silver spoon.

"I hate Mondays," he growled under his breath.

Episode 2

[~ Enter Magical Girl ~]

Take one common item, like a locket or a pen, and give it the ability to change your regular clothes into a magical costume. Then hand it to a girl between the ages of ten and seventeen, and what do you get? The magical girl. They're mysterious super-heroines that run around a town or city, carrying overpowered magical weapons—they take down bad guys, fight ugly monsters, and save the world. What makes their stories interesting is that they run on high emotions of love and justice, and the power of friendship. It becomes their tenacity, determined to protect the people they love and the world they care for from the forces of evil.

April 9, 2002

In the afternoon, Kaori walked north on Grove Street towards I-Man's, Seizon in hand. Dressed in workout clothes, she was returning from sword practice. As she stood in front of a crosswalk, waiting for the light to change, she felt a buzz in her pocket. She sighed under breath and took out a cell phone. It read 'Hino-san.'

"Damn it, can't he ever give me a break?" Kaori took a deep breath, and her anger subsided. As she flipped the phone open, a large backpack bumped her. She saw a tall, muscular man with short blond hair, dressed in a buttoned blue shirt, khaki shorts, and an explorer's hat. The giant backpack he carried bent his body backward and bumped into people who tried to walk around him. Kaori noticed an advertisement from the store in his hands.

"Kaori, are you there?" Hino's excited voice spoke from the phone.

"He has it," the man said softly, within earshot of Kaori. He crushed the ad. "I will break him."

Kaori closed her cell phone and followed the tall man to a restaurant with outdoor dining. She watched him take the backpack off, and when he set it down on the ground, the tables, chairs, and windows all rattled. She even felt the sidewalk shake. She heard a phone ring. The man pulled out a large cellular phone the size of a brick from his backpack—it was small around his hands by comparison—and answered.

"I'm in Denfair City now. New Jersey smells as toxic as always. You better have my money ready when I retrieve the spoon." The man reached into his backpack, taking out a picture of the lion-headed silver spoon. She saw the picture set next to the advertisement, unaware of his eyes tracking her. Worried, she kept going and left him. As she waited at an intersection for traffic to stop, a shadow covered her body from behind.

✳ ✳ ✳

Meanwhile, at the shop, Michael handed a young boy a manga, receipt, and change. After waving goodbye, he picked up a newspaper and read an article about a mysterious person fighting crime the night before. He shrugged it off, looking out to Yuki, who was waiting to tape a poster of next week's new release of Huge Robot Nogaida on the window. As Jamal came out of the storage room with a new roll of tape, Michael felt something appear in his pocket. He pulled out the spoon, and scratched his head.

"You still have that spoon?" Yuki said, taking the tape from Jamal.

"It's weird, because everywhere I go, it ends up in my pocket, or right next to me."

"You just like the thing, that's all," Jamal said, walking back to the storage room.

"I don't like the spoon, Jamal. I tell you, this thing is stalking me."

"Yeah, yeah," Jamal said, and he entered the storage room. "Everybody is after you. I thought you'd be used to it by now."

"I'll never get used to it." Michael leaned back, and noticed Yuki was concerned.

"Is everything okay, Michael?" she said. "Who's after you?"

"Everyone." Michael looked up at the ceiling and nodded. "Yeah. Just about everyone."

"How?"

"It's just the store's popularity. We got bigger than we can handle."

"I see," Yuki said, approaching the counter. "Just let go of the spoon." She placed her hand on Michael's wrist, and he released the spoon.

"That's it," she said, leading him out from behind the counter. "Now come on and help me with the posters. The spoon won't hurt you."

Michael followed her to the window, carrying folded stepping stairs. He unfolded the stairs and watched Yuki climb up to the top, holding onto the poster. As he did, the spoon glowed red, and the top step buckled under Yuki's feet. Michael caught her, and together, they fell to the floor. When Michael opened his eyes, he felt something soft and squishy. He saw his right hand on her chest, and heard Yuki's growl. Her elbow had struck his temple, shifting his head to the side. Michael lay flat on the floor.

"Sorry, Yuki," he moaned, as Yuki stood up, crossing her arms with a blush.

"I hope this won't be a part of my services, Michael."

"Services?"

"Yes. Services. Your mother told you about this."

"My mother talked to me?"

"Yes. She called you on the phone."

"My mother called me?" Michael tilted his head up, trying to remember. He patted his forehead, struggling to recall.

"You're not serious?"

"Well…yeah." Michael stood up rubbing the back of his head, laughed for a moment, and then made a serious face, his hand under his chin. "Seriously, my mother never called and talked to me about you."

Yuki sighed, placed her hands on her hips. "I'll explain everything," she said, but as she was about to tell her story, Jamal rushed out of the storage room.

"Hey, Michael, it's time. You have a conference call now."

"Oh, I almost forgot." Michael appeared behind the counter from out of nowhere, grabbed the phone underneath, and placed it by the register. He turned to Yuki, who was crossing her arms and staring like a deer. It was like she'd witnessed something unusual. He waved to her to wait a moment. When he dialed the phone, he looked out the window.

Outside, the tall blond man with the large backpack waited across the street. It looked like he could see Michael staring at him through the window, since he was signaling him to come out. So Michael did.

"Aey!" he said loudly, from across the street. "What do you want?"

"My name is Wolfgang," said the blond man. "I want the spoon."

"Spoon?"

"Yes, I-Man," Kaori said, who was hanging on a rope above Wolfgang. "The spoon."

"Kaori? How did you get up there, and what are you talking about?" As Michael said this, Yuki stepped outside, watching Kaori.

"What's going on?" she said.

"Kaori's tied up again, Yuki," Michael said, forgetting that Yuki was in her second day on the job. "This isn't like you, getting captured this easily."

"Well, excuse me, I-Man, he was too fast. I just wanted to make sure he wouldn't hurt you."

"Coming from the one who wants to hurt me," Michael said with a smirk. "I feel even safer now."

"Enough!" Wolfgang yelled, crossing the street. "I want the spoon. I have a group of auctioneers interested in it, and they're waiting for me to retrieve it."

Michael lifted his head, since Wolfgang's shadow covered his body. He hadn't expected Wolfgang to be that tall.

"Look, even if I did have the spoon, it's not on me right now. See?" Michael emptied his pockets, showing his wallet, keys, and the spoon. Wolfgang leaned close to his hand. Michael saw the spoon and screamed in shock. He noticed Wolfgang had gone into a hypnotic trance. He chuckled as Wolfgang stared at the spoon.

"Go ahead, take the spoon," he said, facing Kaori. "Then go away and leave us be."

From the corner of his eye, Michael saw Wolfgang lift Seizon over his head, even though the tall man was still fixated on the spoon. Seeing Kaori's sword in Wolfgang's hand shocked him. With a scream, Michael ran off.

Wolfgang blinked once, and saw that Michael had already reached the end of the city block and crossed the street. He raised an eyebrow at what Michael did, but kept focus. He started to chase after Michael, but Yuki tripped him to the ground. He turned around and watched Yuki kick the sword to the side. Since Michael was already in the distance, he got up, punched Yuki in the stomach, and followed him.

"You run fast," Wolfgang said to himself, "but not fast enough!"

He unlatched his backpack, and it dropped to the ground behind him with a loud thud; the sidewalk cracked, and everything vibrated. A small sonic boom at his feet allowed him to gain speed, but just as Michael turned the corner, Wolfgang grabbed his collar and slammed him to the wall. With ease, Wolfgang lifted him up and pinned him to the wall, curling his hands into fists.

"Now, Mr. Impossible Man, the spoon."

"The."

"What?"

"You left out 'The' in The Impossible Man. Always apply the 'The' in my name."

Wolfgang's eyes twitched. "You idiot…give me the spoon now!"

"You don't have to give him anything at all, citizen," said a female voice from out of nowhere.

"Who's there?" Wolfgang said, and he turned around.

From down the street, a young woman emerged out of the shadows. She wore a one-piece pink, red, and white short dress with a belt. Her knee-length boots and elbow-length gloves matched the outfit. She held a pink and white staff, with a winged ball as its headpiece. A pair of white, wing-shaped hairpieces with blue jewels propped up her silver hair.

"Yuki?" Michael said under his breath. "I don't believe it."

"Who are you?" Wolfgang said.

"I am the deliverer of justice!" called Yuki, stretching her right arm out. "I am the definition of courage, the essence of love!" She held her staff over her head, spun around like a graceful ballerina. "I am the magical girl…"

She stopped spinning and lifted her right knee up in the air. "Scarlet Sorceress!" Then she pointed at Wolfgang. "Beg for mercy now, and I shall grant you that wish."

As Michael and Wolfgang both stared at Yuki, a sweat-drop appeared over each of their heads.

"Did I just see white panties?" Michael said, and Yuki bashed her staff on his head.

"Think straight, citizen! It's a leotard, not panties."

"I don't care!" yelled Wolfgang, pulling Michael closer, face to face. The putrid scent of rotten alcohol and milk from his mouth made Michael gag. "I want my spoon!"

"I want to go home!" Michael said. With a growl, he gritted his teeth. "What's so special about a dumb utensil?"

"Like I would tell you."

"Put him down now!" Yuki said, raising her staff up in the air. She watched Wolfgang wrap his left hand around

Michael's neck and drag him toward her. The winged ball on her staff glowed, and she prepared to cast a spell, but hesitated out of fear of hitting Michael. Wolfgang grabbed her collar and slammed her against the wall beside Michael before she had a chance to defend herself. Now, with both Michael and Yuki subdued, Wolfgang squeezed their necks.

"Some hero," Michael said, "you turned out to be."

"Shut up!" Yuki replied. "Show some support."

Then the buzzing sound of a watch stopped everyone, and Michael looked at his watch.

"I'm late," he said. "We have to go back now!"

"What's wrong, Michael?" Yuki said, and covered her mouth.

Wolfgang growled. "So you know him."

"No time to explain!" Michael took her hand, and they ran away from Wolfgang, leaving him behind still in choking position. "I have to make that important call. Let's go!"

Wolfgang, meanwhile, looked at his arms, grabbing the air as though Michael and Yuki were still there.

"What?!" He stumbled back, trying to figure out what had happened. "Impossible!"

※ ※ ※

Michael held Yuki's hand as they ran back to the shop, but Yuki became tired from running. He felt her hand slip away, and he stopped. As she tried to catch her breath, he jogged in place. "Yuki, we don't have time."

"I'm not Yuki," she said, and took a deep breath. "I'm Scarlet Sorceress."

Michael stared at her, and she sighed.

"How did you know?"

"Your silver and black hair, for one thing."

"Any girl could have silver and black hair."

"And your voice and your face are too obvious as well."

"My face?" Yuki pressed her fingers to her face and turned to Michael. "Wait…how did you know I have black hair?"

"When you were unconscious yesterday, I saw some of your black hair underneath." Michael crossed his arms.

Yuki was shocked. She pulled her hair down, trying to cover the black strands.

"It's cool," Michael said, and Yuki blushed. "What I can't figure out is how Wolfgang couldn't recognize you."

"No one does. Trust me, secret identity is part of being a magical girl."

"Aren't you eighteen? Please tell me you're legal."

"What? Of course I'm legal! Where'd you get that?" Yuki thought about that for a second, and realized that she wasn't a kid. "Oh, right."

She leaned back on the wall and crossed her arms, her staff in hand. "I work for the Order of the Magical Girl. Magical girl is the title of my position. You could say it's like a cadet in law enforcement."

"Cadet?"

"Yeah, well, you see, we start training at age ten. As kids we go through tests, homework, physical education, typical school stuff. We also have on-the-field training starting at eleven. In our final year we have what we call a Promotion Test since we can't really be magical girls, because we're not little girls anymore. So I was supposed to get a promotion since I'm eighteen now, and, well…"

As Yuki tapped her fingers together, looking away, Michael waved his hand. "Go on."

"I failed my promotions test. So I was going to be designated an officer, but our mothers got into a fight and that prevented me from becoming an officer according to the conditions of their duel. Now I'm stuck as a magical girl. Since this is a unique situation and I have no experience in global matters, this means I am designated as re-training from scratch instead of working my way to a magical detective promotion, which is what I wanted."

"Okay," Michael said. He sat on the hood of a parked car, crossed his arms. "May I see your staff?"

Yuki hesitated, then handed him her staff. She saw the curiosity in his eyes as he twisted and turned it in his hands. Michael struggled to comprehend the pink and white staff, and the winged ball attached. It looked like a toy.

"It's name is Tsubasa. The staff was given to me by my grandmother," she said. "Actually, it's a magical brooch that turns into a staff, and changes my clothes when I chant the magical words. I can cast mostly elemental spells and light-based spells with it. It has protected me many times. So many battles. So many creatures." Yuki's hands shivered, and with a smile, she curled them into fists.

"Have you bashed anyone else over the head with it

in combat?" Michael swung the staff violently, but Yuki snatched Tsubasa and raised her fist at him. He shielded himself.

"This is a very sensitive magical weapon," she said. "You can't just go around banging it on people's heads."

"Coming from the one who bashed my head with it."

"Well, I...shut up! It's not supposed to actually be used for bashing."

"Then it's a useless weapon."

"It's not useless. I need it to protect..." Yuki paused, as Michael raised an eyebrow. She leaned on the car next to Michael. "I have to protect you. That's why your mother sent me."

Michael rubbed his eyes. "Okay, let's get this over with. How did this arrangement happen?"

"The Order of the Magical Girls' combat rules state that if a mother defeats another mother, then the losing mother's child must serve the winning mother's child."

"I have no idea what you just said."

"Your mother fought my mother and won. As a result, I became your personal bodyguard. To help me make a living here in America, your mother hired me to work in your store as the security guard."

Realizing he and Jamal had taught her how to take on customers, he lowered his head. "We have mistrained you."

"That word doesn't exist."

"Anyway, Yuki," he continued, "what would have happened if my mother had lost?"

"Then you would have been sent to Japan, where we

would have permanently transformed you into a magical girl and made you serve me for the rest of your life as my bodyguard."

"If I refused?"

"Then we would kill you by removing your testicles and letting you bleed out."

Michael's eyes grew wide at the thought: a choice between death by castration, or turning into a servant girl.

"And by 'serve' do you mean…"

"No." Yuki dropped her arms. "Maybe, over time… okay, it has happened before."

"Being your servant would be awesome," Michael said, with a straight face.

"Of course you would choose that over death. I can see it in your eyes." Yuki walked away from Michael, throwing her arms up in the air. "I tell my mother all the time that that ultimatum never works with a man."

"Hmph. Well, if that's the case," Michael said, leaning on the wall next to Yuki from out of nowhere and startling her, "I can make you service me any way I want."

"If you try to use force while I serve you, you will then have to become a magical—"

"Ha!" Michael pointed at Yuki, having exposed another loophole. He smiled as she shook Tsubasa in her hands out of frustration and turned around.

"How did the Order manage to last this long?! I told her the rule was dangerous." Yuki stomped her foot. "Look, my job is to be your bodyguard, nothing else. I still have a right to live my life accordingly."

"Then what's stopping you?"

"Eh?" Yuki faced Michael.

"I don't need a bodyguard…and since you protected me from that weird guy, I don't need you anymore."

"What's that supposed to mean?"

"It means your duty is complete. Finished. Done. Mission accomplished. Now, I'm in a hurry." Michael walked away with his hands in his pockets.

The dismissal caught her off guard, so she hurried up alongside him. "Does that mean I'm not working for the store either?"

"If that's what you want."

Michael and Yuki faced each other. They were quiet for a moment, and she answered, "No." Her eyes followed him as he walked faster. Something about him made her curious. The Impossible Man, she thought, what an odd name. She expected him to take advantage of her as his servant, yet she felt a little rejected that he did not need her, going against the rules of the Order. Still, she felt something about him that she liked. No one had complimented her hair before. She felt good about that. She wanted to know more about him. "I want to work for your store."

"Okay."

"Just don't tell anyone about my powers. They're supposed to be a secret."

"All right, but don't be surprised if Jamal recognizes you."

Michael reached out to Yuki, and she grabbed his hand and blinked. When she opened her eyes, to her surprise, she saw the shop. Michael released her hand, and they saw Jamal carrying a ladder toward the store and Kaori picking up her sword.

"Wait, weren't we just…" Yuki trailed off and looked back down the street, in shock at finding herself at the store already. She tried to comprehend what had just happened.

"Kaori," said Michael, "I see you stopped playing with yourself on the rope."

"I'll make sure to put it back in your closet next to the rubber woman."

Michael stood before Jamal and Kaori, and they stared at Yuki. When he began to speak, Yuki covered his mouth, laughing. The two struggled as Jamal and Kaori became impatient from the horseplay. Jamal punched Michael in the back of the head and dragged him inside the store.

"You got to call that freak," he said.

Kaori placed her hands on her hips. "And don't tell that mutant I'm here, Michael. I don't need his creepy advances to pile on my already bad day."

"Freak?" Yuki said, tilting her head in confusion as Kaori approached her.

"Who are you, and why are you with I-Man?" Kaori stood in front of Yuki, balancing Seizon on her shoulders.

"I am the Scarlet Sorceress." She tightened her grip on Tsubasa. "I was just protecting him from Wolfgang."

"That's my job," said Kaori, leaning closer to Yuki and pointing at herself.

"Your job?"

"I was hired by his mother to protect him at all times."

Yuki was shocked.

"…as the public relations manager."

"Oh," Yuki replied, "Well…I…" She scanned through her thoughts, making sure not to reveal her secret and expose the Order of the Magical Girl to civilians. "I was sent here from my organization to protect Michael. It's my mission."

"Really?" Kaori tapped the wooden blade on her shoulder and walked around Yuki. "I-Man doesn't need help from a cosplayer like you."

Yuki felt Kaori's intimidation and responded in kind. "Really?" She tapped her magical staff on her shoulder and walked around Kaori. "I never knew Michael was into bondage like you."

"Bondage?"

"You looked like you were having an orgasm, tied up there."

"At least I don't prance around in miniskirts like a prostitute." Kaori leaned close to Yuki's face.

"You think Michael wants you?" Yuki inched her own face closer to Kaori's forehead.

"At least I know The Impossible Man. You're just a fan."

Yuki's mind cracked. She realized she knew nothing about Michael. Kaori smiled, and behind her, Yuki saw Wolfgang in the distance. He rushed towards them at high speed, grabbed their necks, and slammed them on the ground. Yuki and Kaori both dropped their weapons, struggling to break free, unable to call out for help.

Inside the shop, Michael picked up the phone next to

Jamal. After dialing and listening to the phone ring, he noticed that Yuki and Kaori were gone.

"Where did those two go?"

"Who? Kaori and that strange girl?" Jamal said.

Michael was about to respond, but as he did, someone answered the phone on the other end.

"Aey!" Michael said and proceeded to speak in Spanish to the caller. "What's going on? What? Are you crazy?"

He covered the phone speaker and made funny faces to Jamal while the caller talked, then continued the conversation.

"You know I won't do that!" he said. "Up yours!" Michael covered the phone. "Jamal, he wants to know if you want to sell hentai in the store?"

"Hell no!" Jamal said. "We're a family store. We'll lose customers if we sell porn."

"Ha! Two to one. Kiss my butt!" Michael reached into his pocket to get his keys, but he pulled out the spoon. He growled under his breath and threw it across the store; it landed on the table by the window.

Meanwhile, outside the store, Yuki and Kaori punched Wolfgang at once, causing him to stumble back on his feet. They stood up, unaware of a red glow behind the storefront window. Yuki and Kaori both gasped for air as Wolfgang regained his sense of direction. The women reached for their weapons, but a fire hydrant that glowed red gushed out water, pushing the weapons out of reach. Yuki and Kaori looked at each other, and as they did, Wolfgang grabbed them by their collars and threw them in front of the store window. Michael and Jamal had their backs turned, focused on the phone.

As the red glow inside the store disappeared, Yuki used the window to get to her feet, while Kaori struggled to get up. She noticed that Michael and Jamal weren't paying attention, but before she could swing her hand to slap the window, Wolfgang punched her in the face. When Yuki landed next to Kaori, she saw her eyes glowing red; her pupils were gone.

"Are you okay?" Yuki saw Kaori get to her feet, and Seizon, in a red glow, floated to her hand. She sensed something powerful near her. "Where is that energy coming from?"

Yuki searched to find the source of the power, but she could not sense its location. She turned to Kaori and saw the wooden sword swing downward. Yuki shifted to the side and watched the blade cut the air. She stumbled back and saw Tsubasa resting on the street, past Wolfgang. Yuki rolled between them and hurried to her staff, but before she picked it up, Wolfgang slid his arms under her shoulders. She felt her body lifted into the air and her knees slamming into the ground. Wolfgang crossed his fingers to lock her in place, and when she lifted her head up a little, she saw Kaori standing before her, with Seizon pulled back.

"Hey! Snap out of it!" Yuki screamed, and the sword struck her in the waist. She screamed, feeling her energy draining. Again and again Kaori struck her, each blow making her wince and yelp. When the attacks stopped, she coughed up a little blood.

She lifted her head and saw Jamal pushing at the door, but it wouldn't open. There was a red glow around the edges keeping it locked. As Jamal pressed his hands on the window, staring outside, Yuki saw Tsubasa to her left: out of reach. This caught Kaori's attention, and she dropped her sword. "Please don't."

"Shut up!" Wolfgang said, and he pushed her head down, straining her neck. Kaori stood before them with Tsubasa. She struck Yuki's head with the end of the staff and made her scream.

"Stop it!" Yuki said and opened her eyes. She found herself sitting on her knees with Tsubasa in hand. She looked to the side—there, Kaori and Wolfgang stared at each other in the same positions in which they'd attacked Yuki. Everyone heard a door open, and there was Michael, watching them.

"And keep it down out there!" he continued. "I'm on the phone!"

Amazed, Yuki wondered how he'd broke the mysterious red glow around the door. She stood up, stumbling a little from the pain. She raised Tsubasa over her head; it glowed bright blue.

"Healing Light!" she yelled. Some of her wounds healed, though a few cuts remained, and the pain went away. She took a deep breath as the glow disappeared, then stared at Kaori and Wolfgang coldly.

"We're doomed," Kaori said, in a hypnotic voice.

"What do you mean, we're doomed?" Wolfgang said to Kaori, pointing to the staff sparking with electricity.

Inside the store, Jamal looked out the window as Michael continued talking on the phone.

"Nah," he said. "I'm not going to bet on the hockey championship this year. Jersey got eliminated in the play-offs, and they won't be fighting for the title."

"Electric Mayhem!" yelled Yuki from outside.

As if watching a television screen, Jamal saw the light of the electricity flash through the window, x-raying Kaori and Wolfgang's bodies. He only heard Wolfgang scream, but saw both run off to the right, with Yuki chasing them. "Kaori?"

"Fire Bane!"

Jamal saw Kaori and Wolfgang run left, across the window, chased by a large flame that engulfed them. He shielded his eyes, and when he opened them, Yuki hopped in front of the window, chasing them. He saw Kaori and Wolfgang running to the right, across the window, charred and smoldering.

"Watery Wave!"

A large tidal wave splashed past the front door, and for a moment, Wolfgang and Kaori floated in front of the window like fish in an aquarium. Once the water receded, Michael lowered the phone.

"Watch the windows! They're expensive to replace!"

Jamal saw Yuki peek into the store and gave a two-fingered victory sign. He then watched Kaori and Wolfgang, burnt and wet, run across the street. There Yuki stood before the front window, covered in bright light.

"Excuse me a moment," said Michael into the phone. He set the phone on the counter and stood next to Jamal by the window. Together, they pulled out pairs of sunglasses from their pockets and put them on. Yuki's light engulfed the entire store.

"Shining Light!" The light exploded on Wolfgang and Kaori, sending them high into the sky, until a pair of stars flashed in the distance and disappeared. Yuki collapsed onto her knees, as the pain from her injuries caught up to her. Her costume turned back to her regular clothes, and Tsubasa turned back into a brooch. She noticed Michael standing over her before she closed her eyes.

"Yuki is the magical girl?" Jamal said from the door, as Michael carried her.

"No, she's the magical fairy princess looking to grant us wishes." Michael turned to Jamal for a moment, then back at Yuki while Wolfgang's backpack behind them glowed red and vanished, leaving behind a crater on the sidewalk. "Now I get why she wore that school uniform yesterday."

"What?" Jamal said.

"Magical girls are commonly schoolgirls. You know, secret identity, superhero stuff."

"That makes sense," Jamal said, opening the door for Michael, "for a kid."

"I think she has a fetish," Michael said, as he carried Yuki.

"I don't have a fetish," Yuki said, opening her eyes. She saw Michael's face and found herself in his arms. She blushed. Michael stood Yuki on the sidewalk, and her knees buckled, so he grabbed her arms to hold her up.

"Easy now."

"I'm okay," said Yuki. She covered her waist, nursing the pain. Suddenly a window opened from the apartment across the street. An old man stuck his neck out and said in Japanese, "What's with all the noise outside?! I'm watching Courtroom!"

Another window opened and a woman stuck her head out. "Why are you screaming?! My baby is sleeping!"

A third window opened up and a shirtless man shook his fist. "I gotta work the night shift! Keep it down outside!"

The old man pointed at Michael. "It's The Impossible Man! He's causing trouble again!"

The woman looked down at the store. "You better not have blocked the street again for an ad shoot! I have to drive and pick up my kids from school!"

As the neighbors yelled at Michael, Yuki scanned them and realized they were all Japanese. Her eyes grew wide. "This is not like back home."

"Ah, urban life." Michael crossed his arms with a smile as he heard the neighbors curse his name in Japanese. "Don't worry, they came from the City."

"The City?" Yuki followed Michael and Jamal inside, her eyes blurred. When she blinked, she saw a chair next to her that hadn't been there before. She bowed a little, and sat down. "Thank you."

"It's what we call New York City here." Michael picked the phone back up to finish his conversation. "Okay, you … where were we? Uh-huh. What? What?! Don't tell me that!"

"Thank you," Yuki said, receiving a cup of water from Jamal.

Yuki looked up to Michael, as his hair rose up and his teeth clamped down.

"You…hold on! Jamal, we have bad news."

"What is it?" Jamal said, and Michael covered the phone.

"He lost his job."

"No. That means—"

"He's coming to work full time," Michael said, and they lowered their heads.

"I never thought this day would come," Jamal said, shaking his head. "Again."

"Who's coming?" Yuki said.

"Our silent partner," they answered in unison. Then Michael went back to the phone. "Fine!" he yelled. "Tomorrow! Good night!"

Then he spoke calmly. "Oh, and don't forget to bring back my manga, okay? Thanks." He slammed the phone down, and Jamal and Yuki jerked their heads back from the impact. Michael turned to them and sighed.

"His name is Dōm Coquí, Yuki."

"What an odd name."

Jamal crossed his arms. "So should I get…the flies?"

"Flies?" Yuki said.

"Yes." Michael lifted his head up and turned to Yuki. "Where's Kaori?"

"I don't know," Yuki said, looking out the window. "Something happened to her and she turned on me. Some strange energy got control of her mind and made her attack. So I sent her away with Wolfgang before she killed me."

Yuki cracked a guilty smile, her hand resting on the back of her head, as Michael tilted his head.

"Huh?" Michael turned to Jamal, who nodded in agreement, and thunder rumbled outside.

That evening, it rained. Michael sat on his couch in his apartment, next to the answering machine, watching television. He skipped a lot of messages—they were mostly him answering the phone at the last minute, but finally he heard his mother.

"Hi, son," she said. "How is everything? Japan is great as always. Listen, something big happened here. I found this strange town run primarily by women. Crazy, isn't it? Well, it turned out that they had a little secret I wasn't supposed to know about. They all have magical powers. The girls looked so cute in their costumes. I couldn't stop hugging them and taking pictures. Though they were getting annoyed and said I was obnoxious…ahem…anyway, to make a long story short, their leader challenged me. So I won, and as a prize for my victory, I'm sending you the leader's daughter. I tried to refuse, but they would have turned me into a magical girl and made me serve the leader.

"As awesome as it sounds to be young again, and wear those cute magical outfits, I really don't want to go through another childhood. Oh, sorry, I'm rambling again. Right now, the leader's daughter is with me. Her name is Yuki Shimizu and we're working out her visa, finding an apartment for her to live in, and filling out her employment application for your store. I hope you don't mind. When she comes over, she'll be your bodyguard, and work as the store's security guard, so take care of her.

"Please, for the love of God, accept her, or you and I will be turned into magical girls and serve Yuki and her mother forever—awesome as that may be. Make sure to pick her up at Newark when she arrives in a couple of months. She has no idea how to get around the U.S. Well, I have to finish my world tour. You and Yuki stay out of trouble and have fun. Love you."

"End of message," the answering machine said. "Tuesday, February 5th, 2002."

Michael turned off the machine and leaned back on the couch. As he stared at the ceiling, he felt a headache from this new ordeal his mother had put him in. The television got his attention, and the evening news showed firefighters helping Wolfgang off a tree branch, and Kaori lifted in a gurney by a helicopter.

"Oh boy. She's going to try to kill me … again." Michael got up off the couch and grabbed his keys, but then the doorbell rang. He looked out the window and saw Yuki standing there, wiping water off her face. She noticed him outside and waved. He went to a speakerbox with two buttons on it, next to the apartment door. Michael pressed the talk button. "State the nature of your business."

"Seriously!?" Yuki said over the speaker. "It's raining outside!"

Michael pressed the open button to let Yuki in, and he opened the front door. She was soaking wet, with a suitcase set behind her.

"The apartment your mother got me closed down," she said. "I have no place to live."

"What do you mean, closed down?"

"The landlord sold his building and threw everyone out. I never even got a chance to get furniture."

Thinking about what his mother had said about the consequences, Michael opened the door wide and welcomed Yuki into his home. Before entering, Yuki removed her shoes and placed them by the door.

"Whoa," she said, touring his apartment to find nothing but basic furniture underneath piles of mess. "I expected to see all kinds of anime and manga stuff, like posters and figurines."

"I have a store for that," said Michael, walking to his bedroom. "I'll get you the sheets. The couch is there. The refrigerator is here. I have mustard if you're hungry."

"Mustard?"

"Yeah, the premier food of bachelors." Michael walked to his room.

Yuki watched Michael enter his room, and when the door closed, she took her brooch in her hand. With a light tap, it glowed.

"Supervisor, I've infiltrated The Impossible Man's home. I am now undercover."

Episode 3

[~ Silent Partner ~]

Mascots. Japan has a lot of them, just like we do here. They're cute for kids, and moneymakers for companies. They can also represent an entire city or region in Japan, known as Yuru Chara. Now, Denfair City has one as well. The worst thing that will happen to me is that I have to face off—once again—against one of the most annoying, most freaky, most indescribable characters I have ever faced, in my entire life, living on this Earth for all time…

…and in anime, they aren't even human.

April 10, 2002

Michael opened up shop and welcomed Jamal into the store, but when he saw Jamal's straw hat, he stood by the register in disbelief. The apartment door opened behind them, and Yuki came out, approaching Jamal.

"Did you just come from his apartment?" Jamal said.

"Yes," she replied.

"Just checking." Jamal stepped aside, not asking any further questions.

"What's that for, Jamal?" Yuki pointed at the straw hat.

"For when Coquí arrives, Yuki. I just want to stay on his good side."

"There'll be no good side," Michael said.

"He still hasn't forgotten about that dominoes game, Michael?" Jamal said.

"No, he hasn't."

"Dominoes?" Yuki said. "What's that?"

"It's a game," Michael said. "Well, how can I explain it? Think of it as cards, but with small rectangles that have numbers in them. There are two teams, you see, and each of them take seven dominoes to start as their hand. The player to get rid of their entire hand ends the round. After that, whatever dominoes are left from his opponent's hand will be counted as the score of that player or team that won the round. Of course, each game has a set score of the player's choice, like one hundred."

"And Michael had a communication problem with his partner," Jamal said.

"Hey, he had fives and I followed suit."

"You left him with six dominoes in his hand. How could he have done anything?"

"That didn't give him the right to gorge the dominoes and spit them at me."

"Gorge?" Yuki said. She wanted to ask what they meant, but feared she would not understand the explanation. "I think I'll keep out of dominoes. It sounds too violent."

"Look at us, Michael," Jamal said, taking the hat off. "Even when he's not here, he somehow gets us arguing."

"We have to watch out for that."

"Deal." Jamal and Michael shook hands, and Kaori entered the shop, slightly limping on one leg. Everyone stared at the bandages wrapped around most of her body. She seemed okay for the most part, since she was strong enough to curl her injured hand into a fist.

"Look, it's the mummy," said Michael, smirking and leaning back. Kaori stood right in his face. "I see you're okay this morning."

"Shut up!" Kaori said. "I want the girl."

"What girl?"

"That silver-haired girl."

"What do you want?" Yuki stood before Kaori, and the swordswoman sneered.

"Not you," Kaori said, and Michael and Jamal lost their balance. "The girl that blasted me off into the sky with that crazy guy."

She grabbed Michael's collar and pulled him close to her face.

"She's not here," said Michael, smiling with twitching

eyebrows. "Have you tried calling the commissioner? I heard he got a new signal in the shape of a giant…"

Kaori kneed Michael's groin, dropping him to the ground.

"Don't patronize me. I'm not through with you."

"Okay…" Michael crawled away from Kaori in pain, and Jamal raised his hands, stepping aside from her frightening stare. Michael reached for a seat, and Yuki helped him sit down. After relaxing from the pain, he saw Kaori in Yuki's face.

"So what do you have for I-Man?" Kaori said.

"Just leave him alone," Yuki replied, crossing her arms.

"This isn't any of your business, little mouse."

"It's my business now." Yuki's eyes caught Kaori's attention. Those eyes had the look of a person who had fought wars. That alone made Kaori nod in understanding. Without paying any attention, Michael stood up between them.

"Please," he started, "there's no need to—", but Yuki and Kaori pushed him back into his seat.

"What are you, a fan?" Kaori said. "Do you know who you're up against?"

"I get it now," Yuki said with a smirk. "You're jealous."

"Jealous?" Kaori placed her fingers on her chest. "What makes you think I'm jealous?"

"You just told me."

Kaori jerked her head back, as Yuki stroked her hair with a smirk. They were staring each other down when the sound of cats hissing broke the silence.

"Did you bring cats into my store, Kaori?" Michael said, and Jamal leaned close, whispering into his ear.

"That's not actual cats we're hearing," he said, pointing at the women. Michael tilted his head. "Michael, it's best not to interfere."

"Believe what you want," Kaori said to Yuki. "But I'll see to it that The Impossible Man never has his day of rest."

"That doesn't make sense," Yuki replied. "What did he do?"

"He still has to answer for that bachelor party mix-up."

"Bachelor party?" Yuki said, and Michael stood up out of his chair.

"Would you both just—" he started again, but Yuki and Kaori pushed him back to his seat. He lost his balance, fell over, and banged his head on the counter. He blinked his eyes twice as Yuki and Kaori sat on their knees next to him. They tried to help him up, but all they did was bat their eyes at each other.

"Look at what you did," Kaori said.

"Me? You're the one who…"

"Enough!" Michael was—from out of nowhere—on his feet behind them, rubbing the bruise on the back of his head. He looked up at the ceiling. "Two days. Just two days in already, mother."

He looked at both women, still on their knees, and stepped away from them. He took a long, deep breath that made Kaori jerk her head back. "Okay, okay. Kaori, take the rest of the day off and get healed. I'll need you well-rested tomorrow for the next advertisement."

Kaori nodded without saying a word. He watched her leave the store, waving goodbye in guilt. He turned to Yuki, startling her.

"I'm … I'm …" Yuki could not get her apology out.

"Just go get some posters. We're running low on them in the rack." Michael watched her quietly nod and go into the storage room.

✳ ✳ ✳

In the storage room, Yuki passed by the lion-headed spoon, which was lying next to some tools on a shelf. When she noticed it, it looked weird among the tools rather than in the kitchen. She figured it was just Michael being ridiculous again. As she went into a couple of boxes, she wiped tears from her face, wondering why that had happened. She felt stupid for acting the way she did. Especially since her duty was to protect Michael, yet she could not help but think about him and his abilities.

"Who is The Impossible Man?" she whispered, moving a small box to the side. Yuki at first thought he just had tele- portation powers, but it wasn't like that. This was something she'd never seen before. "I'll have to call supervisor and get some advice."

She found the rolled posters in a box and was bending down to reach them when suddenly, a hammer flew over her head, striking the wall. Yuki lifted her head up and saw the hammer lying on the floor. She picked up the tool and examined it, but when she scanned the room, she saw noth- ing out of the ordinary. She took both the hammer and the posters, placing the hammer back on the shelf next to the spoon. A strange feeling overcame her when she saw the spoon. It was as if the eyes of the lion were looking at her like a person. She reached for it, but the sound of screaming outside caught her attention.

Yuki jumped out of the room with her brooch in hand, ready to transform. She saw Michael and Jamal standing before the storefront window. As Yuki approached them slowly, the people outside ran away. She noticed that Michael and Jamal stood unfazed. She wasn't sure whether she should transform or wait.

"Yuru Chara! Yuru Chara!" A little boy pointed down the street, and his terrified mother pulled him away. Yuki stood next to Michael; him and Jamal were wearing sunglasses. They both had droplets of sweat sliding down their faces, fear projecting from their eyebrows. She found herself holding a pair of sunglasses. "Where? How?"

"Put them on," Michael said. "Remain calm and face front. As this is your first encounter, you need time to break into looking at our partner."

Yuki put the sunglasses on and looked out the window, past the store's frog emblem. Everything was tinted.

"He can't be that scary, Michael," she said, but never got a response. "Is he?"

"You'll see," answered Jamal.

Yuki turned to him, while more people ran by.

"It took us a while to get used to him," Michael said. "Who am I kidding? We're still not used to him."

Kaori limped her way back into the store, fell to the ground, and gasped for air. She crawled behind the manga shelves and poked her head up. She saw Yuki looking back at her, but Michael and Jamal coughed to return her attention.

"Why didn't you tell me he was coming?!" Kaori said.

"Oh, I'm sorry," said Michael, tugging his ear. "It's very hard to remember when people chase me with swords."

"Well, maybe if you hadn't put me in such a perverted situation, I wouldn't have to chase you."

"By the way," Michael said with a smile, "why did you come back here? You knew this was where he was headed."

"Damn!" Kaori lifted her head up in shock, then ducked back down. "Why didn't I think of that? Don't tell him I'm here."

"Don't have to. He can smell you." Michael shifted his eyes to Yuki. "Are you ready to meet him, Yuki?"

"I've faced monsters before. How scary could he be?"

Jamal pointed with his thumb. "Then prepare to say hi."

When Yuki faced the window, she saw the store's frog emblem move. There was the reflection of a short person walking by on her sunglasses. She blinked her eyes once, and saw that the emblem had not moved. The sound of the door opening and feet squishing on the floor left her frozen. Her heart raced while she stared out the window, not wanting to move her eyes to the creature next to her. Suddenly she remembered her eleven-year-old self in a magical battle, on her knees, screaming out loud in tears. She took one deep breath to snap out of it, and Michael and Jamal lowered their eyebrows.

"Yuki, Dōm Coquí," Michael said. "Dōm Coquí, Yuki."

"Nyah bu raya," croaked Dōm Coquí. He had two

webbed green feet and was dressed in a yellow muumuu, staring back at her with his frog face and sunglass-covered eyes.

"It talks!" Yuki screamed and fell on her butt, stumbling backwards and bumping into one of the aisle shelves. Removing her sunglasses, her hands shivering, she lifted her head up slowly. She saw Coquí's webbed hands reach out to her, trying to help her stand up, but instead she screamed again and crawled backwards, bumping into Michael's legs. She climbed to her feet up his legs, clutching his clothes like a ledge, until she reached his collar. Then she shook his shirt violently until his head rocked back and forth and his eyes turned to spirals.

"What kind of freak is this?!"

"Qwani sha monplemo?" Dōm Coquí pointed at Yuki in anger, and Michael shook his head, straightening his vision.

"Relax, Coquí. She's never seen someone like you before."

"You understand him too?" Yuki's eyes trembled. The fact that Michael nodded yes made her mind snap. She fainted and collapsed to the floor.

"You killed her, frog," said Michael.

Dōm Coquí pointed to himself. "Mio?"

Yuki opened her eyes and found herself on the floor. She pulled her knees to her chest, hugging them, as Dōm Coquí rolled his eyes and shook his head in disbelief. Yuki turned away, trying to calm down, and Michael knelt before her.

"You okay?" he said. Then he sat down across from her as she shook her head no.

"Ar ya kay bo?"

"Don't," said Yuki, raising her hand to quiet Dōm Coquí. "Don't say a word, please."

"He just wants to know if you're all right," Michael said.

"Do I look all right?"

"It's okay," Jamal said, standing next to Dōm Coquí. "He's a nice person."

"Person?!"

"Person?!" Kaori echoed, and covered her mouth. She saw Dōm Coquí's eyes light up. Kaori crawled along the aisle, looking past the DVDs. She watched Yuki bury her face in her knees as the frog walked past her. Kaori crawled in the opposite direction, only to bump into a pair of frog legs that landed before her. She lifted her head up and saw Dōm Coquí lower his sunglasses to check her out. She freaked out at his blinking eyes, alternating left to right, then right to left, then together at once. Kaori stood up, walking backwards, as he placed his hands over his heart.

"Hi, Coquí, how are you doing?"

"Kaori," he said. "Mazugi."

"Kaori. My love," Michael translated, as he came out of nowhere to stand behind Dōm Coquí.

"Stop it, I-Man."

"Lo pui jo venkana."

"You are a lily pad and I'm the body that sits on you."

"Shut up!" Kaori's eyes shifted to Michael, leaning against the wall beside her. She felt her hand held by Dōm Coquí's webbed fingers, which made her hair stand on end.

"Gen."

"Let us go to the back so I may do things found only in Hentai," said Michael.

Dōm Coquí turned around with angry eyes. Kaori pulled her hand away from him and stepped aside.

"I-Man teke ven detu."

"No, I'm not making things up. I'm just trying to enhance the mood."

"Syi aun yar! Gome teke ven detu."

"I swear I'm not. Why are you always trying to bend the truth?"

As Michael and Dōm Coquí argued, Kaori walked past Jamal, who was rolling his eyes from the argument, and Yuki, cradling herself like a baby from shock. She reached for the door and looked back.

"Well, I have to go home and rest these injuries," she said. "I'll be at the agency tomorrow to do the commercial. Bye."

"Where do you think you're going?" Michael, out of nowhere, stood between Kaori and the door.

"Home! Injuries! Remember?!"

"Oh, right ... I forgot."

"Idiot."

"Well, we have an emergency meeting."

"Oh, come on! Why?"

Michael pointed at Yuki on the floor.

"So?" said Kaori.

"She's your new co-worker."

"Co-worker?"

"Mo-werter?" said Coquí.

"Yeah." Michael leaned on the counter.

"Your mother?" Kaori asked.

"Aey! No insults." Michael saw Kaori cross her arms.

"I'm asking if your mother hired her."

"Oh. Yeah. Well, it's a long story." Michael smiled, and Kaori and Dōm Coquí rolled their eyes. "Look, just introduce yourself before you go."

"Fine," said Kaori.

Michael extended his hand to Yuki, and she took it and stood up. Dōm Coquí waved hello to her from across the store, but she looked away, shivering.

"I'm scared of frogs." She clenched her brooch, took a deep breath, and whispered to Michael, "I was eleven when I was eaten by a monster frog. I was lucky to survive." Yuki's shivering eyes said it all, and Michael nodded.

Kaori approached her and introduced herself. "I'm Kaori Saito...I handle the store's public relations, and I am Japan's number one idol."

"In America," Michael added.

"Don't you..." Kaori turned to him, and he stepped back with a smile.

"Hey,' Yuki's eyes lit up. 'I remember seeing you in advertisements back home a couple of years ago, but you're here in America? How?"

"That's because of Coquí over there," said Kaori,

pointing to the frog. Everyone saw him leaning on the wall, latching his tongue onto a fly, sucking it into his mouth, and swallowing it. He smiled sheepishly.

"Idiot," said Kaori.

"Let me explain, Yuki," Michael said.

It had happened two years ago. Michael was eighteen and had just finished establishing his store. He returned from Puerto Rico, having visited relatives, carrying a frog called a Coquí. Coquí are rare frogs from Puerto Rico. They are a unique species in that when they croak, it sounds like they are saying "Coquí."

Held in a plastic container, this frog jumped around happily. On his way back from the airport, Michael stopped at a gas station across from a chemical plant on the other side of the road. When the gas attendant finished filling the car up, Michael found the container tipped over and the frog gone. He was unaware that the frog had hopped freely toward the chemical plant across the way; he never saw it again.

A few months later, on a hot, sunny day, a four-foot-tall naked human-shaped Coquí walked into the store with going out of business signs and passed by Michael and Jamal, without a care in the world. They followed him into Michael's apartment, where he looked into the fridge, took out a beer Michael's mother had left behind, and drank it.

"And so," he said, "in the first few months of the store's existence, we were not getting a lot of customers. Not a lot of people were into anime and manga. We became a sort of niche store. We were strapped for cash to pay back the business loan. Somehow, Coquí got random jobs and provided money for us to help keep the shop up. That's when I came up with the idea of Coquí being a Yuru Chara."

"Really?" Yuki said.

"Yes," said Michael. "He's a character loosely representing our store." He stood by the frog emblem on the store sign. "We posted some videos on our website to promote the store. It caught attention in Japan and became very popular. The fans actually believed that Coquí was Denfair City's own mascot, and so the three of us received an invitation from a Japanese show called Outside Japan. On that show, we met Kaori while she had her interview about her career as Japan's current number one teen idol. Then suddenly—"

Kaori waved Michael off, but he kept talking. "So Outside Japan had the idea of Kaori coming to America to promote my store, and give cultural insight to Japanese television viewers. We're their sponsors now, and my mother didn't hesitate to hire Kaori as our public relations director here. Coquí then took on the role as our mascot to continue to help make money for the store. Behind the scenes, though, Coquí likes to be a pain. So we let him get odd jobs, just to stay away from the store, but now that he's out of the job again, he'll be working full time as our mascot."

"Funny," Kaori said. "I thought your popularity was because you got punched in the face by that female customer after using your Rhythm."

"The what now?" Michael said, ignoring his friend's wide eyes. "Oh yeah, that day. Those customers did spread rumors, but you and Coquí gave the store its exposure."

He smiled at Jamal, and was met with a displeased head shake by his store partner. Michael waved his hand to signal Jamal to say nothing else.

"Rhythm?" Yuki said, staring at Michael's suddenly blank expression. "So how can Dōm Coquí talk? And what is he saying? How do you understand him?"

"He just picked up the languages easily," Michael said, suddenly appearing next to Dōm Coquí. "The problem is, he picked them up too easily and learned English, Spanish, and Japanese at the same time."

"What he speaks isn't any one of those languages."

"To you. The thing is, he absorbed so much of all three languages at once that he … waffled it."

"Waffled?"

"In other words," Jamal broke in, "he speaks three different languages at once. Coquí makes no sense unless you speak all three languages. Since Michael is trilingual, he knows exactly what Coquí says. The good thing is that you, Kaori, and I can pick up a Japanese or English word or two from time to time."

"Freaky, eh?" said Michael, appearing suddenly next to Yuki and smiling at her. They both leaned on the counter, and Yuki tried to comprehend this insane world in which Michael's mother had placed her.

Kaori walked towards the door. "Listen, I'm going home to rest these wounds."

"Okay." Michael waved to her, and she left the store.

"Poime!" Dōm Coquí said. He tried to chase after her, but Michael stood in the frog's way and crossed his arms.

"You got things to do. Jamal?"

"I got him," said Jamal, and he took Dōm Coquí to the storage room as Michael turned his attention to Yuki. She held her hands to her head.

"I'm used to a lot of strange and weird things in my life, Michael, but between you, the idol, and that thing…" Yuki pointed at Dōm Coquí as he came out of the storage room, wearing a chalkboard sandwich sign advertising the latest release for the Torako Trading Card Game on one side and the latest Kuru Kururi-chan manga on the other. She clenched Michael's shirt, watching the frog standing before the front door, ready to go outside.

"I don't get it, Yuki," Michael said. "You're a magical heroine who's faced all kinds of monsters, and you're scared of him?"

"Mahogical hiroko?" Dōm Coquí said, with eyes wide open.

"Yeah. She beat the crap out of this guy named Wolfgang yesterday."

"Prove it," Yuki said.

"What does it matter? Jamal knows you have magical powers. He saw you transform back to normal yesterday."

"Keep me out of this, Michael," Jamal said, walking up to Dōm Coquí with a broom. He handed it to the frog and watched him slip on his sunglasses.

"Gilu xu," said Dōm Coquí. "Janu me tah deki." He waited for Michael to translate.

"He says 'Your secret is safe with me. Besides, no one will understand me with that oversized trunk of a mouth.'"

Dōm Coquí stomped on Michael's foot, and received a slap on the head in return. They both stared each other down, with fists raised, ready to fight. The two growled at each other and Jamal stood between them, pushing them back. Michael and Dōm Coquí turned to each other's backs with arms crossed, like a pair of girls.

"I don't know what I'm going to do with you two," said Jamal. "This store is more important than your petty argument."

"It's like I'm watching two children," Yuki said, from the far end of the aisle.

"Yus je en wer."

"Here we go with the dominoes again." Michael turned to Coquí. "I told you, I had fives and I followed your move!"

Jamal threw his hands up in frustration and walked away from them. Suddenly, Michael felt something in his pocket. He reached in and found the spoon in his hand. He growled at it and threw it past Dōm Coquí, and as he marched into his apartment, the frog stood over the utensil.

"Qwani nok ne?"

"What?" Yuki said to Jamal, while walking to the counter. "I picked up the word 'what' from him."

"Qwani nok ne?" Dōm Coquí picked up the spoon and lifted it in the air, so Yuki would understand his question.

"Oh, the spoon." Yuki sat on the chair behind the counter and controlled her fear. "Michael claims the spoon is following him."

"Yoco," said Dōm Coquí. He tossed the spoon aside and took the broom outside.

"Yeah…yoco. Whatever." Yuki leaned back, sorting out her mind. "And I thought the monsters I fought were insane."

"Believe me, Yuki," Jamal said, standing across the counter from her. "You'll get used to all of this."

Yuki watched Dōm Coquí sweeping the sidewalk, while people read the chalkboard sign hanging over his body. She looked skeptically back to Jamal. "You're not helping."

※ ※ ※

After the store closed that day, Michael looked around his apartment and realized the piles of mess were gone. In their place were things he'd never seen before. A couch and coffee table, a floor, lamps, coasters on the table, and both his and Yuki's shoes by the door.

"I didn't know I had a chair there," he said, looking at the seat along the wall. "And where did this table by the couch come from?"

He slid two of his fingers across its surface, and noticed there was no dirt. "Where's my dust?"

He lifted his head and saw Yuki in a bathrobe, opening her suitcase.

"No, no, no," he said, approaching Yuki. "We can't have this."

"What?" Yuki said.

"This." Michael showed his two fingers to Yuki.

"Your fingers?"

"No. Clean." Michael waved his hand, presenting his apartment. "This is not natural."

Yuki crossed her arms and tapped her feet. "I can't protect you if I'm going to be living in a filthy mess."

"Who said you were going to live here?" Michael placed his hands on his hips. "You're going to read the classified ad I brought from the store so you can find a place to live."

"And I will, when I'm done getting dressed."

"You've been debating what to wear for a long time. You're not going anywhere, so just put something on."

"I don't want to waste my clothes for nothing."

As Michael opened his mouth, he heard a knock on the window. He signaled with his hand to stay quiet and turned back to her. She took her suitcase and ran to his room. Michael pulled the curtain back, looking through the window, and saw Jamal waiting outside on the porch. He pressed the talk button. "I'm not attracted to you."

"Open the damn door."

Michael pressed the open button to let Jamal into the building, then opened the front door and shook Jamal's hand.

"Aey, Jamal, what happened?" Michael let his friend in and watched the young man cart his suitcase inside. Michael's smile turned to a frown as he stared at the traveling case.

"I got kicked out of my apartment."

"So your mother finally sent you away?"

"Idiot." Jamal sat on the kitchen chair. "Where did this chair come from?"

"I know, right? I never realized I had a chair there."

Jamal stared at Michael, shook his head. "Anyway, my

landlord sold his building to corporate contractors. So now I have no place to stay."

"This is really a bad time."

"Why?" Jamal saw Michael's shoes alongside women's shoes at the door.

"Hello, Jamal," Yuki said, and Michael lost his balance. Jamal turned his head lightning fast, seeing Yuki in her robe. He looked back and forth between his friends for a moment, then got up out of his seat.

"I'll leave you two alone," he said. He got up, but Michael and Yuki stopped him.

"It's not what you think," Yuki said.

"Really?" said Michael. "Because I…" He was interrupted by Yuki's elbow poking his ribs. He quieted down, and Jamal took his suitcase, heading for the door.

"Wait," Michael said, pressing his hand on the door to stop Jamal from opening. "I hear something."

Voices came from outside the hallway. "You crazy old man!" said a woman.

"I expect my rent money ten seconds ago!" came a man's voice.

"It's Mr. Tanaka," said Michael, his eyes shifting toward Jamal. "You guys can't be here."

He heard the sound of footsteps outside.

"Hide," he whispered. Jamal grabbed his suitcase and pushed Yuki into Michael's room, just as there were knocks on the door.

"I know you're in there, gaijin! Open up!"

As soon as Jamal and Yuki disappeared, Michael opened

the door. He leaned on the frame with his arms crossed, staring down at Mr. Tanaka.

"I heard people other than you."

"You have a hearing dysfunction, on top of your erectile dysfunction, Mr. Tanaka."

Michael felt the cane of the landlord strike his leg. He stepped aside, nursing the pain, as Mr. Tanaka toured the clean apartment. He saw the shoes by the door.

"This is not like you, gaijin." Mr. Tanaka turned around, and the shoes were gone.

"Unlike your sticky hands, I do have a sense of cleanliness."

"Prick." Mr. Tanaka walked past Michael, toward the bedroom door. "Is that washed up whore staying in your apartment again?"

"Her name is Kaori, and she isn't here."

Behind the bedroom door, Yuki's eyes went wide and she took a step back, unaware of a lamp by Michael's bed dimming its lightbulb. She turned to the lamp and the light shined bright. She heard Michael speak again and hurried to Jamal's side. "And I'd appreciate you not to insult my friend, or Kaori will slice your pants off like last time."

Outside, Mr. Tanaka leaned close to Michael and aimed his cane at his face. "Remember, if you have other people living here, I will triple your rent, then evict you and keep your deposit."

"Yeah, yeah." Michael waved off Mr. Tanaka. "How else are you going to pay for all those gigolos you hang out with?"

"Be careful, gaijin," said Mr. Tanaka, looking back at Michael with the corner of his eyes. "I know men from prison that can make a woman out of you."

"Yeah, well, you'd know that from experience, right?" Michael smiled, slammed the door in Mr. Tanaka's face, and breathed a sigh of relief. He looked out the window, watching the landlord outside the building tapping the porch light to get the bulb to stop dimming, then saw his friends peeking outside from the bedroom. "Come on, the coast is clear."

"Wait," Yuki said. "Take your shoes off, Jamal."

"Really?"

"Respect a cleanly home." Yuki crossed her arms and Jamal took his shoes off.

"Yeah, respect a cleanly home." Michael covered his smile, and Yuki's and Jamal's eyes pierced him.

After placing their shoes by the door, Jamal and Yuki sat down on the kitchen chairs, and Michael handed them one page each from the classified ads. In the living room, the lion-headed spoon sat on the table.

It glowed a red color… with intentions.

Later in the evening, Kaori returned to her apartment with a bag of medicine. The injuries she'd received from that blast were too much to bear. Her anger at what the mysterious girl had done made the pain even worse, but the pain was the least on her mind. Knowing that there was a new girl working at I-Man's annoyed her to no end. Though she knew it was Michael's mother who'd hired Yuki, she couldn't help but feel slighted.

"There has to be a reason Mrs. Garcia hired her." Kaori stopped for a moment and had a flashback to the first time she'd met Michael, when she was seventeen at the taping of Outside Japan. Her left eyebrow twitched. "He's the cause of this."

As Kaori reached for her keys, wincing from the pain, she saw a blue light slide over her hand like a glove. It enveloped her body and had a gentle warmth overlaying her skin. Her muscles felt relaxed, and the pain eased up. She lifted her arm up and was able to move. "How?"

Kaori removed the bandages, and despite still feeling bruises, the bulk of the pain was gone. The ki energy from her sword-wielding abilities activated, and she looked up to the sky. There was the Scarlet Sorceress, watching from the rooftop.

While Yuki was put off by Kaori's confrontation regarding Michael, her intuition told her that Kaori was neither a threat to him nor a cruel person. "I'm sorry about blasting you away with my spell yesterday," she said, and bowed. "You were the victim of a mysterious power that controlled your mind against your will. I should have been more careful with my actions."

She jumped away under the bright moonlight before Kaori said anything, leaving her behind in quiet reflection.

Episode 4

[~ Rumble Under the Jungle ~]

There is a legend that alligators live in the sewers. I know, I know, there's no such thing as alligators in the sewers. In fact, there are many legends about the sewers that are improbable. Like, for instance, monster humans that live under New York City and snatch people from the surface. Large maze-like structures. Animals that turn into humanoid martial artists. Maybe that's fiction. Also, breathable air. Lots of shows, comics, and video games—especially video games—love the sewers for some reason. I don't. It smells.

April 14, 2002

Clouds floated high in the sunny sky over Denfair City when the city street suddenly shook, causing the alarms of parked cars to sound off. Further down the street, as shoppers went about their business, a couple of cars crashed into each other. While the drivers argued, a crack in the ground separated them and slowly collapsed. The two drivers hurried to the sidewalk, and everyone in the area watched the cars fall in the hole. A woman looked down and saw a stream of water. A large green tail slid by. She screamed, and the creature below roared.

At I-Man's, though, the day started without a problem. Yuki stood in the manga section, reorganizing the books. Jamal restocked the anime DVDs. Dōm Coquí stood outside in his chalk sandwich board, sweeping the sidewalk, and Michael was at the counter, watching an Internet review of the recent episode of Moving Outfit Sundam Side X. A couple of teenage boys approached him with their merchandise, ready to purchase. Michael overheard their conversation.

"No way, Sundam Nighthawk is the best mecha in the series," said the boy on the left.

"Are you kidding me?" said the boy on the right. "Sundam EX-561 is lightning fast and will take out Nighthawk anytime."

"Boys, boys, you've been here all morning," Michael said. "When were you going to let me in on the whole Sundam talk?"

"Sorry," said the boy on the left. "What's your favorite Sundam?"

"Sundam Davaross."

"Aw, come on!" both boys said.

"How predictable," said the one on the left, taking out his money.

"Always the mainstream American dubbed versions, never the classics."

"Seriously." The boy on the left received his change. "And the pilot is always whiny with daddy issues. Freaking shoot something for once."

Michael took the money and brushed them off. After making the sale, he sat back on his seat and relaxed with a smile. Everything was good so far. Even the sudden appearance of the spoon, relaxing in a reclined position over a magazine, did little to ruin the mood, despite it glowing red to get his attention. That was until Dōm Coquí came inside and stood before Michael.

"Lu peh cingo-ju pekalar?

"What do you need fifty dollars for?"

"Rix ni heparto."

"Fix your apartment?" Michael lifted one eyebrow. "You got your own money. Use that instead."

"Uz xe ye ATM."

"Why can't you go to the ATM?" Michael crossed his arms.

"Iz faer."

"It's not that far, you lazy little toad. Go away." Michael waved Dōm Coquí away, and leaned the back of his head on his hands.

"Jawu."

"Up yours."

"Why do you two always argue over little things?" Yuki said from across the store.

"It's in their nature, Yuki," Jamal said, standing to his feet.

"Mind your business," Michael said, getting off his chair.

"You just can't bear the fact that it's true," Jamal said, approaching the counter.

"Mos het laz xiv." Dōm Coquí turned around, crossing his arms with his eyes closed.

"What was that, Coquí?"

"Leva miz."

"Yeah, I thought so."

A sweatdrop appeared behind Yuki and Jamal's heads; they found the argument ridiculous, as well as confusing to human language. The two continued taking care of the store, while Michael and Dōm Coquí called each other names and pulled each other's cheeks. When they finished, Michael turned on the radio. He switched stations, searching for music, and instead got breaking news reports. He turned up the volume, and everyone listened.

"Small earthquakes throughout Denfair City have residents scared. Streets are falling into the sewers below. Residents are advised to stay indoors until the city workers stabilize the streets. Everyone is asked not to drive their cars at this time. This just in, there are reports of a giant alligator in the sewers. City officials have no comment on this situation."

"Wow, there's an alligator in the sewer," Michael said, lowering the volume.

"Alligators in the sewers?" Yuki replied, clutching her brooch. "Maybe I should investigate to make sure."

"There's no such thing as alligators in the sewers," Jamal said. "It's an urban legend. Think about it. One, alligators can't survive in sewers, and two, if they did, then they wouldn't fit. Sewers are mainly cramped tunnels and portholes, filled with gases that would kill you."

"How could you not believe it?" Michael said. "Just look at Coquí."

"What about him?" Jamal faced Coquí.

"He's a frog, four feet tall, ugly looking. Even an ugly woman would put a brown paper bag over him, if they were in bed to begin with."

A large tongue smacked Michael in the face and knocked him to the ground. Michael saw the tongue retract into Dōm Coquí's mouth. Michael stood—from out of nowhere—towering over the frog, and chased him out of the store. As the two ran down the street, Yuki stood outside, watching them, while Jamal locked up the shop.

"Come, Yuki," he said, "before those two kill each other."

Dōm Coquí and Michael ran along the sidewalk, navigating around the people. The frog saw a pair of movers carrying a couch to a truck. He leapt on top of the couch and croaked, then jumped again, high in the air, to create more distance between him and Michael. He landed and ran, and Michael passed the couch without even jumping over it or running around it. The frog screamed.

As Dōm Coquí turned the corner, he saw Jamal and Yuki

behind Michael and prayed they would stop him. When he looked back, Michael was right on his back. As Dôm Coquí picked up speed, he saw a crack in the sidewalk follow alongside him. As he felt Michael's hand reach out for him, the street and sidewalk collapsed under them, taking a parked car into the sewers below. They both fell in. Michael grabbed the edge of the street, but Dōm Coquí fell into the water below. He popped out of the water and looked around, while the shadow of a giant tail moved in the distant tunnel.

Then the edge of the street Michael was holding onto broke loose. "Look out below!"

He splashed into the water, and Dōm Coquí floated over the giant wave his fall had created. Michael looked up at the hole and saw Jamal and Yuki above. Jamal laughed, while Yuki covered her mouth.

"You're all wet, I-Man," Jamal said.

"Michael, zer wil fe."

"Yeah. It really stinks here. Just like you."

Dōm Coquí pushed Michael's head underwater, and Michael pulled him down. They both surfaced, gasping for air. Then they looked at each other, growling and splashing water.

"Are you children done fighting down there?" Yuki called down.

Jamal watched on beside her with lowered eyebrows. "Do you know who you're talking to, Yuki?"

"Aey," Michael called out at the hole. "Help us up."

"I don't know," Yuki said, leaning her face on her hand. "You two make a cute couple floating in the sewer."

"Yeah," Jamal said. "I say let them soak a bit."

"Michael will probably stink up the apartment."

"You're right. Let him sleep in the bathroom."

"Good idea."

"Screw you two!" Michael clenched his fist up at them. He smelled his arm, and the rancid scent overwhelmed a bit. He shook his head. "Fine! I won't fight with Coquí... for today. I don't know who's worse, you or them."

Dōm Coquí gave a large, cheesy smile, showing his teeth, and Michael rolled his eyes. He looked around and found the tunnel to be very large. He swam to the wall and tried to grip it, but the surface was too smooth, so he floated back to the center of the hole.

"Great," he said to Dōm Coquí. "I'm going to have to do this the hard way. Grab my shoulders, hang on, and don't break my concentration."

Dōm Coquí's eyes were trembling, and his body was floating away. He looked up at Jamal and Yuki, who shrugged their shoulders in confusion.

"Coquí, what's wrong?"

"Reter!" Dōm Coquí swam away.

Michael heard a light growl behind him. He turned around and saw a large green island with yellow eyes inching towards him. "Whoa!"

The gator followed Michael—it took twenty seconds for that large body to swim past the opening.

"It's longer than a bus," Jamal said, as Yuki slid her body over the edge. "Yuki!"

"I have to help Michael and Coquí," she said, climbing down the hole, but Jamal grabbed her hands.

"Wait! You don't understand. Michael could just..."
Jamal lost his grip, slid down the hole, and bumped into
Yuki. As they fell down, Yuki sensed a strange aura. The
water below twisted, distorted, and changed into solid cob-
blestone ground. She used her arms to shield her face and
crashed onto this ground. When Yuki lifted her head and
saw she was in a large tunnel with pipes and no landmarks,
Jamal landed on her back. He rolled off of her, and they lay
side by side, knocked out. The lion-headed spoon flew over
them and around the corner, to another tunnel.

Michael was swimming as fast as he could away from the
gator when he saw Dōm Coquí dive underwater and gain
speed. Michael felt his body lifted up in the air. He flipped
over and saw the jaws of the gator, which were wide enough
to swallow him whole. It snapped its mouth at him, but all it
got was air. The force of nature looked up at Michael hanging onto the pipes on the side of the wall. Their eyes locked,
as though they had both remembered who they were and
had never forgotten what just happened here. Suddenly, the
gator's head jerked out of the water and snapped at Michael's
foot, but he pulled his legs up in time.

"Ut fe ey!"

"No, Coquí! Don't draw it to you! Get out of here!"

The gator floated toward Dōm Coquí, and the frog
swam away. He picked up speed while Michael jumped back
into the water to follow them. Ahead of Dōm Coquí was a

ladder leading into a large tunnel. The frog caught the rusted bar. As the gator opened its mouth, Dōm Coquí used the wall to leap up the ladder, landing in the tunnel, crouching. When the frog looked down, he saw Michael swim to a tunnel across the underground river, climbing up that ladder.

"Are you okay, Coquí?"

"Mun ha yu ke po?"

"You ingrate! How can you be asking for my stereo when I haven't even died yet?!"

"Thi foh ih!"

"Not unless I make you bait first!"

As the two argued, the gator swam in a circle, watching and waiting for them to jump back in. It growled impatiently as Michael felt something in his pocket. He reached in and found the spoon in his hand. Just as it was about to glow and help them escape, Michael screamed and threw the spoon at Dōm Coquí. As the spoon flew over the river, the frog used his tongue to deflect it. The utensil fell down into the water.

Michael and Dōm Coquí watched as the gator chomped down on the spoon, spinning its body as though it were drowning the utensil. They got up, shrugged their shoulders, and walked into their respective tunnels. The gator stopped spinning; the spoon in its mouth was gone, but it was covered in a red glow. It looked up with glowing red eyes and saw that Michael and Dōm Coquí were gone. The gator turned its head up, sensed something else in the sewer, and swam downriver in that direction.

❋ ❋ ❋

Yuki, meanwhile, took Jamal's hand and stood up. As she looked up at the closed ceiling of the tunnel, Jamal walked ahead with awe at the size of the tunnel.

"This can't be possible," he said, placing his hand on the moist brick surface of the wall. "You know how many tons of this it would take to build this place?"

"I don't understand," said Yuki, tilting her head at his attitude. "You've been with Michael a long time. How can you be so skeptical about being in a large sewer?"

Jamal saw the look in Yuki's eyes. Despite his skepticism, he noticed that she was not in shock at standing under the city, rather than dying and suffering from the sewers.

"Yuki, you're a magical girl, right?"

"Yeah. Well…it's a title." Yuki crossed her arms. "So?"

"Think about it. Kaori has a wooden sword that can rip through existence itself. Dōm Coquí is a mutant frog. I'm standing in an improbable tunnel with a giant alligator the size of a bus…and there's Michael. So…"

"You have no powers." Yuki's eyes opened in shock, and she realized that out of all the people in the store, Jamal was the most normal. He must have seen things that most people would not believe. That would drive a person insane. "You really have no powers?"

"All I can do is martial arts, and no, I can't do that ki energy channeling fireball throws, either. Just good old-fashioned martial arts."

"Maybe you can. I mean…anything is possible."

Jamal just stared at her.

"I'm sorry," she said. "I didn't consider your feelings."

"Don't worry about it." Jamal looked up at the corner where the ceiling and wall met. He noticed a line of lights flickering on and off. "Electric lighting?"

There was a continuous row of lights all along the tunnel, leading in both directions. He saw Yuki standing before an open grate, her hair blown back by wind.

"Fresh air," Yuki said, and Jamal stood beside her, reading an engraving on the metal that read "City of Denfair Sewage Department."

"Why would the city make the sewer system this big?"

"I don't know, Jamal." Yuki faced him. "Maybe we should find a way out and see if Michael and Coquí got out safe."

"Right," Jamal nodded as Yuki noticed a tunnel junction up ahead. He followed Yuki to the tunnel, but she stopped.

"Could you give me a minute?"

"Why?"

"The gator is still here, and I can sense a strange magical presence nearby." Yuki looked back from the corners of her eyes. "I have to transform."

"Okay. Do it."

"Not in front of you."

"What?" Then he remembered why. "Of course, the secret identity."

Jamal leaned back on the wall, his arms crossed, as Yuki entered the tunnel alone. He let out a sigh, thinking how strange things had gotten recently, and finally relaxed.

"Forever…Heart…Rave!" yelled Yuki.

"Rave?" Jamal said, and at that moment a light enveloped

the tunnel and air burst out. It rattled his nerves for a moment as the sounds of swishing and swooshing echoed through the tunnel. The light changed into an array of colors, like a rainbow, and thirty seconds went by. He whistled in sync with the transformation light as another change of colors occurred. More sounds of twinging and twanging echoed out of the tunnel. Then the light died down and disappeared as Jamal's whistle climaxed at the end.

"I am the deliverer of justice. I am the definition of courage. I am the essence of love. I am the magical girl ... Scarlet Sorceress! Beg for mercy now and I shall grant your wish."

Jamal stopped whistling and peered into the entrance of the tunnel. "Who are you talking to, Yuki?"

Yuki poked her head out in her magical outfit, rubbing the back of her head with a smile. "Sorry," she said, "it's kind of automatic after transforming."

"I see," Jamal said. "Well, let's get going."

The sound of growling echoed from within the tunnel. A pair of red eyes glowed behind Yuki. She threw her staff, Tsubasa, in the air, then clamped her hands on Jamal's shoulders and did a cartwheel over his body as the gator's jaws snapped where she'd once stood. When she landed beside Jamal, Tsubasa spun right back into her arms. As she aimed her staff at the gator, Jamal jumped in the air out of reflex. Yuki watched him spin his body and stretch out his left leg, moving it in a wide arc. Jamal's leg slammed on top of the gator's upper jaw. The kick disrupted its senses, and Jamal fell on his back due to the gator's thick skin.

"Amazing," Yuki said.

The gator headed out of the tunnel, and Jamal flipped himself back to his feet. There was hardly any room to get around the gator, and there was only one direction to go. Yuki raised her staff, but the gator lunged at them, forcing a retreat. It chased them down the tunnel, snapping constantly, running unusually fast for its size.

"Those are the same red eyes Kaori had when I fought that Wolfgang guy," said Yuki as they ran.

"Really?" said Jamal, then fell on the ground.

Yuki stopped and watched in horror as the gator's snapping teeth came close to him. Instead, the gator's legs stretched up and ran over Jamal, never stepping on him once. Yuki jerked her head back, realizing she'd become its sole target, and she ran. Faster and faster she went, turning left at a nearby fork in the tunnel. She could feel the snapping jaws brush her legs. Startled, her feet unexpectedly stumbled over an exposed pipe. As she fell toward the floor, and the jaws of the gator enveloped her body, she heard the sound of a snap and screamed.

"Aey, I got you!"

Yuki stopped screaming and opened her eyes. The gator on the floor below was watching her with a growl, while a pair of arms hugged her waist gently. Yuki turned her head around and saw Michael hanging upside down on a pair of pipes.

"Miss me?"

"Michael!" Yuki realized they were very high up. "How did you get us all the way up here?"

"That's not important. What's important is that we find the frog and get out of here. Is Jamal with you?"

"Yes."

The gator jumped up and snapped its jaws at them. Yuki realized the creature may get lucky with the next jump, and she suddenly felt her body slide a little. Michael smirked at her.

"No, you're not…"

"You got the weapon," he said, and released her.

The gator opened its mouth, ready to eat her, when she aimed Tsubasa at it.

"Fire Bane!" A large fireball blasted out of the staff and into the gator's mouth. It snapped the fireball into its mouth, and its face turned red. It spat out the flames like a dragon. As it stumbled away, roaring from pain, Yuki flipped her body over and landed on her feet. She stood in shock, taking short breaths, as Michael stood directly behind her.

"I knew you could do it," he said, and Yuki bashed his head with the winged ball of Tsubasa.

"Don't ever do that to me!"

"Yes…ma'am." Michael stumbled back, nursing his wound, and Yuki saw the gator turn the corner.

"It would be best if we captured that gator."

"Why?" Michael said.

"I felt a strange aura around it when it attacked me and Jamal. Jamal…" Yuki lifted her head up.

"What is it? Where is Jamal?"

Yuki walked past Michael and looked down the tunnel behind him. Then she turned around and looked at the tunnel behind her. "Jamal and I got separated, and now I don't know which way I came from."

"It's okay," said Michael, placing his hands on Yuki's shoulders. His gentle grip brought a light blush to her face. They started walking. "We'll find him. I'm surprised he even came down here. He usually can't handle illogical things."

"He's a lot stronger than you think," said Yuki, turning the corner with Michael; he raised an eyebrow at her. There was a strange confidence in her eyes regarding Jamal that made him smile. Yuki turned back at Michael and saw him laid flat on his face. She knelt down and placed her hand on his back. "Michael, what happened?"

"I don't know," Michael said, using Yuki's arms for leverage to stand up. His hands trembled.

"We've been walking for a long time now. Maybe we need some rest."

"Walking?" Michael looked back at where he was for a second. He felt his memories catching up, and remembered they had walked around a couple of corners into other tunnels. "What were we talking about?"

"Michael?" Yuki led him to a large stone alongside the wall and sat him down on it. "Are you alright?" She leaned closer to his face, watching his eyes tremble. She saw his eyeballs physically shift left to right, as though they were dislocated from the socket.

"Is this…energy?" He whispered, while staring at his hands.

Yuki placed her hands on Michael's cheeks, scared for him, and they heard the sound of screams at the far end of the tunnel. She kept her guard up as Michael blinked twice and regained focus.

"Jamal," Yuki said, and began to head down the tunnel.

"Coquí," Michael said, and grabbed her to stop her from running. "Not that way."

"Why? It's where they're screaming."

"That's the echo." Michael turned to the opposite direction. "They're this way. Come on."

Yuki heard it in his voice. It was so serious that she was compelled to listen. She made no argument as they ran down the tunnel. It was the first time she had seen him like this, and she did not know how to react.

✳ ✳ ✳

Jamal and Dōm Coquí ran down the tunnel, with the alligator snapping right behind them. The walls began to thin around them, forcing the two in a single file, Dōm Coquí was in the lead. The ceiling got higher, but not out of reach of Dōm Coquí. The frog picked up speed. He jumped up and grabbed a pipe hanging from the upper wall. He saw Jamal and stuck his long tongue out.

Jamal jumped and reached out, but his hands flew past the tongue. The gator was now on top of him. The corridor forced Jamal to turn left, and he felt relief that the alligator wouldn't fit. Suddenly, he slid down an incline. After rolling to the bottom, he checked himself for injuries. The gator roared and watched him from above. Shocked that it fit, Jamal trembled at the gator looking down at him, unaware of an armored woman standing behind and above him at the edge of a tunnel.

The alligator's red eyes fixated on the woman. She was dressed in a one-piece blue suit that covered her entire body, and white and blue cybernetic armor, plugged into the suit. The armor around her chest covered a white vest with a yellow jewel on the front, just below the neck. Her blue and white helmet covered her cheeks, tugged her shoulder-length red hair that looked like it was electrocuted, and a blue visor hid only her eyes, not her lightly tanned cheeks and chin. There was a badge on her shoulder with the initials A.C.E. on it. The gator's red eyes glowed upon analyzing her and nodded.

As it turned around and walked away, Jamal turned around, and no one was there. Jamal stood up, tilting his head and rationalizing what had just happened. He began his climb back up. "Gotta get Coquí."

Jamal slipped along the slope when a tongue snapped his wrist. He saw Dōm Coquí pulling his tongue up with his hands, like a rope. Jamal made his way, and they both sat down. "Where's the gator?"

Dōm Coquí nursed his tongue. "Reter ko te beh un se wi."

Jamal stayed silent and forgot the language barrier. He watched Dōm Coquí pantomime while talking.

"Reter jo qa li uw vah." Dōm Coquí pointed to the ceiling where he was at and made a gesture with four fingers, representing the alligator passing by in a hypnotic state.

"I don't know what you just said." Jamal stood up, and he and Dōm Coquí went back the way they'd come from.

Upon passing by a large tunnel, the gator jumped back behind them and resumed the chase. "Why me?!"

※ ※ ※

Running alongside Michael, Yuki saw Jamal and Coquí ahead.

"Jamal!" Yuki yelled. She waved as he and Dōm Coquí slowed down, and both ran in place. "I'm glad you're both alright."

"Not really," said Jamal. He and Dōm Coquí saw the gator with its red eyes at its brightest running in the distance, with Michael standing in front of it.

"Michael!" everyone said, and he looked back from the corner of his eyes. They stood in quiet shock as Michael lifted his right arm up, made the peace sign extending his thumb out, and smirked.

"The Impossible Man," Jamal whispered.

Yuki saw something in Michael that she was witnessing for the first time. Somehow, he was standing there while at the same time leaping over the gator. His arms were pulled back, his feet rotating in the air as though he was pedaling a bike, then at that same moment he was behind the gator, running down the tunnel.

"There's three of him?" Yuki closed her eyes and clutched her aching head. She could not handle the image she'd just seen. Her mind automatically blocked it out from shock. It became amnesia.

"Yuki," said Jamal, grabbing her as she collapsed. "Are you all right?"

"I don't remember." Yuki saw in Jamal's eyes that something had happened, but he did not want to say anything yet. "Where's Michael?"

"The gator is chasing The Impossible Man right now."

"The Impossible Man?"

"I-Man!" Dōm Coquí said, running after him, and Yuki realized they'd stopped calling him his real name.

Michael ran as fast as he could, with the gator snapping at his legs. He ran so fast that he was soon at the end of the tunnel. Before him was a large opening, and a chasm right below: total darkness, with no ground in sight. There were three other open tunnels across the chasm, and the ceiling above was carved into a dome shape. The gator charged at him as his friends followed behind. He stood there with a smirk, then found himself face flat on the ground.

"Damn…" Michael stood to his feet, his hands trembling, as the gator opened its mouth for one last charge. "Fine!"

He leapt backwards into the chasm, and the gator followed over the edge. They fell down into the darkness, with his scream and the gator's roar fading into silence.

Yuki, Jamal, and Dōm Coquí stood over the edge of the tunnel and looked down in horror. Yuki dropped to her knees and made Tsubasa act as a flashlight, but the light could not go far down the hole.

"I-Man," Dōm Coquí said.

"Michael…" Yuki's eyes welled with tears.

"He couldn't have fallen down." Jamal looked at the tunnel, and saw there was no place for Michael to have grabbed anything. "I don't see him in the other tunnels across the chasm. He had to have used the Rhythm."

"The what?" Yuki turned to Jamal as he continued to search for Michael.

Michael suddenly stood next to his friends, looking curiously down the chasm. "What a good waste of gator meat." He shrugged.

Yuki stared at him, as though she had not seen him in forever. She embraced him, they both fell on the floor, and she tightened her hug. "I thought you were…dead."

When she pulled her hands away, she saw the chasm.

"I saw you…I heard you…" Yuki's tears streaked down her face. She realized she was on top of Michael, and pushed herself off, facing away. Her face became red as Jamal and Dōm Coquí greeted him.

"Michael, don't scare us like that," Jamal said.

"Sorry about that."

"Reter u thad?"

"I just let it fall into the chasm."

"Good," said Jamal. "Now let's get out of here." He led the guys away, laughing as though nothing had happened.

Yuki stood there, watching them talk about what to do at the store today. She didn't get it. They'd just spent a long time in the sewers, being chased by a gator, and now they seemed unfazed. She could even see it in Michael's smiling face, where just moments ago he'd gone from shivering to confident and heroic, and now, casual. She could not shake this feeling of a blank memory in her mind. All she could do was ask. "Is this why you're called The Impossible Man?"

The guys stopped and saw her standing there, unmoved. As Michael crossed his arms, wearing sunglasses, Jamal and Dōm Coquí turned to each other and nodded.

"Hey, Yuki," Jamal said. "That can only be answered by observing."

"Observing? Are you serious?"

"Yeah." He waved her over. "Come on. It's okay. It will take time, but you will know."

She looked at Michael as Jamal and Dōm Coquí reached out for her. She wanted in her heart to know more about him. She wanted to know more about The Impossible Man. With a smile, she nodded and ran towards her friends.

✳ ✳ ✳

By night's end, everyone was all cleaned up. The store closed with the lights out, and everything was quiet. Yuki stood before the store's computer, typing away on a search screen to investigate the sewers, and scrolled through maps of Denfair City. She saw Jamal approaching her from the apartment, and he leaned on the wall.

"Yuki," he said, "about what happened today." He crossed his arms as she kept typing. "The Impossible Man cannot be explained. You just have to observe him to get it."

"There's no harm in telling me what makes Michael tick."

Jamal sighed. "Look, it's best if you don't try to find

out who he is. You may not like the truth. It's too difficult to handle. You'll lose all sense of rationality and reasoning. Trust me, his power can damage the mind. It's why I have to be skeptical about everything else in the world. Like the sewers."

"Or you doing that improbable spin kick?"

"What?"

"Forget it. You were right to be skeptical, Jamal." Yuki stopped typing as Jamal pushed off the wall and leaned close to the monitor. "The sewer system you were thinking of is impossible to go through."

The map on the screen showed the entire sewage system. Each notation pointed out where the methane gas was at, what pipes the water and toxins flowed through, where a person could crawl, and what was inaccessible.

"Then where were we just at?"

"Here." Yuki clicked on another map, within the very sewer system itself. When she reduced the size of the webpage, it became the shape of a perfect circle. There was a smaller circle in the center, with four lines stretching outward to form pie wedges. Inside the smaller circle itself were only two intersecting lines. Yuki pointed to that center. "We were right here, where Michael and the alligator fell into the chasm."

"What is that place, Yuki?"

"I don't know," she said, "but when you place this design over the map of the surface…" She moved the blueprint of the expanded system and overlaid it on the city. "… it matches."

"The pie wedges are over the boundaries of the four outer districts," said Jamal sliding his finger over the streets that formed the crooked boundaries in wedge-like shapes, "and the center circle is Little Edo." His eyes grew wide. "Those two intersecting lines in the middle are Main Street and Grove Street."

"The center of Denfair City itself," Michael said, standing behind Yuki and Jamal from out of nowhere, startling them.

"Don't do that!" Yuki slapped Michael on the shoulder; he rubbed his head with a smile.

Everyone calmed down, and Yuki and Jamal explained their findings to Michael. He stood there, confused. "So we were directly underneath my store?"

"Yes." Yuki nodded.

"Nothing more I can do."

Yuki crossed her arms. "Aren't you concerned? This is your store we're talking about."

Jamal approached Michael. "If that alligator hit something, like a gas line or a water main, we could have lost everything."

"I'm moving on." Michael began to walk back to his apartment. "I'll just file that under 'P' for plot hole."

"You know I hate it when you talk like that!" Jamal said, and Michael stopped. "It freaks me out to know that you could actually do that."

Yuki looked at Jamal, entranced. There was only the sound of the disk drive humming as everyone became quiet. There was no quick response. No sarcasm. No weirdness in the air.

Michael took one deep breath, and without looking back, he spoke. "You're too late... I've already filed it."

Yuki covered her mouth as Jamal slammed his hand on the counter. "Damn it, I-Man!"

"Gotcha," said Michael. He looked back with a big smile, then ran back to his room, laughing. He left Jamal and Yuki behind, their faces in total disbelief, now wondering if he was really serious or just joking.

"Scary," Yuki said, looking at her trembling hands gripping her brooch, unaware of how quickly she was ready to transform. Jamal growled, and shook his fist.

"Aey!" Michael said, inside the apartment. "What are you doing here?"

Yuki and Jamal hurried inside the apartment, and they saw Dōm Coquí standing in the front door with two suitcases, his large smile gleaming at Michael.

"Lut he tu vet," Dōm Coquí said.

"Did he say he has no home or has no fish?" asked Yuki.

Dōm Coquí lost his balance, and Jamal looked at Yuki, wondering why she even tried to understand the frog. He sighed. "I'm surprised you let him in, Michael."

"I did it so I can throw him out."

"Qwani?" Dōm Coquí growled as Michael pointed to the front door, but Jamal and Yuki pulled in his suitcases together, vetoing his demand.

"You owe us for your antics, Michael," Jamal said.

"If you hadn't chased Coquí," Yuki added, "we wouldn't have ended up in the sewers."

Michael stared at Dōm Coquí, and the frog smiled back.

The door behind Dōm Coquí slammed on its own, sending a brush of wind after it closed. Everyone stood there, frozen, as the sound of the television turned on in the living room. Yuki, Jamal, and Dōm Coquí peeked inside and saw Michael on the couch, flipping through the channels with a bowl of popcorn from out of nowhere.

"Don't make too much noise," Michael said without looking back, "or the landlord will know you're here, frog."

"Syi." Dōm Coquí removed his shoes naturally, and left them at the door.

As Jamal helped Dōm Coquí settle in, Yuki stepped outside to the hallway. She tapped her brooch, and it glowed. "Supervisor, this is Scarlet Sorceress with my latest report on The Impossible Man."

Episode 5

[~ Step into the Squared Circle ~]

Guess what, sports fans? There happens to be a variety of sports-themed manga and anime shows as well. Especially popular American sports like basketball and baseball. Even American football has been featured in anime and manga, either through characters or settings, but the one thing that stood out the most for me was an anime series that started airing here on Saturday morning television, alongside American cartoons dedicated to wrestling…

…and I don't mean the Greco-Roman style, either.

April 16, 2002

As Kaori stood in front of the bookstore's entrance with Seizon attached to her hip, she stared at the latest magazine from Japan, Nihon Teen. The front cover featured twin teenage girls named Reya and Rena Urashima, the music duo called ReRe. Their latest album had been released, and the magazine announced an interview with them. Kaori saw an image of herself at their age, with a big smile and similar headlines. She placed her hand on the cover and took a deep breath. "Soon, I will make my comeback."

Kaori saw the reflection of herself in the window, and noticed Yuki in that reflection. She turned around and saw Yuki carrying groceries down the block. She wondered why Michael's mother had hired her. Not much was said to her, but she did trust the Garcias, given their gesture to help her situation. Kaori grinned at the opportunity to tease Yuki about Michael.

"Hey, Shimizu-san!" Kaori waved as Yuki stopped, then ran towards her.

Yuki knew Kaori wanted to start trouble, so she kept walking. As she reached the intersection, a black car pulled up, blocking her. Yuki stepped back as Wolfgang emerged from the backseat, dressed in a business suit, his face scowling at her. He towered over her. She reached for her brooch to call Tsubasa, but her trinket was not on her blouse. Shocked by her mistake, she found her face smothered with a handkerchief around Wolfgang's hand. She punched him in the face and tried to grab his arm to twist it into a submission hold, but her eyes closed to the scent of the cloth. She dropped her bags.

Kaori, meanwhile, rushed at Wolfgang as he placed

Yuki in the backseat of the black car. When she reached him, she swung Seizon at the back wheel, but missed and cut an opening in the air instead, and the car drove off. She chased after the car, as fast as she could across the city, but the distance was increasing. Kaori saw a bicycle chained to a parking meter. She used Seizon to slice it free and started riding after Wolfgang.

✳ ✳ ✳

At I-Man's, Jamal and Dōm Coquí each set down a box. Jamal cut open one of the boxes as Michael read the shipping order. After opening the box, Jamal removed some of the Styrofoam popcorn and picked up imported music CDs.

"This is it, Michael?" he said.

"Yeah," Michael said, "anime soundtracks and J-Pop CDs. Are you sure this is a good idea, Coquí? This is uncharted territory for us."

"Syi. CD sa stoa geth bi. Qwar de zerf mi."

"So our competitors in Little Edo are selling their own shipments of Japanese music CDs? Good job spying on them."

"Where can we put this, Michael?" Jamal said, while scanning the store. "There doesn't seem to be enough room on the shelves."

"We can move the old release anime to along the walls, and use those shelves for the CDs."

"Okay."

"Coquí," said Michael, folding up the inventory slip, "you're going to set this up."

"Me re Yuki? O meh veh…"

"She went to the store to get the food. That's why I gave her the day off."

"Iyo bierveza?"

"You know she can't get you beer," Jamal said. "She's eighteen."

"What happened to the beer supply you had last night?" Michael said.

"He drank it all," said Jamal.

"Coquí, you glutton." Michael rubbed his eyes.

"Waka!"

"What was that?!" Michael towered over Dōm Coquí as the frog turned around and whistled lightly.

As Jamal restrained Michael, a loud bang vibrated from the window. The trio looked at the glass, which stretched back and forth briefly until it stopped. Michael screamed, then appeared outside from out of nowhere, watching the black car drive around the corner.

"Get back here and face me like a man!" he yelled.

"They can't hear you," Jamal said, opening the door.

"I know!"

"Michael, du ka le." Dōm Coquí knelt down and picked up a red brick with a picture attached to it. He handed it to Michael while Jamal checked the window.

"What?" Michael's eyes opened wide. In the picture, Yuki was tied to a bed, her eyes filled with anger and her mouth wide open, as though she were yelling at someone.

"She looks like an anime character in this picture," Michael said.

"Idiot!" Jamal said. "Yuki's been kidnapped!"

Michael flipped the picture over and saw a note written on it.

Dear The Impossible Man,

    I have your precious Yuki. If you want to see her alive and in good health, you will fight my associate in a wrestling match. You will submit to the beating of your life. You will suffer. You will cry. Then you will give me that spoon. Meet us at the Ninth Street Gym. By meeting my wishes, you will be with your girlfriend again.

Signed,
Wolfgang

P.S. Ha ha! Ha ha ha! Ha ha ha ha ha … and ha!

Michael lowered the photo with a blank look on his face. "Girlfriend? Since when did she become my girlfriend?"

"Who cares!?" Jamal said. "Yuki's in trouble."

"Don't worry," Michael said, walking inside the store. "Qwani?"

"Are you crazy?" Jamal followed Michael into the store with Dōm Coquí, where Michael now stood by the counter with a smirk. "This guy is after that spoon. What exactly is it about that thing?"

"I don't know. He just wants it for an auction. So he can have it, if it stops following me."

"And you're not going to bother to go after Yuki?"

"Yuki has her brooch, Jamal," he said. "She'll kick his butt in no time and come right back soon."

"You mean that brooch?" Jamal pointed at the counter.

Michael followed Jamal's finger, and his smile turned into a frown. He saw the brooch and gasped, as though someone had punched him in the stomach. He picked up the magical trinket and raised it up to his face.

"Okay. So if this is here, then what is Yuki going to do, Jamal?"

"Be a prisoner, you idiot!"

"Oh."

"Don't make me hurt you."

"Waka."

✳ ✳ ✳

The Ninth Street Gym in the northern district of Plainsland. It was the training ground for some of Denfair City's most popular and famous athletes, like World Boxing Champion Joe "Thunderclutch" Wilson and the champion wrestler, the Flex. Within these legendary halls, the sounds of training like in the days of old echoed. Photos and newspaper clippings tacked onto billboards in the locker rooms served as inspiration for future athletes.

Michael stood by the front entrance with Jamal and Dōm Coquí. When Jamal pulled the door, he found that it was locked. He stepped aside, letting Michael approach it. He just opened the door normally.

The trio entered the building, where there were multiple hallways. As Jamal looked in one direction, Michael faced the other and spoke. "We should split up, Jamal."

"I don't like this, we should stick—" Jamal turned around and Michael was gone, unaware of a pair of ropes glowing red aimed at him and Dōm Coquí, and a portal through a door revealing a row of chairs, with the sound of Michael screaming and the roar of a crowd within.

✳ ✳ ✳

In the infirmary on the second floor, Yuki struggled to break free from the rope tying her to the bedpost. She stopped and heard footsteps outside. Then she braced herself as the door opened. Wolfgang stepped inside, followed by Kaori.

"Saito-san?" Yuki did not expect to see her co-worker here.

"It seems she is still under that mind control thing from my first encounter with The Impossible Man," said Wolfgang. "She makes a good servant."

"What? How?" Yuki tilted her head as Kaori shifted her eyes at Wolfgang, giving a signal. She remembered that Kaori was a performer and not under any mind control. Yuki stayed focused.

"Wolfgang," Kaori said, in a hypnotic voice. "You know The Impossible Man will just pop in here and free her."

"And what makes you think he'll do that, puppet? I have his girlfriend."

"Not anymore," said Kaori, pointing toward the bed.

Wolfgang turned around and saw only rope on the mattress. He stepped outside and saw Michael walking alongside Yuki. "He ended my conflict this fast!?"

"That was a lame idea, Wolfgang," Michael said, without looking back. "and Yuki, you shouldn't leave your brooch behind like that."

"I know." Yuki lowered her head. "I forgot."

"Aey Kaori, let's go."

"Okay," she said with her regular voice, tiptoeing behind Wolfgang to get away. "I told you that wasn't going to work."

Wolfgang's left eyebrow twitched. "I had anticipated this potential side effect."

"Eh?" Kaori stopped and heard Wolfgang snap his fingers. A large door opened wide, and standing before Michael and Yuki was a masked wrestler covered in a cloak.

Kaori's eyes grew wide, while Yuki jumped in front of Michael as a shield.

"Say hello to El Lobo de Muerte. Or Lobo for short. The reigning champion of the Mexican Wrestling Federation Association. Go on, say hello to Lobo."

"Hello," Yuki said, as Michael clutched her shoulders.

"…and goodbye." Michael smirked, as Lobo's eyes tracked him with untold speed and threw his arm out of his cloak, parallel to his shoulders. Then Michael appeared out of nowhere on his muscular arm, carrying Yuki. Michael was in shock as Lobo shook his muscular arm up and down. He released her, and she fell on her butt, then he tightened his grip on Lobo's arm to hold on.

Wolfgang sighed. "This is tiring. Puppet?"

"Yes?" Kaori said, returning to a hypnotic voice, and hoped Wolfgang had not figured out that she was acting.

"Get him off Lobo."

"Yes," said Kaori. She stood before Lobo as the wrestler stopped shaking his arm. She winked at Yuki, then slid the tip of Seizon across Michael's back.

"Heh heh…that tickles."

"I can't use Seizon if you two are in the way," Kaori whispered into his ear, and Michael stopped laughing. She then spoke aloud in her hypnotized voice, continuing her act. "Give up the spoon and we'll let you go."

"Take it," Michael said. "It's in my pocket."

Kaori reached into Michael's pocket and rummaged around, but found nothing inside other than his wallet. "I'm free?"

"Nothing," Kaori said to Wolfgang, and showed him the wallet.

"I'm free!"

"If you won't hand me the spoon," Wolfgang said, standing behind Kaori, "I'll beat it out of you. Take him, Lobo."

"Let me be free!" Michael said, struggling to break out.

"To where?" Kaori said, as Wolfgang took Yuki by the collar and dragged her away.

"To the ring."

Wolfgang led Lobo as Yuki kicked and screamed. The wrestler carried Michael on his arm, with Kaori following them.

They arrived in front of a pair of giant doors, with the

roar of a crowd blaring inside. Wolfgang opened the door, waving, as the cheers grew louder and Kaori stood in disbelief.

Empty seats.

Nothing but empty seats around a boxing ring, all arranged as though Wolfgang had expected an audience in this small training room. Instead, there was only the referee in the ring, waiting for the fighters to step inside, and a table with a small radio playing the sound of the cheering audience. As everyone walked past the seats, the lion-headed spoon flew past them underneath the ring, creating a red glow.

Wolfgang sat Yuki on a chair in the front row and tied her up again. Then he led Kaori away from Yuki by the hand, and she shivered. Wolfgang signaled Lobo to enter the ring. Everyone watched the wrestler throw Michael over the top rope with ease, and Michael landed on his face.

"You didn't say anything about a fight!" Kaori said, covering her mouth and forgetting her act.

"So what if he has to fight, puppet? When he's softened up, you will kill him."

Kaori tightened her grip on Seizon and growled under her breath. With the opening she had, she raised the sword at Wolfgang, ready to strike, but his hand clutched her wrist as he kept his eyes on Lobo climbing into the ring.

"It would appear that your heart for The Impossible Man has broken you free from the mind control."

Kaori and Yuki lowered their eyelids halfway, listening to Wolfgang's stupidity. They heard a loud thud, and everyone looked up at the ring. Inside, Michael laid face-down on the canvas, his head lifted up in shock.

"I didn't ring the bell yet!" Wolfgang said.

"It wasn't Lobo, sir," said the referee. "He just appeared on the floor out of nowhere."

Kaori and Yuki gasped. They could not understand what had happened and why.

Wolfgang crushed Kaori's wrist to force her to drop the sword. She struggled to break free, reaching out to Michael.

"Focus!" she called out. "You can do it!"

"We can't have cheerleaders on the sidelines," Wolfgang said. He then tied her up next to Yuki, with tape over her mouth. As she struggled to break free, Wolfgang walked past them with a smile. He sat behind a scorer's table by the ring with a microphone, a bell, and a radio that played the sound of the crowd. He set Seizon on the table before him.

Everyone watched the referee pat down Michael and Lobo for any illegal objects and give them their instruc-tions. "Watch the low blows, no illegal holds allowed, any-thing goes. Understand?"

"No," Michael said.

Wolfgang pressed stop on the tape player, then moved the microphone close to his lips and tapped it to see if it was on.

"Testing." The microphone shrieked. "Ladies and gen-tlemen," he said, his voice amplified, "it is time for our main event."

Wolfgang pressed play and the crowd roared.

"Very crazy," Michael said in Spanish to Lobo.

"Yes, mister," Lobo responded in Spanish, "but he pays good money."

"In the blue corner…" The crowd roared to the sound of heavy metal, Lobo's entrance theme song. "…all the way from Cancun, Mexico. Standing at 6 foot 10 inches, 310 pounds…the reigning champion, the hero of Tijuana, our beloved El Lobo de Muerte!"

Wolfgang turned up the volume; it was deafening. Lobo pulled his cloak off his back and threw it into the air, revealing his purple trunks and flexing his muscles in front of everyone. The crowd changed to the sounds of women screaming out for Lobo, some begging him to marry them.

Michael turned to Kaori and Yuki, shrugging his shoulders. Their eyes trembled in fear for his safety. The crowd became silent; a kazoo played from the tape as Michael's entrance theme song.

"…and in the red corner, The Impossible Man." Wolfgang switched tapes, and the sound of crickets echoed throughout the room. Wolfgang laughed out loud as Kaori struggled to break free.

The bell rang, and Lobo rushed at Michael, his eyes tracking him. Michael tried to escape, but the wrestler turned around and grabbed his shirt, pulling him back from out of nowhere. The masked wrestler looked down at Michael with a smile, and Yuki shook her head in shock.

"How?" she said.

"Whoa," said Wolfgang, like a commentator, "a nice effort by The Impossible Man, but Lobo just got hold of him. Your analysis, Wolfgang?" He shifted his body as if he were talking to someone next to him. "As you can see, Lobo has a distinct height advantage and reach over The Impossible Man. That will prove to be the difference in this matchup."

Wolfgang shifted his body to the right and nodded in agreement.

"I see," he said, focusing his attention back to the ring. "And now Lobo has The Impossible Man in a headlock."

At the moment, Michael was flailing his arms as Lobo pushed him downward. He felt himself lifted off the ground and spun upside down. His head slammed into the ground, he flopped flat on his face, and felt an elbow jammed into his back. Michael's scream was unlike anything Kaori and Yuki had ever heard.

"Michael…" Yuki said, as she and Kaori struggled to break free.

"That was a nice elbow slam on The Impossible Man," continued Wolfgang, "and Lobo now has his opponent trapped in the corner."

Michael used the turnbuckle in the corner to stand up, but as he did, a shadow covered his body. He turned around and saw Lobo climbing on the ropes over him. The wrestler pulled his head back and threw punches at his face; the fake crowd counted each punch thrown. Michael heard the referee count up to nine, but Lobo let him go, snarling.

"Don't mess with me, Lobo," the referee said, "or you're disqualified."

Lobo flexed his muscles again as the crowd in the recording cheered him on and the women screamed. He heard a loud thud, and Michael was across the ring, flat on his face.

Michael shivered, and used the ropes to climb back up. He looked down at Kaori and Yuki, wondering why they would not stop spinning.

"Michael, what's wrong?" Yuki said. "Why do you keep falling on your face? You should be able to do whatever it is that you do."

"Trying... pain hurting..."

"Where's my brooch?"

"Brooch... oh yeah..." Michael took the brooch out of his pocket and tossed it to her, but it fell on the floor outside the ring. He smiled in pain at Yuki as she noticed her brooch on the floor and felt a strange aura coming from under the ring.

"What's under there?" she said, as Kaori looked closely. "You sense something in there, too?"

Kaori nodded as they heard Lobo roar, his footsteps stomping on the canvas like a charging rhino. They lifted their heads up and there was Michael, ready to dodge him.

Lobo's eyes tracked him again. He crouched and slid along the ground, his hand curled into a fist. He swung an uppercut, and Michael appeared out of nowhere—his body and clothes turned pinkish purple—crumpling onto the ground. Lobo stepped back while the referee stepped between them and began a ten-count. Lobo flexed his muscles again while Michael struggled to one knee. At the count of nine, Michael stood up, the pinkish purple color having disappeared, and the referee waved his hand.

"Fight!" He stepped back as Michael and Lobo approached each other, fists raised.

"It would appear that The Impossible Man's weird methods are not working, folks," said Wolfgang into the microphone. "How will he survive this match?"

Kaori inched her seat closer to Yuki and did her best to talk to her. "Et his ape op my ace..."

"Get the tape off your face?"

Kaori nodded as Lobo lifted Michael by his waist, bent his body back ninety degrees, and slammed him into the ground.

There was only one idea Yuki could think of to get the tape off. She hopped over to Kaori and stretched her face close to her lips, and Kaori pulled herself back. "Do you want to try and save Michael?"

Kaori nodded, unaware of Jamal and Dōm Coquí tied up and falling through the portal. Their screams ignored, they landed gently on the chairs on the other side of the ring.

"This is the only way." Yuki and Kaori came close together, face to face. Yuki opened her mouth and struggled to grab the tape with her teeth. She used her lips to gently rub on Kaori's face. Their lips connected, even though the tape was between them, and they both lightly blushed as their innocent eyes locked in place. Yuki grabbed the tape and peeled it off. The girls smiled at their success, as they heard nothing but silence in the room. They faced the ring, and there was Michael in a headlock, being punched in the head by Lobo, having watched them. The referee just stood there in shock; Wolfgang was wiping sweat off his face.

"It's not what you think!" Yuki and Kaori said together.

"Ladies and gentlemen, that was an exciting two minutes of hot action, and now…the match resumes." Wolfgang rang the bell as Michael screamed.

"Idiots," Yuki and Kaori said together under their breath.

Lobo grabbed Michael by the hair to stand him up. The wrestler took his arm and made him run to the ropes. As Michael bounced off the ropes and ran back to Lobo, the wrestler jumped up and kicked him in the face. Michael landed on the floor, groaning and covering his head in pain.

"Amazing," Wolfgang said, pressing play on the recorder to make the crowd boo. "The Impossible Man is still alive. Why is that, Wolfgang?"

He shifted his body to the side. "You see, Wolfgang, The Impossible Man is not human. He is some freak of nature, which enables him to live the way he does, and furthermore…"

"Would you stop talking to yourself?" Kaori said.

"Kaori," Yuki interrupted, staring at the canvas, "there's something under the ring that is keeping Michael from doing that thing he does to get us out!"

"What thing?"

"You know, when he pops up out of nowhere. That ability that lets him escape. What did Jamal call it? The…the…"

"Oh, you mean his Rhythm." Yuki nodded and Kaori continued. "Yeah, I'm sensing something under there too."

"Are you using magic energy to sense under there?"

"No, I have ki energy from using Seizon." Kaori turned to Yuki. "Did you say magic energy?" But before she received an answer, Kaori and Yuki felt the energy under the ring getting stronger, as another thud shook them. Michael crawled towards them, stretching his arms out for help.

"Where are Jamal and Coquí?" Yuki said, hopping towards her brooch.

"Jamal and Coquí? Is that a drink?"

"You idiot!" Kaori said, hopping toward the ring. "You came here without them?"

"Where am I? Oh, yeah, they're on the other side of the ring…"

"What?" Kaori said, as Michael rolled his body to the side. Across the ring, Jamal and Dōm Coquí sat tied up, and both were hopping towards the scorer's table. Kaori and Yuki tilted their heads in disbelief.

"How!?" Kaori said.

Jamal lifted his head up. "You two were too busy kissing each other to hear us fall and scream."

"This is not the time, Jamal!"

"We both arrived with Michael and split up," he replied. "Strange ropes wrapped around us on their own and pulled us through the doors. How did we get here?"

"Kode hi asmo," added Dōm Coquí.

"What?" Kaori said.

Michael landed on the ropes and looked at Kaori. "He said it felt… like he skipped time falling. Though, Kaori… I think Coquí got excited watching you kiss Yuki."

"You disgusting frog!" Kaori said.

Yuki growled. "That was not a kiss!"

"Te yi ko wef gu op?"

"Did he say we're lesbians?" Yuki said.

"Don't encourage him," said Kaori.

"We'll get your sword," said Jamal seeing Seizon on the table with Wolfgang. "Help Yuki get her brooch."

"Brooch?" Kaori turned to Yuki. "What's so special about that?"

Yuki saw her brooch and hopped towards it. "Just a little further."

Kaori followed Yuki.

Lobo pulled Michael back to the center of the ring. The wrestler's eyes tracked him, and Michael reappeared on the canvas, his back under Lobo's boot.

I don't get it, Michael thought. It's like he can see me before I execute. If I try to leave the ring, I fall on my face. I have to figure a way out of this.

Wolfgang's laughter rattled Michael's ears as Lobo grabbed his waist and jumped into the air. Michael felt his body flipped upside down and his back aimed at the canvas below. They were high in the air, so that everyone below looked like ants. The force of the fall closed Michael's eyes. When they landed, his back struck the ring, and a gust of wind blew everyone's hair back. When everyone opened their eyes, Lobo had wrapped his arms around Michael's neck and face, locking them in place.

Michael stared at Yuki and Kaori, hopping towards the ring. His eyes shifted to Jamal and Dōm Coquí, who were hopping towards Wolfgang. The referee lifted his hand. It dropped to the mat. He saw the referee point one finger to Wolfgang and lift his hand up again, but again it dropped to the mat.

Michael's eyes began to close. He heard Yuki and Kaori, faint and distant, yelling to him. His sight blurred as the referee pointed two fingers to Wolfgang and lifted his hand up one more time. His memory flashed. He remembered being face first on the ground as the alligator rumbled toward him, just like now in the ring. Whatever it was that made him fall to the ground, the choice he made to overcome it to beat the alligator became an epiphany. The referee released Michael's hand, and was about to slap the canvas for the final time.

Yuki and Kaori lifted their heads, with tears splashing out of their eyes, and called together with one voice:

"DO THE IMPOSSIBLE!"

Mere millimeters from the canvas, Michael stopped his hand. He rolled his hand into a fist and pounded the ground in frustration. His eyes lit up, and he landed face flat on the other side of the ring. He lifted his body up as Lobo and the referee blinked in surprise.

They remained in the same posture they had Michael in, and turned in his direction. Suddenly, Michael's body began to stretch. The sound of bones cracking throughout his body rattled everyone's nerves. His arms, legs, and body wobbled like an inflatable tube-man at a car dealership, until his bones and muscles strengthened. They finally fit back in place.

The ring struggled to glow red. It was fighting for control.

"What's this," said Wolfgang, "a second wind?" He turned up the volume, and the sound of the crowd's boos grew louder. While Wolfgang focused on the fight, Dōm Coquí lifted his head up and stretched out his tongue towards Wolfgang's table. He wrapped his tongue around Seizon, and as Wolfgang slammed his hand on the table and missed, the frog whipped the wooden sword over the ring; it landed by Kaori's feet.

"Thanks, Coquí!" Kaori and Yuki both fell over on their seats, landing next to Seizon and the brooch. Their fingers touched their items at the same time. Kaori angled her sword around to cut herself free, while Yuki made her trinket glow.

Michael, meanwhile, smirked at Lobo, and the wrestler nodded. They both ran at each other. The wrestler's eyes tracked Michael and caught nothing but air. He saw Michael bounce off the turnbuckle, across the ring.

I don't know why this happening, he thought to himself, but if I can't go forward to get around him, then maybe…

Lobo charged at Michael by the turnbuckle. He saw Michael take one step forward. His eyes tracked again and he swung his arms. Michael was not there. Lobo felt a tap on his head and looked up at a foot. He stumbled back. There was Michael standing on the top turnbuckle with his arms crossed, struggling to keep balance.

"I'm feel in control again."

He heard Jamal and Dōm Coquí cheering him on, and Yuki yelling from the other side.

"Forever… Heart… Rave!"

A bright light shined outside the ring as Michael jumped and rammed his feet into Lobo's face. They both had landed on their backs when, out of nowhere, Michael fell on top of the masked wrestler, his elbow striking Lobo's chest.

Yuki raised her arm up in the air. "I am the deliverer of justice."

She swung her arm over her face, revealing her eyes. "I am the definition of courage."

She pressed her hands over her heart. "I am the essence of love."

Finally she spun gracefully, and stopped standing on one leg. "I am the magical girl...Scarlet Sorceress! Beg for mercy now," she said to Wolfgang, "and I shall grant your wish."

"Who are you talking to?" Michael said, and Yuki stood straight up with a smile while rubbing the back of her head.

"It's a reflex."

"Focus, Shimizu-san," Kaori said, with eyes frozen on her. She shook her head and pointed to the canvas. "We have to get whatever is under the ring so I-Man can have full control over his Rhythm."

She and Yuki lifted up the curtain attached to the ring. They saw nothing but frames and posts. The spoon slipped out from the far end of the ring, and the energy went away.

"Whatever it was, it's gone," Yuki said.

"We'll get it next time," Kaori said, helping Yuki to her feet. They watched Michael appear out of nowhere in mid-air, behind Lobo. Their awestruck eyes followed his movement as he landed on the canvas and lifted his head up heroically. They clasped their hands and gasped with a smile.

Wolfgang, meanwhile, jumped out of his seat with a roar and made his way to the ring. He stopped in front of Jamal and Dōm Coquí as their ropes glowed from Yuki's spell, removing them from their bodies.

Wolfgang clenched his fist, but was too slow. He felt their fists in his stomach. He dropped to his knees and crawled past them to reach the ring, but Jamal and Dōm Coquí pulled his legs to slow him down.

"No!" said Wolfgang, distracting the referee, as Lobo approached the rope to see what was going on outside. "You fools! Don't take your eyes off him!"

Michael, out of nowhere, tapped a folded metal chair on the canvas. He slid right behind Lobo and slammed it on the wrestler's back. Lobo contorted his back as Michael slid the chair to Kaori, she pulled it out of the referee's sight. Michael jumped on Lobo's back and placed the masked wrestler in the same hold that had been used against him.

"I don't believe it," Wolfgang said, and everyone tilted their heads in confusion. Lobo, faking pain, dropped to his knees.

Lobo fell onto his stomach, struggling to break free. The referee turned around, held his hand up once, and let it fall to the canvas. Michael tightened his grip as the referee raised Lobo's hand a second time, then a third; it slapped the ring. The referee waved for the bell, and Dōm Coquí hammered in three dings.

"Winner!" the referee said, raising Michael's arm.

Everyone cheered as Wolfgang sat on his knees, shaking his head in disbelief at what had happened. Michael stood outside the ring from out of nowhere, collapsing onto the ground, as everyone gathered around him. Jamal helped him to his feet, and Michael screamed from the pain all over his body.

"Hey," Lobo said, climbing out of the ring. "You live up to your name, Señor."

"Gracias," Michael said, and watched Lobo and the referee leave the gym together.

Wolfgang flipped the table over and grabbed Michael by the collar.

"How!?"

Michael groaned. "You don't want to know. Oh ladies?"

Michael appeared out of nowhere behind Kaori and Yuki as they raised their weapons at Wolfgang.

Kaori swung Seizon at him, and his pants shattered like glass, exposing his underwear, with the smiling face of a teddy bear. She stepped aside as the Scarlet Sorceress aimed Tsubasa at Wolfgang. Everyone stood behind her and slipped on sunglasses, as a ball of bright light formed.

"Shining Light!" The light exploded on Wolfgang, and he crashed through the ceiling into the sky. A single star flashed high above the clouds. When the light disappeared, Yuki turned around and raised her staff at Michael.

"Healing Light!" A veil of light surrounded his body, and some of his injuries healed. "Feel better, Michael?"

"Yeah," Michael said, standing in front of Yuki, but Kaori got in between them.

Kaori stared at Yuki and remembered she'd healed that night. "Yuki, you're the Scarlet Sorceress from the news reports?" she said, and Michael lost his balance.

Yuki nodded and saw Kaori's angered eyes. She expected a fight, but instead was met with a relaxed nod.

"Thank you for healing me, Shimizu-san." She bowed, and before Yuki could reply, Michael stood up.

"Are you blind, Kaori?" he said, and Yuki smiled and winked at him.

"Well, excuse me, I-Man," Kaori said. "She doesn't exactly look the same."

"What? She looks the same. Her face is the same, her hair is the same color. You're so dense."

"Who's dense, Michael?" Kaori pointed her sword at him.

"Don't worry about it, Michael," said Yuki, taking him by the arm. "Let's go home."

"Eh?" Kaori turned to Yuki as Michael's face froze in shock. "What do you mean, go home?"

"As in, Michael and I go to his apartment together."

"What!?" Kaori's eyes tracked to Michael's face, his forehead turned blue.

"Kaori," Jamal said, approaching them with Dōm Coquí right behind. "I'm living in Michael's apartment too. We all got kicked out of our own homes. Right, Coquí?"

"Syi."

Kaori ignored Jamal and Dōm Coquí, raising Seizon over her head. When she blinked once, Michael was already running.

"Get back here, Michael!" howled Kaori, and gave chase.

"Give me a break!"

Episode 6

[~ The Chupacabra is Out There ~]

As part of this cultural exchange, I would like to share a legend known in Puerto Rico and throughout Latin America. This one is very well known and very popular. Chupacabra, the goat-sucker. It loves goats, it has appeared in some sci-fi shows on television, and there are many different drawings of it. It even appears on t-shirts. I, for one, love this legend. In my opinion, it's one of the coolest and most superstitious. Unfortunately, it also became a problem…

April 18, 2002

Kaori stood before a camera on the sidewalk, a microphone in her hand. Standing beside her was a man in a business suit with sunglasses, scribbling notes in his schedule book. She took a couple of deep breaths as he closed the book. "Are you finally done, Hino-san?"

"Yes. I have your schedules adjusted so you can conduct your interview with the circus," said Hino. "You should have no problems today and tomorrow. Sunday, we will head to the recording studio to get the final draft of your new songs. Be sure to dress nicely, we want to impress the producers."

"Okay," said Kaori. She nodded, and Hino approached his car down the street.

"Before we meet the producers, I'll have your assistants do some anger management exercises so we can keep your temper under control. Remember, this is your chance at a comeback."

"Yes." Kaori felt her right hand shaking violently in reaction to what Hino said. She'd closed her eyes to calm down when Hino spoke from a distance.

"And remember to smile. People love smiles!"

Her director stood in front of her, blocking Hino's view. She realized he was shielding her from him, and she felt relaxed. "Sasuke?"

"Don't worry about him. The parade is coming now. Let's hurry up."

Kaori nodded as the parade marched through Main Street. She had received final touch-ups from her makeup artist, and now she looked like a model. Dressed in a skirt and blouse, the outfit matched her athletic physique. Her high heels made her taller before the camera.

"I'm ready, Sasuke." She faced her director as he counted down with his fingers. When she was ready, she took a deep breath and smiled.

"Good morning, everyone. Japan's Number One Idol, Kaori Saito, reporting from Denfair City, New Jersey. Today, Troy and Hanley's Much Too Awesome Circus have come to town, and as you can see behind me, they are making their way through the Little Edo District. I'll be giving a behind-the-scenes tour of the amusement rides, the big tent, and some of their exotic animals. Then on Saturday, I'll be interviewing the visitors for their reaction to the first night of the circus."

"And ... cut," Sasuke said. He approached Kaori. "Good job. We're going to head to the fairgrounds later to talk to the ringmaster."

"Okay," she replied. "I'll be in my trailer." She walked to her trailer, and as she opened the door, she saw residents and business owners coming outside to see the parade. Clowns handed balloons to little children, while the adults looked up at the elephants walking by. Suddenly, a large cage covered in a tarp marched along, pulled by four muscular men.

Standing on top of the cage was a teenage girl with shoulder-length brown hair and her arms crossed. There was a sign on the side that read "Tangerine and her Amazing Pet." Kaori found it strange when she noticed the flap lifting a little, and furry fingers tapping on the covering.

"What was that?" she said, watching the cage roll on.

It was mid-afternoon by the time Kaori and her TV crew arrived at the North Fields of the Plainsland District, one square mile of open grassland on the northern border of the city used primarily for circuses, school trips, and city events. It was where Grove Street ended and split off into the northwest-bound Hopatcong Road and northeast-bound Bucks Highway towards the city's extreme borders. Kaori stepped out of her parked trailer and watched all the circus employees work. There was awe in her eyes as she walked toward the site, but a security guard stopped her.

"Sorry," he said, "but we can't allow non-personnel on the site during construction."

Sasuke hurried to Kaori's side and talked to the guard. "It's okay, we have an appointment."

"I'm Kaori Saito," she replied. "I will be interviewing Ringmaster Joseph Hanley." She presented her ID and watched the security guard pick up the phone. She passed by everyone building up kiosks for carnival games, tents for haunted houses, and odd creatures. Rising high above them all was the big tent. As Sasuke signed the clipboard the guard had presented him, she saw a chubby man with a mustache, smiling and waving.

"You must be Kaori Saito," he said, shaking her hand. "I'm Ringmaster Joseph Hanley. Welcome, everyone."

"A pleasure to meet you," she replied with a bow. "This is my director, Sasuke Kurosawa."

"Good to meet you." Hanley shook Sasuke's hand, and Sasuke bowed in return. "Please come to my office."

As everyone followed the ringmaster, Kaori noticed the teenage girl from the parade who'd been riding the cage. She watched her walking along behind the tent, towing a goat behind her.

"Excuse me, Ringmaster Hanley," Kaori said, and everyone stopped. "Who is that girl?"

"Oh, her?" Hanley said, opening his office door with an unhappy look on his face. "Tangerine's our youngest animal trainer."

"Really?" Kaori watched the girl turn the corner with the goat. She smiled at the idea of interviewing her for her segment. "Is it okay if I interview her?"

"Sorry, I'm afraid I can't allow that. Please come in and we'll discuss who you can talk to."

Meanwhile, Tangerine walked along the tents, avoiding the ropes and tools lying on the grass. She arrived at the animal pens, where the sounds of elephants, lions, and horses drowned out all other sounds in the area. Tangerine passed by one of the animal trainers, who was watching her carefully.

"It's feeding time, Tangerine," said the trainer. "You have the meal ready?"

"Yes," Tangerine said, walking by. "And my name is Angela."

"Be careful what you say. After what happened last time, the ringmaster won't tolerate another mistake."

"I won't mess up like last time," said Angela, turning around with angry eyes. "You'll see."

She made her way to an isolated area, standing before the tarp-covered cage with sadness in her eyes. With a deep breath, she took the keys out of her pocket. She placed her hands on the cover. "Mom, I miss Hanley Senior, he was always nice. If you and Dad were here, you would push the ringmaster around. Well, it's feeding time, Ely." She flipped the tarp up and saw the lock fall onto the ground. She picked it up, saw the cage door crack open, and climbed inside. "Uh oh."

"Baaaaaa..."

✳ ✳ ✳

The next morning, Dōm Coquí was watching the local news on the big screen in the store when he saw a report of an animal attack at a petting zoo in the Plainsland District. The frog watched a zookeeper holding up a goat's skin with three holes punctured in the neck. He screamed and ran to the storage room.

"The hell do you want, frog?" Michael said inside.

"Reevee ha nebunteka," said Dōm Coquí. He came out, pushed Michael to the counter, stood him before the television, and pointed to the screen. "Milu!"

"What's in the news?" Michael looked up. "Traffic?"

"There are delays on Root 80 East from Denfair City to Parsippany," the newscaster said, and Dōm Coquí lost his balance. After standing straight again, the frog took the remote and changed to another newscast. This time, there was another zoo that had a goat attack.

"Strange."

"Eds shubacadra, Michael."

"Chupacabra?" Michael turned to the frog, shocked.

"Chupacabra?" Yuki said, coming up behind and glancing at the news. "What's that, Michael?"

"It's a creature that eats goats in Puerto Rico and some Latin American countries."

"Really?" Yuki approached Michael, but Jamal stopped her to get her attention.

"Don't listen to him," he said, looking at Michael and Dōm Coquí. "Chupacabra doesn't exist."

"Oh yes it does, Jamal," Michael said, and Dōm Coquí nodded.

"Mu ce."

Michael turned to Yuki. "Chupacabra was first sighted in Puerto Rico in 1995. It sucked the blood of eight sheep."

"I thought it ate goats?" She said.

"Well, that and other farm animals."

Jamal placed his hands on his hips. "It's just a myth, guys. A superstition."

"Oh yeah?" said Michael. He and Dōm Coquí approached Jamal and Yuki, and she hid behind Jamal from the frog. "Then how come two goats have been sucked dry today?"

"Probably a giant bat."

"I don't think so." Michael crossed his arms and looked at Dōm Coquí.

"Well, there could be a logical explanation," Yuki said.

Michael took her hands. "I'm glad you understand that it's the chupacabra."

"That's not what I said." Yuki smiled.

"Don't get them into it, Yuki," Jamal said. "Come and help me with inventory."

"O—okay." Yuki pulled her hand away from Michael and used Jamal as a shield to get past Dōm Coquí.

"Yuki," Jamal said, while walking with her. "You shouldn't be scared of Coquí. He's a nice guy."

"I know. It's just that frogs are scary."

Dōm Coquí stood there, frozen, next to Michael. "I have to agree," said Michael, nodding. "You're ugly and scary."

Dōm Coquí was ready to strike Michael, but he raised one finger in the frog's face. The mascot stopped and smiled at the shopkeeper.

"What do you say?" said Michael. "We go capture chupacabra and get a reward for it?"

"Rento di?" Dōm Coquí's eyes grew wide with encouragement.

"Yeah."

"Syi!" Dōm Coquí shook Michael's hand in agreement.

"By the way, Coquí, I get ninety percent of the reward."

"Qwani?"

"Let's go." Michael looked back at Yuki, who was carrying a box out of the storage room, while Dōm Coquí opened the front door. "Coquí and I will be back. Watch the store."

"Wait," Yuki said, watching the door close. "We just opened."

Michael and Dōm Coquí walked down the street, passing by staring onlookers. The two made their way to a single sign that read "Bus Stop to Downtown" and stood next to it. As they waited, cars drove by and people passed, talking on their cellular flip-phones. The wait was long. It wore out Michael's patience, and the sound of a croaking hum rattled his ears. Michael looked down at Dōm Coquí, watching the frog's throat vibrate, making the sound "Coquí." The creature's head swayed side to side in joy. It was peaceful to Michael's ears until the song reached high-pitch levels. It became irritating and Michael could not take it anymore; he curled his hand into a fist and swung it.

"Michael milu!" Dōm Coquí pointed to the nearby intersection, and Michael stumbled past the frog, missing his punch.

He looked up at where Dōm Coquí pointed and saw a teenage girl crossing the street, not watching the moving traffic. A truck came barreling towards her.

"Ely!" the girl said with her hands to her mouth, like a bullhorn.

"Michael!" Dōm Coquí said, and heard a thump behind him. He turned around and found Michael lying on the floor, facedown, and Coquí helping him up. Michael stared at his hands in shock.

"What the … ?"

They heard the sound of the truck's horn, and the girl screamed. Then a shadow landed beside the girl, jumping away with her. They saw Kaori land on the sidewalk.

"Kaori!" Michael and Dōm Coquí said, running towards her.

"I-Man?" Kaori watched him just run towards her.

"Are you okay?"

"Yes. Did you ... did you just run?" Kaori heard a moan, and refocused her attention on the girl. "Hey. Are you all right?"

"Yes, thank you," the girl said, and Kaori helped her to her feet. Suddenly she recognized her.

"You're Tangerine, the young animal trainer from the circus," she said.

"Yes, and my name is Angela." She crossed her arms. "Tangerine is my stage name. I'd like to keep it on the stage."

Kaori looked at Michael, who shrugged his shoulders. "Okay," she said.

"Sorry," said the girl. "I'm Angela Rodriguez. Everyone calls me Tangerine, but I want you to call me Angela."

"I'm Kaori Saito," she said with a smile, and looked back at Michael and Dōm Coquí. "Introduce yourselves."

"I'm Michael Garcia."

"Piku ha Domingo Coquí. Dōm Coquí pur shurto"

"Coquí," Michael said, "you shouldn't say anything to her. She's probably in shock at your ugliness."

He smiled at Kaori, expecting Angela to freak out. Angela's hands shivered, and she lifted them closer to her face. Then she clenched her hands into fists and smiled happily.

"A talking frog! Cute!" She hugged Dōm Coquí, and Michael stumbled to the wall, slamming his hands on the bricks.

She actually hugged him, Kaori thought, and her left eye twitched.

"Dōm Coquí is a silly name," Angela said, pulling herself back. "Who gave that to you?"

Dōm Coquí pointed at Michael.

"You're really good with names," Angela said to him.

"Really?" Michael was confused by Angela's remark. "Well, I am a genius, after all."

"A genius of what?" Kaori said.

"Ed la wei."

"What was that?" Michael stood over Dōm Coquí, and Angela repeated the frog's statement.

"He said you're a genius at talking out of your—"

Kaori covered Angela's mouth, while Michael stared down Dōm Coquí.

"I heard what he said, Angela," he said. He paused for a second, then looked at Angela. "Did you just understand what he said?"

"Yes."

"Angela," Kaori said, turning Angela around by the shoulders. "That means you're trilingual."

"I learned Japanese in my spare time, and I grew up speaking English and Spanish from my parents before they passed away from a circus accident."

"My condolences," Michael said, and everyone nodded.

"They 'joked' to death."

Kaori spoke. "You don't have to push yourself to tell us. Choking to death is a horrible thing."

Angela tightened her hug around Dōm Coquí, like a doll. "I know. One day during rehearsal, my dad was suffocating with a pie in his face while spraying my mom in the face with a seltzer bottle, drowning her. They were the best circus clowns."

Michael's eyes widened. "Whoa, talk about 'joking' to death."

Kaori punched Michael in the back of his head and his face planted on the ground. "Show some respect!"

Michael slowly raised his arm in pain. "I got...what Angela meant."

"My parents left behind a will that said I am legally emancipated, so long as I work for the circus."

"So Kaori," Michael said, leaning on the wall. "Why aren't you at the store? Didn't you finish taping this morning?"

"Yes, I was on my way there when Angela..." Kaori leaned close to Michael's face. "Wait, why aren't *you* at the store?"

Michael smiled, leaning back, with his hands up.

"Coquí and I have to get something really important. Right?" Michael saw Dōm Coquí running away. "Don't you leave me behind with this psycho!"

"Psycho, eh?" Kaori leaned close to Michael, and he felt the presence of Seizon...even though she did not have it in her possession.

"Wait for me, Coquí!"

Kaori and Angela watched Michael suddenly appear next to Dōm Coquí, far away. Angela stood there, her eyes wide open.

"How did he get over there so fast?"

"Don't worry about those two," replied Kaori. "Now, how about I take you back to the circus?"

"No, I can't go back yet."

"Why?"

"I have to find my pet, Ely." Angela clenched her fist. "The previous ringmaster, Jeremiah Hanley, retired and his son Joseph took over. He is not nice. If I screw up, he'll fire me and I'll lose my emancipation rights. I'll have to go to an orphanage. So I can't give up."

Kaori saw the determined look in Angela's eyes, and she took the girl by the hand. "I'll help you, okay?"

Kaori saw Angela's smile, and with a nod, they began their search. "In exchange for an interview?"

"Okay, sure."

"So what does your pet look like?"

※ ※ ※

By noon, Michael and Dōm Coquí had returned to the store, each carrying a plastic bag. They set the bags in front of Jamal. Yuki walked behind the counter, keeping her distance from Dōm Coquí.

"Kaori isn't here yet?"

"Saito-san called," Yuki said. "She told me she'll be late. She said she was helping a girl named Angela search for her lost pet. She'll be in during the afternoon."

"I see," Michael said, opening his bag. He noticed Yuki leaning on the wall, staying away from Dōm Coquí. "Yuki, when are you going to give Coquí a chance?"

"I'm standing near him, aren't I?" Yuki said, though Michael noticed a large distance between the two.

"That's not the point."

"I'll be fine." Yuki waved as Dōm Coquí took out a spray can. "What is that?"

Dōm Coquí stretched the can out toward Yuki, offering to hand it over. They stared at each other for a moment, waiting for some movement. Finally Yuki slowly stretched out for the can; her fingers grasped it, and Dōm Coquí let it go.

Yuki read the label. "Chupacabra Scent?"

She pressed the nozzle, and the ensuing stench turned the air around her stale. The residue stuck to her face. She covered her nose as the canister somehow ended up in Michael's hands without him reaching over.

"Hey, don't waste the scent!" he said. "We need it."

"What is that smell?" Yuki wiped her face.

"It's the smell of a chupacabra. Juan said that the best hunters in Venezuela use this stuff."

"Michael," Jamal said, rubbing his fingers over his eyes as Yuki struggled to wipe the scent off her face. "How does Juan, or anybody for that matter, know what a chupacabra smells like?"

"See, we asked the same question, and Juan said they found a puddle of chupacabra urine with some hair. They extracted the scent from it."

Yuki ran to the storage room, screaming. The guys listened to the sound of water running in the sink and Yuki gagging from horror.

"You two are unbelievable," Jamal said, pulling out a package of Chupacabra Flypaper and waving it in front of Michael. "Really? You're going to catch it with this?"

"Actually," Michael said, as Yuki came out drying her face with a small towel, "that's just to slow it down. We're going to catch it with this net."

He pulled out a package containing a folded mesh net. Jamal stared in disbelief as Yuki took out a sack from one of the grocery bags, pouring brown marbles onto her hands.

"That's rotted goat meat and dry chupacabra dung," Michael said, and Yuki immediately dropped the sack and without touching anything, walked back to the sink in the storage room. "See, we lay out this goat meat mixture on sticky paper, spray the scent out in the air to attract it, and then when it's tangled in it, we throw the net and catch it. Simple."

Yuki came out of the storage room, drying her hands, as Michael and Dōm Coquí smiled. She stood next to Jamal, pale and in shock.

"I see," Jamal said, with his arms crossed. "Well, it's your money."

"We actually borrowed—"

"From where!?" Jamal towered over Michael and Dōm Coquí, cracking his knuckles.

"We're in budget."

"Syi," said Dōm Coquí, nodding. Yuki held Jamal's arms back as he struggled to strike them with his fists.

"It's an investment. For the store."

Jamal's growl grew louder.

"Chupacabra will be on display." Michael cracked a smile, and waved his arms outward at the store. "Just you wait, Jamal. We're going to be rich with merchandising."

"We can do that without a 'real' chupacabra!"

"And maybe we can think about reconsidering letting you in on the reward."

Michael turned around and found Yuki struggling to hold Jamal's punch back, while he dragged her along.

"Though your reward will be two percent of Coquí's cut."

Dōm Coquí growled, and Michael waved his hand at him.

Jamal lowered his hand and calmed down. "The day you capture chupacabra will be the day I crow like a rooster."

"Is that a bet?" Michael said, crossing his arms with a smirk on his face. Jamal's left eyebrow twitched.

"Fine," said Jamal. "And if you don't capture chupacabra, you'll crow like a rooster."

"Deal!" Michael and Jamal shook hands, and Dōm Coquí pulled out a contract from his pocket.

Yuki saw the contract set down on the counter. She picked it up and read it aloud, unaware of the store lights flickering above.

"The loser of this contract will dress and crow like a rooster on Sunday." She set the page on the counter. "You're really serious? Are you two going to sign this in blood?"

"That could be arranged," Michael said, holding a knife from out of nowhere, preparing to cut his finger. As he brought the blade close, Jamal and Yuki grabbed his left hand to prevent him from using it.

"It's not worth it!" Yuki said.

"Just use a pen, you idiot!" Jamal added.

After Michael and Jamal signed the contract, they

stared each other down, and then Michael and Dōm Coquí gathered the hunting equipment and left the store together. As the two would-be hunters walked past the storefront window, Yuki realized something.

"They forgot we're still open today."

"Idiots," said Jamal, his left eyebrow twitching while his fist shook.

✳ ✳ ✳

Michael and Dōm Coquí spent all afternoon wandering the city, carrying their hunting supplies. They checked the alleys where cats jumped off garbage cans. They visited the zoos where the attacks had occurred, looking for clues. They even checked out the meat markets that sold goat meat. They set up one of their chupacabra flypaper traps and goat meat mix, and waited for three hours.

Nothing.

By nightfall, they sat on a park bench in Little Edo. Michael leaned his head back. He sprayed the can of Chupacabra Scent, and the wind blew the mist back on his face.

"We'll have to try again tomorrow, Coquí," he said, watching the clouds cover the moon in the sky. "I'm going to lose the bet big time."

"Xe dib il beke."

"Yeah, I know making the bet was dumb." Michael shifted his eyes to Dōm Coquí. "But hey, at least I got Jamal to put his money where his mouth is."

Dōm Coquí slapped his forehead.

The bushes behind the bench shook. Dōm Coquí and Michael turned around, watching the shrub sway side to side. A pair of red eyes glowed within the darkness of the plant, staring at them as though studying their movements. The eyes shifted to the hunting equipment they carried. When Michael and Dōm Coquí noticed what it was looking at, they smiled, hiding the devices behind their backs.

"Do you think it noticed?" Michael said, as Dōm Coquí's lips trembled in fear. The eyes leapt at Michael, and when the creature hit him, they both rolled onto the ground. He screamed as Dōm Coquí pulled out a flashlight from the bag and shined the light on them. Lying on top of Michael was a small, furry green creature, with red eyes and a pair of arms and legs. It took a long sniff of Michael's face, and must have recognized Chupacabra Scent, because it nuzzled his face and hugged him. Then it lifted itself up, and when it smiled, its mouth went wide and its fangs became visible.

"It's gonna suck my blood!"

The green monster nuzzled Michael's body until it no longer felt him in its arms. It saw Michael hiding behind the small frame of Dōm Coquí; the frog held the unfolded mesh net. The monster stood on its two feet, a round green furball with legs and arms. Michael and Dōm Coquí faced each other.

"Shubacadra?" Dōm Coquí said, pointing at the monster.

"No way. Is it really chupacabra?"

"Chupa! Chupa!" said the creature, and a single sweat-drop appeared on the back of their heads.

"Throw the net!" Michael said. Dōm Coquí threw the mesh net, but it landed on the ground in front of the frog's feet. Michael looked at the frog with lowered eyebrows. "The hell was that?!"

"Efryort."

"You call that effort?!" The chupacabra charged them, and Michael and Dōm Coquí screamed, running down the hiker's path. Up ahead was a parked pickup truck with a goat tied by a rope in the back. Michael tripped over himself past the truck, and as Dōm Coquí picked him up, they watched the creature stop before them and turn to the goat.

Michael and Dōm Coquí watched the monster climb up to the back of the pickup truck. The duo looked away, cringing in pain, as the goat screamed to the sound of a loud slurp, as if from a straw. They saw its skin draped over the side of the pickup truck. The creature jumped off the truck and smiled at Michael with loving eyes.

"It's definitely chupacabra," he said.

"Lu po da qwe."

"Good idea! Let's rush it together."

Michael and Dōm Coquí took one step forward when suddenly the chupacabra ran at them. The duo stepped backwards, went left, and ran toward the building with the chupacabra gaining distance. Once they turned the corner, Michael grabbed Dōm Coquí by the arm. When the creature followed them around the corner, no one was there. Tears welled up in the chupacabra's eyes. It walked away, leaving the park.

Michael and Dōm Coquí leaned on the wall of a building outside the park, each catching their breath. Michael noticed Kaori and Angela at an intersection waiting to cross. He waved at them, catching their attention.

"We got lucky," Michael said as they got near.

"Hey guys," Kaori said. "You two look tired." Michael and Dōm Coquí ran up to her, embracing her like scared little children.

"Kaori, it was horrible!"

"Syi," added Dōm Coquí. She clenched her fist and punched both of them on the head, so they let go of her. Kaori crossed her arms as Angela giggled.

"They're funny."

Kaori tapped her finger on her arm. "Yeah, until they wear out. So what are you two doing out here?"

Michael opened his mouth, ready to tell her what had happened in the park. Instead, he looked at Dōm Coquí and shook his head side to side. He realized she would not believe him if he told her.

"We're just taking a walk," said Michael, and he looked at Angela. "Did you find your pet?"

"No," Angela said, lowering her head. "Ringmaster Hanley is going to be mad at me."

"Don't worry," Michael said. "I'm sure you'll find it. Who knows, maybe your pet found its way back home and is waiting for you."

"Really?" Angela looked up with hopeful eyes.

"I-Man," Kaori said. "You shouldn't say hasty things. You still have your limits."

"Oh. Yeah." Michael faced the sky, as Kaori remembered his running earlier in the day during a critical moment.

"About this morning—"

"Sorry, I have to cut you off," he interrupted. "Coquí and I have to go back to the store. Let's go." Michael grabbed Dōm Coquí by the collar, and out of nowhere was already halfway down the street. Kaori and Angela watched them turn the corner, and Angela tilted her head in confusion.

"How did Michael get there so fast?"

"Don't worry about him." Kaori took Angela by the hand. "Let's take you back to the circus grounds."

✳ ✳ ✳

Saturday evening, Michael, Dōm Coquí, Yuki, and a very happy Jamal went to the circus. They played the carnival games and hopped on the rides. They ate cotton candy and popcorn. Yuki enjoyed every event she tried. Michael watched on; she didn't pay much attention to Dōm Coquí, but the two did challenge each other in a game of Pop the Water Balloon.

"She's getting there, Jamal."

"Definitely." Jamal nodded. "So where shall I have you crow tomorrow?"

"I told you, we found chupacabra."

"Sure, sure." Jamal waved Michael off.

Yuki approached them. "You're still trying to convince Jamal you saw it?"

"We did, right, Coquí?" Michael turned to Dōm Coquí, who was eating cotton candy.

"Syi. Te mu ko cer."

"Coquí," Jamal said, "I have no idea what you're saying, so your story doesn't count."

"I swear I'll get you, Jamal." Michael shook his fist and his friend walked away, waving him off.

Later, as everyone headed for the big tent to watch the main event, they saw Kaori in front of the camera, finishing an interview with a little girl and her mother. Everyone approached Kaori as she signed off for the evening.

"Everyone," Kaori said. "you're all here."

"Of course!" Michael replied. "It's a rare night off."

"I've got good news. Angela's pet came back, just like you said, I-Man."

"Really?" Michael said. "Just like that?"

"Yep. So now she's going to get to do her performance tonight."

"Well, that's good to hear," Michael said, and Kaori wrapped her arm around his right arm.

"Let's go and watch," she said. She escorted him inside, looking back at Yuki with a smile.

"Okay," Michael said, noticing Yuki run up to him and wrap her arm around his left arm. He jerked his head back as the ladies escorted him inside. Jamal and Dōm Coquí shrugged their shoulders.

As the night went on, Michael and his friends watched the clowns perform, jugglers flick fire sticks, and trapeze artists perform high above them. Then Ringmaster Hanley stood in the center of the ring, his arms opened wide.

"Now I introduce to all of you one of the most legendary

creatures on the face of the Earth. It is a frightening creature, but don't worry, our special trainer, Tangerine, will keep this mysterious beast under control. Give a round of applause for Tangerine and her pet chupacabra… Ely!"

"What?" said Jamal, in shock.

"Pet…" Michael turned to Dōm Coquí.

"…Shubacadra?" Dōm Coquí turned to Michael.

"There's no such thing as a chupacabra, eh, Jamal?" Yuki leaned close to Jamal.

"Really, Yuki," said Jamal. "It doesn't exist."

The lights shined down at the opening, and four muscular men pulled in a large, tarp-covered cart. Angela stood on top of the cart in her costume, her arms crossed and a serious look on her face. Once the men moved the cart to the center of the ring, they lifted Angela and set her on the ground. She waved her arms up at the crowd and spun around to the tarp.

"Angela looks amazing," Kaori said with a smile.

"It's not the kid I'm amazed about," Michael said.

"What's the matter?" Kaori looked at Michael as Angela took a rope connected to the tarp and tugged it. The tarp opened, slightly revealing a pair of red eyes. Everyone gasped in horror as they watched the gate open, and Ely jumped out, spinning over Angela. It landed in front of her and raised its arms up like a gymnast. The crowd cheered. As the creature stood on Angela's shoulders juggling bowling pins, it noticed Michael hiding behind a man in the seats. It smiled, hopped off Angela, and ran towards the seats to the screams of the spectators.

"No!" Michael jumped out of his seat and ran for the exit.

"Where are you going, Ely?" Angela said, watching her pet chase Michael.

Kaori, Dōm Coquí, and Yuki sat quietly as Jamal rubbed his green hair in disbelief.

"I lost the bet."

"No," Yuki said, patting Jamal's back. "After all, he was supposed to 'catch' it, right?"

※ ※ ※

When everything settled down, and the circus ended for the evening, Kaori watched Ringmaster Hanley scold Angela. Angela stood before the man, her suitcase on the ground before her, Ely standing next to her.

"To make things worse, Tangerine, I have to pay for the dead goats Ely ate yesterday. You know how much money I lost altogether? I warned you. You're fired. Now go!"

"I'm sorry."

"I said go!" Hanley threw Angela's suitcase out into the street, chasing her and Ely out.

"Hey!" Kaori called out, as the ringmaster kept walking. "Why don't you act like a man and pick on an adult!"

Hanley never looked back, and Kaori turned to Angela. Despite her angry face, Angela wiped her tears, and as she reached for her suitcase, Kaori took it.

"Let's go home," she said, reaching out to Angela.

Angela hesitated, asserting her independence.

"I'm not going to let you live in the street," Kaori said. "Come on."

Angela looked at Kaori's hand and took it. Upon taking her hand, she saw a familiar expression in Angela's face. As Kaori led Angela away, she remembered that face in her reflection at that age.

The next day, in the afternoon, Michael stood out in front of the store, dressed in a rooster costume and crowing into the street. He received laughs from the passing crowd and customers. He even heard Yuki, Jamal, and Dōm Coquí laughing from inside the store. He turned around with a frightening stare to quiet their laughter. He then stood there with his feathered arms crossed as Kaori arrived with Angela and Ely, her sword Seizon in hand and a folder marked "Child Services" in the other.

Angela spoke. "I can't wait to meet your friends."

"They'll be your friends too."

Jamal waved to Kaori and Angela. "How did it go?"

"Pretty good," said Kaori. "I didn't think adoption would be this complicated, but thanks to Sasuke, Angela has a chance to keep working as an entertainer."

Everyone noticed the folder, and Kaori raised it up to them. "Well, it's the only way Angela can work towards her dreams. Though Hino-san isn't happy, because having an adopted child would ruin my image."

Michael continued flapping to the crowd. "Just say it's the Adopt a Sister program. Problem solved."

Kaori thought it over, but she lowered her head. "It might work, but the producers in Japan may not buy into it."

"Don't worry, Kaori," he said with a smile. "You'll find the right words and convince everyone, and your Number One Idol image won't be questioned."

Yuki stood there as Kaori faced Angela with a smile. At first she thought it was Kaori trying to make a move on Michael, getting him closer to her side like a hero, but she realized there wasn't anything in the conversation attracting them. He was encouraging a friend in need. Yuki blushed. "So kind."

Angela approached Michael. "Why are you a rooster?"

Kaori smiled. "I-Man, you bet against Jamal and lost again?"

"It's not right!" Michael said, pointing the tip of the feather with a flapping motion. "I proved the existence of chupacabra."

"Yeah," Jamal called from the opened door. "but the deal was to capture chupacabra."

"Capture?" Kaori turned to Jamal and he crawled back inside the store, scared at the Pandora's Box he'd opened.

"You tried to capture Ely?" Angela's surprised eyes caught him off guard.

"Well, I, uh…"

"Michael," Kaori growled, unsheathing Seizon and aiming the tip at him.

"Kaori, it's a misunderstanding!" Michael felt something hug his waist; Ely was nuzzling him. He screamed as Kaori swung her sword at him and missed. With Ely hanging on, Michael ran away from Kaori as everyone watched. "Get this thing off of me!"

Episode 7

[~ It Always Comes Back ~]

There's chaos and there's nightmares. When they collide, all hell breaks loose. There's no escape. No hiding. No way to understand what this has brought. The fact that I must reveal this may break everything, but if I must, then I must. I will prepare you, dear witnesses. It's the only way to preserve your minds for what will be. I shall explain.

It is the classic trope of American cartoons—born from the Golden Age of American Animation, when animation aired exclusively in theaters—that coexists within this world of Japanese anime. It's not eye-popping shock or the jaw dropping to the ground. No, this cartoonish ability is beyond science fiction transporters. You don't see fancy flashes of lights that send you to the surface of the planet, or special effects where smoke puffs into the air and you're in another location. It's a little simple thing that makes everyone ask "How?" This...is my greatest and favorite skill. The Offscreen Teleport. Just turn around the corner while I'm far behind you, and there I am in front of you.

And I have met my match. The object that would not leave, that would not be destroyed, that would always appear out of nowhere, the object that is...

...the spoon.

April 23, 2002

When Michael stepped out of his apartment one morning, he saw two movers carrying a couch outside. He pulled out his keys and walked out to open the gates to his store. A young man was placing his suitcase in the trunk of his car. Michael noticed the determination in his neighbor's eyes; he wanted to leave right away.

"Aey, Hiro," Michael said, unlocking the gate. "You're moving out?"

"Yes, Michael." Hiro closed the trunk. "That blasted Tanaka accused us of not paying back rent, but my wife has all the endorsed checks as proof. Then he started harassing us for the rent money."

"Well, yes, he does that all the time."

"There's more," said Hiro, helping Michael lift up the gate and exposing the storefront window. "Fumiko caught Tanaka sneaking into our apartment and looking through our private things."

"The hell is wrong with him?"

A young pregnant woman stepped out of the apartment behind Hiro. "He's a bastard, is what's wrong with him."

"Good morning, Fumiko," Michael said.

Fumiko walked down the porch, using the rails as support. Hiro hurried to her as she took her time. They approached Michael, opening the door, and Jamal turned the lights on inside with Dōm Coquí and Yuki waiting.

"Good morning," said Fumiko. "I can't take any more of Tanaka's antics. The stress is taking a toll on my baby."

"Yep, Mr. Tanaka is a handful."

"I'm amazed at how you can take it, Michael."

"Because he's scrawny."

"I heard that, gaijin!" said Mr. Tanaka, marching down the block and looking at the movers. He stood before the tenants, leaning on his cane. "You can't leave. You owe me rent."

"We owe you nothing," Fumiko said, as Hiro took her shoulders and led her away.

"Go to the car," said Hiro. "I'll handle this." He watched his wife wait by the car, her arms crossed.

Michael stepped aside, seeing his friends pretending to have been in the store early, trying to fool the landlord.

"Mr. Tanaka," Hiro said. "We don't have to stay here. We paid you all the rent and we expect our deposit back."

"You're not getting your deposit back. You, gaijin, and Shinichiro are the only tenants left."

"You should have thought about that before you snuck into our private drawers!" Fumiko said.

"Wait," Michael broke in, "there's no one left in the apartment building?"

"Where have you been?" Fumiko said. "Everyone has been leaving because of this pervert."

"Who are you calling a pervert!?"

"I am, you old fart."

"Fumiko, please," Hiro said. "Wait in the car. I don't want the baby to get hurt."

One of the movers gave the signal to Hiro that they were finished. Hiro ran back inside to check the apartment one more time. As Michael and Mr. Tanaka stared at each other, Hiro came out of the building and walked past them.

"Michael," he said, "word of advice, get out of here quick."

"Yeah, okay."

"Mister Tanaka," Fumiko said. "You can take this dump and shove it."

"Screw you!" said the landlord. "I still keep the deposit."

"Forget the deposit, Fumiko," said Hiro. "Let's just get out of here. You'll be hearing from our lawyer, Tanaka."

Michael walked up to Fumiko, gave her a goodbye hug, and gave Hiro a farewell handshake. He watched the young couple drive off, the moving truck right behind them. When he tried to enter his shop again, Mr. Tanaka stood before his door, his arms crossed.

"What do you want, old man?" Michael said from his counter, leaving the landlord standing in front of the door.

"I know you have people living in your apartment," Mr. Tanaka said, turning around and hearing the whistles of Michael's friends. He entered the store and stood before him. "If they want an apartment, they can have one."

Michael opened his mouth, but Tanaka talked over him.

"I expect my rent money from all of you, right now." He held his hand out over the counter and smiled, moving his fingers back and forth to get Michael to hurry up. Instead, the landlord received a low five slap.

"You'll get your rent money after they move into their apartments."

"Fine," said Mr. Tanaka. "You all have twenty-four hours to move in and give me my deposit and this month's rent." He left the store and walked in front of the window, glaring at them from the corner of his eyes.

Once he disappeared, Michael turned to his friends. Their eyes glowed like little children receiving gifts, and as Michael walked into his apartment, they all followed him. Once inside, they saw him standing by the door, opened wide and showing them the way out.

"You all get the day off."

"All right!" they cheered together.

"Just be careful with Tanaka."

Jamal, Yuki, and Dōm Coquí ran to the second floor. There were three one-bedroom apartments there. Yuki took the one overlooking Michael's apartment at the back of the building, Jamal took the apartment to the left from Yuki by the stairs, and Dōm Coquí took the apartment by the stairs to the third floor. They cheered happily for their new homes.

Michael closed the door to his apartment and leaned on the wall. It was quiet now, until he saw their stuff was still lying around. He sighed.

By lunchtime, he temporarily closed the shop so he could go into his apartment to eat. He sat before his dining room table, eating a sandwich. Then he heard everyone moving around outside his apartment door.

"Coming through," said Jamal.

"Careful, I'm moving the couch," said Yuki.

After finishing his meal, he saw the spoon sitting before him on the table. He leaned close to the utensil and stared at the lion's eyes. Then he grabbed the spoon and threw it into the garbage can. He tied it up and opened the door to the hallway.

Outside, he watched Jamal carry a folded table upstairs. Dōm Coquí stepped aside on the top steps, and then leapt down to the bottom to go outside. Michael saw Yuki at her apartment door, struggling to push a sofa inside. It was wedged in and stuck. Michael appeared beside her out of nowhere, leaving the garbage bag behind.

"Need help?"

"Michael?" Yuki jumped back in surprise. After she calmed down, she nodded. "Yes."

Together they tilted the couch to the side and gave one big push. Once they got through, Michael moved the couch to the wall where Yuki wanted it.

"Thank you," she said, walking past the broom leaning on the wall.

"No problem," said Michael. "I'm just surprised that you all got the furniture here so quickly."

"I guess your Rhythm rubbed off on us."

"Rhythm?" Michael tilted his head in confusion.

"Well, yeah. Isn't that what you do?" Yuki saw the dumbfounded look on Michael's face. She didn't understand. He had to know that was what people called his powers. It was what Kaori had told her. Fearing that she may have upset Michael, she kept on topic. "It wasn't hard to get the furniture. We did save up a lot of money."

"Well, that's good to hear," Michael replied. "I just hope that you all won't have a hard time with Mr. Tanaka. He can be a pain."

"I know, but you have to have your privacy too, Michael. Thank you."

"It was nothing. I knew Mr. Tanaka—"

"No, I mean," Yuki interrupted, blushing at the thought of Michael's kindness since she'd come here. "Thank you for letting me work for you, even though your mother hired me without your knowledge."

Everything became silent. Michael and Yuki stared at each other, and finally Yuki took one step forward, closer to him. It felt like a long time since they'd met that day, but Yuki's heart thumped hard and her cheeks blushed. She did not know what was going through Michael's mind. She wished she could read past his oblivious face. What was so special about him that the people around him would tolerate such powers? Her eyes lulled.

"Who is The Impossible Man?" she said with a hypnotic whisper, but a loud knock on the door snapped her out of her trance.

She turned around; there was the landlord, watching them from the open door and waiting for something to happen. It felt perverted.

"Yes, Mr. Tanaka?" Michael said.

"My rent money. Now!" He extended his arm, like a beggar wanting a handout.

"Sure," said Michael, standing before Mr. Tanaka out of nowhere and noticing his garbage bag sitting by the door below. The landlord saw the bag and growled.

"Why is that garbage bag in my hallway!?"

"What garbage bag?" Michael crossed his arms.

The landlord looked down the stairs and saw nothing. When Mr. Tanaka faced Michael again, Michael presented the cookie jar and took out the check…and the spoon. Michael's eyes grew wide at the spoon in his hand, while Tanaka stared at it with lowered eyebrows.

"Is this a joke?"

The check sat on Yuki's hand, and Michael stepped aside, trying to bend the utensil. Mr. Tanaka then waved at Yuki to hand over the check. She wrote two checks, one for the deposit and one for the rent, and after receiving the check, Tanaka saw Jamal walking down the hallway. He began to chase him down for his money, too.

Yuki, meanwhile, approached Michael. She saw the intensity in his eyes as he stared at the spoon. This was a cause for concern. Ever since they'd found that spoon on top of their pizza pie, all kinds of weird things had occurred, or at least weirder than things normally were, based on the stories she'd heard from Jamal. She stretched her hand out, wanting to take the spoon from Michael, but the sounds of Jamal and Mr. Tanaka arguing outside distracted her.

As Yuki headed to the door, the spoon glowed. The broom on the wall fell over before her feet. She tripped over it and saw the floor right in her face, but she never hit the ground. She looked back at Michael, surprised. She felt his hands on her chest, standing her up. Out of reflexive shock, she pushed his hands off, and crossed her arms with a blush.

"You're welcome," Michael said.

"Wait, I didn't ..." She turned around to Michael, but he was no longer behind her.

"It's okay," he said at the front door, "as long as you're not hurt. Are you?"

"No," said Yuki, her heart thumping hard again. "I'm not."

"Good. See ya."

She watched Michael close the door, then stood there, unable to move. She thought about the little mishap. Yuki knew he was just trying to help, and she felt stupid for over-reacting. She then heard Michael argue with Dōm Coquí beyond the closed door.

"Ko do di mu!"

"You're the one who bumped into me!"

She smiled.

Just before the end of his lunch break, Michael arrived at the post office. He took a box in hand and slid the spoon inside. Then he closed it, wrapped it in brown paper, and wrote down an address in the Galapagos Islands. He waited in line for a long time; the employees looked miserable and angry as they tended to each customer.

Michael shook the box to make sure the spoon was still in there, and it rattled. Within the hour, he made it to the teller and paid for the stamps. The postal worker took the box and violently threw it against a wall. The impact dented the corner of the box, which fell on top of a pile of dented boxes.

"Wow, good arm," Michael said, walking away from the counter. "Well, spoon, have a good time on the island."

He ran out of the post office laughing hysterically, people looking at him with sweat drops hanging from their heads. He was unaware of the armored woman watching him from the roof above. She tracked him with her visor, and it recorded him suddenly appearing across the street from out of nowhere. When she replayed the video, it was only static.

Once Michael returned to his shop, Angela arrived with Ely tied to a leash. She noticed the joy on his face.

"Hi, Michael," she said, walking up to him.

"Hi, Angela," he replied, stepping away from Ely's advances.

"Down, Ely," Angela said, and Ely obeyed, crossing its arms. "Sorry about that. I think we should hurry and shop."

"It's okay, Angela. You can take your time."

Angela walked down the manga aisle, using her finger as a guide to read the titles on each spine. Her eyes turned to Michael, who was smiling at something on his computer. She thought his smile was cute, but Ely growled at her for a moment, and Angela snapped out of her thought and found the book she was looking for.

"Oh," she said. "What's this?" Angela reached behind one of the books. "Michael, why is there a spoon in your shelves?"

Michael's face fell. He appeared in front of Angela out of nowhere, catching her and Ely off guard. He leaned closer and saw the lion-headed spoon in her hand.

"Is it part of a rare set?" Angela asked.

"It's not for sale," said Michael, disgruntled that the spoon had returned. His tone frightened Angela. When he saw the look on her face and noticed the manga in her hand, he calmed down. "Is that what you would like to purchase?"

"Y—yes." Angela shielded herself with a blush as Michael walked past her.

"Come on," he said, "let's ring it up."

Angela smiled and followed him, her grip on the leash loosening.

Michael appeared behind the counter from out of nowhere and opened the register. After he took the money and bagged Angela's purchase, Ely broke free, jumped over the counter, and hugged Michael, nuzzling on his chest.

"Get off me!" cried Michael.

"Chupa. Chupa." It tightened its hug as Angela pulled its arms off.

"Leave Michael alone, Ely," she said, tugging her pet's face and opening its mouth.

Michael saw its fangs, its tongue dripping with drool, and screamed even louder, but when he felt the spoon in his hand, an idea popped up in his mind. Michael reached for Ely's mouth and widened it even more, creating the sound of creaking door, then crammed the spoon down Ely's throat and closed its mouth shut. He heard a loud gulp, and Ely released him.

"I'm so sorry, Michael," said Angela. She dragged Ely out of the store, and when the door closed, he snapped out of his shock and saw that she'd left her manga behind. With a sigh, he placed the book under the counter and closed up shop for a fifteen-minute break.

Michael went into his apartment to calm his nerves. He sat on his couch and rested his head back, but when he looked over, he saw that sitting next to him on his couch was the lion-headed spoon, dripping with Ely's drool.

He grabbed the spoon and tried to crush it with both hands, his eyes hysterical. He rushed out of his apartment and stood by the corner of the street, where there was a storm drain to the sewers. He threw it down, watched it fall into the water below, and walked away whistling, as though he'd done nothing wrong.

"I-Man!" Kaori called from across the street, waving to him. She caught up with Michael and walked alongside him. "Did Angela come by your store just now?"

"Ah, yes," Michael replied, smiling with glee. "She left her manga behind. Would you come by and take it to her, please?"

"Sure." Kaori was worried. She'd never seen Michael like this before. "Are you okay?"

"Yep, now that I'm rid of that spoon."

"Spoon?"

"Yes," said Michael, but he felt something appear in his pocket. He pulled it out. "This spoon." His sanity had reached its limit. "This spoon that is in my hand right now, when it should be in the bottom of the sewers. Why won't you leave me alone!?"

He ran away from Kaori, screaming like a lunatic. Once he'd disappeared from her sight, she saw the keys to the store on the ground before her feet. She saw a couple of customers looking at the store entrance and opened the door for them. "Welcome to I-Man's."

Michael never returned for the rest of the day.

The next morning, Yuki's apartment door opened and Mr. Tanaka was thrown outside, landing on his face. Yuki stood in the doorway, dressed only in her towel. She saw Jamal and Dōm Coquí peeking out their doors.

"Take care of this, pervert!" she yelled, slamming her door shut.

Mr. Tanaka leaned on the wall as Jamal and Dōm Coquí approached him. He ran downstairs and the two chased him. With the door coming closer, and escape within reach, Mr. Tanaka fell on his face. He flipped his body over and saw Michael standing behind him from out of nowhere. Michael's leg was stuck out.

"You tripped me, gaijin!" yelled Mr. Tanaka.

Michael stared down at him, not wanting to deal with the landlord's antics. His stare would send chills down anyone's spine. With the spoon in his hand, Michael was ready to hurt Mr. Tanaka. That was until Jamal and Dōm Coquí got ahold of the landlord.

"You do this again, Mr. Tanaka," Jamal said, "and we'll get the city to investigate you."

"If you do that, you'll be out into the street," replied the landlord. He brushed Jamal's hands away, and his threat froze everyone in their tracks. Mr. Tanaka walked out of the apartment building, brushing the dust off himself.

Jamal and Dōm Coquí turned their attention to Michael. They'd never seen him in this state before. They had a crisis on their hands, and he was too tired to listen.

"Tanaka snuck into Yuki's apartment and watched her bathe," said Jamal finally.

"I see," Michael said, staring at the lion-headed spoon.

"You have to stop Tanaka."

"I see." But Michael was thinking about where to get rid of the spoon. He growled out of frustration.

"Ba wed mun cux."

"My balls are not broken, you web-toed freak!"

"Glad you're with us, Michael," said Jamal. "So are you going to take care of Tanaka?"

"Yeah, when he gets back," said Michael, handing Jamal the keys and leaving the apartment. "Open up shop, please. I'll be back in a little while."

Michael left the apartment building and walked down the street. He saw construction workers on Main Street, spreading out an asphalt patch to plug a pothole, and noticed a worker starting up a steamroller and driving it up the newly patched street. Michael walked towards it, spoon in hand. He threw the spoon on the asphalt pile, right under the path of the steamroller. The wheel rolled over the utensil, stretching it outward until it was perfectly flat. The lion head's lips were a straight line, its eyes a perfect circle. As the construction workers stared at the spoon, Michael ran off laughing hysterically.

While the workers were distracted by Michael, the armored woman stood over the flattened spoon. She watched it return to normal. She slowly lifted her right arm up; it was like molasses. A device materialized over her arm and a projection appeared in mid-air. It was a video of Michael crossing the street. The spoon observed. Watching the static, it glowed in frustration. As the woman's shivering hands reached out to the spoon, as if to capture it, her breathing struggled to let her scream. The utensil's glowing eyes struck her, turned her into a ball of red light, and pulled her in. The spoon vanished before the workers turned around.

Michael returned to the shop, passing by Dōm Coquí sweeping the front. Inside, Yuki and Jamal restocked the week-old released anime DVDs on their "Pick of the Day" shelves. Michael slouched over the counter, exhausted. He looked to the right, and when he did he was ready to cry; there the spoon lay on the counter, returned to its original state with a little tar residue.

"Are you okay, Michael?" Yuki said, approaching him.

"That…" He pointed to the spoon as Jamal and Yuki leaned in closer.

"What about the spoon?" Jamal said.

"I can't get rid of it."

"Let me help," Yuki said, reaching out for the spoon.

"No," said Michael. He grabbed the spoon and ran out of the shop, causing Dōm Coquí to stop sweeping.

"Weh konde et su?"

"Far away!" He ran through town until he arrived at a junkyard by the city line in the western district of Metalworks, where Main Street ended at the border and State Highway 51 resumed up an incline into the forested mountain. Michael stood over a hydraulic compactor, turning scrap metal into cubes. With hate-filled eyes, he threw the spoon into the compactor as a crane dropped another load of scrap metal behind him. The machine spat out the metal cube with the spoon inside it. Michael ran as fast as he could, passing by a pair of newly built giant metal legs with knee joints attached to them, and out of the junkyard. As soon as he reached the end of the street, he felt his pocket shimmer. He reached inside and pulled out the spoon.

Michael saw an old man sitting on the bench with a smile. He handed the spoon to him, waved for a taxi to stop, and when it did, he hopped in. The taxi drove for a while, finally arriving at a train station. At the platform, a train to Newark Airport arrived, and he boarded. It took ninety minutes, but he arrived at the airport and bought a ticket to Los Angeles. After a four-hour flight, he took a bus into the city. When he got off the bus at the beach, he checked his pockets and felt nothing. No spoon. None whatsoever.

"Finally," he said. Michael went to a beachside restaurant and sat at a table. A waitress arrived, placed a set of utensils wrapped in cloth by his side, and handed him a menu. He stared at the cloth, expecting a surprise, but when he unfolded it, he found a regular, ordinary spoon. How nice that was to see.

A limo pulled up, and Michael watched the chauffeur open the door. His smile dropped, and his eyes grew wide. This surpassed everything his mind could handle. This was more than just a nuisance, this was a travesty, for on the backseat of the limo, there it was. Its lion head stared at him. It actually had traveled across America.

Michael made one final effort. Later, he stood atop a cliff overlooking Los Angeles. It was a long drop below, and Michael almost slipped and fell. He grabbed the spoon out of his pocket and tossed it over the edge, watching it fall all the way down. It took a while, but a little plume of dust finally appeared at the bottom. When Michael turned around, he felt the spoon in his pocket.

"Damn you, spoon!"

The armored woman below the cliff watched on. A video screen appeared on her visor replaying his actions. It was still static. The static affected her mind. She lifted her hands up to look at them, but when the video ended, her body glowed red and turned into a ball of light again, returning to the spoon.

※ ※ ※

By nightfall the next day, Michael had returned home. He saw the lights on at the shop, and didn't understand why. The "Closed" sign hung on the locked door, but everyone was there. Angela waved to him, and Kaori unlocked the door to let him in. He walked to the counter, avoiding Ely as it slept on the floor, and slumped over the counter like a piece of clothing hanging over a rail.

"Michael…" Yuki said, reaching for him, as Kaori wedged herself between the two.

"Are you okay, I-Man?" she said.

Without saying a word, Michael reached into his pocket and took out the spoon. He dropped it to the floor and turned his hand over. The spoon returned to the palm of his hand, completing its fall, and everyone gasped. He threw it again, but this time the utensil did not go far; it reappeared in his palm again. Worn out, he released the spoon.

It disappeared in a fraction of a second, leaving his very skin and reappearing on the palm of his hand.

"Stop it!" Yuki said, touching Michael's shoulders. The spoon suddenly released itself from Michael's hands and disappeared from the room. She stepped back as Michael lifted himself up.

He felt like he was back to normal. He checked his pocket, and felt only his wallet and apartment keys. He turned to Yuki with a smile and hugged her tight.

"Thank you, Yuki."

"Lucky," Kaori said, as Angela was disappointed by the hug.

"I'm your bodyguard," said Yuki. "It's my job to make sure you're safe." She smirked to Kaori, showing that she had an edge over her, but found herself separated from Michael as he looked down at her.

"Again with the bodyguard talk, Yuki?" He held her shoulder, but saw Kaori and Angela, so he released her and leaned back on the counter. "I thought I told you I didn't need a bodyguard."

"Well, I..." Yuki saw the smirk on Kaori's face, and she turned around, crossing her arms and closing her eyes. "Fine then! Go insane with the spoon. See if I care."

Michael shrugged his shoulders as the door opened, and Mr. Tanaka entered the store with a sheet of paper, looking triumphant.

"What's this crap?" said Michael, examining the paper.

"Eviction notice."

"What!?" everyone said.

"Why?" said Yuki.

"Because I felt like it," Mr. Tanaka replied. "I'm taking everything back. Even the shop."

"The hell you are!" Michael leaned forward, crushing the paper, towering over the small landlord.

"Don't try anything," said Mr. Tanaka. "You have until this Sunday or I'll have the police throw you out." He left the store, marched past the storefront window, and immediately bumped into Michael, who'd appeared out of nowhere.

"Hey, Tanaka, what's the matter? Can't look at your tenants face to face?"

"I can't afford this place anymore because of you and your punk friends," said Mr. Tanaka, looking back from the corner of his eyes as everyone exited the store to watch. "I want all of you off my property, immediately!"

"I have a better idea," Michael said. "How about I buy your property?"

"Ha! Do you have five hundred thousand dollars, gaijin?" Mr. Tanaka waved his finger in Michael's face. "That's how much you'd have to pay to buy the entire building with your store."

Michael was shocked. The price was not what he'd expected.

"Well, do you, gaijin?"

Michael turned around to his friends, waiting for his answer. He looked up at the apartment building and thought about what his neighbors were going through. How they were chased out of their homes because of Mr. Tanaka. Michael could not comprehend the difficulty of such a life-changing decision forced upon them. He faced Mr. Tanaka. His stare made the landlord take a step back. With a smirk, he flashed the palm of his right hand in Mr. Tanaka's face. The landlord flinched. He then made the two-fingered victory sign and extended his thumb. The lights in the store flickered briefly.

"I'll get the half a million dollars by 11:59 p.m. Saturday."

Yuki's eyes grew wide. "That's forty-eight hours! Are you—"

Jamal raised his hand up, silencing her. Yuki and Angela saw the determined look on the faces of Jamal, Kaori, and Dōm Coquí. It was like they'd been called to arms.

"Forty-eight hours?" Mr. Tanaka said. "You must be nuts."

"No, Mr. Tanaka … I am The Impossible Man." Michael stared down the landlord with confidence. He knew Mr. Tanaka had nothing to lose. With a nod, they shook hands.

"Fine, but you'll be out in the street before you know it. Fool." Mr. Tanaka walked away, laughing, as Michael headed to his friends.

"I-Man?" Jamal followed Michael inside the store. "You've never attempted anything like this before."

"Relax, I got this under control."

"Even so, we're talking about five hundred thousand dollars."

"I know."

"Qwani wu ce qe lu, I-Man?"

"I'm going to dip into our emergency supply," said Michael, smiling at Dōm Coquí as Jamal and Kaori shook their heads in refusal.

"No," Jamal said. "We can't. We don't have that kind of manpower. Remember last time?"

"Yes," Michael said. "And we can. We do have that kind of manpower. Remember last time?"

"And look what happened the next day," Kaori said, and Jamal leaned on the counter, rubbing his green hair.

"Even so, Kaori," he said, looking at her, "preparation takes time. We only have until tomorrow to get everything in place. Then we only have Saturday to sell all the items."

Jamal stared at the counter. "There has to be another way."

"It's the only way, Jamal," said Michael, as Yuki and Angela tried to understand what was going on.

"Fine," said Jamal. He stood up and walked past Michael. "I'll call for a permit tomorrow. I'll owe a lot of people on this one. You owe me big, I-Man."

"Kaori…" Michael turned to her.

"I'm right on it, I-Man." Kaori took out her cell phone, flipped it open, and called up Sasuke. "Coquí, get the inventory book."

"Syi," said Coquí, running to the storage room.

"Angela," Michael said, "would you like to help us out this Saturday? I could use the extra manpower."

"Really?" Angela smiled in excitement at the opportunity to help.

"If you want to."

"Yeah. I'll give it my best."

"Michael?" Yuki said, and everyone went silent. Angela looked around at them, trying to figure out why. Yuki took a deep breath. "I-Man?"

Everyone resumed, Angela stepped back confused, and Yuki clenched her fist while maintaining her composure. "What are you going to sell that you'll get all that money for in such a short time?"

Dōm Coquí returned with a thick book, handed it to Michael.

"Are you nervous, Yuki?" said Michael.

"Is it going to be bad?"

"Only if we panic." Michael opened the inventory book and showed Yuki and Angela the product.

They both gasped in awe, then looked at each other with a giggle. Their eyes had an innocent glow. They nodded, determined to make it work.

Yuki watched Michael walk behind the counter to work on the computer. She felt relieved that he was back to his old self, but was still wondering what the spoon was and where it had come from. It was gone for now, and there was nothing she could do about it. She felt she had to be ready for anything it did from here on out, and she was determined to protect Michael.

So she left everyone and entered the storage room. Yuki tapped her brooch and paused for a second, then felt something: a presence.

"Scarlet Sorceress report," said a woman's voice. Yuki panicked and looked at the door, hoping no one had heard her.

"Supervisor, I need research into a magical object."

"Your mission is to observe The Impossible Man."

"I know, ma'am." Yuki watched the door. "But I believe this object is related to my case."

"Very well," said the woman.

Episode 8

[~ Sale of the Century! ~]

In Japan, there is a very popular doll, so popular the world fell in love with it. Even here in America, it's still revered to this day. It appears in all kinds of merchandising, like books, toys, and clothing. There are people dressed in large mascot suits. It even has its own store, not just in Japan, but over in the City as well, right on up in Times Square. Here's the kicker, it even had an American Saturday morning cartoon show back in the '80s. Not a single person walked the streets of Japan without knowing that doll's name. Without further ado, to keep the introduction short—ladies and gentlemen, say hello to…

…Ohayō Kitten.

April 27, 2002

Twenty-four hours had passed since Tanaka issued his challenge to Michael to claim the apartment building. Everything in the store was in place. The sun shone down on Denfair City and broke through the shades of Michael's room as the clock struck seven. He lifted up the shades and saw Kaori's camera crew setting up outside the store. After he cleaned up and ate breakfast, he picked up an extra-large purple T-shirt with the face of a kitten on the front.

There was a knock on his apartment door. When he opened it, there Jamal and Dōm Coquí stood, in the same purple T-shirts. They were exhausted from prepping the store. Michael let them inside, and following behind them was Yuki, who took her Ohayō Kitten sneakers off before entering. She wore the same shirt, though it was pink.

"This is such a cute shirt, Michael, I mean…I-Man," Yuki said, stretching her arms up purposefully so Michael could see a little of her belly and her chest perk up.

"It's to help the customers know that we're the employ-ees," Michael said, oblivious to Yuki's advances.

"Yeah," said Yuki, pouting.

Michael stood before Yuki and presented her an orange armband with the words 'Security' stitched in Japanese kanji.

"Really?"

"We're depending on you to keep everyone in check. We don't want anyone fighting."

"I'll do my best." Yuki slipped the armband over her left shoulder and then stood with her hands on her hips like a superhero. "Security Guard Yuki is on the case."

Michael walked past her with a smirk. "Oh, how cute."

"Hey!" Yuki followed him, and Jamal walked right behind them.

"Seriously," Jamal said, "do we have to wear this again?"

"Yes," Michael said. He opened the back door with energy, and everyone entered the store.

"I-Man, uy er ad ij ok."

"Yeah? Well, you look like two different-colored grapes with that shirt on."

"I hope you two aren't going to argue today," Yuki said, passing by Michael at the door and slipped on her sneakers. "We have a job to do."

"Yeah," Jamal said, following Yuki. "Like making you live up to your name, The Impossible Man."

Once everyone had entered the shop, Michael turned on the lights. The room shined lavender and purple; there was Ohayō Kitten merchandise everywhere.

❇ ❇ ❇

Ohayō Kitten: a small, cute lavender kitten. Millions of the official dolls were sold throughout the world. Yet its humble origins go back to Osaka, Japan, where a young woman named Rumiko Hasegawa sewed a doll for her little daughter to help calm her when sleeping fifty years ago. The child adored it so much that it never left her side. When a friend of Rumiko's daughter saw the doll, she wanted one too, and Rumiko went ahead to make more. She watched the girls make the dolls greet each other with "Ohayō," or good morning, and thus established the doll's name: Ohayō Kitten. As those dolls spread around the city, they attracted more little girls, and before Rumiko knew it, it reached the whole world. She'd never believed that was possible.

At I-Man's, Ohayō Kitten products were displayed all across the store. Posters hung from the ceiling and on the wall. Anime and manga of Ohayō Kitten had replaced the store's current lineup on the shelves. Music soundtracks were stacked along the storefront window. Bookbags, notebooks, and various school supplies sat in the corner. Boxes of mugs, statuettes, toys, and other memorabilia were lined up on a table. T-shirts, pink painter hats, and a line of clothing hung high from a closet in display.

Behind the counter, Ohayō Kitten jewelry worth up to five hundred dollars sat safe and secure, alongside a box of rolled-up posters. Finally, the highlight of the store sat in the center of all the displays. Stacked fifty boxes high, from the floor up, were boxes of Ohayō Kitten.

Yuki picked one up, stared at the plushy, lavender-colored doll. Its soft pink t-shirt felt like the actual shirt she was wearing. Its innocent eyes made her giggle, but its softness made her skin crawl.

"Cute!" she said in Japanese, hugging the box tightly.

Michael smirked at Yuki's cheer as he put in a DVD and started up all the television sets in the store. "Hey, Yuki, why is the sun smiling?"

"Oh no," Jamal said, and Dōm Coquí gulped, but Yuki's eyes lit up like a little child.

"It's happy morning time!"

Michael pressed play, and Ohayō Kitten's face appeared on the screen. A jingle began, and a female sang in Japanese:

It's happy time
Let's come out and play a game today
The sun is smiling
Let's get together and jump hooray...

"To a place so far away," Yuki sang along with a smile, her head swaying with Ohayō Kitten, as Jamal and Dōm Coquí covered their ears and screamed in horror. "You're my best friend every day. Yay!"

"They're about to open!" said a girl's voice from outside the store.

When Yuki stopped singing, and looked out the window, she saw little girls, teenage girls, and women emerge from the ground like zombies rising from the grave. Some folded up chairs, while others rolled up their sleeping bags. A mother and daughter folded a blanket together. A couple of girls leaned their faces on the gate, trying to peer into the window.

Michael took an official Ohayō Kitten megaphone, grabbed Dōm Coquí by the collar, and dragged him outside the store.

Yuki, meanwhile, watched from inside. "You have got to be kidding me."

"What's up?" Jamal said, attempting to take the box from Yuki's hand so he could return it to the display.

Yuki yanked it back. "How long have they been waiting outside?"

"Since last night," said Jamal, still trying to pry the Ohayō Kitten box from her hand.

"They actually slept out there all night to buy an Ohayō Kitten doll?"

"Yep," said Jamal, finally giving up and leaving the doll in Yuki's hands.

Through the window, Yuki saw Michael start up the megaphone as Dōm Coquí set up a large chalkboard ad, welcoming customers to the Ohayō Kitten event. She also saw Kaori and Angela, wearing the same pink T-shirts, emerge from the van, with Ely wearing a painter hat like the doll. Emerging from behind the van was a woman dressed in an Ohayō Kitten mascot costume. After fixing the head, she stepped out to the crowd and waved. Their appearance arose a roar from the ladies outside, though the reaction sounded like there were a lot more of them than the number of customers in front of the store. She felt Jamal's hand grab her wrist, and he jerked his head, signaling her to come along. Yuki followed him out of the apartment and heard the loud screams from the crowd outside again. As she got closer to Kaori and the camera crew, she saw a man in glasses talking to Angela.

"Who's that?" Yuki said to Kaori.

"Hino-san, my agent. Our agent."

"Are you ready, Tangerine?"

"Angela," she said, her face lacking a smile.

"This is going to be your co-hosting debut. Just follow Kaori's lead and remember to smile. Everyone loves a smile." Hino waited. "Come on, you can do it, Tangerine."

"Angela," she said again, crossing her arms and looking away. She saw Kaori standing there, and thought she was burdening her by pouting. So Angela turned to Hino and smiled, unaware that Kaori had become concerned. Suddenly, Sasuke came between her and Hino.

"We have to film," he said, as Kaori took Angela by the wrist and pulled her away. "I need you off the set."

"Of course, director, of course." Hino walked past Kaori and Angela, and he made a gesture to smile. They did. He opened the door to his car and looked back. "Tomorrow, Tangerine, we'll look through today's recordings to see where to analyze your performance."

"It's Angela!" she said, with her hands curled in a fists and shivering, and Hino looked to Kaori.

"Make sure to teach Tangerine how to control her temper. We can't have her repeating your mistakes." He jumped into his car and drove off.

As Angela took deep breaths, she felt Kaori's hands on her shoulders. She looked at her and became calm. Angela received a microphone from her co-host and turned to camera with a smile. With Kaori by her side, they watched Sasuke give the signal to begin.

"Meet The Impossible Man's Anime and Manga Shop's newest members," Kaori said. "Yuki Shimizu and my new co-star, Tangerine, with her pet chupacabra, Ely!"

"Pleased to meet you, everyone." Angela bowed with a smile, but felt empty inside as the camera stared back at her.

The crowd roared as Michael, Jamal, Kaori, and Dōm Coquí gathered around Yuki, Angela, and Ely. They all stood in front of the mascot and waved at the camera. Yuki bowed with a blush, a little shy in front of the camera, while Angela and Ely smiled and waved more.

Everyone turned to the crowd. Yuki's face froze in shock. As she walked behind Michael, he lifted up the megaphone.

"Good morning, ladies!"

"Good morning, The Impossible Man!" the crowd yelled in unison, as Yuki looked past the line. It went far, with no end in sight, almost as though it could lead out of the city. People of all types, but mostly females, waited in line for their chance to purchase an Ohayō Kitten doll. Police cars stationed at each block kept the crowd under control. Port-o-potties stood lined up along the edge of the sidewalk.

"Why is the sun smiling?"

"It's happy morning time!" yelled the crowd.

"Are you all ready for the greatest adventure of a lifetime?!"

"Yes!" yelled the crowd in hypnotic unison. "We are ready to buy! Open the store already! We don't have all day! We would like to get our errands done before nightfall! Plus, we don't want to get stuck in traffic on the way home! We can't stress enough how annoying Jersey traffic can be on a Saturday!"

"I see," Michael said, his hand under his chin. He lifted

up the megaphone and addressed the crowd again. "Well, let's get that loud cheer!"

The roar of the crowd deafened the neighborhood. Yuki covered her ears, and as the noise died down, she felt a pat on her back. She turned around and saw Kaori with her cameraman, holding the microphone up.

"Would you tell us a little bit about yourself, Shimizu-san? How did you get hired by The Impossible Man?"

"I...ah..." Yuki was speechless. She became shy and lost the words she wanted to say. Of course, she had to be careful not to mention that she was the Scarlet Sorceress. "His mother hired me."

Kaori turned to the camera. "And there you have it, everyone. Shimizu-san, the newest member of The Impossible Man's Anime and Manga Shop."

"And...cut," Sasuke said, and his cameraman turned off the spotlight. "The live feed is over. We'll be recording the rest for tomorrow's recap."

"Thank you, Sasuke." Kaori bowed, and he reciprocated. She then turned her attention to Yuki.

"Wow, you're lame, Shimizu-san," said Kaori. "You need to lighten up, like Angela and Ely." She directed Yuki's attention to the two, who were giving a little performance that made the crowd clap.

"But they're professional entertainers," Yuki said. Kaori shrugged, walking away.

"Okay, everyone," Michael said through the megaphone, holding up a lavender card with Ohayō Kitten's face on it. "Only those of you who receive this entry card will be permitted to enter the store to purchase Ohayō Kitten merchandise. Children twelve years and younger must be accompanied by an adult at all times."

Some children jumped out of the line and ran home. "We close at eleven."

"So…the official dolls are limited to one per person per purchase. That means if you are one single person, you do not get two. Only one. Not two. One. Even if you're in a group, only one person can hold one doll. It does not matter if you have to run to the bathroom, you do not hand off that one doll to a friend who already is holding one doll, so that friend of yours ends up holding two."

Michael planted a bucket, from out of nowhere, onto Angela's hands. Fifty Ohayō Kitten entry cards were piled up inside.

"Due to the size of the store, and by city safety ordinance, we can only allow ten people at a time. Angela and Ely will be coming down the street and handing out one entry card per person. These entry cards are limited to one per person. That means if you are one single person, you do not get two. Only one."

Jamal lifted up the gate, Yuki unlocked the front door, and Sasuke and the cameraman went inside to take footage of the first members of the crowd. Dōm Coquí swept the front, while Kaori hung a bucket at the door that read 'Place Entry Card Here.' Jamal gave the signal, and Yuki and Kaori led the first group of ten inside.

As the customers walked in, Michael continued talking. "…who already is holding one card, thereby that friend of yours ends up holding two. Thank you, and enjoy shopping at The Impossible Man's Anime and Manga Shop. Jamal, open the gates."

When he turned around, he jerked his body back in shock, watching the crowd already in the shop. He appeared behind the counter, out of nowhere, handing the first official doll to a little girl with her mother in front of the cameras.

She showed the Ohayō Kitten doll to the cameraman with a giggle, raising it up over her head. All the customers inside gathered around and reached out to it with a low murmur of awe. The morning light outside shone over the plushy doll.

"Thank you, The Impossible Man," said the little girl. As she left the store with her mother, she raised the doll up to the screams of the crowd. She walked over to Kaori with a second cameraman and began doing an interview as the next person entered the store.

By nine o'clock, the soundtrack rack had emptied out completely. Angela hurried over with a box and replenished the stock with Ely, while Kaori replaced the mugs. Jamal took down a poster on the wall and rolled it up. He handed it to a little girl, and she ran to her mother to purchase a doll. He watched Yuki take the money and give change back in return. He smiled with a nod.

Outside, Dōm Coquí swept the floor, clearing out the garbage, while Michael addressed the crowd through the megaphone.

"How many people do not have an entry card?" he called out.

The people at the corner raised their hands. Michael got Dōm Coquí's attention and handed him the basket of entry cards. With a nod, the frog hurried down the block, passing the cards to the people with their hands raised.

"Yuru Chara!" one of the teenage girls said in the crowd.

The crowd of women and girls roared, swarming around Dōm Coquí like ants on candy. "Cute!"

Dōm Coquí screamed for help as Michael took the broom inside. As he did, Jamal exited the storage room with more products to display. Michael hurried to help him as Dōm Coquí arrived at the front door, collapsing to the ground in pain.

"How's the inventory keeping up?" Michael said, and Jamal opened the box.

"So far so good, I-Man," he said, while Michael took out diaries and placed them on display. "Our accountant will be arriving this afternoon to monitor the totals for the end-of-day sales."

"Great," said Michael. "We need to start monitoring the money soon so we can be ready to buy the apartment building. Do we have enough dolls to sell? It feels like everything is going fast."

"Don't worry, we have enough until lunch."

"Call at 11:30 so the shippers can arrive before one o'clock."

"Okay," said Jamal. "You know, we might just pull this off."

"I told you, Jamal."

"Just don't start gloating in my face."

"I won't." Michael patted Jamal's shoulder with a smile and continued re-stocking.

By one o'clock, the heat had overwhelmed the crowd, and the truck pulled up on the sidewalk. Police officers stood in front of the vehicle as the shippers lifted up the back door, revealing cardboard boxes filled with dolls. Jamal and Michael took the shipping packages into the storage room as Kaori and her camera crew taped the crowd's reaction. Michael, Jamal, and the shippers deployed the boxes quickly, and didn't make the crowd wait for long. Michael and Jamal paused for a moment when they saw Mr. Tanaka watching them from the corner of the street, and as they stared at him, Yuki stood at the edge of the sidewalk with her arms crossed. The landlord saw her orange armband and ran off without saying a word.

"Ignore him, I-Man," said Jamal.

"Yeah," Michael said, passing the box. "Eyes on the prize."

He returned to the store as Dōm Coquí passed him by, pushing a cart. The cart had a towel over a block of ice, paper cones, an ice scraper in a cup of water, a triangle shaper, and five bottles of different-flavored syrup. Dōm Coquí saw a teenage customer in line wave at him, and stood before her curious eyes. He revealed the block of ice to the customer. He then presented the different flavors of syrups, and handed her an advertisement that read, "Piragua—Shaved Ice with choice of one of five flavors."

"I'm kind of hot," said the teenager. "I'll take one."

Dōm Coquí grabbed the ice shaver, wiped it on his apron, and scraped the surface of the ice. The frog packed two scoops of shaved ice into the paper cone. He used the triangle shaper to mold the ice, then waved his hand in front of the bottles, revealing a choice of cherry, lemon, orange, grape, or piña colada.

"I'll take cherry."

Dōm Coquí grabbed the bottle of cherry syrup and sprinkled it onto the ice. The frog handed it to her and received one dollar in return.

She took a little bite and smiled. "Delicious."

Soon everyone in the crowd was calling for one, and Dōm Coquí couldn't keep up with the demand. As the customers raised their hands, one after another, a little girl tugged her father from across the street, attracting everyone's attention.

"Daddy, I want an Ohayō Kitten doll!"

"I'm sorry, honey," he said, "but that line is too big and we don't have all day."

The little girl didn't struggle or put up a fight. She watched the crowd with sadness, and the customers felt her pain. That was until the child turned around and saw Michael crouched before her from out of nowhere. Her eyes grew wide as he revealed an authentic Ohayō Kitten from behind his back. They both looked up to her father, and with a smile, he nodded.

"Fifteen dollars, please," Michael said, handing the doll over.

"Here you are." The father took out his wallet and paid for the merchandise. He patted his daughter. "What do you say?"

"Thank you, Mr. The Impossible Man." The little girl gave Michael a hug, all caught on camera, and the crowd was awed by his kind act.

"That was so nice of him," one of the teenage girls said to a woman next to her.

"We love you, The Impossible Man!" screamed another.

Michael, from out of nowhere, appeared before the line. He lifted up his megaphone and addressed them back.

"I love you all too!"

✳ ✳ ✳

Inside, Yuki heard all the teenage girls screaming, and crossed her arms out of jealousy. Her eyes shifted over to Kaori, Angela, and Ely, and their reaction was the same. Yuki took some cash from a female customer as Michael entered the store.

"He's so awesome," said the customer.

"Yeah, he is," said Yuki, slamming the register shut. As the customer walked away, Kaori placed her hands over her chest, blushing at Michael.

"You're so awesome, The Impossible Man."

Yuki growled.

Kaori's eyes turned to hearts. "You're not as annoying as him."

"Him?" Yuki said. "Michael?"

"He's The Impossible Man." Kaori leaned in Yuki's face. "Always The Impossible Man."

Yuki stepped back and Kaori walked to the cameraman. Yuki looked to Michael, trying to understand what Kaori was talking about. "I don't understand. I just want to call him Michael."

A large belly slumped over the counter. A doll landed on the counter, along with posters, DVDs, manga, and shirts. She lifted her head up slowly as a pair of hairy hands wiped the lenses of a pair of glasses, which were soon set in place on a man's face.

"I would like to purchase the Ohayō Kitten Summer Outfit set," he said.

"Uh…" Yuki reached for the box of play clothes hanging next to the television screen. "Yeah, your daughter is really going to love this set."

"Daughter? Miss, I happen to be a collector of Ohayō Kitten memorabilia. I only need the Summer Outfit to have the complete Seasons set."

"Right," said Yuki, keeping her mind focused.

"In case you haven't noticed, this is a limited edition Ohayō Kitten, signed by Rumiko Suzuki, the creator of this doll. This will be worth a lot of money so long as it remains in its box."

"I see," said Yuki. She rang up all the merchandise and received the money. Suddenly Michael stood beside her, out of nowhere.

"Aey, Kenny," he said, startling Yuki.

"Hello, The Impossible Man," Kenny said. "I appreciate the notification on your latest Ohayō Kitten event."

"Oh hey, no problem," said Michael, handing him a certificate. "You almost forgot this voucher. I set it aside for you. Tell no one."

"Well, thank you."

As Yuki watched Michael talk to Kenny, she'd never seen anything like it. She saw a grown man buying kids' stuff, but he was treated with kindness by Michael. She panned the store and saw mostly girls and women. The only males standing around were reluctant boyfriends, fathers with their daughters, and sons with their mothers and sisters.

"I don't understand," Yuki said, getting Michael and Kenny's attention. "Why are you here?"

"Excuse me?" Kenny said, and Michael immediately waved his hand to calm the atmosphere.

"Kenny, she's our new employee Yuki Shimizu."

"Oh…" said Kenny. "Well, this is a hobby of mine. One half of me collects them for fun, the other half collects these because they have a high rarity rate among collectors. In time, I will auction these off and profit. This is an investment."

"Interesting."

"I understand how weird it is, but we do have a community of men and women who are collectors and historians. What Rumiko Suzuki has accomplished is nothing short of amazing. To help bring joy to the world with one simple doll is a remarkable feat. For the historians that collect these dolls, this must be preserved. Once all of this is over, who will remember a mom with a simple idea for her daughter and persevered?"

Michael appeared behind Yuki out of nowhere and leaned into her ears. "He is a valued customer, we like his business."

Yuki's eyes grew wide, and she immediately bowed. "I'm so sorry for my rudeness. I had no right to judge you."

Kenny waved in understanding. "It's okay. If you are interested in our club, you're welcome to join. The more Ohayō Kitten fans we have, the more fun…and profits. Have a good day."

"Interesting customers we have today, eh? We have a lot of different hobbyists for customers." Michael watched Yuki stare at the door where Kenny had just been standing. It was as if she found herself in another world. It was fascinating, but hard to process at how normal it looked to her. He took Yuki by the shoulders and got her to walk.

"Everything is fine, Yuki. I'll take over from here."

At three o'clock, Michael hit the jackpot. A woman dressed in very expensive clothing stood before him with her daughter, holding a doll. She pointed at a necklace and ring selling for a combined $2,100. That attracted the attention of Kaori and her camera crew. The crowd outside spread the word about the purchase, and Michael smiled, teeth exposed.

He said under his breath. "Money…"

As Kaori and her crew recorded the event in the store, Yuki took care of collecting entry cards outside. A man in a business suit approached her, holding a briefcase, and presented her a business card. She read it as he introduced himself.

"Hello, I'm Mr. Smith," he said. "I'm the accountant, here to see Mr. The Impossible Man."

"Oh." Yuki looked inside and saw Michael at the register. "Michael... I mean I-Man, Smith-san is here to see you!"

Michael leaned over the counter, acknowledging Yuki, and he finished ringing up the ladies' jewelry purchase. He waved Kaori over to take the register, then exited the store to greet Mr. Smith.

"Hey, Mr. Smith. Good of you to come." He placed his hands around Yuki's shoulders, much to the jealousy of Kaori. "I'd like to introduce my new employee, Yuki Shimizu, the store security."

"Nice to meet you." Mr. Smith shook Yuki's hand.

"Nice to meet you too," Yuki said with a slight bow, watching Michael lead Mr. Smith to the storage room where Jamal and Dōm Coquí were waiting for them. She'd never seen Michael act with such determination.

✳ ✳ ✳

Inside the storage room, Mr. Smith sat at the desk and analyzed the receipts and inventory list. Michael and Jamal watched as he typed on a calculator, flipped through the pages, and wrote his notes on a pad.

"Impressive," he finally said, and stopped writing. "Well, Mr. The Impossible Man, you only need one hundred and fifty thousand dollars to meet your quota."

"Please call me I-Man, and thank you for your help, Mr. Smith. I assume you will be spending the rest of the day monitoring our sales?"

"Of course. You never cease to amaze me, I-Man. It's a miracle you made this amount today, but at this rate, you'll be lucky to reach five hundred thousand."

"Lucky?"

"Yes. After all, you can't get the whole city to purchase Ohayō Kitten dolls. By the end of the day, the crowd will die down. I'm sorry, but if you don't have a strong finish to go with that strong start, you'll come up short. Also, this line you have here is too slow. People will get tired of waiting."

"I see," said Michael.

"Excuse me, I have to call my wife. She wants to bring our daughters over to purchase Ohayō Kitten dolls."

"You can buy them now if you like."

"Thank you, but I don't have money on me right now. I have to wait for my wife to go to the bank and then visit her mother with the girls."

"Please," said Michael. "My phone is at the counter."

"Thank you."

As Jamal and Dōm Coquí continued reading the charts and inventory papers, Michael stepped out of the storage room and made his way outside the store. Yuki was out there, trying to persuade people to wait in line. As the customers walked away, Michael crossed his arms and tried to think of an idea for how to keep the line going.

"Mich...I-Man," said Yuki, hurrying over to him. "The customers are leaving."

"The waiting is the problem." Michael looked at the officers in their patrol cars across the street. "If I try to concentrate on selling everything outside, it could cause a riot."

"What are we going to do?" said Yuki.

"We have no choice. We have to give it everything we've got."

✳ ✳ ✳

By seven o'clock, the sun was leaving the sky and darkness had fallen. Another shipment of Ohayō Kitten dolls arrived, and the police set up a barrier to prevent the crowd from rioting. The shippers, Michael, and Jamal once again hurried the merchandise inside as the crowd cheered happily at the new wave of dolls. Suddenly, the engine of the delivery truck roared, and it drove away, spilling some of the boxes on the ground.

"No!" Michael said, standing out in the street. "Not the dolls!"

Michael saw the police run to their cars. Unfortunately, someone had slashed their tires. As the officers called in an all points bulletin, Michael ran after the departing truck.

"Shimizu-san!" Kaori came out of the store, Seizon in hand.

"Let's go." Yuki detached her brooch, and together they ran after Michael.

As the truck turned the corner, Mr. Tanaka laughed maniacally behind the wheel. He looked at the sideview mirror and saw no one behind him.

"Now I'll have the whole apartment and the store all to myself," he said.

"I beg to differ."

Sitting beside Mr. Tanaka was Michael with his arms crossed.

"What!?" Mr. Tanaka jerked his head back. "How did you get here?"

"You know my name," said Michael. "Now how about you pull over and lose like a good little—"

Mr. Tanaka slammed on the brakes, and the truck crashed into parked limos, pushing them aside like paper cups. When they came to a complete stop, the vehicle bumped into the last limo and popped its trunk open. A plume of white powder rose into the air. The doors of that limo opened, and men in business suits buttoned their vests and jackets. They approached the truck, carrying bats and chains.

"Yakuza?" said Michael. "Since when did we have a Yakuza in this city?"

"You're going to get it now, gaijin!" Mr. Tanaka jumped out of the truck and ran towards the mob. "Hello, my brothers. He's the driver. He made me do it. I have money!"

Without hesitation, a couple of the mobsters took out machine guns and fired away at the cab of the truck. Mr. Tanaka laughed at the bullets punching holes in the metal, but as he did, he felt an arm placed around his shoulders.

"Don't you learn anything?"

There was Michael, rocking the landlord from side to side as if they were dancing. "Can't you stop doing that!?"

"No."

The Yakuza aimed their guns at Michael, with Mr. Tanaka standing in front. Just as they were ready to pull the trigger, a glowing blue rock landed on one of the gunmen. It was so large that only his arms and legs were visible, waving side to side like a turtle. Everyone looked up at the truck, where Tsubasa stopped glowing. On the roof were Kaori and Yuki, armed and ready to battle.

"Fools," Kaori said, pointing her Seizon at everyone. "How dare you jeopardize my beloved's chances of victory?"

"Beloved?" Yuki said, shaking her staff at Kaori. "Since when did he become yours?"

"Since before you were hired."

"Oh yeah?!"

"Yeah!"

"Hello?" Michael flailed his arms, getting their attention.

"You think you can stop us," Mr. Tanaka said, pointing at the ladies. "Men, get those girls!"

Guns fired and bullets sprayed as the ladies jumped up into the air. Kaori landed right before the gunmen and swung Seizon twice. Though they laughed at her wooden sword, she smiled, and the guns collapsed into little pieces. Then their belt buckles vanished and their pants fell down, exposing their Japanese-style thong underwear called fundoshi. Kaori stood up as Yuki raised Tsubasa over her head.

"Electric Mayhem!" she screamed. A lightning bolt struck the ground around the Yakuza, and they howled in pain. When the electricity disappeared, they stood there charred and smoldering. Then they ran away, their pants around their ankles like penguins, but they were too slow; the police arrived and surrounded them.

Kaori and Yuki hugged Michael with joy. Then the two stared each other down and tried to push each other off him. Suddenly they found themselves in each other's arms. The police officers and the Yakuza whistled and hooted.

Behind the truck, Mr. Tanaka tried to tiptoe away from the scene so he could avoid arrest. With his head down, he bumped into Michael and stepped back, only to find Kaori and Yuki waiting behind him. Surrounded, Mr. Tanaka chuckled.

Back at the shop, the crowd was growing restless, while Jamal, Angela, Dōm Coquí, and the police tried to calm them down. The sound of the horn blared, and everyone went quiet.

There was Michael, struggling to drive the truck, steam spilling out of the grate. On top of the hood, Mr. Tanaka sat tied up in rope, screaming and struggling. Michael, Kaori, and Yuki stepped out of the truck to the applause of the crowd.

One of the shippers approached Mr. Tanaka. "You'll be paying for the damages."

"Curse you, The Impossible Man!"

A news van arrived from the crime scene where the police had arrested the Yakuza. A female reporter, dressed in business attire, stepped out of the van with her news crew and stood in front of Michael.

"Thanks for the scoop, The Impossible Man," the reporter said while signaling her cameraman that she was ready.

"I was lucky that the truck had a radio."

The cameraman perched his camera on his shoulder and waited for the feed to begin. He gave the signal. "Ready, Martha."

"Martha Stone, Local News, live at The Impossible Man's Anime and Manga Shop, where the local Yakuza have been arrested just minutes ago for drug possession," she said. Behind her, the crowd in front of the store cheered and tried to wave to the camera. She approached Michael. "The Impossible Man, could you tell us exactly what happened moments ago?"

Michael smirked, and Kaori and Yuki stepped aside. Everyone watched Michael rub the back of his head, smiling and answering questions into the camera.

"The news should help give the store some publicity," said Mr. Smith.

"Really?" Yuki turned to the accountant.

"Yes." Mr. Smith noticed Yuki in her Scarlet Sorceress costume, and raised his hand to shake hers. "And you are, Miss..."

Yuki smiled as Angela approached her with wide eyes, touching the costume.

"Yuki?" Angela whispered in the Scarlet Sorceress' ear. Yuki placed her finger on her lips and winked. Angela smiled. "I won't tell."

✳ ✳ ✳

Eleven o'clock, and the last customers—a couple of police officers who had daughters—left the store. Michael flipped the "Open" sign over to read "Closed." He walked past Mr. Tanaka, tied to a chair with Seizon and Tsubasa aimed at his face. Michael leaned on the counter as Mr. Smith gave the final total.

"Okay, you're short twenty-five thousand dollars."

"Damn!" Michael pounded the counter.

"Ha ha!" Mr. Tanaka tapped his feet on the floor. "I win!"

"Not so fast!" Kaori said, taking out a blank check. She filled it out. "Here's a check for fifteen thousand dollars."

"Here's a check for three thousand," said Jamal, making out his own check.

"Et ut er tre thusen." Dōm Coquí made a check out as well.

"And here's my check for three thousand dollars," said Yuki.

They all turned around to Mr. Tanaka, with looks that silenced him.

Looking at the pile of checks, Michael had never felt so much support from his friends. They all had blank checks ready in case they came up short. He could see that they were as determined to beat Mr. Tanaka as he was.

"Everyone..." Michael said.

"You're still short one thousand," Mr. Tanaka said with a smile.

So with a smile in return, Michael stood behind the counter from out of nowhere and took out the cookie jar marked "Sweet" from underneath. He reached inside, took out a blank check, and filled it out.

"Here's my check for nine hundred and seventy dollars," he said, slapping the check on the pile. Everyone stood there, with a sweatdrop hanging over each of their heads. "Well, you see, this shirt was on sale for thirty dollars at the mall, and—"

Yuki and Kaori struck Michael with their weapons and sent him flying to the back of the store, where he fell to the ground headfirst. "Leave it to you to mess things up!" yelled Yuki and Kaori together.

"Ha! You're still short thirty dollars," Mr. Tanaka said, tapping his feet on the ground with joy. Then he was interrupted by a knock on the door.

At the door were a woman and two girls. They waved at Mr. Smith and waited for someone to let them in. Mr. Smith smiled and hurried over.

"Ah," he said, "my family has arrived."

Michael appeared by the door from out of nowhere and unlocked it, and Mr. Smith's wife entered. "Honey, are we too late?"

"No, you're not too late," Mr. Smith replied, kissing his wife. "I-Man set aside the dolls, as he promised."

"Yay!" Mr. Smith's daughters ran to the counter, as Michael stood by the register from out of nowhere, and presented them each with an Ohayō Kitten doll. One of the girls spoke. "Grandma held us up with her long story."

"Yeah," the other girl said, picking up a doll clothes set. "It was boring."

After the girls picked up what they wanted to go with their dolls, Michael finished the transaction. Receiving the receipt, Mr. Smith finalized the paperwork and handed the title deed to Michael.

"Congratulations, I-Man. You are now the owner of this building."

Michael turned around and saw his friends standing there with glazed eyes. "We did it!"

Everyone cheered and gathered around Michael to celebrate as Mr. Tanaka suddenly found himself outside, still tied to the chair, crying like a baby. The lights in the store and apartment building brightened on their own.

Episode 9

[~ A Day of Madness. What?! Get Out of Here! No, Really...Go! ~]

Hot springs and bath houses: places where one can relax after a hard day's work. Hot springs are some of the most popular places in Japan, both in the countryside and in the cities. Bath houses are a little different. They're mostly public baths, usually used by people who live in apartments that don't have bathrooms of their own.

In anime and manga, it can be a comedic setting with slapstick and wild jokes, or it can be a dramatic setting where everyone learns about characters, what they think and what they feel.

So of course, there's one in Denfair City: a combo hot spring and bath house. Unfortunately, things can never be relaxing in this city...

April 28, 2002

Everything in the store was back to normal. While Kaori and Angela were at the studio, finalizing the recap of the Ohayō Kitten event for their Outside Japan television program, Michael, Jamal, Yuki, and Dōm Coquí spent the entire day replacing the Ohayō Kitten merchandise with the original store merchandise. Whatever was left of the Ohayō Kitten products was given its own little section in a pocket corner of the store.

It had been an exhausting forty-eight hours for the crew, as Michael spent the day hugging the title deed he'd won from Mr. Tanaka like a doll. He was anxious to use the rest of the day to check out all of the remaining empty apartments vacated by the tenants, due to the old landlord's cruel behavior.

With business as usual, Dōm Coquí swept up the front while wearing his chalkboard sign over his muumuu, and Michael and Jamal went through the anime DVDs, sticking new price tags on them.

"This sure is a long episode title," Jamal said, staring at the back of the DVD case.

"Indeed, Jamal," Michael said, leaning over to look at it. "Why is that?"

"Because that's how the American companies translate it, I guess." Michael took another DVD and read the back cover. It never had occurred to him that most of the anime DVDs had such long episode titles. "Check this out, 'The Day Has Come! Michiko Strikes Back Hard!'"

Jamal received the DVD from Michael and spoke. "Why not a title like 'Endgame' or 'Conquest Day'?"

"Well, some of the latest anime are starting to come out with shorter episode titles. I guess it's to appeal to us Americans, now that anime is gaining popularity again over here. Besides, I like the long episode title better. It's part of the pop culture. Take manga, for instance. When it first came to the States, they had to reverse each page because we read words left to right."

Yuki lifted her head over the aisle, overhearing the conversation. "Really? They did that to manga?"

Michael nodded. "It was done for our convenience, because in the early years people didn't know anything about Japanese comics. It didn't get popular, but it also ruined most of the experience of reading manga, because some English words in the original art panels would get reversed, like a mirror. Now that they started releasing manga in the traditional right-to-left format, I'm experiencing a part of Japanese pop culture I missed out on when I was a kid. It's a completely different experience."

"I see what you mean," Yuki said, looking at the time. "I'm going to get lunch."

"Okay," Michael and Jamal said, watching her leave.

After Michael placed the last DVD on the shelf, Yuki entered the store carrying two bags of food from a Japanese takeout restaurant called Maid in Japan. She placed okonomyaki on the counter, a pizza-like omelette made of flour, eggs, and cabbage, topped with a thin slice of pork, pink flakes called bonito, seaweed flakes, Japanese mayonnaise, and okonomyaki sauce. Alongside it was takoyaki, a pastry ball stuffed with a piece of octopus inside and topped with bonito flakes, mayonnaise, and takoyaki sauce. As Michael, Jamal, and Dōm Coquí gathered around ready to eat, Yuki turned around with a smile and pulled out slips of paper from her pocket.

"What's this?" Michael said.

"Coupons." Yuki handed one slip to Michael. "They were giving them away at Kaminari Hot Springs and Bath House."

"Wow, that's great," Jamal said, taking one himself. "That sounds like a good chance to sit back and relax, after everything that's happened."

"Aren't those hot springs artificial?" said Michael.

Jamal sighed. "So what, Michael? It's still a spa with a Japanese setting. They say it has great service."

"Service, eh?" Michael smiled, and Yuki slapped him with the bag of food over his head.

"Focus, Michael," she said.

"I don't know." Michael placed his hand under his chin, the bag resting on his head. "These places usually come with problems."

"Like what?"

"Like stumbling into the wrong place naked." He smirked at Yuki.

Yuki slapped the other bag of lunch on his head. "This isn't an anime, you idiot! Is that all you think about?"

Jamal crossed his arms. "Don't give him ideas."

As Dōm Coquí stood on his toes, taking one ball of ta-koyaki out of the bag on Michael's head, Jamal presented the store keys to Michael. "Just close the shop early and come. You need to relax anyway."

Michael clenched his fists, nodding in agreement. His eyes shifted to Dōm Coquí as he continued eating his meal from the bag resting on Michael's head. Michael turned around and punched the frog on the forehead, leaving a painful lump.

"Stop eating from the top of my head!"

"Sath's qwani hi shead."

"That's what he sai—why, you!" With a roar, Michael chased Dōm Coquí around the store, the bag falling off his head to the floor.

Yuki and Jamal shrugged their shoulders and sighed.

✳ ✳ ✳

After closing the store early, Michael zipped up his duffle bag, ready to leave for the springs. He walked toward the door, passing by the lion-headed spoon sitting on the table. It glowed red when he reached for the door, and he turned around. The glowing stopped. He opened the door and Yuki was at his door, ready to knock. They both startled each other.

"Sorry, Yuki."

"No, it's okay." Yuki saw Michael looking back inside the kitchen, worried. "Is everything okay?"

"The spoon came back."

"Where?" Yuki hurried inside, taking her sneakers off, and Michael pointed to the table. The spoon was no longer there. Yuki lifted up her hand and focused her powers, but she couldn't feel any magical presence. "Too late."

"Maybe I should have grabbed it."

"No!" Yuki turned around suddenly. With concerned eyes, she feared for his safety. Her heart skipped, and her cheeks blushed. Yuki refocused her thoughts to the issue at hand. "It's best you don't come in contact with it. I talked with my supervisor last night, and she said the best you could do is not touch it. She's checking things out on her end. So for now, avoid it. The last thing you want is for that thing to make you lose your mind again."

"He's already lost his mind," Jamal said, approaching the door with Dōm Coquí.

"This is serious," Yuki said, exiting the apartment, slipping on her sneakers. "The spoon showed up again."

"That thing again? Aren't you going to get rid of it?"

"No," Michael said, locking up his apartment. "I'm going to use it to scoop out your armpits."

Michael turned around and saw Yuki holding Jamal's fist back.

"Ut en er op wud."

"No, I wouldn't do it to you, you toe-licking toad."

"Wert lo na." Dōm Coquí leaned close to Michael's face.

"Screw you."

"Don't start!" Yuki towered over Michael and Dōm Coquí as they held each other's arms in fear. She calmed down and crossed her arms. "We're going to have a good time, and that's that."

"Scary."

"Scaweii."

The Kaminari Hot Springs and Bath House. It was built the first day Little Edo District was established, and soon became a popular spot for many weary residents. Both the hot springs and bath house had two sections: the very expensive private section, and the very cheap public section.

Unlike the private section, where male and female patrons had the choice to share a spring or a bath together, males and females were separated in the public section. Another difference between the two was that the hot springs offered the onsen experience, where a one-night stay featured a traditional Japanese-style room with traditional homemade cooking and a relaxing atmosphere. The bath house, on the other hand, had a more modern communal bathtub, lockers, and bath supplies.

After the crew entered, Michael placed the coupons on the counter. "One hot spring room for four."

He waited for everyone to give the cashier their money when Yuki suddenly stepped back.

"Michael?" she said, as he, Jamal, and Dōm Coquí turned to her. "I really don't like the idea of sharing a bath with men."

The trio forgotten that one little difference between them and her.

"Are you sure, Yuki?" Michael said.

"Yes, I'm sure." Yuki turned around. "I'll go to the public springs with the other women."

"Oh, yes, Shimizu-san, please do that for us."

Yuki lowered her eyes and saw Kaori approaching them, wearing a Japanese-style robe called a yukata. "Saito-san."

"Poime!" Dōm Coquí hopped toward Kaori, his arms wide open, ready to hug her. As he saw her yukata-covered chest come closer and closer, Kaori took his arm and pushed him toward the wall. He slammed into it headfirst.

"Pervert!" Kaori turned to Yuki, still pinning Dōm Coquí to the wall with her foot, and smiled. "Go on to the women's spring with Angie-chan and Ely, while I-Man and I share a room together."

"Ely?" Michael said, looking around scared. "How did you get that in here?"

"We dressed her up," Kaori said.

"Her?" Michael said, and Jamal peeled Dōm Coquí off the wall with a ripping sound.

"Yes, Ely is a girl."

"Then how come she has a boy's name?"

"You see, I asked Angie-chan the same question, and she said she named it after her dead pet cat."

"Was the cat a girl?" Jamal said.

"Yes, it was."

Michael and Jamal lost their balance, as Dōm Coquí wobbled beside them from the lingering pain.

"Shimizu-san," said Kaori, taking Yuki by the hand. "Why don't you join me and Angie-chan in our private section?"

"Sure," Yuki replied with a smile. "That way I know you're not sneaking into Michael's section."

"That's exactly what I had in mind about you."

As the ladies laughed at each other, Michael lowered his head. He felt Jamal pat his back, giving him a sympathetic smile. Michael walked away with Jamal, dragging Dōm Coquí behind.

Rocks lay along the women's side of the hot springs, while paintings of mountains and forests on the walls gave the room an outdoor atmosphere. Bonzai trees stood perched on the corners alongside lamps, and a small stream of water fell into the mouth of a bamboo stick. When it filled up, the bamboo tilted over with a click, spilling the water it had filled.

Yuki slid into the warm, relaxing water. She looked up at the ceiling, painted with a blue sky and clouds, as Angela and Ely floated by. Ely's fur was wet, and there was hardly an actual body on the creature. It looked human in nature, but the head was bigger than the body itself. Yuki shivered.

"Scary."

Kaori sat on a wooden stool, splashing water from a bucket to rinse the soap from her body. "So what do you think of America so far Shimizu-san?"

Yuki leaned on the edge of the pool. "It's strange. The mountains are beautiful here, and yet when I landed in Newark Airport, I saw nothing but buildings, a port and factories. It felt like I never left home. It reminded me of Tokyo when my family and I visited there."

"Not really." Kaori tied her long hair into a ponytail.

"I mean, like a large city with smaller buildings around it for kilometers in forests and mountains."

"I see." Kaori lifted her head up and nodded in agreement. "So what do you think of New Jersey?"

"Well, there are a lot of diners here. I don't understand why there are so many diners. I find it funny that some residents say 'wooder' instead of water, call every restroom a bathroom and you're waiting 'on line' instead of waiting 'in line'. At the bank, I stood in front of a computer waiting to get online until the representative pointed to the line of people and told me to wait on line there. In fact, I've been noticing that people drop r's in their words. It's hard to understand what they say sometimes."

Kaori chuckled. "That's probably the legendary Jersey accent you're hearing. I got confused too when I first heard it."

"Like the Osaka accent?" Yuki smiled and Kaori laughed. "Then there are the local legends like the Jersey Devil, the Mantis Man, the Cat's Eyes of Jersey City, and Clinton Road. I wonder if there are monsters to fight here like back home." Yuki thought about all the cases she could get out of them. She shook her head and continued.

"And the different languages used for buildings, streets,

and lakes. It's fascinating since we only speak and read one language back home. Although we do have English in some parts, but not like here where multiple languages are everywhere in one town or city. How do the residents keep up with it when they talk?"

"I try not to think about it. It reminds me of the frog."

Angela waved her arm at Yuki. "I can help. Which words don't you know?"

"Well for instance, what is a stoop?"

"It's Dutch for a house porch."

"Bodega?"

"It's Spanish for a grocery store."

"Hopatcong?"

"It's Lenape for stone water. Though, local historians are unsure of that."

"Oh." Yuki's eyes grew wide. "Also, nobody waits for the crosswalk light to turn green. Or is it white? Still, watching everyone cross on a red light was weird."

Kaori chuckled. "Let me guess, you stood waiting for the crosswalk to change even though the traffic light above was red and the cars stopped."

"Yes!" Yuki laughed. "Is it broken? Or is that the way they're supposed to work?"

"They're broken, and it's like that all over New Jersey."

Kaori made her way to the spring itself, sliding in next to Yuki and moaning from the warmth.

"Do you have to sound like you're in bed, Saito-san?"

"Do you have to talk like a virgin, Shimizu-san?"

"Hey," Angela said, and she stopped playing with Ely,

leaving it floating across the water. "Why do you two refer to each other by your last names?"

"Eh?" Kaori said. She and Yuki looked at each other, then both turned to Angela. "What do you mean, Angie-chan?"

"Well, Kaori, you call me Angie-chan, and you call Michael, Jamal, and Dōm Coquí by their first names. Same with Yuki, although she hasn't called me Angie-chan yet."

"Well, you see, um…Shimizu-san and I are not…"

"I guess it's custom, Saito-san. I call Michael and Jamal by their first names because Michael's mother told me that it was okay not to address them by their surname. I didn't know Dōm Coquí had a first name."

"He doesn't. Besides, Michael told me that it was okay when he hired me, without using '—san.'"

Kaori and Yuki understood Angela's point.

"Yuki."

"Kaori."

"Yay! Now we're friends, and you can call me Angie-chan, Yuki."

Yuki and Kaori turned to each other and nodded. Then they relaxed, looking up at the painted ceiling.

"Kaori, how did you end up working with Michael?"

"Eh?" Kaori turned to Yuki and looked down. "Well, his mother hired me, but it's…kind of complicated."

Yuki and Angela listened.

"The thing is," Kaori continued, "my producer in Japan reassigned me to America as part of a deal to salvage my career."

"What were you actually doing back home?"

"I was an idol. I sang, starred in commercials, magazine shoots, and more. I was beginning to build a fanbase, but my producer and agent said I had a temper."

"That makes sense," Yuki said, floating away from Kaori.

"Come on. I'm working on it."

"Well, you're not saying everything."

"Michael, Jamal, and Dōm Coquí went to Japan to do a cross-promotional event where Coquí would be declared an official Yuru Chara of Denfair City."

"Yuru Chara?" Angela said.

"An official mascot to represent Denfair City. Many cities and towns in Japan have Yuru Chara representing them in promotional materials. The network was also involved with advertising New Jersey tourism. Doing so would help the city increase the number of Japanese tourists they get. Uh…just to clarify what Michael said when he introduced us; I was joining them on the show Outside Japan for my own interview of my upcoming tour. My first impression of Michael and Dōm Coquí, however, was that they were obnoxious and annoying."

Kaori turned around and rested her head on her arms on the edge of the pool. She closed her eyes.

"They got into an argument during the taping, I lost my temper and…I punched Michael on live television. It made headlines, and the deal would have been cancelled if I didn't apologize and resign as an idol. I don't know how, but Michael found a way to salvage it by saying it was a publicity stunt between us. Behind the scenes, however, my agent and the producers were not happy with me. Afterwards, I got blacklisted."

Yuki tilted her head. "Blacklisted?"

"It's what Americans say when you can't get hired by anyone because of your reputation. I was declared 'hard to work with.'" Kaori buried her face and took a deep breath. "Michael and his mother offered me a chance to recover from my mistakes, and gave me another route to boost my career as their publicist."

"I see," Yuki said, and Angela placed her hand on Kaori's shoulder.

"It's the long way back. I just call myself Japan's Number One Idol as a marketing brand, but it's for here. I'm learning new things about the publicist trade thanks to WMDS-TV in nearby Newton. They are a Japanese-American station that airs only on New Jersey cable, and they hired me for their local shows. The producer knew Michael because he would advertise the store on their network, so Michael got them to hire me despite my reputation. Yeah, that story even reached here. Sasuke, my director and producer, spoke with my agent Hino-san, and they made a deal with Outside Japan to help me get back on top back home. My segments would air on the show in Japan as long as I behaved. I don't know if it's worth it now. Everyone there had forgotten me. No more cover shoots, or interviews, or song recordings. All I have is this mutual business opportunity with Michael and this small local television station that isn't even seen in New York even though the City is right down east on Route 80 across the Hudson."

"Kaori," Yuki said, stretching her hand out. "You'll make it back. Just do your best."

"Hey, Kaori," Angela said, pulling Ely out of the spring; it shook the excess water off its fur. "Once you sing at the Sakura Matsuri in a couple of weeks, you'll be back on top. If it doesn't work, then it's okay. We're in this together, a TV team."

"Thanks, Angie-chan…Yuki." Kaori turned around and sighed. "All this experience I am gaining will show everyone how hard I worked for my dreams."

"You have a song?" said Yuki.

"Yeah, we're starting the recording next week. Hino-san arranged everything at the festival, and Sasuke will have it viewed in Japan."

Angela floated by. "Did you ask Michael about the apartment?"

"Oh," said Kaori. She turned to Angela, slapping her hands together like a prayer and looking down. "I'm sorry, Angie-chan. I completely forgot."

"What happened, Kaori?" Yuki said.

"Well, I have a single room apartment, and Angie-chan has been sleeping on the couch. Pets are not allowed either, which makes hiding Ely very difficult. Since Michael has a couple of two-bedroom apartments on the third floor, I was hoping we could move in there."

Yuki didn't like the idea of Kaori being in the same building with Michael. She knew that Kaori would do anything to be close to him.

"We have to move into a bigger apartment before Child Services does their interview this week," said Angela.

"Child Services?"

"It's the state of New Jersey," said Kaori. "Ever since she was fired from the circus, she lost her emancipation rights. It allows her to live on her own, Yuki. Angela is declared an orphan, and I've been given a chance to take her in, but I have to improve her living conditions. I got a professional tutor. They would prefer her in school, but it's so late now in the season. The school year is not the same as Japan's. We have to wait until September. Having her sleep on the couch isn't going to win them over, either. We have little time. This interview will be their final decision."

Seeing Angela was now living with Kaori, Yuki chose to give her the benefit of the doubt. "I'm sure Michael will say yes. He's not the type to just turn away anyone so easily. Especially friends."

"True."

Kaori turned to Yuki. "How about you, Yuki? You said you were sent here to be Michael's bodyguard. I don't believe it."

"Why?"

"Because ever since The Impossible Man became famous, Michael became a trouble magnet."

Yuki found it strange that Kaori referred to Michael as two separate people, and Kaori's stare made her feel like she was being backed into a corner. Yuki understood that the two had a history together, and Kaori had the look of a lioness ready to defend.

"Kaori…" Yuki took a deep breath. "Who is The Impossible Man?"

"Oh, Yuki." Kaori shook her head side to side. "So that's why you're here."

"You lily-pad-sniffing horny toad!" yelled Michael from behind the walls. "Get back here!"

"Michael?" Yuki and Kaori said together. They could hear screaming, so they swam to the wall, racing each other. They leaned their ears on the wall, and Angela floated up alongside Ely to do the same. They could hear a lot of noise through the wall, and lifted their heads to the barrier as the screaming got louder. The sense of relaxation in the air disappeared.

"Idiots," Yuki and Kaori said together, and Angela smiled.

❋ ❋ ❋

On the other side of the wall, Michael was chasing Dōm Coqu̧ all around the spring. Both wore only towels. Michael had one eye closed, was covered in soap suds, and brandished the bar of soap at Dōm Coquí.

Jamal spoke without any emotion. "Please, stop…don't do this."

Dōm Coquí pulled his lower eyelid down, his tongue sticking out. The chase was on.

Michael reached out to him, but he missed, and the frog dove into the water. The towel flew off and onto the ground. He watched Dōm Coquí leap out of the water onto the rocks, where another towel waited for him. After Dōm Coquí wrapped the towel around his body, Michael stood in front of him out of nowhere.

"Wi borbat," said Dōm Coquí, slapping his forehead.

"Yes, you forgot, didn't you?" Michael smiled while Jamal slid into the water.

"Would you two just stop fighting for one day?"

"Fine, Jamal," said Michael. He slid into the spring across from him. Everything was quiet now, and Dōm Coquí spoke.

"Hochi mei doku ba Hackettstown."

Michael turned to him. "How did you find a house with a pond in Hackettstown?"

"Nebunteka." Dōm Coquí squatted. "Ko tu wei nu."

"Well, just keep saving money and you'll get it."

Jamal leaned his head back on his arms. "Yeah, I feel you, Coquí. I haven't decided yet if I want to start my own business here, or move to Japan."

"Honly?"

Jamal took a moment to process what Dōm Coquí said, then nodded. "Really. No offense, Michael, but I do have my own dreams."

"I'm not stopping you," Michael replied. "Just know you have a job and a place to stay if things don't work out for you two."

Jamal smiled at Michael. "Yeah."

"Syi." Dōm Coquí nodded and hopped into the water. When he surfaced, he heard women giggling. He looked at Michael and Jamal, neither of whom was making the girlish laugh. Dōm Coquí waded over to the wall, and when he leaned his ear on the barrier, he heard a familiar laugh.

"Poime?" he said, and caught the attention of Michael and Jamal.

"Aey, what's going on?"

"Poime des cehin zah lall."

"Kaori's behind the wall, eh?" Michael and Jamal approached the wall and leaned their ears on the barrier to listen. There was nothing but silence. "Did we end up in the women's section, Jamal?"

"No, we followed the arrows correctly."

"Des wo ni et."

"Yes, too quiet. You don't think they're…" Michael and Dōm Coquí looked at each other, while on the other side of the wall Yuki, Angela, and Kaori pulled away.

"I don't hear anything, Yuki," said Kaori.

"You don't think they're…"

"Dōm Coquí is here. I wouldn't put it past him." Kaori stood to her feet. "There's only one way…"

On the other side, Michael stood up too. "…to find out."

Wrapped in towels, Michael led Dōm Coquí out of their room. They both walked down the hallway, towards an intersection that separated them from the women. The duo arrived at an open door, and as they did, Yuki stepped out. Michael and Yuki stood there, looking at each other in their towels. It was the first time they'd ever seen each other like that. They blushed lightly at first, and Yuki tilted her head.

"You don't have much of a body."

"What?" Michael patted his abdomen. It lacked any muscle.

"Uh…you…you shouldn't be here," Yuki said.

"Please," said Michael. "You came out here for the same reason we did. To spy on us."

"Wait a second…"

"Admit it! You would kick our butts if we came over and spied on you, but it's okay if you spied on us because we wouldn't scream."

"What?" said Yuki in surprise. It was nonsense to her. Before she had a chance to respond, Kaori stepped outside in her towel.

"Hey, what's going on?" she said, closing the door behind her. "You two shouldn't be here. The women will beat you guys up."

As Kaori took a step forward, her towel got stuck in the closed door, and it slipped off and revealed her naked body. She stood there as Yuki covered her mouth in shock and Michael watched. Dōm Coquí collapsed to the floor, blood squirting out of his nose and a smile of satisfaction on his face. Kaori crouched, covering her chest with her arms, and screamed. She heard Michael chuckle while pinching his nose to prevent any bleeding, while Yuki went to get Kaori's towel.

"This is not funny, Michael, cover your eyes!" Yuki opened the door a little to free the towel, and Kaori stared at him.

"So you think this is funny!" She grabbed his towel. "Let's see what you got!"

Kaori pulled Michael's towel off, leaving him naked. She laughed, and Yuki blushed bright red like a light. As Kaori pointed at Michael covering himself with his hand, Dōm Coquí sat up and laughed along with her.

"That wasn't smart, frog," said Michael, turning to Dōm Coquí with evil in his eyes. He threw the frog, out of nowhere, over Kaori. The towel slipped off Coquí, and he landed on his back.

"I'm blind!" yelled Michael, and covered his eyes. Kaori and Yuki jumped back from shock at seeing Dōm Coquí naked.

"No you're not," Kaori said to Michael. "You just have your eyes covered."

Michael uncovered his eyes and raised his freed arm up in joy.

"I can see again!"

"Idiot," Kaori said, and slouched her shoulders.

They laughed, while Yuki stood there trying to grasp everyone's random behavior and enjoyment. "What is wrong with all of you? You're all naked."

She handed Kaori the towel. As Dōm Coquí used Yuki's own towel to stand up, she tried to stop him from pulling it, but the towel loosened and fell to the ground. Yuki and Michael now saw each other fully nude. With her hands trembling, as Kaori watched on, Michael shifted his head to the side, trying to look away, even though his eyes would not. The sound of a slap echoed down the hallway, and Yuki went back inside.

Michael watched the door slam. "Damn."

"Ignore her," Kaori said, opening the door with a smile. "She's not used to our style of fun."

✳ ✳ ✳

Kaori followed Yuki back to the spring. She laughed out loud as Yuki slid into the water, covering her chest and blushing. Kaori sat on the edge, with only her legs in the water, and leaned close to Yuki.

"It was an accident."

Yuki remained silent and buried half her face underwater.

"Come on, Yuki, it's not like he hasn't seen you naked at all."

"What are you talking about?" said Yuki, raising her dripping head.

"You were in his apartment before Jamal arrived." Kaori slid into the water right next to Yuki and whispered into her ear. "You have to have had at least a little piece of the I."

"What?" Yuki had no idea what Kaori was talking about. "I don't understand."

"The two of you in the same room … in the same bed …"

Yuki tilted her head up. It took a while, but finally she put it all together and quickly waved her hands. "No, we never did. He slept on the couch or the floor … or upside down on the chair. How did he do that? Anyway, we can't. It goes against the rules of the Order."

"Upside down on the chair? Normally he would sleep on the table when I stayed overnight."

"What?" Yuki's eyes widened.

"Relax, sometimes I work two shifts between the shoot and the store. I can't get home after midnight. So Michael lets me stay overnight."

"Liar." Yuki looked her in the eyes and refocused the conversation. "Look, I have too much respect for him to treat him like an object."

"Yeah right, Yuki. I've seen you make moves on him. Who're you trying to fool?"

"At least I didn't hesitate for a long time. You had, what, a couple of years to win his heart?"

Kaori looked around the room a bit in thought. When her mind caught on, she growled. "I tried."

"Not hard enough, Kaori."

"So is that a challenge?" Kaori raised her fist.

"Yeah. I'll win his heart. Whatever competition you want."

"So much for respecting The Impossible Man," said Kaori, and smiled.

Yuki froze in place and did not say another word, realizing what she'd said. She remembered how much she'd hated being treated like an object by her mother, when she fought Michael's mother and handed Yuki over as a trophy to serve as his bodyguard. If Michael's mother had lost, he would have served her as a bodyguard, magically transformed into a girl forever. Thinking it over, he'd never looked at her the way her own mother did. He made it clear many times that her duty as a bodyguard was over. It was not as easy as she thought...or maybe she didn't understand her own feelings.

"Michael is a nice person, Kaori. Well, when he isn't acting like an idiot." Yuki sighed. "I can't explain it, but…I like him."

"Michael?" Kaori looked up at the ceiling. "Yeah, I like him too. After everything he's done for me."

"Rivals?" Yuki lifted her pinkie finger to Kaori. The act surprised Kaori, but she understood.

"Rivals." Kaori locked her pinkie finger around Yuki's, and they shook on it.

Angela gasped. "A challenge to win a first date with Michael?"

"Yes." Kaori stood up. "Be ready to lose, Yuki, for I will be the one to marry The Impossible Man and have The Impossible Children!"

Angela pointed at Kaori and smiled. "I see you."

Kaori splashed water at Angela and sat back down, resting the back of her head on her hands. "You and the Order of the Magical Girl will never know who The Impossible Man is. Ever."

Yuki looked at Kaori's smile. She was curious why she kept calling him The Impossible Man more than his actual name, but as she opened her mouth to respond, Angela interrupted. "Rules of the Order?" she said, floating with Ely close to the women. "Yuki, you're a virgin?"

Yuki and Kaori turned to Angela, surprised to have heard her say that. Angela smiled, and Yuki swam away.

"I may be fourteen, but I'm not that dumb."

"I guess we'll have a little talk." Kaori floated beside Angela, and Yuki leaned back on the water to relax. "Yuki, don't you want to have a little talk too?"

"I already had my little talk with my mom when I was twelve. You go and have fun." Yuki waved them away and relaxed.

Kaori and Angela giggled. Angela looked around and noticed someone was missing.

"Ely? Uh oh…"

✳ ✳ ✳

"Jamal is taking a long time," Michael said in their room, a red handprint throbbing on his cheek. He relaxed on the wooden chair, examining the soap, waiting for Jamal to return. As he did, Dōm Coquí looked at the wall and sighed.

"You miss seeing Kaori in her birthday suit, eh?"

"Syi."

"The best five minutes of your life?"

"Syi."

"There's always next time."

"Syi."

Michael crossed his arms with a light growl, tapping his fingers on his arm. "I hope Jamal will hurry with the damn sponges."

On cue, the door opened. Michael leaned forward, rubbing the bruise on his cheek. "It's about time, Jamal! Now hand me a sponge." He stretched his hand out, but no one stood in the doorway. Footsteps stopped behind him, and he felt a sponge rub up and down his back. "Why're you rubbing me, Jamal?"

"I'm over here."

Michael looked over, and Jamal stood in the doorway, holding a bucket of sponges. In the other direction, Dōm Coquí shivered with a wide stare. When he turned around, a soggy and skinny Ely was smiling at him. Ely's eyes turned to hearts, and she held a sponge up. Michael rushed out, wrapping his robe and screaming.

Jamal stepped to the side of the door and watched Ely chase Michael down the hall, towards the women's side of the spring.

Angela peeked out the door, seeing Michael and Ely turning the corner. "I found Ely! Stop chasing Michael!"

"Never mind them, we have to finish our talk," said Kaori.

Angela closed the door. "So what does the boy do next?"

As Ely continued to chase after Michael, he ran past some women in their towels screaming. He reached a door and entered, but once he slammed it, he leaned back on it and took a deep breath. When he looked up, he saw a group of angry naked women before his eyes.

"Pervert!"

"You don't understand!" Michael flew out the door, beaten and battered, landing next to Ely waiting for him. As she gave Michael a big hug, he cringed in pain. He pushed Ely off and ran, and as he entered the lobby, she caught up to him.

In the lobby, he rushed past a woman and her boyfriend, who both screamed. Ely followed him, and as she passed, the man fainted into his girlfriend's arms.

Ely ran down a hallway and saw Michael wasn't there. She looked down with sadness, only to get picked up by the back of her neck by Michael. His glare made Ely smile with guilt.

Michael returned to Yuki, Kaori, and Angela's room, where he opened the door with his eyes closed tight. He held Ely up like a grocery bag. "You lost this?"

"Ely, you bad girl," said Angela, jumping out of the water naked. Yuki and Kaori threw their arms up in shock, and waved for Angela's attention.

"Angie-chan, cover yourself!" Kaori said.

"But I am, see?" Angela used Ely as cover while the women lowered their heads in shame.

Michael gritted his teeth. "If you don't mind, keep Ely away from me!"

"Sorry!"

The door slammed, and Angela turned around, laughing with Yuki and Kaori. She sat back into the pool and released Ely into the water. "This has been fun."

"For us," Yuki said, making Kaori and Angela laugh. She leaned back and looked up at the ceiling. Then something flew over her suddenly; she couldn't feel her body move, nor was her mind focused. Her eyes turned red and became pupil-less. Her body glowed red, and that aura left her.

"What was that?" Kaori looked around. "A ki energy?"

She turned around to Yuki, who was in a trance. Kaori and Angela hurried over until the energy grew stronger, which distracted them. The sound of Ely growling caught Kaori's attention, and she saw Angela reaching out to Yuki.

"Yuki, are you okay?" Angela said, placing her hands on Yuki's shoulders.

"Angie-chan, don't…"

Angela's eyes turned red and pupil-less as well. She fell back into the water, and Ely barked and jumped in.

"Angie-chan!" Kaori dove underwater and pulled Angela out, with Ely's help. She rolled Angela out of the water and laid her on her back. When she pressed her hands on Angela's chest to resuscitate her, Yuki grabbed her leg. Kaori looked back as her eyes turned red, and she fell on top of Angela. "I-Man…no…"

✳ ✳ ✳

Michael stuck a bandage on his forehead, as Jamal and Dōm Coquí watched; they couldn't believe it was much worse than the hand-slap.

"You're a pain magnet, Michael," said Jamal.

"This is supposed to be a day for me to relax, eh? I don't feel relaxed."

"You're never relaxed. You're always stressed, and that gets you in trouble."

"Aey, I don't ask for trouble. It always follows me."

"It's your world now. You made it happen." Jamal took a deep breath. "Fine. Come on, Coquí, let's get something to eat. You want anything?"

"Silence," said Michael.

Jamal shrugged. He and Dōm Coquí both slipped into their yukata, leaving Michael alone in the spring. The moment the door closed, he screamed from the bruises he had, then let out a deep breath. "Finally. Peace and quiet."

He leaned his head back, staring at the ceiling for a while. All the chaos that had happened in the past couple of days melted away, and the warmth of the spring soothed his muscles. He closed his eyes, and a smile grew on his face.

Suddenly, a splash in the water opened his eyes. A folded towel now lay next to him, just above the water. Michael raised one eyebrow and lifted the towel up. Underneath it was the lion-headed spoon, leaning back on the edge of the spring, half its body resting under the water. Michael stumbled back, splashing. He watched the towel rest on the lion's head, as though it rested on the head of a human, and it disturbed him.

As it glowed red, he opened the door and threw the spoon outside, the towel still on its head. Michael slid back into the water from out of nowhere and took a deep breath. As he perched his arms on the edge of the spring, he felt a pair of hands cover his eyes. He pulled the arms back and turned around. There he saw Yuki, glowing in light, kneeling before him naked. He quickly raised his arms up, ready to block another slap, but instead he heard her giggling.

"Yuki?" he said, and she dove in, lighting up the water underneath the surface.

Then she emerged from the water and leaned toward him. As Michael floated backwards, made nervous by her sudden aggression, she followed him. The glowing Yuki embraced Michael, only to grab nothing but air. She turned around and found him at the other end of the pool. Her eyebrows lowered in anger, and she swam toward him.

"Yuki, what's gotten into you?" said Michael. Yuki

splashed water at him, and when he blocked it, her hand touched his. Then Michael's eyes turned red and pupil-less. He felt the glowing Yuki shift his head to the side, watched her lips draw closer to his. At first, his lips came close to contact, but then a lightbulb from a lamp by the wall dimmed.

"Damn spoon," he said. His pupils returned to normal, and the glowing Yuki stumbled back. When color returned to his eyes, he saw the figure of light scream aloud and collapse into the water. There he saw the spoon sink to the bottom of the pool. From behind the wall, someone screamed. "Yuki! Kaori!"

"Michael!" Yuki said from the other side. "Angela is hurt!"

Michael jumped out of the pool, a yukata already wrapped around his body. He ran outside from out of nowhere, passing by Jamal and Dōm Coquí.

"Hurry, Angela is in danger."

Jamal and Dōm Coquí arrived at the women's side, where Michael opened their door.

Inside, he saw Kaori giving CPR to Angela as Yuki and Ely watched on. Michael approached the women as Jamal and Dōm Coquí entered.

He hurried past Yuki. "What happened, Kaori?"

"I don't know," she replied, as Yuki stood ignored. "We passed out for a moment, and when we woke up, we found Angela on the floor, not breathing."

Kaori stopped the CPR and looked up at Michael with a nod. "It's time, I-Man."

"Time?" Yuki said, and Dōm Coquí placed a yukata

robe over her back while Jamal took her hand to escort her out of the room. As he did, Michael walked to a nearby lamp.

"Excuse me, but it's a life and death situation," Michael said to the lightbulb, and removed it, gently placing it on the ground. He pulled out an electrical wire from the lamp and split the wires.

Yuki realized what he planned to do as he made the wires spark. She struggled to break free to stop him as he held the wires poised over Angela. "Michael, are you crazy? Let me go, guys! I have healing spells!"

When the door closed, it warped and bent a little. When it all stopped, Michael screamed, and the lights flickered throughout the room.

✳ ✳ ✳

"A dream?" Angela stood on the fifty-yard line of a football field. There was nothing but mist all around. Each breath she took made mist appear like a cold day in winter. Suddenly, she heard footsteps behind her; a shadow in the mist was approaching her, and it was big. A monster. She thought when emerging from the mist was Michael, carrying the large yellow goalpost over his shoulder.

She stepped aside, as each step Michael took was slow and steady. As he passed by her, she struggled to say anything. The mist ahead of them opened up for Michael and the end zone was exposed. As the mist engulfed Michael again, Angela's eyes grew wide. The silhouette of him raising the goalpost over his head scared her. Strange shadows of creatures and people appeared next to Michael, each brightened a light, and Angela ran forward in slow motion, her right arm extended towards him.

"The Impossible Man!" she said, and she watched him stab the end zone with the goal post.

She opened her eyes and found herself in bed, dressed in pink pajamas. The newspaper on the table showed that it was May 1st. She saw Kaori sleeping on a chair beside her, and smelled food cooking outside the room. Angela took her blanket and covered Kaori with it, smiled, and stepped outside. There was Yuki by a stove, cooking breakfast.

"You're finally awake," she said, turning to Angela. "You were out for a couple of days."

"Where are we?"

"You're in my apartment. You've been resting here while Kaori had Michael and the guys move you both into your new apartment today."

"Angela," said Kaori from behind.

"Kaori!" Angela hurried to Kaori, and they hugged each other.

"How are you feeling?"

"I feel better, but … the appointment?"

"I received a call the day after the incident. Child Services pushed our interview date to next week due to a scheduled conflict."

"No…" Angela placed her hand on her forehead. "That can't be right."

"What is it?"

"The Impossible Man. I saw him. I understand. I-Man!"

She dashed out of Yuki's apartment, where outside, she saw Dōm Coquí carrying a chair at the top of the stairs. She looked up the stairs to find Michael, and heard screaming below instead. Downstairs, Michael was outside, running away from Ely. She exited the building, and they both stopped. Angela hugged Michael, and Ely hugged them both, much to Michael's panic. As Angela stared at Michael's face, everything around her became tinted. A pair of sunglasses slid over her eyes, like a rite of passage, and when she stepped back, she saw the bandages on Michael's hand. "You're hurt?"

"The electricity from the lamp fried my fingers, but thankfully Yuki healed most of them. It will take time to heal the rest of the way."

"I understand now why you're called The Impossible Man!" Angela took his bandaged hands and held them tight, though he winced in pain. "Thank you."

"No problem," Michael said, looking at the apartment entrance. He saw Dōm Coquí and Kaori staring coldly, and Yuki tilting her head in confusion.

Jamal stepped outside, waving an order form in his hand. "Did you place an order for Kaijuzoid products?" Suddenly, he saw Angela with sunglasses on, Dōm Coquí and Kaori staring on. He took a deep breath and nodded.

"Yeah, Jamal," Michael said, and Angela's eyes grew wide. "The new series is coming out and I want to get the initial sales."

"You know we'll get backlogged with memorabilia," replied Jamal.

Angela stepped back with her hand over her head, feeling Kaori's hands on her shoulders. "Angela," said Kaori, "are you okay?"

"I can't remember what I dreamed," said Angela, "but The Impossible Man ... I think he did something."

Kaori looked into Angela's eyes. She growled and turned towards Michael, but Angela grabbed her arm.

"Please. I want the interview to work for us."

Kaori looked back at Michael, not realizing that her hand had curled into a fist. She nodded and hugged Angela instead. "Damn him."

"Kaori?"

"We'll be okay. Everything will be okay."

Yuki watched Kaori and Angela hugging each other. She shifted her sights to Michael, who was arguing with Dōm Coquí over the order. She felt conflicted between targeting him or the spoon. Yuki went to her apartment, closing the door a little, and entered her kitchen. Her brooch blinked and she tapped it.

"Yes, supervisor?"

"Scarlet Sorceress, we have concluded our initial investigation. Our sources have confirmed your suspicions about that magical presence in your area."

"The spoon ..." Yuki clasped her brooch. "Let me take this case."

"You're a magical girl. This is outside your field."

"I'm the only one here. It will be too late if we wait for a magical detective." Yuki's eyes lit up and she smiled. "Besides, my investigation on The Impossible Man led me to this magical presence. It only makes sense that the two may be linked somehow."

Yuki waited for a response as she approached the door; the hallway was empty. She looked at the front door to Michael's apartment, thinking of the power he possessed. She leaned on the wall, her eyes closed.

"Very well," Supervisor said, and Yuki opened her eyes. "We'll add this to your current case file. As evaluation, you will report to us every night. We'll monitor from here. Good luck."

"Evaluation?" Yuki's eyes grew wide and her heart skipped a beat. "Thank you. I'll do my best."

The brooch stopped blinking. Yuki stared at the embedded jewel, unaware of the table lamp's lightbulb brightening up. She tightened her grip on the brooch and pressed it to her chest. "I won't give up what I aspired for. It will be hard work, but I will become a magical detective."

Episode 10

[~ Round 1 ~]

With everything going on around the shop, I'm quite surprised that you have made it this far. Even a relaxing time at the hot spring ended up being eventful, but with all the strange things going on around this place, I wouldn't blame you if you left right now and didn't continue on. Please don't leave yet. After all, my crew and I have taken on just about almost everything...

...but the kitchen sink.

May 4, 2002

The past couple of days had been a bit peaceful. The spoon hadn't made any moves since the hot spring. Instead, it observed the store from across the street, analyzing everyone there, searching for patterns. The armored woman used the camera on her helmet to record everyone's activities. Together, they looked up at the top floor and saw the window vibrate.

In Kaori and Angela's apartment, meanwhile, they were almost done unpacking. On the kitchen table lay the file documents for their interview with Child Services. They heard a strange thump through their walls. At first, they thought it was coming from outside, but when they looked out the window they realized it was coming from within.

Then there was Jamal. When he finished drying his face after shaving, the wall in his bathroom rattled. An earthquake? He thought.

At Dōm Coquí's apartment, he heard a loud snore through the air vent. He would croak back at it, but there was no frog on the other side.

Yuki stood in her kitchen and saw the pipes to her radiator begin to vibrate. It shook some of the dust off the ceiling and rained down to the ground.

Michael, on the other hand, never had these problems. In fact, his room was never disturbed. He stepped out of his apartment and heard everyone talking on the third floor. He appeared behind them from out of nowhere, and they turned to him for answers. "What's wrong?"

"This is the third time this week that we've heard that strange noise," said Kaori.

"Now it's in all of our apartments," Jamal said.

"How strange?" Michael said.

Angela spoke. "Maybe it's coming from the fourth floor?"

"Fourth floor?"

Yuki placed her hands on her hips. "Yes, Michael…the fourth floor."

"I didn't know we had one."

Out of frustration, everyone but Angela slapped the back of Michael's head at the same time. Kaori placed her hands over his ears and turned his head to the side. There were a set of stairs before him. Kaori tilted his head, guiding it to the top, where he saw the only door on the floor.

"Hey guys, look," he said, pointing up at the door. "We have a fourth floor."

Kaori tilted his head again and it locked in place.

After Michael pulled away from her and straightened his head, he led everyone up the stairs. Each step they took made a creaking, creepy sound, which made the trip upstairs very tense.

For no reason.

Once Michael took another step, a loud sputtering sound burst out from behind the door. Everyone screamed, and Michael looked back at them with a chuckle. On the next step, they all heard a loud moan. There were not a lot of steps to get to the fourth floor, but Michael was enjoying everyone's fright. He reached the top step and stared at the door.

"You don't have to come, ladies."

"I..." Yuki shivered. "I insist."

"Oh cut it out, Yuki." Kaori pushed Yuki and Michael both aside, marched upstairs, and grabbed the doorknob.

"Come in," echoed a creepy voice from behind the door.

Kaori's forehead turned blue and she ran right back behind Michael. She peeked over his shoulder, and Michael shifted his eyes in her direction with his eyelids half closed.

"My hero," he said.

"Shut up," said Kaori, pushing him forward. "And open the damn door!"

Michael approached the door and reached for the doorknob. He looked back. Kaori and Yuki held each other's arms, Angela hugged Ely tight, and Jamal and Dōm Coquí braced for something big to happen.

The voice spoke. "I don't have cooties, you know."

Dōm Coquí screamed like a little girl and wrapped his arms around Kaori, pretending to be scared and nuzzling her chest. Her cheeks turned red and her eyes grew angry.

"Get off me, you pervert!" She kicked Dōm Coquí's face into the wall. She then proceeded to stomp on his back for a while. When she stopped, the frog went down the stairs like a slinky, and Angela and Ely watched him pass by.

Michael opened the door, slowly, and as he did it made a long screeching sound, scaring everyone. He moved the door back and forth, listening to the creaking.

"I'll have to oil this door, Jamal."

"Just go inside!" Jamal said, and everyone pushed Michael through the doorway before following him inside.

The apartment was pitch black, and everyone heard more moaning. A male voice. The light outside was all there was for everyone to see. A little spotlight appeared in the distance, exposing the wooden floor. It guided Michael and his friends toward the moaning. They looked around the area to see where it was all coming from. When Michael stopped, everyone bumped into him, and they all fell down into the spotlight. As the moaning got louder, everyone sat up.

"Ah, my foot feels better," said the mysterious voice. "My favorite corn doesn't hurt any more...oh, you're here."

Suddenly the sound of the motor echoed in the darkness. It sputtered as it got closer. Songs of a humming choir created a soothing atmosphere. As the motor approached, it made popping and stuttering sounds, stalling to move onward.

"Up! Up! Damn it!" Then the motor sounded better, and a new spotlight appeared before everyone. They were staring out at the light when the squeaky sound above made them all look up. While the humming choir became loud, an old, bald man descended from the darkness and into the spotlight. He wore a Hawaiian shirt with flower designs and long shorts covering his knees. His legs were crossed, and his hands rested in a meditative state. Angela noticed he was held up by two strings. Once he landed on the wooden floor and the strings loosened up, the sound of a vinyl record scratching to a stop ended the song of humming choir.

The old man spoke with a soft and wise voice. "What brings you to my domicile, my children?"

"Yeah, where's the guy with the creepy voice?" answered Michael.

Kaori slapped Michael and leaned into his smiling face. "He's the creepy voice, you idiot!"

"I am Shinichiro Katsuragi. A Reader."

"Hiya, Kats!" said Angela, waving with a smile, and Shinichiro lost his balance.

"I am not a pork cutlet!" he yelled.

"Huh?" Michael suddenly imagined a slice of breaded pork with cat ears and tail attached. "That doesn't look appetizing."

Angela smiled. "You're the famous—"

"Also, do not give me a nickname when we're just introducing each other," Shinichiro said, but Yuki waved for his attention. "Did you say you're a Reader?"

"Indeed I am."

"What kind of Reader?"

"A book reader," Michael said, and Shinichiro threw a book from behind his back at his face. It slid down to his lap.

"I am a Reader of many things, which can see what you cannot."

"Yeah," Michael said, "can you read this?" He stuck out his middle finger at Shinichiro's face, but Shinichiro, giving off little emotion, grabbed the middle finger and twisted it to the side. Michael's body flipped over in a perfect circle, where he landed on his back and stared at Shinichiro. He watched Shinichiro reach into his pocket, take out a long pipe, and light it. With one puff, smoke covered Michael's face, and he coughed. He rolled back to his side of the spotlight.

"How long have you been here?" asked Yuki.

"Since I moved from Japan many years ago, before any of you arrived."

"Oh yeah," Michael said, sitting up and nursing his back. "Well, I don't recall giving you this apartment."

"Oh," said Shinichiro, taking a puff of his pipe. "So you're the shrimp who bought out Tanaka."

"Shrimp?" Michael stood up on one knee, rolling his sleeve back. "Listen here, squatter, you better get out of my place, because this apartment isn't free."

"Make me."

Michael ran toward Shinichiro and grabbed his Hawaiian shirt. After Shinichiro blew smoke into his face, Michael felt his arm twist, and his body flipped over again. He landed on his back. Michael stood up and threw a punch, but Shinichiro sat there untouched. Michael threw a few more punches, yet Shinichiro still sat there, taking a puff of his pipe, never moving his head to dodge. Every attack missed. Before Michael knew it, he flew in the air and landed on his back again.

Shinichiro took another puff of his pipe. "Let's make a deal, since you can't see the simple solution due to your stupidity. If you can throw me out of this room, I will leave in peace. I'll remain here for as long as I keep throwing you out."

"Forget it," Michael said, crossing his arms while lying on his back.

"Chicken?" Shinichiro said in Japanese.

"What?!" Michael said in Spanish. "Why, you…"

He stood up on his feet once again. As he approached Shinichiro, a puff of smoke blew into the air. The door opened by itself, and Michael flew out of the apartment. He rolled down the stairs to the third floor and slid into the wall by one of the empty apartments.

Everyone inside looked at the opened door and then back at Shinichiro.

"Your friend should know that there's a bigger fish to fry tomorrow. That's a free sample reading."

Yuki lifted up her head and looked at the darkness. "This energy."

Kaori nodded. "Yeah, it's spiritual. Do you read souls, Katsuragi-san?"

Shinichiro took another puff of smoke. Looking into Yuki and Kaori's eyes, he saw positive energy within them. Scanning the rest, there was no malice to be found. He chuckled. "If that is what you sense. Living or object, if any of you want a reading, just stop on by. I normally charge a fee for this, but since we're neighbors, I'll give you a one percent discount…and that's being generous. Good day."

Shinichiro floated up into the air. The sound of the vinyl record started again, and the humming choir drowned out the rumbling motor. He disappeared in the darkness and all the noise faded away.

Everyone exited the apartment, quiet for a moment, and the door closed behind them by itself. They did not know what to make of Shinichiro. Everyone walked down to the third floor. They passed by Michael lying on the wall, his eyes spinning in a spiral, without a care to his well-being. As Dōm Coquí dragged Michael by the collar, Angela looked back at the door above and realized something.

"We never told him to stop making the noise."

Everyone stopped and lowered their heads at their failure to complain about it.

In the store, Michael screamed in pain as Yuki rubbed more alcohol on his forehead. He felt Kaori wrapping a bandage around his head as Angela handed him a cup of water. The help was nice until Yuki and Kaori slapped each other's hands away from him. Unfortunately, that led to their hands striking the back of his head. The world spun around him.

"Sorry," they said.

"Katsuragi," Michael said, and his sight straightened out. "He's out of here."

"You may as well not try," Yuki said. "Katsuragi-san obviously is too good and got into your head. Plus, I don't think you can physically handle this one."

"Strange?" Kaori said. "I doubt that Michael ever had a head to work with anyway."

"Watch it, Kaori. Whoa…" Michael held his head in his hands; the world was spinning around him, and he saw copies of Dōm Coquí. "Frog, what is it with you and shadow clones?"

"Qwani?"

Michael shook his head and slapped his face. He rushed back into his apartment, and everyone followed him. He appeared out of nowhere in front of Shinichiro's door, and could hear the footsteps of his friends coming from below. Michael grabbed the doorknob and tried to open it. He found it locked and heard Shinichiro speak.

"Try again tomorrow."

"No," Michael said. "We're going to do this now!"

"I'll only allow you one try a day."

"You sneaky old fart." Michael planted his foot on the wall to add more strength. "Let me in!"

"Push the door, not pull." Shinichiro said, but Michael doubled down to open it.

Michael's hands slipped off the doorknob and he fell back. He sat up and felt the keys in his pocket. With a smirk, he pulled out the master key. When he inserted the key, a jolt of electricity flowed throughout his body. When Yuki arrived, Michael could not let go. He felt her arms around his waist, and the electricity surrounded her body. Together, they gave one big pull. Michael broke free and they fell down together. Their bodies vibrated from the surge, and he felt Yuki hold him tight to get him to stop.

"Stop! You're hurting yourself!"

Kaori arrived and growled at Yuki, giving her a glare.

"Once a day, shrimp," Shinichiro said. "Once a day."

"Ergh…"

Yuki helped Michael up to his feet. She led him to the stairs, and Kaori reached out for him. Yuki and Kaori quietly competed with each other to help Michael. As they released their hold of him, they got physical with each other, and Michael fell down the stairs. They saw him on the third floor, face first on the ground.

"Damn."

The skies darkened over Denfair City, and rain was pouring down. It was closing time. Michael finished logging in the last inventory statements on the computer before closing out the register. He saw Angela help Yuki enter the store—both wearing raincoats to stay dry, and carrying books in plastic bags in their arms. After they planted a pile of books on the counter, Angela walked down the manga aisle, peeking in his direction in secret.

"Thank you, Angie-chan," said Yuki.

"You're welcome." Angela slid her fingers across the binder of each manga book on the shelf without looking in Michael and Yuki's direction.

Michael picked up a book titled Ancient Artifacts of World History. He flipped through the pages and saw pictures of old urns, staffs, and relics.

"What's the book for Yuki?"

"I'm doing research on the spoon. My supervisor told me that neither she nor the Order could find anything about it on their end. So I'm checking out some of these books that were not released in Japan. Maybe they might have something on that spoon."

"Thanks."

Yuki blushed from the compliment and smiled. She saw Angela stand before the counter with a manga in hand and stepped aside.

"I would like to buy this manga, Mikey."

Michael left eyebrow raised from that nickname, but he let it slide. "Ten dollars."

Angela took out some money and handed it to Michael. She stepped back from him, blushing at the fact that she'd bought something from him. Angela never noticed the confused look on his face before she ran out of the store.

"Strange," Michael said, scratching his head.

Yuki giggled. "I can't blame her for feeling like that."

"Huh?" Michael turned to Yuki, oblivious.

"Angela has a crush on you." Yuki looked at the rain. "That's so cute."

"She does know that I'm too old for her, right?"

"I'm sure she does, but you have to remember, she has changed a bit since you saved her life at the hot springs."

"Well, at least I know I'm not too old for you." Michael leaned over the counter, and Yuki turned to him and blushed. He smirked at her, and she realized he was not being serious about her feelings.

"True," said Yuki, flicking her finger on Michael's forehead. "But you're still too immature for me."

Michael slumped over the counter, confirming Yuki's

suspicions. He looked up at her. She giggled and picked up the books. He watched her leave the store.

"I'll research this tonight," said Yuki, stopping and looking back with a smile. "I'll see to it that I stop the spoon from tormenting you."

"Thanks," said Michael. He stood by the door from out of nowhere and waved goodbye to her.

"No problem," said Yuki, waving goodbye in return and leaving the store.

Michael locked the door and flipped the open sign to 'Closed.' After shutting everything down, he entered his apartment. Thunder roared outside, and he turned on the lights to the kitchen. He did not notice the spoon while removing his shirt, but at the sight of his plain-looking body, the spoon glowed red. After changing into a clean white t-shirt, he made dinner and sat in the living room to watch television.

The lion-headed spoon watched him, laughing out at the TV show. There was something about his laughter that made the spoon want to be closer to him. He was relaxed and calm, the first it had ever seen him like that.

Michael got up off the couch with an empty dish. He placed it on a pile of unclean bowls and cups in the sink, and there he saw the silver spoon resting next to the refrigerator. He leaned close to it.

"What are you?" With a growl, he picked up the spoon, ignoring Yuki's warning in his mind, and it glowed. Without thought, he flicked the spoon into the sink and turned on the water to drown it. He stopped the water and walked to his room, turning off the light.

The spoon lifted itself up halfway above the water. It glowed red, targeting Michael. The lightning outside flashed. As the spoon fired a pair of red beams at Michael, the electricity from the lightning surged through the wall. Like a rod, the spoon attracted the voltage and was struck in the back. The thunder was too loud for the noise to attract Michael's attention. As it watched Michael close the door, it slipped underwater, glowing red against its will.

The electricity extracted the ball of red light into the wall socket and followed the electric wires through the breaker and outside. At the other end, a sphere of light grew large and vanished. Red electricity took human shape, and the armored woman materialized in a crouched position. She slowly stood up, and her visor activated.

Michael started his morning standing in front of Shinichiro's apartment door. After a good night's sleep, his anger towards Shinichiro had waned a little, yet he still felt nervous about turning the doorknob to open the door. He patted it a couple of times, and did not feel a shock. He was raising his hand up to knock on the door when he heard Shinichiro's voice.

"Come in."

Michael entered the room—without opening the door—and saw Shinichiro sitting in the spotlight, waiting. As Shinichiro took a puff of smoke from his pipe, Michael rushed at him. Once Michael reached out to the old man, aiming for the collar, Shinichiro raised his hand up and made him stop. A spotlight appeared beside Michael, and Shinichiro offered a seat there. Michael sat down on the floor and remained quiet, unaware of the door opening on its own behind him.

"Let's see what the bones say," Shinichiro said, holding a pair of white dice in one hand and a ceramic cup in the other. With one swift motion, he crossed his arms, slamming the dice into the cup. He spun the cup on the palm of his hand while rotating his arm over his head. Once the cup was above his head, he slammed the cup down, keeping the dice covered.

Shinichiro leaned close to the cup. Michael leaned close to him, and together they stared at the ceramic cup. Shinichiro removed the cup, and they saw the number nine on the dice. The two shifted their eyes toward each other.

Shinichiro whispered. "The bones tell me nothing, goodbye."

Michael flew out of the room. He bounced down the stairs, landing painfully on his back on the third floor. He watched the door close on its own.

"Remember, shrimp, something odd is going to happen to you today."

Michael sat up, rubbing the back of his head. He realized Shinichiro had tricked him. He slapped the floor and got up. He thought of breaking the door down, but instead, he made his way to the store and opened up shop. After turning on the lights, he flipped the Closed sign to Open, and Jamal arrived, ready to set up shop.

"Dōm Coquí got the day off," Michael said.

"Okay. I'll go get the sign stand and set up the new ad outside."

As Jamal went to the storage room, Kaori entered the store, carrying Seizon in her hand. Michael stepped back with his arms raised, and Kaori saw her wooden sword in hand. With a smile, she placed it on top of the counter. Michael sighed in relief.

Yuki ran into the store and bumped past Kaori to get to Michael.

"Michael, I have bad news," she said, leaning her hands on her knees while catching her breath. "There was nothing in the books about the spoon."

"Hey, Yuki, why don't you watch where you're going?" Kaori pushed Yuki aside and hugged Michael's right arm.

"Why don't you get your arms off Michael?" Yuki hugged Michael's left arm.

Michael felt the sudden hate from Yuki and Kaori's eyes flowing around his head like wind blowing around a rock, each connecting with the other.

"Fine!" Kaori said. "Let's play out our cards. I-Man is mine."

"No, Michael's mine."

They both tugged Michael's arms, shifting his body back and forth. The pain his head had taken from the fall made the world go around, and his eyes turned into spirals. He could see multiple images of Jamal shrugging his shoulders in disbelief. Thankfully, it all came to a stop when there was a knock at Michael's apartment back door.

Everyone stopped. The door bulged out into the shape of a lump, as though someone was trying to break it down.

"Is someone in your apartment, Michael?" asked Yuki.

He shook his head and regained his vision. "No."

Jamal stepped back inside the storage room, using the chalkboard as a shield. One screw after the other popped out from the hinge. The doorknob twisted slowly, and when it stopped, the door exploded into dust that spread across the store, forcing everyone to shield their eyes. The sound of tapping on the floor entered the shop. When the dust settled, everyone stood with their eyes wide open, their jaws dropped, for there stood before them...

"The kitchen sink!?"

The kitchen sink stood on one pipe that split apart to act as legs and feet. Its spout bent and twisted, looking around the store. Using the hot and cold water knobs as human hands, it picked up a copy of a DVD and flipped to the back cover, as though it were shopping. The faucet shifted its sight over to Michael, dropped the DVD, and its opening folded into a smile. It charged at Michael, ready to use the hot and cold knobs as fists.

"Michael!" Yuki pushed Michael to the side, and she took a punch in the face from the sink. She fell to the floor and looked up at it.

Kaori grabbed Seizon and jumped in the air with her wooden sword over her head. She swung the sword downward and the knobs clapped on the blade of the sword, stopping her attack. As her feet were about to touch the ground, a burst of water shot out of the faucet. Kaori flew back on top of Jamal and they landed on the ground. The sword flipped back at them, and the blade jabbed into the floor, piercing a piece of existence.

The sink saw Michael already outside running. It pushed the door open and chased after him, firing bursts of water like a fire hose, but each attack missed.

Michael saw the corner of the street and picked up speed. He looked back and saw that the sink had kept up with him, even when he turned the corner. Michael ran around a parked car and u-turned back to the store.

When he arrived, he saw Jamal with a wrench in hand, Kaori armed with Seizon, and Yuki as the Scarlet Sorceress, holding her staff Tsubasa gathering magical energy.

On the roof, the armored woman read her visor screen. It gave her a success probability of ten percent to defeat Michael and his friends at the same time. The visor then locked on to the spoon inside the sink and gave a rescue success rate of ninety-five percent. Suddenly, the armored woman raised her arms, observing the mechanisms attached to her, but her arms dropped and focused on the sink. She remembered she was going to strike Michael last night, but a strange electrical energy struck her in the back. Her eyes grew wide as she realized who she was. The image of the spoon flashed in her thoughts.

"Bo…dy…" she said, looking at her outfit. She then caressed her neck. "Voice…words…I have a body now?"

The spoon closed the woman's eyes against her will and glowed red, accessing her memories to learn language. She could hear the woman screaming at the spoon within her mind. The spoon had no control over her arms as she clutched her head in pain. Then she heard Michael yelling below and stopped.

"Yuki! Fire!" Michael said with a wave, and he fell flat on his face out of nowhere. "Again?"

He flipped his body over and the sink stood over him. A burst of water from the faucet struck his face. Michael opened his mouth and it filled with water. He was drowning, and his eyes rolled up. He saw Yuki raising her hand.

"Energy Pulse!" A yellow ball flew from Yuki's hand, and it struck the sink. It burst into a rippling wave and knocked the sink off Michael.

The spoon observed Yuki and her abilities. She saw her running to Michael with a concerned look in her eyes. The magical energy Yuki had displayed got the spoon's attention, and looking at itself, the spoon felt the limitations of this body in relation to its powers. She knew what she wanted, but realized the plan wouldn't work in her current state.

Yuki ran over to Michael as he coughed water and knelt next to him, but before she could take his hand, Kaori pushed her aside and checked the pulse on his neck.

"He's not dead, you know!" said Yuki.

Kaori looked up. "You never know."

The sink stood up and stared at everyone with a red glow. The neck of the faucet bulged. Like a lump, its neck straightened up into the air.

Jamal ran toward it, wrench in hand, but before he had a chance to wrap the wrench around the sink's neck, the bulge shot out a heavy stream of water, pushing him into everyone so that they all slid across the sidewalk.

The spoon above saw her opening. She jumped and turned into red electricity. The lightning struck the ground and she appeared behind the sink; her visor had an inventory list, selecting Shock Cannon. Red electricity coursed along her back and a slim box attached. A pair of guns stretched out over her shoulders, setting in place. It began to charge up as her visor's targeting system locked onto the sink. Just as she fired a ball of electricity, the sink dodged and deflected the attack with its knob. It flew into the air and vanished due to the atmosphere. As the sink readied for another attack, the woman's visor pointed to the wrench on the ground. The woman materialized behind the sink, reaching for the wrench, but it burst water like a cannon itself and pushed her down the street into a car.

Unaware of what had happened, Michael got up and ran for the corner again. As the sink chased him, Yuki and Kaori attacked it with their weapons. It was not enough to slow it down. Michael saw the sink coming for him and turned the corner. Thanks to the distraction, the sink lost Michael as it turned its faucet around, looking for him. A large shadow appeared out of nowhere and Michael latched the wrench on the neck.

"I got you."

But the sink fired another round of high-pressure water into Michael's face, knocking him to the ground. As Kaori and Yuki raised their weapons at it, the sink stood over Michael. Then it turned the faucet around and blew them back with the water as well. Not paying attention, the sink felt the wrench twist its faucet to the side. It screamed with the sound of scraping metal. It turned once, and there was Jamal, ready to make another twist. Angered from the pain, it sprayed water at him and knocked him away. Suddenly, a slap by the wrench sent the faucet spinning twice. The sink stumbled around, screaming even louder, and it saw Michael smirking at it. The faucet shook side to side, regained its composure, and chased Michael again.

"I'm getting tired of this thing," Michael said, reaching the front door of his store. He rushed inside and slammed the door on the sink. The sink reached for the door with its knobs, but the door pushed open, knocking it into the street. Michael jumped out, carrying a large hammer with two hands. He let out a tribal scream and swung away at the sink, striking twice and denting the edge before the water blew the weapon out of his hands.

Kaori stopped and raised her arms up to stop Jamal and Yuki from advancing as well. "The Impossible Man…"

Michael looked at his bare hands and saw that the sink was holding its knobs up like fists. So he shrugged and lifted up his fists too. They walked around in a circle with fancy footwork. Michael punched the edge of the sink, and he felt a jab from the right knob.

"Southpaw, eh?"

Michael and the sink boxed in the middle of the street, exchanging jab for jab, a fist to the faucet, a knob to the face. A punch to the body of the sink was like a body blow to the stomach. The sink returned the favor with a strike to

Michael's gut. He threw a right hook into the faucet and the sink stumbled to the side.

"You know," Yuki said, watching the sink throw a left cross at Michael's chin, "if it wasn't because it was Michael, I would find this to be very stupid."

Kaori and Jamal looked at Yuki in her Scarlet Sorceress costume. They took one step to the side, creating some distance from her. Everyone watched Michael take an uppercut from the faucet, and he flew in the air, landing on his back. They cringed at his defeat as the sink placed one of its makeshift legs on his chest and clasped its knobs together, shaking side to side in victory. A burst of electricity from down the street struck it and dropped to its knees. As everyone looked down the empty street, Kaori pointed at the sink.

"Now!" Kaori said, as the sink lifted itself to its feet. She led Jamal and Yuki in a desperate charge. They all piled on top of the sink and pounded away on it. Michael appeared out of nowhere next to Yuki, and together, they forced the sink to stay on its knees. Kaori saw Angela and Ely approaching.

"Wow," said Angela, "I'd say that I've seen everything, but that would be an understatement."

Ely smiled and jumped on Michael's back, with a hug, and he screamed.

"What are you guys doing?"

"We're beating up the sink, Angie-chan," Kaori said.

"Why?"

"Because it's evil," Michael said.

"Maybe I can help." Angela approached the sink.

"Don't get near it, or you'll get hurt," said Yuki.

"Don't worry, you all are holding it down." Angela stood in front of the sink and saw the dishes. She noticed the lion-headed spoon at the bottom of the pool. "Hey, it's that spoon you all keep talking about."

She reached inside, and the water sprayed her face and clothes, but the burst did not knock her back. She grabbed the spoon, pulled it out, and the sink fell to the ground. It never moved again.

Everyone stepped back, and Kaori patted Angela on the head.

"Good job."

Michael nodded. "Yeah, thanks."

"No problem, Mikey." Angela handed the spoon to Yuki, but before they could pass it over, the utensil glowed bright red, its eyes drawing energy back. "Oh no."

Yuki slapped the spoon off Angela's hand and pulled her away. "Cover your eyes," Yuki said, and the spoon disappeared. "Are you okay?"

"Yes." Angela looked at herself and Yuki checked her body. "Really? I'm not hurt."

"Just a first aid precaution." As Yuki checked on Angela, Kaori watched her play nurse as the Scarlet Sorceress, and she nodded.

"I'm sorry I let the spoon get away."

"It's okay, Angie-chan," said Yuki, leading her away. "It's over now."

Kaori turned to Yuki as Jamal followed. "The spoon must have found a way to make the sink do that."

Jamal crossed his arms. "But a sink?"

Yuki shrugged. "Who knows?"

As everyone walked back to the store, the neighbors opened up the window and yelled at Michael for disturbing the area.

"You're making noise again, The Impossible Man!"

"I got a double shift starting at midnight!"

"What's with all the water in the street? Are you opening the fire hydrant again to play around in?!"

He ignored them, staring at the sink. He kicked it and walked away. As he entered the store and the door closed, the sink rattled and collapsed into pieces.

Down the block, the armored woman was lifting up her shivering arms. Realizing what the spoon had done to her, she tried to escape, but her body couldn't do what she wanted. As soon as her visor locked onto the spoon, a red beam struck her again, turning her into a red ball and pulling her inside.

The spoon watched Michael entering his store, staring at his friends inside. It locked onto Yuki and its eyes glowed red.

Episode 11

[~ Being Friends ~]

Many will recognize the monster pet genre in anime and manga, in which people, usually young kids and teenagers, capture monsters and train them to battle other people's monsters. Do I have to talk about this?

Really? I do?

There has to be more to the genre than just monsters fighting each other to win the ultimate prize, only to lose to the grand champion, and learn that it's about the journey and not winning the trophy. Ah...the genre also represents the boy and his dog tale, or in this case, a girl and her chupacabra.

Does that even make sense?

May 9, 2002

Kaori was in her living room, on the phone with Hino. She listened to him as she observed Angela fixing her skirt in front of the mirror. His voice was distant as she understood why Angela was doing that.

"Kaori, are you listening to me?"

"Eh?" Kaori lost her concentration and focused on the phone. "Yes. You said ReRe is coming here for the Sakura Matsuri."

"Good to hear you're with me. You will be their opening act."

"Opening act?" Kaori kept watch on Angela.

"Why are you repeating what I said?"

"Sorry."

"This is big. The twins are sitting at number three in Japan and rising. If you open for them here, it will open the door for your comeback. Isn't that great?"

"Yes." Kaori saw Angela approaching the door to leave the apartment.

"I'm going to see Mikey," said Angela.

"Angela," said Kaori, getting Angela's attention. "Don't leave yet."

"Tangerine is there?" Hino said. "Please remind her that I have arranged a photo-shoot with Nihon Teen next week. She will be doing an interview with them. They are very curious about how you and her teamed up as a television duo."

"What?" Kaori stood to her feet. "You're moving too fast. We should sit down together and the three of us discuss this. Japan is very rough."

"Yes, it is," Hino said. "So I expect you to keep your temper in check when Tangerine does the interview."

Kaori growled a bit.

"Kaori," Hino said, and she stopped.

"Yes."

"Good. Talk to you soon." He hung up.

Kaori sat down. She rested her arms on her knees, taking a deep breath. She looked up at Angela as she approached her.

"Is everything okay?"

"Yes, Angie-chan."

"Is it the photo shoot?"

"That's not important right now. Please sit." Kaori moved aside to give Angela space to sit. When she did, Kaori looked her in the eyes.

"Is it about Mikey?"

"Yes." Kaori curled her hand into a fist. "You need to stop calling him that. He's not a child."

"But—"

Kaori raised her hand. "He's too old for you to have these feelings."

"But I lo—like him."

"It's just a crush. You're infatuated with him because he saved your life."

"Just like you."

"Angie-chan!" Kaori's eyes made her duck. "This needs to stop."

"I'm going!" Angela stood up. When Kaori grabbed her hand and she pulled it away. "You're not my mom!"

Kaori stared at the angered eyes of a teenage girl, struggling to say anything more. It was the first time she'd ever had to act like a mother. "You're right. I'm not your mom, but I do have experience in a broken heart. I just want to guide you."

"Not your problem." Angela walked out of the apartment, and when the door closed, Kaori lowered her head.

❋ ❋ ❋

The clear spring day brought the people of Denfair City out of their offices and into the sunshine for lunch. The warm breeze was peaceful, and small bands played out in the open parks. Of course, at a time like lunch, I-Man's tends to be in downtime. Everyone but Michael went off to eat except for Yuki, who made a surprise return with lunch for her and Michael. In fact, she made lunch just for him in a special box imported from Japan. She wrapped it in a blue cloth with feather designs on it.

"I made you lunch, Michael," she said, and smiled.

"I thought it was a present," Michael said, and Yuki's eyebrow twitched, irritated at his oblivious reaction. He untied the cloth and spread it out on the counter. The box was made of wood, handcrafted with a finish that reflected light from its surface. When Michael removed the top, he saw five compartments: one with finely crafted chopsticks, the other four with a complete meal. Tuna rolls, teriyaki beef, rice topped with pickled ginger, and two fried shrimp tempura.

"Your mother told me you would like the bento meal."

"My mother? Where is she now?"

"She heard about the spoon, so she's helping out the Order of the Magical Girl to stop it."

"Oh, that's nice." Michael lifted his head. "Wait, my mother gave you advice on what to feed me?"

"Yeah."

Michael leaned closer to Yuki, and she blushed lightly. He raised one eyebrow, then looked down at the meal.

"So she thinks I'm not eating enough, eh?" Michael slid the box closer and grabbed the chopsticks. "Thank you for the meal."

As he scooped up the rice and ate it, Yuki sighed.

"You see, Yuki, I'm eating enough...and real food on top of that. You could tell her it's the best food I ever ate since mustard."

Michael placed the empty box on the counter and laid the chopsticks across the top of the box. He stepped back. As Yuki stared at the empty box, there was not a single morsel left.

"Any news yet about that spoon from your supervisor?"

"They're still investigating from their end. It's just a little strange the spoon hasn't done anything. Don't let your guard down."

"Okay," said Michael, and presented Yuki with a manila envelope. "By the way, I just received this from my mother, and the note said I had to sign it right away. Did she mention anything about this to you?"

"Uh...I don't know," said Yuki. She waved her hands innocently. "You'll have to talk to Kaori about—"

"Hi, Mikey!" Angela said, entering the store and hurrying to the manga aisle.

"Hello, Angie-chan," Yuki said with a smile.

"I said hi, Mikey." Angela glared back with jealous eyes.

"Please," Michael said, rubbing his eyes. "No fighting."

Angela looked back at the manga, a little embarrassed, but she kept her eyes on Michael as her fingers slid across the bindings of each book.

"So, Michael," Yuki said. "Have you tried to throw Katsuragi-san out today?"

"Not really. I'm waiting until 11:55 tonight to take him on."

"Why?"

"Since midnight is the start of the next day, if I go after him just before midnight and get thrown out, I can then come inside after midnight and catch him off guard."

"You do realize that if you fail, you'll have to wait a whole day to challenge him again, right? Maybe a day and a half…"

"Excuse me, Mikey," said Angela. She approached the counter, shyly, and presented a small box. "I made this for you."

Michael took the box from Angela's shaking hands and opened it. Inside laid a small crane origami with a small string to hang on the wall. He smiled.

"Thank you. It's really nice."

Angela's eyes opened wide and her cheeks turned red from the compliment.

Yuki leaned closer to Michael to look at it. "Hey, you did a nice—"

"Yeah, yeah, Yuki." Angela waved her hand dismissively. "So Mikey, are you going to hang it up?"

Yuki crossed her arms. "Angela, you should be a little more—"

"Mikey, are you—"

"Angela," said Michael, and his voice frightened her. "That was very rude of you. Yuki just complimented your gift. You shouldn't cut people off when they're talking."

"Forget it, Michael," Yuki said, walking to the storage room. "I'll take care of the inventory."

Michael went after her, but he felt Angela's hand grab his wrist. He pulled his hand away. "Are you crazy? You're just a kid."

Angela stepped back, and found herself surrounded by anger. She faced the floor. There was no response. It was as though she were alone. She hadn't meant to make them angry, but she had feelings for Michael that meant a lot to her.

"Mikey, I…" Her tears splashed off her face, and turned his anger to concern. Just as Michael approached Angela to talk about it, she marched out of the store, wiping the tears from her face.

Michael placed his hands on his hips and shook his head in disbelief. "Poor Angela."

"It's that crush of hers," said Yuki. "It's gotten to her head." She turned to Michael and stomped on his foot, then grabbed his ear and pulled him down to her face.

"Go get her!"

"Why me?" said Michael.

"Because if you don't listen to her feelings and give her a proper response, it will scar her for the rest of her life."

"How is that?"

"You're truly dense about us, aren't you?"

"Uh…"

"Go!" Yuki chased Michael out of the store and he screamed. He ran down the block past the apartment door, and Angela came out of the apartment building with Ely, holding back her tears.

"We're going for a walk, Ely," she said.

"Chupa. Chupa."

Angela walked in the same direction Michael had gone and made her way to Main Street. She turned left and found herself surrounded by people entering and exiting the stores. Some of them were on their lunch break, while others were on vacation. As Ely walked alongside Angela, there was not much of a reaction from the crowds, save for the visitors. It was natural for them to see something as strange as Ely walking around.

Angela and Ely arrived at a park, where all kinds of dogs were playing in the designated area. Angela took a stick and got Ely's attention. She threw it out into the grass and watched her run after it. While a dog nearby picked up a ball with its teeth, Ely used her hands to pick up the stick. Angela knelt down as Ely returned to her and handed the stick over. She repeated the game as the dog owners stood there, watching curiously, and then awkwardly smiled with sweeatdrops over their heads at Angela's playfulness with her pet.

Angela walked Ely along the edge of the park and threw the stick over the fence. She watched her climb over the fence like a human and pick up the stick. As Angela ran toward Ely, a net fell on top of her pet, thrown by a dogcatcher. Angela jumped over the fence to stop him.

"What an ugly dog," the catcher said, in a jumpsuit with a patch reading Animal Control on it.

"Wait, please," Angela said, stopping before the man. "That's my chupacabra!"

"Chupacabra? What kind of dog is that?"

"It's not a dog, it's a chupacabra."

"Well, whatever it is, it has no dog license."

"How do I get a license?"

"You buy one at the dog shelter." The dogcatcher placed Ely in a cage with the other dogs roaming inside, whimpering or barking.

"But I don't have any money."

"Then you get no chupacabra, or whatever it is." The dogcatcher slammed the door. Ely held onto the bars. As the truck drove away, Angela ran after it and tripped onto the ground.

Ely watched what happened to her owner, violently shaking the gate to pry it open. Then she turned to the other dogs, and they scurried to the corner, whimpering. It did not take long for the truck to stop. Ely climbed up and looked through the window. She saw another dog running away from the catcher. Ely smiled at the opportunity.

The animals all heard the door unlock, and after it swung open, Ely climbed up the side of the gate next to the door. When she saw the dogcatcher open the gate, she cartwheeled through the opening and pounced on top of him, staring at him with a smile. Her fangs frightened the man and he screamed aloud, releasing his newest capture. All the dogs inside jumped out of the gate, landing on top of him, and ran free. Ely ran with the dogs until she was all alone.

"Ely!" called Angela's voice in the distance.

Ely ran toward her owner and around the corner, finally finding Angela sitting on the sidewalk, crying. Her knee was bruised from her fall.

"Chupa. Chupa." Ely placed her hand on Angela's hair and her friend looked up. Her smile eased Angela's sadness, and Angela hugged her.

"I was so scared I was never going to see you again."

The afternoon moved on, quiet and calm. Angela and Ely crossed a footbridge over a creek, and Angela watched Ely climb onto the railings and do cartwheels. She clapped her hands, and Ely flipped off the rails, raising her arms up like a gymnast. She took Ely by the hand, and they walked out into an open road with more stores.

They entered a candy store, and with very little change, Angela bought small candied fruit. She shared them with Ely, and they sat down on a bench near a fountain. Beside them, a man and a woman held each other's hands, kissing each other on the lips.

"I hope Mikey will get to kiss me like that, Ely."

"Chupa. Chupa." Ely growled.

"Well, he is kind of old. I know I'm just a kid, but he

saved my life. Maybe the way I care for him is not the same as Kaori and Yuki. I don't know. It just feels weird."

Angela watched the couple leave, still holding hands. She imagined herself walking with Michael like that, but her fantasy came to an end when Ely sniffed the air. Angela watched Ely place her hand on the side of her head, listening to the sound more clearly.

"Baaa…"

Ely heard this goat in the distance and immediately ran in the direction of the sound; Angela hurried after her. Ely crawled under a bush, and on the other side of the road was a truck with a goat chained to the back. She walked past a sign that read "Petting Zoo," and as Angela crawled out from the bushes, a branch scraped her arm. Ely reached out for the goat, its tongue draping out of her mouth. Angela grabbed Ely, but she broke free, knocking her owner over.

Angela heard the slurping sound of a straw and the goat's wail. The goat's skin draped over the side of the truck, and Ely jumped off. Angela stood up, shaking her head side to side, and took her pet by the hand.

"Bad girl! You can't go around eating other people's goats." Angela and Ely crawled back under the bushes. They saw the zookeeper arrive and stare at the goat's skin, then lower his head in sadness. "Look what you did! If you were hungry, you should have told me. I would have gotten you food."

✳ ✳ ✳

Later in the afternoon, Angela carried Ely in her arms. She realized that she'd missed her tutor session, and feared Kaori would be mad at her, but there was nothing she could do now. Angela decided to look for a phone so she could call Kaori and let her know she was okay. Maybe even talk to her about Michael.

She entered into a sandlot to cross over to the next street. Halfway through, she saw a couple of teenage boys, dressed in black clothes, one with a skull shirt and the other with a spiral. They stopped talking and began to watch her.

"Hey, Barry," said the boy in the skull shirt. "Take a look at that."

"Yeah, she's a pretty one, Quint."

"Hi, uh, I'm Angela."

"Take a look at this Kaijuzoid," Barry said, ignoring Angela—she stood in place as a sweatdrop hanged over her head—and leaning close to Ely.

"Kaijuzoid?" The word activated Angela's memory of The Impossible Man carrying the goal post. "No way."

"I've never seen anything like this before, Barry," Quint said, taking Ely by the hand.

"This is Ely," said Angela. She stepped back and pulled Ely's hands away from Quint. "She's a chupacabra."

"I never heard of that Kaijuzoid before," Quint said. "Let's analyze it."

"Ely is not a Kaijuzoid." But Angela's words never reached the boys' ears, and Barry took out a strange device. It looked like a remote control with a screen on it, with a variety of buttons to choose from, like Analyze and Main Screen. Angela watched Barry press a button that made a flash, and soon the screen showed a picture of Ely. The words 'No Information' and 'No Rank' appeared.

"No Rank?" Quint said, and Barry smiled.

"Awesome. It's a legendary No Rank Kaijuzoid. It has to be ultra-powerful."

"What's a Kaijuzoid?" Angela said, and the boys turned to her in shock. The question, for some unknown reason, had upset them. Angela stepped back, and Ely struggled to break free from her arms to protect her.

"How could you not know what a Kaijuzoid is when you have one in your possession?" Barry said.

"It's one of the most popular creatures in the world," Quint said.

"Then how come I've never heard of it?"

"Because you're a newbie, and newbies shouldn't have a No Rank Kaijuzoid. Trap-a-zoid!" Barry took out a trap-ezoid-shaped device. He aimed it at Ely, and Angela turned around to run away. "Release Gilla! I want you!"

Barry pressed the "summon" button on the Trap-a-zoid, and a beam of white light flew past Angela and Ely. It stopped before them, and an outline of something huge materialized before them. It stood on two feet, scaly like a lizard, with spikes that curved like a shark's teeth, short stubby claws, a long tail with three spikes at the tip, and a ga-tor's head. When it roared, two large thin ears spread apart, shaking like a baby's rattle.

Angela fell on her butt, and Ely fought hard to break

free from her arms. Her eyes trembled in fear as Quint leaned next to her with a smile.

"You can avoid this fight if you forfeit your Kaijuzoid. You see, Gilla is a Rank AAA Kaijuzoid. Not the type you want to battle against."

"I don't want Ely to fight. Besides, isn't that illegal, to make animals fight?"

"Kaijuzoid are not animals," said Barry, "like dogs or the common cockroach. Kaijuzoid are Kaijuzoid, and they are our best friends."

"Best friends?" Angela looked at Gilla and wondered if it really thought of Barry like that, since it was always contained in a Trap-a-zoid.

"Yeah," Barry said hypnotically, "best friends."

Angela turned to Barry and saw a lull in his eyes. She remembered The Impossible Man carrying that goal post. "Did he do this?"

"Make your Ely a Kaijuzoid." Quint presented a spare Trap-a-zoid. "Put her in this Trap-a-zoid, and you both can be…best friends."

Barry presented her with a Kaijuzoid T-shirt. "And buy all kinds of merchandise."

Quint presented Angela a Kaijuzoid poster. "Merchandise."

"Gilla." The giant Kaijuzoid presented Angela with a doll version of itself.

"No!" Angela pushed them all away, and Ely broke free. She stood in front of her, growling at Barry, Quint, and Gilla.

"Then," Quint said. "I guess my friend's Kaijuzoid will beat your Kaijuzoid to a pulp, then trap it to be his own."

"He can't do that." Angela turned to Quint.

"Actually, he can, since you don't have a Trap-a-zoid and your Kaijuzoid is considered feral."

"But Ely is not a Kaijuzoid. Why won't you listen?"

"Barry, she won't give up the No Rank Kaijuzoid." Quint raised a pair of red flags from behind his back, and his friend stood beside Gilla. "Begin Kaijuzoid Combat. Engage!"

Quint threw the flags down.

Barry pointed his finger at Ely. "Gilla! Tail Swing!"

Gilla swung his tail around, and Ely backflipped to avoid the attack. "Not bad. Especially since it took no orders."

"She doesn't need to take orders," said Angela. "Right, Ely?"

"Chupa. Chupa." Ely nodded in agreement.

Barry pointed his finger at Ely. "See, even your friend talks like a Kaijuzoid."

"Gilla." The Kaijuzoid nodded in agreement.

"Fine!" Barry pointed his finger again.

"Why do you keep pointing?" Angela said.

"Gilla! Power Beam!"

The Kaijuzoid opened its gator-like mouth, and a beam of light ripped along the ground right at Ely. The beam struck her and created a small explosion. When the dust settled, Ely laid on the ground, hurt.

"Ely!" Angela saw her pet lifting her head up in pain. Barry aimed the Trap-a-zoid at Ely, and a purple beam shot out from the device. Angela covered Ely, and so the beam struck her back instead. She felt pain throughout her body, and Ely's eyes grew wide. Angela screamed out loud as the beam failed to trap her, and she collapsed on the ground. Her body felt numb, and the ground turned to sky; she realized Ely had rolled her over. Angela could not move or say a word. Only her eyes trembled. She saw Ely's eyes fill with anger.

"Chupa! Chupa!" Ely turned around and growled. The boys and Gilla froze in place. Each step she took made the trio shiver in fright. Her nails stretched out of her finger-tips. When she roared, drool dripped down her fangs. Barry, Quint, and Gilla screamed. With a leap, her nails dug deep into Gilla's shoulders, and her fangs pierced its neck.

Barry pointed the Trap-a-zoid at Gilla. "Kaijuzoid are not supposed to eat other Kaijuzoid."

Barry and Quint stood in horror as the sound, like a long, slurping straw, went on and on. It felt like a minute had passed when suddenly it all came to a stop. The boys watched the skin of Gilla drape right before them. Neither could move, and Barry dropped the Trap-a-zoid.

The device landed on the "release" button, and all kinds of Kaijuzoid escaped: a giant wingless insect, a six-legged flying turtle, a three-headed winged lizard, a fog monster, and something that could only be described as a small potato with stubby legs walking away. They all turned around, saw Gilla's corpse, and turned their sights on Barry and Quint, growling in anger for the captivity they'd suffered and the death of their friend.

"Run!" Barry said, and the Kaijuzoid chased the boys down the street. "I just wanted to be a master!"

As everything quieted down, Angela shifted her eyes at Ely and smiled. She heard the sound of footsteps approaching fast, and Ely growled. Angela thought for a moment that it was Michael coming to get her, and felt relieved that he was there to rescue her again. She waited for the anxious moment of seeing his smile, that confident look in his face. That power of his that would instantly bring her home and lay her on her bed, his power when he'd moved the goal post. Was that the only way he could save her life?

Her heart skipped at Michael's appearance, but instead, kneeling next to her was a teenage boy. She saw his face, and it became an unforgettable memory; his short hair draping over his ears made him look cool. Looking at him made her heart skip for no reason. As Ely barked at him to get away from Angela, he asked her a simple question.

"Are you hurt?" The young boy took Angela by the hand and sat her up. He took out a small bag, and Angela's eyes locked onto him.

"These are Kaijuzoid treats. I don't know if your pet could eat it, since it's not a Kaijuzoid. Would you mind if I feed her?"

"I …" Angela's voice was raspy from the beam strike. She nodded as permission to let Ely eat the treats. Ely sniffed in the bag and returned it, rubbing her belly. As the skin of Gilla laid out like a rug, they realized Ely was full.

"My mother is a veterinarian," said the boy. "She could take a look at your pet, if you don't mind."

Angela saw the wounds on Ely from the Kaijuzoid's

attack and agreed. She tried to stand up, but the young boy gave her the leverage she needed to get on her feet.

"My name is Ryonosuke," he said, picking up the Trap-a-zoid. "My friends call me Ryo for short. What's your name?"

"Angela," she said with a scratchy voice. It was painful, but it was getting better.

"That's a nice name," Ryonosuke said.

Angela picked up Ely and followed the young boy to his mother's clinic.

✳ ✳ ✳

Elsewhere, Michael walked around the city, keeping an eye out for Angela. He saw Kaori and her sword Seizon in the distance, and she spotted him. As she ran towards him, Michael ran, too.

Kaori reached out to him. "No, wait! I just want to talk!"

"Yeah, with that sword of yours!"

Kaori kept up with him on the longest city block; the next corner was a long way. She got close enough to grab his arm. That got Michael's attention, and he slowed down. They fell to the ground, taking deep breaths. Kaori leaned on the wall and placed Seizon on her lap.

"I know about Angela," she said.

"I swear I didn't do anything bad."

"Would you relax!? I know she has a crush on you." Kaori turned to Michael. "Yuki told me what happened."

"I didn't mean to hurt her feelings."

"I know that! She's still a young girl. Angie-chan is just learning about love. I told her not to get too attached to you."

"Well, it obviously didn't work." Michael leaned his arm on his knee.

"Ever since you saved her, she feels secure around you. I can't blame her really. That's how I—"

Kaori clenched her sword, and held back her tears. She felt Michael place his arm around her shoulder. She blushed, looking at the sky, tears trickling down her face. "I'm scared. The interview is tomorrow, and I want her in my life. Somehow, I just know someone has hurt her. I can feel it in my heart. I've never felt so…so…"

"Vulnerable?"

"Some samurai I turned out to be. Japan's Number One Idol, doing something stupid again."

"You're only human."

Kaori turned to Michael and saw him looking up to the stars. A flash of memory of him standing before her with a door between them opened her eyes, but it was not him she was with now, it was The Impossible Man. She leaned on Michael's shoulder and sighed. "Damn…how do you do it, I-Man? How can you make all of us feel the way we do when we're around you?"

"I do what now?"

✳ ✳ ✳

It was a short walk from the sandlot. As they traveled, Angela's voice got better, and she started feeling Ely's warm fur in her arms. She explained everything that had happened.

Ryonosuke understood. "The beam that struck you causes paralysis," he said. "It's kind of a failsafe to prevent people and non-regulated animals from becoming Kaijuzoid."

"I could have become a Kaijuzoid?"

"Yeah," Ryonosuke said, watching the regular birds fly in the sky. "In theory, though. It's said that your mind is rewritten and you only take commands. That could happen to Ely."

"Scary." Angela hugged Ely, and they arrived at the clinic. She followed Ryonosuke inside, and they stood before the receptionist's desk. Angela saw the receptionist smile at first, and then look shocked. Angela did not realize she was covered in dirt and bruises, nor had a cut on her arm. It was because of the numbness in her body that masked the injury. The experience was scary enough as it was, and the receptionist led Angela and Ely to a room.

Angela sat on the chair, holding Ely. She saw a female doctor enter inside, with Ryonosuke waiting by the door.

"Hello, I'm Doctor Saki Aizawa. I'm Ryonosuke's mother."

"Hi, I'm Angela Rodriguez."

"Now normally I wouldn't look at humans," the doctor said, while taking out some bandages. "But I think I can fix up that knee and arm of yours. Ryo, please wait outside."

"Yes, mother." As Ryonosuke stepped away, Angela leaned her head to watch him.

The doctor blocked her view. "Here we are."

"Thank you." Angela released Ely, and the doctor tended to her wounds. She watched Ely jump up and down, and smiled, though she felt the sting of the iodine rub over her arm and knee. "Will you help Ely?" she asked. "She got hurt by a Kaijuzoid."

"Those creatures again! Taking care of them is such a chore. I get them a lot here. It's a good thing your chupacabra is not a Kaijuzoid."

"Those boys thought she was and tried to capture her."

"They definitely don't understand the rules," said Aizawa. "Your pet would never be caught by them." She stood before Ely and tended to her wounds. "I have to admit, Ely is very healthy. Her coat is very shiny. You've done a good job taking care of her."

"She's always by my side. I love her a lot."

"Chupa. Chupa." Ely nodded in agreement, and Aizawa finished bandaging her.

"I would like to give your pet a thorough examination," she said. "But before you do, you'll have to fill out the forms at the receptionist."

"But I need Kaori to help."

"Is she your mother?"

"She's my guardian…" Angela thought about Kaori. She'd forgotten about the interview tomorrow with Child Services. With her wounds, they might get the wrong impression. "Do you have a phone?"

"Of course." The doctor turned the phone on the desk to the side, set it up, and left the room.

The phone rang for a while, and she heard the message recording of herself, Kaori, and Ely requesting to leave a message after the beep. She was silent. Angela did not know what to say. There was not a single word she could think of. Everything that had happened today overwhelmed her, and all she could do was cry. Ely hugged her.

"I'm coming home, Kaori. I'm sorry." Angela hung up and wiped away her tears. She picked up Ely and opened the door. Doctor Aizawa escorted them to the exit.

"Here's the appointment card, Angela. I expect to see you and Ely in three weeks, with your guardian to fill out these forms, okay?"

"Okay. Thank you again." Angela stepped outside, and there she saw Ryonosuke leaning on the wall, trying to look cool.

"Leaving?" he said.

"Yeah, though you look stupid, trying to act cool like that."

"What?" Ryonosuke pushed off the wall, and Angela walked away. "Wait, what school are you from?"

Angela stopped for a moment and looked back from the corner of her eye.

"I have a personal tutor right now, but I'll be going to Memorial Academy in September."

"Really? I mean..." Ryonosuke blushed lightly, trying to act cool again. He heard her giggle and she smiled at him.

"You go to Memorial Academy?" she asked.

He answered with a nod.

"I'll see you in three months."

"How about the summer?"

Angela smiled, bumping her back on the wall. She chuckled awkwardly, and left Ryonosuke and the clinic behind. Without looking back, she realized that she'd forgotten about Michael. Her feelings for him changed. He'd never come to rescue her, as she hoped. She felt that she held him in too high regard, and was not fair to him. Angela felt she owed him an apology, and Yuki as well. Yuki was always nice to her. She allowed her obsessive crush to upset them, and never even thought if he was okay with her calling him Mikey. Angela wanted to set things right. She took Ely by the hand, and they ran back to the store together.

✳ ✳ ✳

When Angela and Ely returned to the store, they saw Kaori and Michael together, walking toward the store across the street. She realized they were searching for her.

"Kaori!" Angela ran to them, and Michael braced himself for her hug. Instead, she ran right past him and hugged Kaori, leaving Michael tilting forward. As Angela and Kaori held each other, Ely hugged Michael, and they heard his scream. They giggled together.

Kaori examined Angela's wounds and wiped the dirt off her clothes. "Angie-chan. What happened to you?"

"I'm fine." Angela watched Michael struggle to get Ely off.

"Aey," said Michael, and pushed Ely's head back. "I'm sorry for yelling at you like that."

Angela shook her head, rejecting his apology. "I'm sorry for the way I acted. I should have considered your feelings and…our age differences. You were right, Kaori. Is Yuki around? I have to apologize to her."

"She's in the store." Kaori placed her hands on Angela's shoulders. "It's all right now. We should focus on finding a way to hide these bruises by tomorrow."

"I got you covered," Michael said, pushing Ely's hands off his shoulders. "You won't have any problems in the morning."

Angela heard what he said and thought about that goal post. She looked him in the eyes. "Thank you, The Impossible Man," she said, "but…Kaori and I can handle this, and…and I like Michael as a brother. He saved my life and he just wants to help us out, that's all."

The feelings she had for him, the way Yuki and Kaori had for him, were gone. She understood her feelings for him now were sisterly, and that was the way she wanted it. Angela stared The Impossible Man in his eyes, not Michael.

He nodded.

"Kaori, can we talk?" she said.

"Sure." Kaori looked at Angela, then at Michael. She understood, and smiled at Angela. "Of course," she said, "but first, let's get you and Ely cleaned up. We have a big day tomorrow." She took Angela by the hand, and they both peeled Ely off Michael.

"Ely, leave Mikey—I mean, Michael—alone." Angela carried Ely inside, and her pet tried to reach for Michael.

Yuki opened the door and Angela bowed in apology. Yuki hugged her to ease her pain.

✳ ✳ ✳

It was now 11:55 p.m., and Michael stared up at the fourth floor at Shinichiro's apartment. He saw Angela and Ely watching from their apartment and cheering him on. They both monitored a watch for him.

"You can do it, I-Man!" called Angela.

Michael gave the peace sign with his thumb extended and climbed up the stairs. As he entered the door, Kaori stepped outside below to see what was going on.

"Angie-chan, what are you doing out here this late? We have to wake up early for the interview. Plus, you have to make up for missing this afternoon's tutor session."

"I-Man is going to get Kats."

"Again?" said Kaori, as Ely jumped in excitement.

"Chupa. Chupa."

Michael screamed, flying down the stairs. He landed on his back and everyone closed their eyes from the impact. He stood up.

"Time?"

"Midnight," Angela said, looking at her watch.

"Perfect."

Kaori smiled. "Good luck."

Michael appeared on the top step from out of nowhere. He opened the door and saw Shinichiro stare at him, but Michael caught him off guard and appeared behind him, pushing Shinichiro to the door. Just as they arrived, Shinichiro set his feet on the ground, his toes just short of the outside.

"Very clever," he said, clenching Michael's arm. "But not clever enough!"

Michael found himself flying through the air and landed on the steps, bouncing like a ball onto the third floor. He moaned. The door closed by itself, and Angela sat on her knees next to him.

"Next time, shrimp, I won't underestimate you."

"Kats…" Michael groaned.

Angela helped him sit up. "I got you, Michael. I'll help you back to your apartment."

"Thank you, Angela."

Angela and Ely gave a sympathetic smile to Michael. They both helped him to his feet and guided him downstairs to his apartment.

Kaori watched on, smiling, happy that Angela was growing up. However, Ely was another issue, as she gave Michael a big hug and he screamed in pain from his new injuries.

✳ ✳ ✳

Early in the morning, Angela sat on a chair in the orphanage hallway, playing a portable video game and ignoring all the kids running around outside. She tried not to remember being out there, back when she was in an orphanage in her hometown before her parents' will emancipated her.

She increased the volume, unaware of her heartbeat rising. She looked at the bandages she'd gotten yesterday, scared that they were going to reject Kaori. The door opened, and her caseworker—dressed in business attire—waved her to come inside.

Angela approached, kept her nose buried in the game, but then she stopped, looked up, and saw Kaori sitting in one chair. There was an empty one to her right. The caseworker led Angela to the chair and she sat down, turning off the game. Angela watched the woman read through the documents. Each page she flipped echoed in her ears.

"I confirmed with Doctor Aizawa regarding the Kaijuzoid incident and your injuries," said the caseworker. "And as for running away, I also confirmed with Michael Garcia and Yuki Shimizu about what had happened. Angela, you are still young, and experiencing crushes is part of growing up, but running away is not how you face that. He apologized to me for putting your adoption at risk and pleaded for leniency... in his own way."

Kaori lowered her head. "Please, Yuki, I hope you kept him in check."

"Hm?" The caseworker turned to Kaori, and Angela spoke.

"I'm sorry for causing so much trouble yesterday."

The woman turned to Angela. "What's important is that you're safe now and will be okay." As she continued flipping through the pages, she spoke again to Kaori, but her voice faded away.

Angela was ready to say goodbye to Kaori for the last time. Looking at her arm, she realized she hadn't seen the big picture. What she'd put at risk.

Being alone again.

Kaori reached out, took a pen, and signed a document, and Angela's eyes welled up. Once the caseworker stamped it, Angela only heard one word.

"Congratulations."

Tears welled up in her eyes, and Angela cried in Kaori's arms. "I am home," she said in Japanese.

Kaori shed tears, too. "Welcome home."

Later in the morning, Michael finished his breakfast and looked out the window. He saw Kaori and Angela well dressed for today's promo shoot, stepping out of the car with their director Sasuke. Kaori carried documents in hand. Yuki stepped outside and they all cheered. As Jamal and Dōm Coquí stepped outside to congratulate them, Michael cracked a smile. He entered his living room and approached the packaged envelope his mother had sent him. He sat down before it, unaware of the spoon watching over him from the kitchen. He opened it. Inside, there was a file and a note attached. It had one simple sentence.

"Angela is your new intern, sign it and be nice."

When he opened the file, he saw Angela's name on it. The form was completely filled out and signed by Angela and Kaori, as her legal guardian.

"Damn, Mom, you work fast." Michael just stared at the note. Once again he felt the sting of his mother having taken actions without consulting him.

"No. I won't sign it."

With his head down, he signed it.

Episode 12

[~ Howling Woobles ~]

Horror in anime is very diverse, from classic American-style vampires to old Japanese folktales. The Japanese legends here in America are unknown unless you're from Japan, know Japan well, or love Japanese pop culture. In every way, horror in anime is the same thing, no matter what is used. Fright, death, and suspense. Fear of the unknown or mind-breaking monsters that we would never think would exist. Whether it's vampires or the oni, we all are going to get scared eventually...

May 11, 2002

The dead of night.

The moon lit bright.

A young couple about to face fright.

They walked hand in hand along the street. The morning sun had yet to rise, even though it could pass for daylight if not for the night sky. The couple nuzzled and played with each other, a light giggle from the girlfriend, a chuckle from the boyfriend. Both passed by a dark alley, unaware of the pair of green eyes that popped out one by one, as though someone had flipped a light switch.

The eyes leaned to one side and whispered. That sound followed the couple. Step by step, closer and closer, the whispers grew louder and louder. Finally it towered over them. They turned. They screamed.

All that was left...

...were the whispers.

✳ ✳ ✳

Later that morning, Yuki entered Shinichiro's apartment. She approached the spotlight and stood under it. Observing the darkness of the room, she wondered where the walls were. Is this some spiritual realm or another dimension? she thought, given the energy emitting around her. Her thoughts paused, and she heard the sputtering sounds coming closer. A loud bang startled her.

"Left! Left!"

The spotlight shone before Yuki as the humming choir

echoed in the apartment. She saw Shinichiro floating down in the open spotlight, his butt planted on the ground. Yuki sat on her knees and the choir faded into silence. Her eyes blinked twice as Shinichiro remained silent. She was about to speak, but Shinichiro raised his hand to stop her.

"You are here to be read. Yes?"

"Actually, I…"

"I see you are in need of…help."

"Yes, I…"

"Wait, I'm not finished." Shinichiro folded his fingers together, pressing his index fingers to each other. He focused his mind and hummed under his throat, trying to give his reading.

"But Katsuragi-san…"

"Yes, it's about a young man."

"Yes, it's…"

"Please, my child, the bones are talking."

"Would you listen?!" Yuki towered over Shinichiro and made him roll out of his spotlight. She crossed her arms and watched him crawl back into his spot.

Shinichiro sat down, crossing his legs. "I have lost contact with the bones."

Yuki rubbed her eyes in frustration. "Enough with the bones. I need you to analyze something."

"I don't analyze. I read."

"Whatever. I need you to read a spoon."

"Spoon, eh?" Shinichiro took out his pipe and lit it. "Sounds very challenging. Let me see it."

"I wish I could."

"Well, why not?" Shinichiro took a puff of his pipe.

"Because it's stuck to Michael. If I try to take it, it disappears from him. If he lets go, it comes right back to him."

"Then bring him over so I can look at it."

"I can't."

"Why not?"

"Because your barrier blocks him from coming inside."

"Oh, is that all?" Shinichiro took another puff from his pipe. "Then tell him to bring the spoon tomorrow so I can look at it."

"Can't you do it today?"

"I have to honor my challenge and keep him out until he tosses me out. I have to admit, his powers are…impressive. His strategies are getting more and more inventive each day."

Yuki stared at Shinichiro. She didn't know if he was serious, or if he even cared. It was very agitating, since she had to watch Michael lose his mind every day trying to get the spoon away from him. She was running out of options.

A flash of light struck Shinichiro's mind, like flipping a switch. He pulled out a pair of dice and a ceramic cup. He tossed the dice into the cup and slammed it face down on the ground, then lifted the cup, revealing a pair of ones. "The bones tell me that someone, or something, will be coming soon."

"You can tell by looking at the dice?"

"Also, the bones say that two individuals will be the key tomorrow."

"Wow, really?"

"I doubt it."

"This is serious, Katsuragi-san!" Yuki leaned into Shinichiro's face, and he raised his hands with a smile.

"Okay. Okay. Tell me about this spoon. I will try to understand its spiritual energy."

✻ ✻ ✻

At the store, Jamal gave a customer his change, Michael washed the storefront window, and Dōm Coquí—dressed in his muumuu—swept outside. After the customer left, Jamal read the newspaper. The lead article was about the mysterious monster that had attacked the couple before dawn. The couple had been found naked in the street, unconscious. There were eyewitness reports of monsters in the city, but even Jamal could not buy into that.

"The couple were hospitalized with bites.", the article stated.

Jamal rolled his eyes and turned the page.

Behind the music rack was a pair of green eyes. It whispered very calmly and watched Jamal read the paper, approaching the counter slowly. When Jamal turned the page, the whisper leapt over the counter, and Jamal screamed.

"Qwani meh?" Dōm Coquí entered the store. He saw Jamal with his shirt ripped, standing on a chair and hanging onto one of the shelves on the wall.

"It's down there," said Jamal, pointing to the floor.

Dōm Coquí leaned over the counter and saw nothing. He looked up to Jamal and shrugged his shoulders, then helped Jamal down. Michael appeared, out of nowhere, beside the counter.

"What happened?"

"A monster attacked me," Jamal said, shaking in fear.

Michael noticed Jamal's tattered shirt, then Dōm Coquí. He had no idea what had happened, but made a guess.

"You both could have held your private sex party in your own apartments."

Jamal and Dōm Coquí punched Michael in the face together, but without budging, Michael stood there and crossed his arms with a nod. They both removed their fists and calmed down. Jamal stumbled. The world blurred, and Michael leaned close to him.

"Aey, Jamal, you don't look so good."

"Everything is so stretchy." He saw Dōm Coquí's face twist.

"All right, let's get you to your apartment. Coquí, watch the store."

"Syi."

Michael acted as a crutch for Jamal. It was a difficult climb up the stairs. They both stumbled on the steps when Yuki came down from Shinichiro's apartment.

"Jamal!" Yuki walked a few steps down. "Are you alright?"

"I got attacked by some creature," Jamal said. Looking at Yuki, her face melted. "You look like putty."

"What did it look like?" Yuki said.

"It...happened too fast...why am I the first to go?" Jamal collapsed into a slumber.

Michael stretched Jamal's face to open his eyes, and turned to Yuki. "The monster took him out first. That's just plain wrong."

"Let's get him to his room," said Yuki. She helped Michael lift Jamal up, and they carried him to his apartment. Yuki took Jamal's keys from his pocket and they entered inside. They navigated around weights, a punching bag, and martial arts magazines on the floor. As Michael laid Jamal on the couch, Yuki lifted Jamal's shirt and examined his belly. She saw a bite mark near his belly button, and placed her brooch on his forehead. With her hand on the jewel, her body was covered in a calm blue light. "He's hot. I can't heal him."

"Perhaps this bite may be why you can't heal him and may have caused his fever."

"What is it, Michael?"

"It's when an infection causes your body temperature to rise, but that's not impor—"

"I know what it is!" she broke in.

"Can I…can I finish my reference?"

"I don't know what you're referencing." Yuki shook her head and focused. "Why are we having this conversation!? We have to help Jamal! That's important."

"Yes, what's important right now is that we have to find this thing and kill it."

Yuki slouched with her eyes half closed. "Really?"

Michael and Yuki tended to Jamal; Yuki placed a cool, damp rag on his forehead while Michael threw a blanket over him. They left the apartment, and as they did, Yuki stopped.

"Katsuragi-san wants to see the spoon tomorrow."

"Oh really?" Michael led Yuki downstairs. "How do I know he won't toss me again?"

"He won't do it until he finishes reading the spoon."

"Alright, I can live with that." Michael and Yuki reached her apartment. Michael leaned his arm on the wall, and Yuki opened the door.

"I told him everything that happened so far."

"What did he say?" Michael said, crossing his arms as she stepped inside.

"He said you're hopeless." Yuki giggled while closing the door.

Michael stood frozen. He turned around and walked downstairs, unaware of a pair of green eyes popping up from a dark corner behind him.

The whispers hesitated to go after him, sensing a frightening presence; they shivered like a frightened animal, staring at him. Instead, it looked around and shifted its sight upstairs. It heard a door open on the third floor, and leapt upstairs. Near the top step, the whispers watched Angela and Ely step out of the apartment. Ely growled in its direction, and so it ran to the second floor as Angela petted Ely to calm her down.

Kaori spoke from inside the apartment. "Angie-chan, don't forget the milk."

"I won't," Angela said through the open door.

The whispers watched from the dark corner on the second floor. Angela grabbed Ely's hand and ran down the stairs. The whispers looked below and saw how fast Angela hurried out of the apartment. The sound of a door closing gave the whispers a last-minute decision. It hurried up the stairs and leapt at the closing door, but bounced back. So it waited in front of the door.

✳ ✳ ✳

Outside the store, Dōm Coquí waved the broom at Michael, while ignoring Ely hugging him.

"Te li nu qe!" he said to Michael.

"I told you, I don't know what attacked Jamal," Michael said, as Angela struggled to pry Ely off his waist. "If I knew, I'd tell you."

Michael planted his hands on his hips, feeling his waist tugged side to side. His body shifted left as he tried to keep composure and not freak out over Ely's grip.

"Qwani un ohn?"

"I don't know what we're going to do," Michael growled at Ely. "Would you get off of me!?"

"Come on, Ely, we have to get to the grocery store and get food." Angela gave another tug. "Kaori will be mad if we don't do this."

Ely looked at Angela with innocent eyes, but Angela stood her ground. So Ely released Michael and stepped down. Facing the ground, she raised her hand, and Angela took it. They walked away, and Ely watched Michael argue with Dōm Coquí.

"What do you mean you won't go back to the store?"

"Mo pit za shin en dere."

"I need you to take inventory while I restock the manga."

"Nie." Dōm Coquí turned around with his arms crossed.

Yuki came out of the apartment building and walked past them without a care.

"Frog, I'll kick you inside if you don't get in there!" yelled Michael as she passed.

As she closed the door, Yuki saw the spoon resting on the counter. She approached it carefully, leaned close to the utensil, and stared at the lion's head. She wondered if it was a symbol of an organization.

"Just what are you?" she murmured. Then she heard a loud scream outside. She turned to the window and saw Michael chase Dōm Coquí across the street and out of sight. While Yuki watched the chase, the spoon glowed red, and a DVD case struck her on the back of her head. Yuki turned to the spoon, but it was gone. She leaned over the counter and saw nothing there. "That energy was the spoon."

On guard, she picked up the case that had hit her. It was a copy of the anime, *Endless Heart*. Looking at the case, she remembered the first day she'd come into this store and taken this DVD out of its shipping.

"It's been a month now," she said to herself. Yuki looked around the store and saw a reflection of herself on the glass counter; she smiled. When she turned around to return the DVD to the shelf, another case struck her in the face. Once she regained her bearings, every DVD case flew at her, pounding every part of her body. She dropped to her knees, screaming aloud, and Dōm Coquí screamed for his life outside, running down the street.

Dōm Coquí saw Michael chasing him. He picked up speed until he saw Michael was within inches of grabbing him. Dōm Coquí jumped up in the air, his feet touching the windowsill. Using the momentum, he jumped one more time, and his hands caught the edge of the roof. Dōm Coquí struggled to climb over the ledge. A pair of hands helped him over. He lurched over his knee, taking short breaths, and a shadow hovered over him.

"Tharicias," he said.

"You're welcome."

A familiar voice turned Dōm Coquí's forehead blue. He saw Michael smiling in front of him. Suddenly, Dōm Coquí found himself in a headlock, dragged away to the rooftop stairwell and struggling to break free. With each thump down the stairs, his webbed feet flopped on the steps. With every attempt he made to slide his head out of the arms, the grip tightened. As they crossed the street to a grocery store, Angela stepped out, carrying a bag. Michael stopped, and Angela held Ely back.

"I see you got D.C.," she said.

"Yep," said Michael, and Dōm Coquí let out a big smile.

"So what are you going to do to him?"

"You know, I have no idea."

"Ute wi soco poi."

"I doubt Michael is going to squat by the bushes."

"You little…" Michael squeezed Dōm Coquí's neck until his face turned blue. While he was distracted, Ely broke free from Angela and pounced on Michael. He felt Ely nuzzling his waist and screamed. Michael released Dōm Coquí so he could push Ely off. Dōm Coquí lowered his right eyelid and stuck his tongue out. "Why, you ... get back here!"

Angela tried to peel Ely off Michael, and Dōm Coquí ran away. Once she succeeded in freeing Michael, she held Ely to her chest, and they watched Michael chase Dōm Coquí. They smiled. She picked up the groceries and headed back to the apartment. When she and Ely passed by the store, they saw Yuki on the floor. Angela hurried inside to help Yuki stand up.

"Yuki," Angela said, placing the groceries on the floor. "What happened?"

"Video cases..." Yuki pointed at the aisle, barely holding her arm up. She saw a bruise on her arm. "attacked..."

Angela saw the cases scattered across the aisle. She led Yuki to her apartment, and they struggled up the stairs together. They took one step at a time. Once inside Yuki's apartment, Angela laid her on the couch. She didn't realize that Yuki had passed out during the trip. The door creaked open, and Angela heard Ely growl. The sound of whispers came from the broom resting on the wall. She watched her pet leap to the door, and heard a struggle.

"Ely!" Angela heard her pet yelp, and watched Ely limp toward her, so she scooped the chupacabra into her arms. Ely closed her eyes. She looked toward the sound of the whispers. It rushed her, and Angela screamed loud enough for Kaori to jump out of their apartment, armed with Seizon.

"Angie-chan!" Kaori looked down the stairs and saw Angela swinging the broom. She couldn't get a good look from where she was to see what was attacking Angela.

As Angela pushed the door closed, the whispers forced itself inside. Angela ran out of the apartment and met Kaori at the bottom of the stairs. They ran upstairs, with the whispers chasing them. The sound of a stampede came closer behind. They made it to the top of the steps, but the whispers jumped Kaori.

Angela saw Kaori covered in black fur, screaming. Kaori's hand punched out of the fur, reaching out, and Angela grabbed her, but a black furball jumped onto her wrist. Angela screamed and flicked her arm, slamming the creature into the wall. As she watched the furry thing bounce on the floor, another furball jumped out from the pile and landed on her shirtsleeve. The ball looked like night, its green eyes the only light, and a dot for a nose. The creature chomped the sleeve and bit her arm at the same time. Angela slapped the fur off her, and Kaori stuck her face out of the pile.

"Angela, get inside!" Kaori used whatever strength she had to push Angela into the apartment and closed the door.

Angela leaned on the door, and the furballs banged against it. Kaori screamed, but Angela covered her ears as the whispers drowned the scream out. Sweat dripped down her face, and her body felt like it was on fire; she hugged her knees and cried.

"Someone...help..."

Everything became silent outside.

Angela breathed heavily, reaching for the doorknob. She leaned her ear on the door and heard nothing. Trembling, she turned the knob, and with a little light on her face, she saw Kaori curled naked on the floor. Angela crawled to her, shaking her to wake her up. She heard Kaori moan, looked at her hand, and felt a sticky residue. Angela heard voices downstairs. Barely able to move, she crawled close to the stairs and saw Dōm Coquí in front of Yuki's apartment.

"Yuki is knocked out," Michael said from inside the apartment. "Probably from whatever happened in the store, but Ely has the same fever as Jamal."

"Te re o yut fe?" Dōm Coquí said.

Michael stepped out of the apartment, shaking his head from side to side. "I don't know what's going on here."

"Michael…" Angela said with a weak voice, just enough to get their attention. She felt her body turn around and saw Michael looking over her.

Dōm Coquí hopped up the stairs.

"Angela, are you okay?"

"Kaori is…hurt…"

Michael and Dōm Coquí saw Kaori on the floor. Dōm Coquí knelt beside her, his webbed hands shivering in fear. Michael sat Angela up on the wall and went into her apartment. Inside, he found no sign of a struggle.

"Kaori…" Dōm Coquí said, and Michael stepped out of the apartment. He tossed the frog a bedsheet.

"Fi eb er," said Coquí, covering Kaori's body.

"Just like Jamal and Ely," Michael said. As he was about to scoop Kaori up, Dōm Coquí raised his hand and carried her instead. As he took Kaori inside, Michael took Angela's hand, startling her. "Come, Angela. I'm going to take you to your bed so you can rest."

"What's wrong with me?" Angela said, cradling her waist, and Michael carried her in his arms.

"You have a fever, that's all." Michael stood before her bed from out of nowhere and laid her on the mattress. He saw Dōm Coquí walk past the room closing Kaori's door, heading outside.

"Don't leave us…" Angela closed her eyes.

Michael heard a strange thump outside. He appeared beside Dōm Coquí. The sound was coming from the fourth floor. Michael laid on the top steps from out of nowhere, climbing up, and the whispers grew louder. He peeked at Shinichiro's door. There was a pile of fur balls bouncing back from the electric shock.

Louder and louder the whispers got as they tried hard to break in. When one of them turned around toward the stairs, there was no one there.

Michael leaned on the wall behind Dōm Coquí, his eyes trembling, his hand clenching his heart with each breath he took.

"Qwani es et?"

"I don't know."

"Kats yi saven?"

"Yeah, he's safe, for now."

They heard the sound of footsteps below and saw Yuki covered in bruises, climbing up the stairs. Michael reached out to her and she slipped on a step. He helped her up.

"Are you okay?" Michael said, leaning her on the wall.

"Yeah…" Yuki stretched her body. "I think the spoon attacked me in the store. Is it with you?"

"No, but we'll deal with it later. Right now, we have a bigger problem."

"What?"

"Woobles!" Dōm Coquí said.

"Yes, they are furballs, but what are they?"

"Woobles!" Dōm Coquí pointed up to the fourth floor.

Michael and Yuki saw the furballs watching them from the top step. Everyone stepped back, and the creatures jumped at them. As Michael and Dōm Coquí closed their eyes, Yuki took her brooch and held it in the air.

"Forever…Heart…Rave!"

A light shone out over the floor, and a blast of air blew Michael, Dōm Coquí, and the Woobles away from her. The blinding light kept all their eyes covered, and the swishing sounds deafened everyone in the building. It took a while, but the light finally disappeared, and everyone opened their eyes. Yuki pointed her finger at the Woobles, while they rose up to the ceiling like a wave of water.

"I am the deliverer of justice. I am the definition of courage." Yuki found herself pushed to the floor by Michael as the Woobles flew past her. "I am the essence of love. I am the magical girl…"

She pulled herself away from Michael, knelt on her right knee, and stretched out her left leg with her arms crossing each other, making a peace sign in front of her chest.

"…the Scarlet Sorceress!"

She pointed at the Woobles. "Beg for mercy now and I shall grant your wish."

"Do you have to do the whole pose and speech thing?" Michael held Yuki's arm, and they stood.

"It's a free move in Japan."

"It's not a free move here!"

The Woobles blinked, staring at Yuki's costume. The pink, red, and white colors of her outfit hypnotized them. Little strands of drool seeped out of their mouths. The sounds of tiny stomachs grumbled one by one. The noise made Yuki step back with a smile. Each of the tiny creatures smacked their lips, with tiny purple tongues hanging out.

"Why are they looking at me like that?"

The Woobles gathered around and became a giant black ball, forming a mouth, a pair of stubby hands, and feet. When their mouth opened, the sound of whispers made the trio cover their ears. Within the whispers was one word. "Hernandez!"

Each step they took shook the building like the sound of heavy machines pounding the floor. As the monster reached out to them, Yuki aimed Tsubasa.

"Electric Mayhem!" she shouted.

The staff glowed, and electricity entered the mouth. The monster's body expanded like a balloon and burst. Furballs rained on the floor, bouncing off everyone and rolling along. Yuki watched the Woobles gather around, shivering in the corner. They scurried down the stairs, rushed out of the apartment building, and slammed the door. Yuki felt the bruises she had from the spoon's attack catch up to her. Casting her spell blurred her vision. She dropped to the ground and collapsed into Michael's arms.

As Michael held her, he stroked her silver hair to the side, revealing her black hair underneath. He saw some of the bruises on her legs and forehead. He wondered what had happened in the store. The sound of Shinichiro's apartment door opened. Michael and Dōm Coquí looked up the stairs at the darkness inside.

"Bring her to me," Shinichiro said from his apartment, but Michael hesitated due to their deal. "This is a truce."

Michael stood in Shinichiro's spotlight, watching Yuki float. She looked peaceful curled up in the air. He stared at her soft, calm face and tilted his head. Looking at her lips and silver and black hair, he took a deep breath. He stood there quiet, while Dōm Coquí sat in another spotlight leaning on his hand.

Shinichiro spoke from within the darkness. "Nice display, isn't it, Shrimp?"

"Aey!" said Michael. "You better not be hurting her."

"Relax. This young lady is injured and needs a little rest."

"You're just an old pervert, Kats. I know you're looking up her skirt." Michael sat down on the floor, looking up her skirt, and Shinichiro arrived, floating in his spotlight to the song of the humming choir, while wearing an Hawaiian shirt with surfboards on it.

Once he landed on the floor, he took out his pipe and lit it. After taking a puff and blowing smoke into the air, he snapped his fingers. A spotlight appeared next to him, and a furball chained to the floor. They all watched it struggle to break free.

"Do you know what that is, Kats?"

"It's a Wooble."

Michael and Dōm Coquí fell over, and Shinichiro took another puff of his pipe. They sat up and growled in anger.

"Yes, we know it's a furball."

"Upo a rit?"

"Did he say point?" Shinichiro said.

"Yes…the point," Michael said, pointing his finger at Shinichiro. "The very same point that will be shoved straight up your—"

Suddenly, Michael screamed, flying toward the open door. As the light outside approached, Michael stopped short, landed on his feet, and turned around. There he saw Yuki floating in the air, her staff aimed at him. Her light smile calmed Michael, and he returned a smile to her.

"Please," said Yuki, turning to Shinichiro. "Tell us about these Woobles."

"We don't know much." Shinichiro took a puff of his pipe. "But we do know it eats clothes."

"Why?" Michael said, returning to his spotlight.

"Food."

"Food?"

Shinichiro smoked his pipe. "Yes…food, you one-celled bacterium."

"Do I have to hurt you?"

"Please, stop it!" Yuki raised her hands between Michael and Shinichiro, and she got silence from them. "Go on, Katsuragi-san."

Shinichiro tossed his dice into the ceramic cup and

slammed it onto the ground. When he lifted the cup, the dice had rolled a six and a five. With a nod, he faced everyone.

"The good news is that the toxins in your friends are only there temporarily. It's nothing more than a tranquilizer."

"You got it all from that?" Yuki said, pointing at the dice.

"Actually, I heard it from the afternoon news." Shinichiro pulled out a remote, and everyone lowered their eyebrows halfway. They watched Shinichiro turn the television off in the darkness. "They will be physically fine in twenty-four hours. However, their spirits will have nightmares as they sleep through recovery. It's not permanent damage, though. Now I suggest to all of you to find those Woobles and capture them before they wreak havoc on the city."

"Why us?" Michael said.

"You're The Impossible Man, right?"

"Yeah, and?"

"Michael," Yuki said, getting his attention. "We have to do this."

Michael saw it in her eyes, the need to do the right thing. Her job. With hands to his hips, he nodded at Shinichiro.

"All right, fine, but will you be okay, Yuki?"

"I'm feeling better, even though I have no idea how to get out of the spotlight."

"Don't worry," Shinichiro said. "I'll take care of that."

Shinichiro took the remote control and aimed it up in the air. He clicked on a button marked 'Down' and Yuki felt herself lowered to the floor. Her skirt flipped up, revealing her white leotard. She pushed her skirt down, and Shinichiro's and Dōm Coquí's noses bled. Yuki used Tsubasa to fire an electric bolt at them, and Michael smirked, his nose pinched.

"Aey, that's what you two get for looking up her skirt, you slimy perverts."

Yuki slammed Tsubasa on Michael's head. When she lifted the staff, Michael stumbled around.

"And you're the king of them all!" She crossed her arms, tapping her foot on the ground, and Michael rolled onto his back. As she stood over Michael and he sat up, the Wooble broke free from its chain and pounced on Dōm Coquí. She and Michael watched Dōm Coquí lay on the floor, tranquilized, as the creature ate up his muumuu, then the Wooble ran out the door. As Dōm Coquí laid naked, a sweatdrop hung from the back of their heads.

Episode 13

[~ March of the Steel Giant ~]

In my opinion, the flagship genre of all anime and manga is mecha. Machines as big as buildings or as small as human beings, these vehicles are piloted in either warlike settings or to fight giant monsters. Some can transform into objects or creatures, while others can be servant robots, pets, cyborgs, and more. Some mecha series have shared the same theme: the dangers of man and science, experiments going wrong, the effect of war on the human psyche, and ethics. Despite there being so much mecha in anime and manga, this genre tends to find itself reinvented time and time again. Not a single fan can say they have never come across mecha…

…or at least that's what I'm aware of.

May 12, 2002

The sun rose up over the junkyard in the Metalworks District. A laugh blared across the sky. The echo ripped through the canyons of twisted metal and garbage, and the only light in the junkyard shined in the center of the area. Sitting on one of the mountains of discarded items like a throne was a giant robot. It had a round belly, long legs with stubby feet, and long arms with stubby hands. The dome-like head had a mouth that frowned, eyes that looked angry, and a window in the center of the forehead where the cockpit was. A tiny ladder rested on the side of the head, where the left ear acted as a door. The light shined on the flat platform the ladder was on, and suddenly, stepping out of the shadows, was Wolfgang wearing a lab coat.

A phone rang from his backpack. He reached in, took out his large brick-sized cell phone, and spoke. "Yes?"

He listened. "I understand the last auction had the buyers walk out when they learned the spoon would not be there. I underestimated The Impossible Man and his friends, but now, I have a way of retrieving it. I will have the spoon for your next auction."

Wolfgang listened, and a bead of sweat slid down his face despite his calm demeanor. "I see. Then if my life is at risk, tell me what the spoon does?"

The phone hung up on him, he looked at it in frustration, and he put it back in his bag.

"Very well. Thanks to Professor Bates, my invention is now complete. Let's see The Impossible Man stop you. Yes, my little brainchild…the Clipperstein Mark 100 Version

Beta II X Turbo! We'll crush The Impossible Man and take the spoon as ours! I will have my dream! Screw the auctioneers!"

The shadow of Wolfgang threw his arms up in the air with a maniacal laugh. Thunder blared in the morning sky to accompany Wolfgang's joyous moment. The only problem was that the thunder did not come from the sky. Instead, it came from the ground, the sound of a stampede followed by the slam of a cockpit door. Wolfgang stood before his robot. The entire platform shook like an earthquake, and the robot's engine started, as loud as a plane. The cockpit lights turned on and the machine moved.

"Hey! That's mine! Make your own mecha!" Wolfgang looked down at his bare feet and tattered pants, twiddling his toes like fingers. "And what happened to my shoes?!"

His feet smoldered on the platform. The heat from the machine built up. He hopped up and down in a circle, and Clipperstein stood up. It turned its head east, looking out over Little Edo. With its first step, the earth shook, and it cracked a car's window. It marched onward.

Wolfgang climbed down the series of ladders and hopped one foot at a time over the garbage and metal. When he reached the bottom, he watched his robot crush and punch everything in its path.

"No fair! I wanted to do the stomping and punching! And I want my shoes back!" Wolfgang jumped into a car and followed Clipperstein. Each step the robot took made the vehicle jump. It would fly in the air, as though it had jumped off a ramp. He watched people run away, and the machine's foot crushed a parked car, causing an explosion. He came to a stop when Clipperstein kicked a taxi into a building. The sirens of police cars blared in the distance. Wolfgang leaned closer to the windshield and saw the robot's head turning side to side, as though it were looking for something. Wolfgang took a CB radio on the passenger seat, stepped out of the car, and turned on the microphone.

"Identify yourself," he boomed. "And how did you know how to pilot that thing?"

Wolfgang received only whispers in response, and the robot turned around to his direction. He screamed. The robot stomped its way toward him. Wolfgang jumped back in the car and drove in reverse, whimpering like a child, as each foot landed before him. He lost control and crashed into a parked car. When he lifted his head, he saw the left foot cover him and the vehicle, but the foot stopped short, the leg moved back, and the robot stood straight. After feeling his body for damage, Wolfgang laughed. He stumbled out of the car with his radio. "Hey! Whoever you are? Could you at least go to Little Edo and smash The Impossible Man?"

With no answer, Clipperstein walked away, triggering a car alarm down the street. It kicked that car so the noise would stop.

Wolfgang saw a street sign that read "To Heliport" with a direction arrow. He ran very fast in that direction, with a spurt of a sonic boom. Wolfgang stood before an open area where a helicopter was parked. As more destruction from his robot wrecked the city, he smiled.

Flying in the air, Wolfgang floated just above Clipperstein, while reading the helicopter operations instruction book. As the robot bumped into a building by accident, he tried to get a visual at the cockpit. The robot looked at the debris falling down, then at its arm, as though it had touched wet paint. Wolfgang saw something bouncing in the cockpit. He could not make out who it was, so he tried the radio again.

Unfortunately, the robot stepped on a car and stumbled backwards toward the helicopter. Wolfgang pulled up, seeing Clipperstein's chest open wide. Once the machine landed on its back, a cannon stuck out its chest and fired a cannonball into the air. Wolfgang watched it arc over the city, then turned to his robot. It crawled on its hands and knees, feeling the ground, as if it had lost a pair of glasses, making holes in the street.

"What kind of pilot are you?" Wolfgang pulled up higher into the air. Clipperstein stood to its feet and made its march to Little Edo. With a smile, Wolfgang followed right behind it. "There you go."

✳ ✳ ✳

Moments beforehand, Michael and Yuki woke up in the store. The doors were all locked, in case the Woobles returned. They were exhausted from their long night patrolling the city. After washing up, they checked on their friends. All of them were sleeping in their beds. Yuki placed damp, cold rags on their hot foreheads while Michael sat on the steps, trying to keep his eyes open.

"Another day, another store shutdown. My poor profits."

"Focus, Michael," Yuki said from her open apartment. "This is important."

"I know."

Michael was ready to go back out and search for the Woobles. He hoped to find the little critters so he could open the store. Unfortunately, Yuki had to fulfill her duty as the Scarlet Sorceress, and Michael was not too thrilled with the idea of her going after those things. He knew worse things could happen if Yuki's mother found out that something bad had happened to her. Much worse.

"Ready, Michael?" Yuki walked down the stairs in her magical costume.

Michael's eyes followed her until she stood before him. His stare made her blush. He could see the heroism in her posture, one who had seen many battles and was used to what they were about to face. He saw the determination in her eyes.

"Yeah," Michael said. "I'm ready."

"You don't sound like it."

"That's because I'm not a hero like you." Michael opened the door and let Yuki out first.

"With a name like The Impossible Man, you should be." She stepped outside, and Michael closed the apartment door behind her. She looked back at Michael for a moment. Why had he come up with that name if he wasn't a hero? Although it was obvious that name had made him famous, what she found perplexing was the fact that he wore his store's name as though he was born with it: an identity unto himself.

Michael turned around. "The spoon hasn't been around."

"Good. We don't need it to add to our problems. Let's go."

Michael and Yuki walked around Little Edo, far from the store. They crossed the street and saw a large crowd gathered at a small restaurant with open windows. Inside, the crowd watched the television above the bar section playing a news report. Michael and Yuki slipped through the crowd and reached the front. They watched the television as the waiter raised the volume. On the screen, the giant robot walked through the streets of Denfair City, and everyone listened to the reporter.

"The giant robot has been marching through the neighborhoods, destroying everything in its path. It's horrifying! It's a tragedy!"

"The hell is that?" Michael said, and the robot on the screen lost its balance with an open chest.

"It's a giant robot," Yuki said, and watched Clipperstein fall on his back, firing a cannonball into the air. "You actually have those here in America?"

"Why, you have those in Japan?" Michael stared at the television as the cannonball bounced by the front of the restaurant. Out of sight, it exploded and launched a parked car into the air, bouncing in front of the restaurant. As the crowd turned around to look outside, the parked car slid past the restaurant. Michael and Yuki continued watching the television.

"Lots," Yuki said, watching the robot stand on its feet. "The government just keeps them out of public view and says it's for a television show if questions are asked. That's why you never see them in person."

"Awesome."

"Wait," said the news reporter. "It would appear that the giant robot is heading in the direction of Little Edo District. Citizens are advised to leave the area immediately."

Michael and Yuki turned around and found the restaurant completely empty. They walked outside and the earth shook. Another loud thump, and cars jumped. Car alarms deafened everyone in the area. The duo glanced down the street and saw police cars flying in the air. A giant right foot landed in the intersection, and a gust of wind blew them to the ground. The windows shattered. Michael and Yuki opened their eyes. She found her back laying on top of Michael, his hands clasped around her chest. Michael realized what he held onto and made an awkward smile.

The sound of the slap made Clipperstein turn in that direction. Its monitor closed in on Yuki, and statistics of her costume appeared on the screen. Clipperstein spun, knocking pieces of a few buildings over. The debris rained down, with a big chunk heading toward Yuki.

Unable to react, Yuki screamed, only to see the giant robot suddenly become smaller. Her feet planted on the street, and Michael's right arm wrapped around her belly. The experience overwhelmed her thoughts again, and she lifted her head to look at Michael.

"How did you..." She tried to hold onto that memory,

but it slipped out of her mind, like amnesia. She held her head. As Michael held her shoulders, her brain could not process the experience; that piece of memory disappeared.

"Aey, Yuki?" Michael shook her shoulders, and she lifted her head up. "Did you hurt your head?"

"What happened?" Yuki shook her head. "Why do I feel like I've been through this before?"

It was a weird feeling, similar to what she had when she was in the sewers. Her memory was now a déjà vu in thought only. She felt her body shake in Michael's arms.

"Yuki, are you okay?" Michael felt her hands pull his cheeks to make him stop.

"You're going to scramble my brain if you keep shaking me," said Yuki, and Michael let go of her. "I'm fine. Thank you."

As the earth shook with each step he took, Clipperstein approached Michael and Yuki. She raised her staff Tsubasa, which glowed, and closed her eyes. Aiming at the machine—reaching at her with its hand—she opened her eyes.

"Electric Mayhem!"

Bolts of crackling electricity struck the robot. As the sparks spread throughout the metal body, it stumbled back a little. The spell ended, and Clipperstein dropped to its knees. Yuki turned around to Michael and smiled.

Clipperstein's hand shot out like a cannon. It was connected to a tether. The hand slammed into Yuki and pushed her along the street, and its fingers closed up around her. Yuki screamed, and the hand flew past Michael, connecting back to its arm.

Clipperstein stood up to its feet and climbed up a small apartment building. As Yuki struggled to break free, the robot saw news helicopters flying around it. It placed Yuki on the roof and swatted at the helicopters while they flew around in a circle. It turned to Yuki, and she ran and entered the rooftop entrance of the building. It leaned close to a window and saw her running through the hallway.

Clipperstein bashed its hand through the window and grabbed her again, pulling her out of the building. She waved her arms, kicked her legs, and screamed, but when Clipperstein opened its hands, there was a mannequin with a tape recorder attached, playing a woman's scream.

Michael and Yuki stood on the rooftop, five buildings over, watching the robot drop down to its knees, searching the ground. As Clipperstein sat on its knees, rubbing its chin in wonder, Michael and Yuki stood there with a sweat-drop hanging over the back of their heads.

"Only in America," Michael said, and a wind picked up.

Michael and Yuki heard a motor blaring above them. They turned around and saw a helicopter hovering there. They tried to talk to each other, but the noise overpowered their voices. The helicopter landed, and the sound of Clipperstein destroying Denfair City continued.

Wolfgang screamed at the radio as he opened the door. "The next time you build a giant robot professor, make it magic proof!"

He slammed the radio and stepped out of the helicopter to stand before Michael and Yuki, who didn't look surprised at his hunting outfit under his lab coat.

"Silence Field!" Yuki tapped Tsubasa on the ground, a green circle spread out canceling the noise within their area, and spoke. "It's just him."

"Just him?" Wolfgang replied, jerking his head back. "Don't you know who I am?"

"Hot air." Yuki crossed her arms.

Michael spoke, pointing at Wolfgang. "Don't waste your time on him. Besides, I'm not in the mood to deal with his sexual fetish with that spoon."

"I'll show you a fetish!" Wolfgang ran toward Michael.

"Light Wall!"

Wolfgang bounced off an invisible wall. He stumbled backwards onto the ground, and saw Yuki holding her staff between them.

"Down, boy," she said.

Michael took a step forward, but Yuki's eyes told him to stay. "Look, Wolfgang, I told you I don't want the spoon. You can have it."

"Then why won't it leave you?"

"The hell should I know? You're the one hunting it. Don't you know what it does?"

"If I did, I would have taken it already instead of trying to kill you."

Yuki turned to Wolfgang. "Does it have to be a kill?"

Wolfgang looked up to the sky, pondering the question, and faced Yuki. "Yes."

Another explosion in the background made the ground rumble. Everyone turned to a plume of smoke rising from the buildings. Clipperstein was trying to put the building back in place. Once fixed, the robot walked away from the disfigured building with its arms behind its back, emulating a whistle blow, and acting innocent.

Yuki slouched. "The pilot has issues."

"That's my robot." Wolfgang sat up and crossed his bare legs. He brushed the tattered pants. "The Clipperstein Mark 100 Version Beta II X Turbo. I built it so I can take the spoon from you."

Michael and Yuki just stood there for a moment. They were trying their best to set aside the fact that Wolfgang had built the machine to retrieve a spoon Michael had just said he would love to get rid of.

Yuki held Tsubasa to his chest. "Well, Wolfgang, I have to keep that spoon away from you."

"What?"

"It's a dangerous item and it's causing problems."

Michael pointed his thumb at Clipperstein. "Yeah, like that thing over there. If that robot's yours, then why aren't you piloting it?"

"Because someone stole it."

"Who?" said Yuki.

"I don't know. I was ready to pilot it when someone just slipped past me and started to drive it...and look what he did to my socks and shoes." Wolfgang lifted up his bare feet and tattered pants. The dirt on his soles was black as night and mixed with crusted oil. He twiddled his toes, making the crust fall to the ground. The act disgusted Michael and Yuki. "It's as if they were eaten."

"Eaten?!" Michael and Yuki said in unison, and they

noticed the bite marks on Wolfgang's legs. They turned around and watched Clipperstein back on its knees, lifting a SWAT car and peeking in the windows like a curious child.

"The Woobles are in there?" Yuki said, and Wolfgang tried to understand what she meant.

Michael nodded. "If they are, they probably wanted something to protect themselves while they go after you."

Wolfgang looked at Michael, now lost in the conversation. "But why?"

"They eat clothes." Michael turned to Yuki. "Your outfit must be filet mignon to them. Rare and succulent."

Michael and Yuki stood still for a moment at that revelation.

"You put them up to this, didn't you?" said Yuki to Wolfgang.

He stood to his feet, towering over her. "Do I look like I know what a Wooble is?"

"You look like you can't tell the difference between turning left and right."

Michael smiled after hearing Yuki say that. "So this Frankysty—"

"Clipperstein!" yelled Wolfgang indignantly. "It's called the Clipperstein Mark 100 Version Beta II X Turbo!"

"What is it with the stupid long name?" said Yuki, standing on her toes to get close to his face. "This isn't a fighting arcade game! It's as bad as ranking something SSS."

"What?" Wolfgang said, and shook his head in a double take. "It's not stupid. I designed it specifically to take The

Impossible Man out. No way he can use whatever it is he does to beat Clipperstein."

Michael turned to Wolfgang. "What thing everyone is talking about?"

"Uh…guys." Yuki reached out to Michael and tapped his back to get his attention. When he turned around, Yuki slipped behind him as a shield. "The Woobles are looking at us."

Inside the cockpit, the Woobles viewed the monitor, whispering. One of them hopped on a button on the control panel and made the camera zoom in on Yuki, hiding behind Michael. The furballs hopped excitedly. Outside, Clipperstein jumped up and down, shaking the earth.

The Woobles turned to the pilot's seat, where only one of them sat. Next to a large instruction booklet titled *So You Think You Can Pilot Clipperstein Mark 100 Version Beta II X Turbo Eh?* with Foreword by Professor Armond Bates, that creature had a tiny helmet with a white mask, covering only its eyes, and a red cape. The ones overlooking the monitor waited for their orders from their masked leader.

The leader shifted its body, as though it had arms, and moved the red cap to the side as though it was swinging its arm. It signaled the order to commence. The Woobles simulated a hand salute and moved Clipperstein forward.

✱ ✱ ✱

Back at the rooftop, Yuki's Silence Field spell ended. Michael and Yuki heard the helicopter launch. They crouched, watching Wolfgang pull up into the air. As the building shook with each step, the helicopter flew over their heads. Suddenly, Clipperstein stopped short of the building. Michael and Yuki stepped back, worried about the robot, and a large blue beam from a distance struck the helicopter.

From a faraway rooftop, the armored woman made a laser gun attached to her right arm disappear. The spoon floated beside her, and they watched the helicopter swerve all over the place, like a fly with no sense of direction, then crash in a nearby park. The spoon turned to the armored woman with glowing red eyes, and as the armored woman's eyes turned to the spoon, it made her disappear.

Clipperstein turned its attention to Yuki; she and Michael were gone. The robot slapped its forehead. Michael stood before the helicopter out of nowhere, planting Yuki's feet on the ground. He dropped to his knees, struggling to breathe. Yuki rubbed his back with her hand, and he was startled. Before she could say anything, they saw the helicopter with its tail snapped in half. The cockpit was intact, and there was no sign of fire.

Michael got up to his feet, and Yuki reached out to him but paused. He opened the door, hearing Wolfgang moan. When Michael pulled him back, Wolfgang's eyes spun in a spiral and he was covered in sweat.

"Is he okay?" Yuki said.

Michael saw Wolfgang's feet covered in bites. "The bites finally caught up to him."

"How did he last this long without passing out from the fever?"

"When you're insane," Michael said, turning to Yuki, "you feel nothing."

"Like you?" Yuki noticed something odd about Michael. His hand made a victory sign, and he extended his thumb. "The Impossible Man?"

He nodded, and the sound of destruction in the distance sent a flash of realization to Michael. "We need to get the Woobles out of that machine, or they'll destroy my apartment building…and everyone in it."

"You just figured that out now!?"

"Hurry!" Michael grabbed Yuki's wrist and led her back to Clipperstein.

The spoon emerged from behind the tree. It floated over Wolfgang, observing him. With a nod, it vanished.

✳ ✳ ✳

Back in Little Edo, Michael tied a rope around a lamppost, taking short breaths. He ran past Yuki across the street, leaving some slack. Suddenly, Clipperstein arrived, looking around with its hand over its forehead, shielding the sun from its eyes.

"This isn't going to work," said Yuki.

"Why not? All you have to do is use a spell to make me super strong, and I'll trip Clipperstein with this rope."

"Why can't you use your Rhythm?"

"My what?" Michael said, taking a deep breath. "You're not making any sense."

"He's not serious," Yuki said under her breath, watching him shake his head to refocus.

"Fine," said Michael, wrapping the rope around his arm to reinforce it. He braced himself. "I'll do all the work. You just stand at the end of the street, lure the robot, and when it trips over, you cast a spell."

"Have you lost your—never mind." Yuki ran to the nearest intersection, waving her arms and Tsubasa in the air to get Clipperstein's attention. The robot looked in her direction.

Then Yuki stood still as the earth shook and glass around them shattered. She aimed Tsubasa at Clipperstein, focusing her magical energy, and saw Michael pull the rope. Her hair was blown back by the wind, stronger and stronger. Her skirt flipped up, and she pulled it down with her hands. Shielding her face, Yuki saw Clipperstein fall on its belly. A loud bang made a few buildings crack and a faint scream grew louder. Yuki looked up in the air, and Michael's body crushed the roof of a parked car. "No!"

Michael lifted his head up, with the sound of bones cracking at every movement. He took Yuki's hand and pulled himself out of the wreckage. He brushed the dust off his clothes and took one long stretch, snapping his body back in place. He never noticed Yuki's concerned look. Michael turned to Clipperstein lying on the ground and patted Yuki's shoulder with a smile.

"Great work, Yuki."

"I didn't do anything."

"What?"

"I didn't cast a spell."

"But your hair was blowing and everything like a special effect!"

"That was the wind caused by Clipperstein tripping over itself."

Clipperstein's feet were crossed over each other. The rope had never even tied around them. Inside, the Woobles were all on their backs, their eyes shaped like spirals. They shook off the pain and regained their composure. With a whisper, the furballs hopped up and down on the buttons. Clipperstein slammed the palm of its hand and curled it into a fist, pushing itself up to its knees. When it lifted its head up, Michael landed face first on the street. When the monitor turned on, the Woobles saw a red glow in the air. The cameras zoomed at it, but the glow disappeared. Clipperstein turned to Michael and Yuki.

"Run!" Michael said, turning to Yuki, and saw that she already had a head start. Michael ran beside her from out of nowhere. He took Yuki's hand and turned left at the next intersection. He landed on the sidewalk face first with Yuki lying next to him in his arms, and Clipperstein stomped past them down the street.

"What happened?" Yuki said, lifting Michael up.

"I don't know." Michael clenched his teeth with a long inhale. "It's happening again."

Yuki felt his hand turn cold through her gloves. She rubbed his hands to warm them up. That was when she realized that he was not losing his breath from exhaustion; he was losing breath from exposure to the cold. She realized his weakness. "We have to get you somewhere to rest and regain energy."

Clipperstein returned to Michael and Yuki. When it leaned close to them, they both smiled at its face. The Woobles bounced in excitement at the monitor's close-up of Yuki's costume, and accidentally hit the switch to move the arm. Upon impact with the ground, a gust of wind blew Yuki's skirt up, exposing her white leotard. Yuki screamed on the screen, and Michael held his nose to stop the bleeding. The Woobles' dotted noses bled as well, and they watched Yuki bash Michael over the head with Tsubasa. They hit the rewind button on the monitor, and it replayed the moment the wind blew up her skirt. They put it in slow motion and wooed in whispers.

The Woobles moved Clipperstein's arm closer to Yuki. As Michael lay on the floor with his eyes in a spiral, the hand opened up, ready to snatch her. It stopped. Clipperstein lifted its head up and saw in the distance, in the Metalworks District, a clothing factory.

Still lying on the floor, Michael looked at the factory upside down. "Well, whaddya know?"

"A clothing factory?" Yuki smiled at the opportunity and waved at Clipperstein. "Hey! Would you Woobles like to have a factory full of clothes to eat?"

The Woobles looked at each other, debating the prospect in whispers. Three furballs pointed to Yuki with a small group, nodding. They all turned to their masked leader, sitting alone in the pilot's seat.

After making its decision, the leader shifted its body as though it had arms and shifted to the side, as though it was swinging its arm. It pointed at the factory and simulated rubbing its belly. The Woobles who wanted the factory bounced up and down, while the ones who wanted Yuki's costume lowered their heads in defeat.

"Yoo hoo, Woobles!" Yuki waved and got Clipperstein's attention. "Hungry?!"

Clipperstein nodded.

"Then follow me to the factory."

The Woobles whispered with joy, bouncing inside the cockpit as Clipperstein followed Yuki to the factory. The robot skipped along with each step, shattering more glass and sounding off more alarms. At each intersection, the police cars stopped.

Clipperstein sat on one knee and ripped off the roof of the factory. Workers ran out the front door, screaming for their lives. Clipperstein reached in and took a handful of clothes. Its head split apart, exposing the cockpit, and it threw the first pile of clothing inside.

"Talk about brain food," Michael said behind Yuki from out of nowhere, and she smiled, with a sweatdrop over her head. They watched Clipperstein smile, and the Woobles inside enjoyed their buffet. Michael and Yuki turned their heads to the sound of sirens.

"Michael, is law enforcement always this slow to respond?" Yuki turned to Michael and received no answer.

She figured it would be best for him not to explain and trigger any new unwanted events. She could see in his eyes that he'd had enough for one day, let alone two. Upon closer inspection, she saw some of the sweat on the side of his forehead frozen into droplets of ice, melting from the spring warmth. She led Michael away from the scene. "I'm surprised the government hasn't shown up at all today with all that news coverage."

The spoon hovered high above, glowing bright red, watching Yuki smile at Michael as she tended to his wounds with her spells.

Very late in the evening, Yuki stood on the rooftop watching crews and first responders sift through damaged buildings and collapsed rubble. She struggled to keep her energy up. Even looking at Tsubasa in her hands, she could barely hold it up, but her education reminded her that she needed rest in order to help the people. Yuki made her way back to the apartment and snuck in from the rooftop entrance. As she made her way downstairs, she passed by each apartment. Yuki thought of what happened to her friends and wished to apologize to them for getting knocked out by the spoon so easily. She would have protected them from the Woobles.

It was quiet in the hallway when she arrived at her apartment. She looked down at Michael's apartment and wanted to talk to him, but after seeing him struggle from becoming cold due to overexertion, she felt she needed to let him rest and clear his thoughts.

Yuki entered her apartment and let out a big yawn. Without thought, she made her way to her room, ignoring the fact that she hadn't removed her boots. Despite her thoughts saying she had to remove her boots, her body was completely out of energy. She entered her room, standing before her bed, and dropped Tsubasa. Yuki remembered her childhood and how she always slept in her costume. She equated it to her pajamas, always trying to sleep in them despite her mother's objections. Yuki collapsed onto the bed with a smile, curling up in a ball in her outfit.

She opened her eyes. There was mist all around her. She stood in the middle of an intersection, holding Tsubasa. Buildings and rubble were all around, barely visible. The mist felt cold, thickening to block what she saw. Each breath she took pushed out a cold mist like it was winter. A shadow appeared. Yuki squinted to get a clear view. It was Michael. She smiled as he walked toward her, but he didn't react. Yuki tilted her head and stepped aside as he passed by. She noticed him walking with a pair of files in each hand, the letter "P" marked on both.

She watched him re-enter the fog and saw a pair of shadows waiting for him. As he presented the files, her thoughts flashed back to the day she'd discovered the mysterious tunnels underneath the city. What was it Michael said to Jamal? Her hands shivered, her eyes trembled, and her mind became paralyzed. As she watched Michael pass the files to the two shadows, the buildings behind her rebuilt themselves.

The feelings in her thoughts and her heart became all too familiar. She raised Tsubasa to stop the hand off, but when she did, she realized she was aiming them at an adult woman. She was dressed in a black gown with gold trim. She was tall, and her eyes were like daggers piercing armor. Her nails were long, and her brown hair was long and airy. Yuki looked at her hands on Tsubasa. They were small and familiar. When she heard her voice, it was a child's.

There she stood at age twelve, conflicted with fear and bravery, facing down the woman with the entire planet behind her, rotating on its axis. She cast her spell at the woman, and the woman cast hers as well. Two beams of light struck each other, and held in place. Yuki watched the woman's ears became pointed, and her teeth grew fangs. It was hard for her mind to take as a monster formed before her eyes. The woman's spell was so strong it pushed down to Tsubasa.

Yuki closed her eyes, focusing all her energy and all her thoughts, as she felt the woman's spell reach over her. Sparks of electricity from the clash of their spells slid over Yuki's hair, turning layers of strands from black to silver. The pain of the sparks ingrained into her memories. Summoning all energy, she repelled the woman's spell back to her, vaporizing her into nothing. Victory was Yuki's as she collapsed onto the ground and watched the earth rotate freely. The ground became her bed, she aged back to adulthood, her eyes glazed over. It was dawn.

Yuki got out of bed, with the dream so confusing, but she realized she had to go back and help with the recovery of the city. Without worrying about cleaning herself, she went to the rooftop ready to begin. She watched the sun rise over the horizon, and tears fell down her face.

The city was fully repaired.

Yuki jumped around the rooftops, exploring the city. Everything and everyone was back to normal. No sign of devastation. She saw Clipperstein in the distance, sitting on its scrapped throne. Fearing she may have been asleep for days, she ran to the nearest news stand. There was the newspaper. She read the date: May 13, 2002.

"Excuse me," Yuki said to the cashier. "Is this an old newspaper?"

"No, this is today's paper."

"Are you sure? This is the right date?"

"What is this, a joke? Are you going to buy it or not?"

Yuki stepped back. She spun around, looking at the people walking by without any care or worry. She ran away as fast as she could and returned to the rooftops. Yuki stopped and collected her thoughts. She remembered her dream; there was only one image. The files marked "P" and the cold mist. In that instant of visualizing those folders, she dropped Tsubasa, the same flashback of her battle with the woman returned, and she remembered the pain she'd experienced as her hair changed color.

It became clear to Yuki that whatever she saw, it attacked her mind, and now forced her to remember a traumatic moment in her life. The shock overwhelmed her. She collapsed to her knees, and covered her face with a childlike whimper.

Episode 14

[~ Ki to Wisdom ~]

Martial Arts anime and manga: one of the most popular genres. While many other genres utilize Martial Arts in their shows, Martial Arts also has its own genre, where it is the primary focus. Sometimes these stories are filled with nonstop action. Other times, they may delve deep into philosophical thought. They might even channel fantasy elements with inner energy, like "ki," with feats of strength or energy blasts that make explosions, but in the end, for those of us who love this genre, we expect one thing and one thing only…

…awesome fight scenes!

May 15, 2002

Jamal was completing a customer's purchase as the clock closed in on noon. When he finished, he flipped through his newspaper's classifieds section. There were apartment buildings with retail space available in the southern district of Downtown, but the prices were very high. As he read, Yuki exited the storage room. He circled a phone number, and noticed Yuki was reading with him.

"Sorry," Yuki said. "I'm just curious."

"I was looking for a place to start my own store."

"Oh? What kind of store?"

"I haven't decided yet. I was thinking of a martial arts supply store, or maybe a sporting goods store. I don't know."

Yuki smiled. "You'll figure it out."

Jamal stared at the newspaper for a moment, then realized they were alone. As Yuki walked away, Jamal said, "Why are you here?"

"What?"

Jamal stared at her intently. "Why are you here?"

"I work here."

"No... I mean, why were you sent here?"

"To be Michael's body—"

"This is not a game." Jamal stepped around the counter and approached Yuki.

"Jamal, what has gotten into you? What's wrong?"

"Michael was fine before you got here, and that spoon showed up on the same day."

"I see." Yuki crossed her arms. "I have something to do with that thing?"

"Maybe. I don't know." Jamal turned aside, his hands on his hips. "What I do know is that once you arrived, so did trouble, again."

"How dare you?!"

"Oh please!" Jamal faced Yuki. "You, a 'magical girl,' shows up the same day as our shipment of Endless Heart DVDs."

Yuki stepped back and looked over at the last case of the show on the shelf. There was an image of a girl in a magical costume, holding a staff. "That makes no sense."

"Exactly!" Jamal walked past her and picked up the DVD. "Just like how the Kaijuzoid came back after he ordered a shipment. The same week he told Angela who he is, and Kats... what are the odds of him being a reader? It's the timing that's driving me crazy."

"He's been here before any of us got here, before Michael built this store!" Yuki's eyes grew wide. "Are you saying Michael can bend reality and change us? Who we are?"

"It... it feels like it." He growled. "I don't know if it's The Impossible Man, or just one big coincidence. I need to know if you have something to do with this, and not him."

"Jamal..."

"What do you think?" Jamal leaned on the counter. They were silent for a moment. People outside were passing by. As he looked at his hands, Yuki turned to her brooch and closed her eyes.

"No." Yuki approached Jamal and looked him in the eyes. "I know who I am. My life has always been this way, since the day I was born. I didn't come here to hurt Michael, or you, or anyone else. Michael, The Impossible Man... whoever he is, he had nothing to do with what happened with my mother and his back in Japan."

She scanned Jamal and tilted her head. "I sense energy in you. When did you start doing martial arts?"

"Irrelevant!" Jamal stepped away and turned his back.

"Yes, it is relevant."

Jamal turned to Yuki. Her eyes demanded an answer.

"Since I was ten."

"And when did you meet Michael?"

"College." Jamal lowered his head. "Still, I never had this energy before."

"Or maybe... you just weren't aware of it when you were ten."

"Or maybe he reset time, and made everything like this."

"Jamal?" Yuki placed her hand on her chest. "I didn't sense magical energy until I was ten, and I never knew there was a person named Michael Garcia."

"It doesn't matter if you knew him or not, he just has to change the world without any of us knowing." Jamal looked up at Yuki; her eyes were tired of his apprehension. His eye twitched, the struggle within him. "I... believed I could do anything when I learned martial arts, but then when I met Michael, I started seeing the possibilities, and yet..."

"Jamal." Yuki took his hands.

"It was just a childhood fantasy. It's not real."

"I'll be fair and say he did do all this. He made you

channel ki and made me a magical girl. Why would he do this to us? His friends?" Yuki clutched her brooch and her eyes trembled. "What is his purpose for making us into something we're not? Something we didn't deserve?"

Jamal lifted his head up and tried to think of anything negative about Michael. He couldn't. Yes, Michael was a pain and got everyone in trouble, but Jamal knew that Michael had done nothing to him directly that hurt him. "I'm…I'm scared."

"I understand how scary strange things can be. This world of Michael's is scary, but I have been down this road before. I have seen things…" She took a deep breath and gently placed her hand over his. "I have seen things that broke my mind."

"What?" Jamal felt Yuki's hand shaking. He turned his head and saw her eyes were like glass, and vacant.

"I've seen a world where shapes move freely. Circles, triangles, squares. People who would turn into monsters. With my sensei at my side, I fought against things that should have killed me. Even my hair color magically changed permanently from these experiences. I was never the same again. I felt my life was wrong." Yuki clutched her shoulders. "It was all so painful. So seeing Michael as The Impossible Man…the kind things I saw him do for people, helped people, not even a single hand of his raised at me… why would he make me into someone that gets hurt by all those horrible things, monsters?"

Jamal rested his arms on the counter and relaxed. He felt Yuki's hand resting on his back.

"If Michael, The Impossible Man, did do this, as you said," said Yuki, tightening her grip on her brooch, "then I believe it was not with malice, but with a kind heart…and someone or something took advantage of what he'd done and brought evil to our world."

"Yuki."

"Until that is confirmed, I am a magical girl, and I am trying to become a magical detective...and you?"

Jamal lifted up the newspaper. "I want my own store. My own business. It's my dream, but…"

Yuki placed her hand on Jamal's shoulder. "You know yourself better than anyone else."

Jamal wiped a tear from his stoic face. "Thank you."

✳ ✳ ✳

During lunchtime, Jamal stood before the register and read the manga Flying Fist of the East on the counter. The cover had a martial artist breaking a wooden board. A young lady stood before the counter, placing a DVD case before him. He stared at her blonde hair and green eyes. Her presence triggered a hazy memory. He had seen her before, but couldn't place her at a moment. Her smile at least welcomed him. After completing the transaction, they continued looking at each other while she walked past the storefront window.

"She's got her eye on you," Michael said behind Jamal.

"Ack." Jamal jumped to the side. "Where did you come from?"

"Out of nowhere," Michael said, waving his hand like a magician. "And yet somewhere."

Jamal felt like whacking him, but the thought of the young woman changed his mind. He looked outside, and there were only passersby and cars driving by.

"I know I've seen her from before. I just can't remember where. Or when."

"Ask her out when you see her again."

"How do you kn—" Jamal turned to Michael and did not dare finish his question. "Forget it. Looking at her, it's as though she's calling out to me."

"Then call back."

"I will."

"When?"

"When I feel like it."

"You virgin."

Jamal punched the back of Michael's head, sending him to the floor. He rubbed his fist, and Michael stood to his feet, rubbing the back of his head with a smile.

The door opened, and Jamal turned to see who was coming in. A young man with blue hair stood before the counter. His eyes were inflamed, and shifted side to side from Michael to Jamal. Jamal stood there, his eyes half opened. Michael just stared.

"Which one of you is Jamal Jones?"

"He is," Michael said, pointing his finger at his friend, but he felt an elbow to the stomach.

"Idiot!"

"I'm Sam Stone, and I'm here to challenge you to a duel."

"Duel?" Michael and Jamal said, turned to each other, and shrugged their shoulders. Michael said, "You're going to play trading card games?"

Jamal sneered in Michael's face and made him step back.

Sam pointed his finger at Jamal's face. "You, Jamal, have de-blossomed my beloved Julia."

"De-blossomed?" Michael said. He rested his chin under his hand.

"I don't know what you're talking about," Jamal said, crossing his arms.

"De-blossomed…" Michael said.

"You know what I'm talking about. Friday, at the party."

"De…blossomed…" Michael leaned closer to Jamal. "Is that even a word?"

"Who cares!?" Jamal said.

"Surely you remember the party."

Jamal shook his fist, and his face scrunched. He struggled to make a clear picture of what had happened that night.

"I said I would fight you for Julia's heart."

"Now I remember!" Jamal pounded his fist in the palm of his hand.

"Really?" Michael said. "For a moment, I thought you were going to crap in your pants."

Jamal struck Michael with the back of his fist and sent him flying onto his back. He slammed the palms of his hands on the counter, leaning over the surface.

"I was talking about European politics when you suddenly—"

"That's not what happened!" Sam said. "We were all having a conversation with flying pink elephants when you—"

"Flying pink elephants?" Jamal shook his head. "Now wait a minute, we talked about politics."

"Pink flying elephants."

"Politics!"

"Elephants!"

Michael stood to his feet. "When does Julia come in?"

"Stay out of this!" Jamal and Sam hovered over Michael like giants, and he waved his hands at them.

"Fine, you walking Christmas ornaments." He stepped back, leaning on the wall. Jamal stared at Sam's blue hair, and Sam stared at Jamal's green hair. As Michael smirked, Jamal and Sam shook their heads and regained their focus.

Jamal spoke. "Fine, I accept your challenge."

"Good," Sam said, walking to the door and opening it. "I'll see you tonight at the Ken Smith Park near the Glory Estates in Suburbia."

When the door closed, Jamal placed his head in his hands in pain.

"Who's Julia?" said Michael. "His girlfriend?"

"No, it can't be, Michael. Can it?" Jamal turned to Michael and received a shrug as a response.

"Aey, you're the player in all this," said Michael.

"I should start up my training and be ready for tonight." Jamal left the store through the apartment entrance, leaving Michael alone.

"Sure, Jamal," Michael said to himself. "You can take the rest of the day off."

Jamal arrived at Shinichiro's apartment. When he was about to knock on the door, it opened on its own. A spotlight in the darkness waited for him. Once he stepped into the light, another spotlight appeared, as the sound of a struggling motor echoed throughout the apartment.

"Come on. Start, damn you," said Shinichiro from the darkness. Then the motor started, and the song of the humming choir began. Shinichiro appeared in the spotlight and landed on the wooden floor. He pulled out his pipe, lit it, and took a puff. "May I help you?"

"I have come to terms with the fact that I have ki energy, and I have accepted a challenge to a fight tonight. I would like to know where my opponent's ki level is at compared to mine."

"Ah, a ki reading. I haven't done that in a long time. Come closer." Shinichiro folded his hands together and stuck out his index fingers and thumbs in the shape of a gun. With Jamal standing before him, Shinichiro closed his eyes and took a deep breath, then exhaled. He repeated this process until his thoughts cleared and he saw a vision of Jamal and Sam. Both fighters had a faint glow; Jamal in blue, Sam in green. Shinichiro noticed that their colors opposed their hair dyes. To make things even stranger, they both swerved side to side. The sound of inhaling and exhaling overwhelmed the vision. As the noise grew louder, the two fighters faded into nothing.

"Wake up!" Jamal said into Shinichiro's ear, and a bubble burst from Shinichiro's lips. "Are you through sleeping, Kats?"

"Sorry." Shinichiro cleared his throat.

"Well?"

"Both of your ki levels read drunk. Full of alcohol."

Jamal's head dropped. He exhaled frustration, and the song of the humming choir began. Shinichiro floated in the air, with strings around him. Jamal stepped back to avoid getting tangled.

"Don't worry, the truth will hurt." Shinichiro faded into the darkness. As he vanished from Jamal's sight, he lost balance, ready to fall down. "More power. More power!"

Shinichiro straightened out and disappeared in the darkness. The spotlight turned off, and Jamal walked away, shaking his head from side to side. He left, trying to figure out what had happened that night. The door opened on its own, and Jamal walked past Michael waiting outside with his hands in his pockets.

"He's all yours, Michael."

"Kats…" Michael said, standing in the doorway. "You're mine!"

Michael ran inside, screaming like a madman, and Jamal shrugged his shoulders, rolling his eyes.

Jamal stepped down to the third floor and saw Kaori carrying Seizon, with Angela and Ely. He stood there for a moment and noticed that Kaori was in her kendo uniform, her hair tied back in a ponytail. Jamal was speechless; he shook his head. "Wow, Kaori, what's with the costume?"

"It's not a costume," Kaori said, and Angela giggled. "It's my practice uniform. I'm going to show Angie-chan how I use Seizon."

"Really?" Jamal looked over at Angela and saw a camera strapped over her shoulder.

"Yeah, Jamal," said Angela, lifting up the camera. "I'm also going to take pictures of her in action for her portfolio."

"That's really nice."

"Kaori's grandfather is going to send me one of his old cameras so I can learn how to film movies."

"That sounds fun."

"Hey!" Angela walked around Jamal, examining his physique. "You're into martial arts, right?"

"Yes, I am."

"I'll use you and Kaori for a martial arts film."

"Angie-chan," said Kaori, "you should ask first before making decisions for people. Jamal could be busy right now."

"I'm sorry." Angela looked down.

Jamal raised his hands up and shook his head, showing he wasn't offended. "It's all right. I wouldn't mind being in your film."

He gave Kaori a thumbs up.

Angela's eyes lit up, and she smiled. "Thank you, Jamal."

"No problem."

Michael screamed like a woman from the fourth floor,

and his body crashed before them. His moans went ignored by Jamal and Kaori, but Angela looked at Michael's twitching body.

"Say, Kaori," Jamal said. "I have some training to do for a fight tonight."

"A fight?"

"Yeah. I still don't know why, but you don't mind if I join you two?"

Michael reached out. "Help…me…"

"In fact, I kind of want to learn more about ki energy."

Kaori's eyes lit up, and she nodded with a smile. She took one step down the staircase. "You can tell me all about it on our way."

"Okay. Let's go." Jamal followed Kaori downstairs. "Michael, I'll be back in a little while to take Coquí's shift."

Angela knelt down, reaching out to Michael. "Are you okay?"

"I…yes…"

Kaori stomped up the stairs and pulled Angela away. As they made their way downstairs, Ely jumped out of Angela's arms and hugged Michael. He screamed from his injuries.

"Get Ely off me!"

At Blossom Park in Little Edo, the cherry blossoms were blooming, and the fragrance of the grass and plants brought calm and serenity. A stream trickled through a trench, where a small bird drank. Ely knelt before the bird and watched it turn its head to the left, then to the right. The chupacabra reached out to pet the bird, but it hopped once, putting distance between them. Ely stepped forward and the bird flew up in the air. As she chased it, she bumped into Angela, holding a camera.

Angela dropped the lens cover. "Ely! Watch where you're going. I almost dropped the camera."

"Chupa. Chupa." Ely ran off, and Angela picked up the cover. She ran past Jamal, who was standing before the stream and shaking his fist.

"Who the hell is Julia?!" Jamal stepped onto the flat rocks and followed the path to the middle of the stream. He raised his fists up and shifted his leg back, scooping the water into the air; the liquid shattered into droplets. As they fell back to the stream, Jamal threw a flurry of punches, bursting each little drop until it formed a splash of water. He stood there, his fist lined up with his eyes, then took a deep breath and heard clicking by the stream's bank.

"That was awesome!" Angela said, taking another picture. "I hope I got all of the punches."

"Not bad," Kaori added, kneeling down before Seizon and bowing to it. She took the sword, placed it at her hip, and stood up. Then she closed her eyes and listened to the sounds of the leaves, the songs of the birds, and the water of the stream. She could sense the ki around her, even Jamal's. She saw the ki energy within him. It was very strong, but its exterior created the illusion of absolute weakness. Whatever was surrounding his ki made it feel like he had no energy at all. She opened her eyes. "Strange."

Jamal looked at Kaori. "Hm?"

"Nothing." Kaori refocused her thoughts. A brush of wind blew a leaf off the tree and flew past her from behind. She swung the wooden sword to the side, and Angela caught the moment with her camera. It looked as though Kaori had missed, but when the leaf flew upwards, it had been sliced in half.

"Amazing," Angela said, lowering her camera. With a smile, she took pictures of Jamal punching and kicking the water he flung into the air, and Kaori swinging her sword up and down by the bank of the river. She imagined Kaori standing on top of a cliff, with ocean water splashing up, swinging her sword. Angela took many pictures of Kaori and Jamal, herself practicing to capture this moment with perfection.

After fifteen minutes, they were finished. Jamal came back to the edge of the stream and sat next to Kaori and Angela, while Ely chased after a squirrel. He lay on his back facing the cloudless sky. The sun's heat conflicted with the cool wind. It was warm and relaxing.

Kaori looked up at the sky with him. "Jamal, how come you don't channel ki energy?"

"What do you mean?" he replied. "I thought I already was using ki energy."

"I see. You're holding back."

"What?"

"You're holding back the ki energy within you, and not realize it. I saw it. Something is blocking that energy. Fear? Denial?"

Jamal's eyes opened wide.

"The Impossible Man?"

"He didn't change me, all right?" said Jamal angrily. "I know who I am!"

"Oh geez, Jamal. Seriously?" Kaori watched Jamal stand up and walk toward the stream. "You're better than this."

"Come on, Kaori, this…this world is not right."

"No…NO!" Kaori stood to her feet, and Angela watched on.

"You've been with him longer than I have, and according to the story, you were practicing martial arts before you ever met Michael, before he became The Impossible Man. He did not create any of this. It just happened."

Jamal lowered his head and rubbed his hair, remembering his conversation with Yuki. Kaori stopped him and lifted his head. "You sound like Yuki. She said similar things."

"I see." Kaori stepped back and held Seizon tight. "You're not being fair to Michael," she said softly. "He's your friend. He would never hurt you. Hurt us."

"Yeah." Jamal nodded. "I know I…if I'm going to do this ki energy thing, I want it to be done by me…with my own hands."

"It will be done by you. Just stop locking your brain out from everything. Stop thinking about it and just do it. It's fun."

"Fun? Until we get hurt."

"Sit." Kaori pointed her finger to the ground, and he complied without hesitation. She took Jamal's hands and they sat down. "Cross your legs together."

"Now?"

Kaori nodded, sitting on her knees, and Jamal crossed his legs. "Just close your eyes and empty your thoughts," she said. "Don't think about anything. Not even The Impossible Man! Ignore everything around you and just feel the wind first. Breathe steadily."

Jamal took a deep breath, ignoring the playful sounds of Angela and Ely. The songs of birds drifted into silence. The water came to a stop. He no longer thought about Sam and Julia. He stopped thinking about The Impossible Man and his powers. Not even the store. Nothing but total silence. All he felt was the wind, blowing over his head, pushing his back, caressing his hands. He followed the flow throughout the field.

It led him to Angela and Ely, and he sensed the joy in them. It guided him to the birds, and he felt the freedom of flight. It took him to the swaying trees, where he felt their patience. It sent him to the water, where he sensed its serenity. For some reason, something about the stream caught his attention, but that came to a crashing halt. He heard a man's voice, a friend from the past.

"Jamal."

He opened his eyes, and his younger self sat in a dojo. Standing before him, looking down, was a man in a yellow karate gi with a black belt, and an afro with long sideburns.

"Sensei?"

"What is the one thing you should never do?"

"Tell a mob boss he came straight out of a comic book?" Jamal smiled.

"Oooi!" Sensei's fist came right to Jamal's face, making him flinch, but its strike never connected. "Don't overthink." Air waved around the fist like water. "Let the world around flow through *you*."

Jamal thought too much. He lost control and felt like he was falling right back into his body. He bounced off the ground in pain.

"Damn!" Jamal punched the grass and got up to his feet, ignoring Kaori reaching out to him. He placed his hands on his hips and kicked a small rock into the water. The sound of the drop burst in his thoughts, and he paused for a moment. He shook his head side to side and regained his composure. "I felt...this stream."

"Jamal," Kaori said. "Jamal?" She waved her hand in front of his face, getting his attention. "You've been practicing martial arts for years. I think you'll channel ki to its fullest much quicker than expected."

"You think so?"

"Your ki will unlock. It'll be sudden, but it's all there, waiting for you."

Jamal smiled as Angela took pictures of Ely just a few feet away, who was posing by the rocks like a supermodel.

Kaori stood up and held Seizon. "Why don't we spar?"

"What?" Jamal turned around as Angela approached them.

"Why not? Maybe a little combat could wake up your ki."

"But you're using a sword."

"Here, Angie-chan." Kaori handed Seizon to Angela.

She approached Jamal and took a stance, raising her hands up, palms wide open.

"Are you sure, Kaori? I don't want to hurt you."

"Do you even know who you're talking to?" Kaori smiled.

"Okay then."

"Oh boy, a fight," said Angela and Kaori showed her how to attach Seizon to her hip. She readied her camera and stepped back to get both in frame.

Jamal raised his hands up, curled into fists. He slid his feet forward, and Kaori stood up with patience. Jamal threw a punch with his right hand, and Kaori grabbed it, pulled him forward, and slapped his back. He stumbled to the ground and slid along the grass. He turned around and saw the grass stain on his shirt. Jamal saw Kaori back to her fighting stance, ready for another attack. He got up, approached her, and threw a left hook. This time, she grabbed his arm, twisted it, and led him in a circle until he slid back onto the grass. His arm released, Jamal slapped the dirt and turned around.

"Feel your ki energy when you throw a punch," said Kaori calmly.

"No fair! You know Aikido."

"Of course, Jamal. Do you think I'm all about weapons?" Kaori winked, and Jamal nodded.

"Yeah, but Aikido has its limitations," he said. He got up again and swung his right leg forward, aiming for Kaori's hip.

Kaori caught the leg and pushed Jamal down on his back. She swung the palm of her hand to his thigh, stopping just short of dislocating his leg. She saw Jamal taking short breaths, with eyes wide open, and she patted his leg. "You're right. If you weren't telegraphing your attacks, I would have switched to Jujitsu. Here."

Kaori reached out for his hand and grabbed it to stand him up. Not paying attention, she felt his arm pulling her down, and his foot planted on her belly. She found the world upside down and realized he was flipping onto the ground to win. Kaori adjusted her body to counter his throw, landing on top of him instead.

They tumbled around on the grass until she pinned his arms down. She looked Jamal in the eyes. They were nice and relaxing. Jamal and Kaori leaned close to each other, but then Kaori thought of The Impossible Man. She rolled off his body and looked away, blushing.

"I'm sorry, Jamal." Kaori placed her hand over her chest, and Jamal took a deep breath clutching the dirt.

"It's okay." Jamal sat up. "It was just the heat of the moment."

"Yeah, that's all."

"Aw…" Angela said, lying on her stomach on the grass with Ely. "It was getting good."

She felt a little pebble bounce off her head, and she made a big smile.

"Angie-chan, don't you have pictures to take?" said Kaori receiving Seizon.

Angela ran off with Ely, and Kaori saw Jamal walk back to the stream to continue practicing.

Kaori placed Seizon on her shoulder as Jamal threw

punches in the air. She wondered what would have happened if she'd kissed him. That would mean giving up The Impossible Man to Yuki, and she refused to do that. It made her wonder if Yuki had similar thoughts too with someone else. Knowing how nice Michael was despite his obliviousness toward their advances, pinning Jamal had thrown her feelings off. She declared Yuki a rival concerning Michael, and she refused to give up on him.

Jamal, on the other hand, was more focused on the fight than anything else. He glanced back at Kaori practicing her swings. Watching her in action gave him second thoughts about her. Beautiful, popular, and headstrong. She knew martial arts, but never gave that quality a second thought due to her role as the so-called "Japan's Number One Idol." Whenever Michael acted stupid, Kaori straightened him out. He really felt out of his league with her, and decided to let it go. He wondered if Julia was worth it, but he would not know until he found out from Sam.

Back at the store, Yuki was in the storage room, trying to grab a box on a high shelf. Michael entered and saw her on a stepladder, reaching for the box.

"Oh, hey Michael," she said, focusing on grabbing the box. "I'm trying to get these labels, but they're so high up. I think Coquí said he needed it for inventory."

"It's actually for a sale." Michael looked inside one of the boxes and took out a receipt roll.

"Oh, well, anyway. I was thinking about this new manga series coming out in Japan we could sell." Yuki stretched her arm further, unaware of Michael lifting his head up when he heard her say "sell." "It's called *Break Rush*. It's about skateboarding."

As Yuki explained about the series, Michael scanned her feet, her legs, her waist, her back, and her hair, and though that got his attention, he was focused on hearing every detail she said about the series. Her idea had his attention more than her appearance. As the lights in the room flickered a little, her soft voice projected business words. He felt something about Yuki, hearing her speak. When Yuki shifted her head, he saw her light smile at the idea she'd presented. He felt his hair stand up, and he snapped out of his trance.

"Michael?"

"What just happened?" Michael tapped his ear. "Was that called listening... I just did?"

"Huh?" Yuki tilted her head. "What are you talking about?"

"Are you thinking of selling it as an import, or if it comes here translated?"

"Oh." Yuki turned her attention back to the box. "Well, we could try import. There have been some neighbors who requested it. They wanted to read manga in Japanese rather than English."

"Okay, I'll run this through with Jamal and check the budget. Imports are very expensive. We may have to wait until next month."

"Okay." Yuki turned to the box and realized Michael was beneath her. With a smile, she pushed on her toes. Her skirt flapped up and down, revealing her lavender-and-white striped panties.

Michael leaned on the wall with arms crossed, watching her struggle for the box.

"You're looking up my skirt, aren't you?" Yuki continued pushing on her toes, waiting for him to freak out.

"Actually, I was wondering if you were going to really get the box."

Yuki stopped hopping with disappointment. "Yeah, well, I did."

Michael placed his hands in his pockets and pushed off the wall. "How did you get the name Scarlet Sorceress?" His right eyebrow jerked at the sudden question.

"Eh?" Yuki looked down at Michael, catching his attention. He looked confused that he asked the question. She wondered what she said to get him to ask that, but she had little time as attention waned. Her mind said *Chance!*. "When I was enrolled into the Order of the Magical Girl, I had to have a unique costume for my secret identity. My mother made my outfit but it was white, blue, and lavender because it was the family colors when we enroll into the order."

She turned around to resume reaching for the box. "I was not happy with it. It did not feel like me. I remembered my grandmother always calling me her little Scarlet Sorceress, so I registered that as my alter ego. The name contradicted with the colors and my mother was not happy.

One year later, I grew out of my first year outfit and I got the colors I wanted with the new outfit."

As her fingertips tapped the edge of the box, her shoulder muscles stretched. She saw Michael's hands grab the item and handed it to her. Yuki took the box and climbed down the stepladder, but as she did, she tripped, bumping Michael into another shelf, and a box fell onto the door, knocking it shut. She rubbed her shoulder. "Great. My muscle is tense, and it's all your fault."

"Then you should have asked for help."

"Why should I when it was pretty obvious I was struggling!"

"Nobody said you had to struggle!"

Yuki lifted her arm, poking his chest, ready to counter his argument, but the pain from the pulled muscle caused her to wince. She turned around, grabbed the box, and rubbed her shoulder.

※ ※ ※

Outside, Dōm Coquí handed a customer a copy of an anime DVD. After the customer left, he approached a shipment of dolls that were cross-eyed with tongues stuck out. As he straightened out the display, he heard a woman moaning. Dōm Coquí looked around a bit and realized the noise was coming from the storage room.

"Michael…" said Yuki.

"Relax, it'll be alright," called Michael, sounding annoyed.

Dōm Coquí leaned his ear on the door and heard Yuki moan again. His eyes grew wide.

"That feels good, Michael. Yeah, that's it…"

Kaori, Angela, and Jamal entered the store and approached Dōm Coquí. They saw him panic and lean his back on the wall, covering his mouth.

"What's wrong?" Kaori approached quietly and heard Yuki's voice.

"That hurts…"

Kaori's eyes grew wide. "What?!"

Dōm Coquí covered Kaori's mouth, and Yuki's moaning continued from the storage room.

Jamal crossed his arms. "What's happening in the back?"

"Ite ni med ol, Jamal," Dōm Coquí said, and everyone turned to Angela.

"He says they're going at it in the back."

"This feels weird," Yuki moaned.

"Yeah, tell me about…" Michael answered.

"No…that little whore." Kaori clenched her fist.

"…why did they package the rubber in these boxes so hard?"

Everyone lost their balance for a moment, and Yuki's moan continued.

"You're good, Michael."

"I'm a natural."

Kaori rolled up her sleeves and held Seizon. "I'll be the judge of that."

Everyone stopped Kaori, heard Yuki moan, and yelped some more. They all put their ears to the door.

Ely growled from behind, hearing Yuki and Michael together. She grabbed the doorknob and turned it. The door opened and everyone fell inside, piling on top of each other on the floor. They all found Michael massaging Yuki's shoulders while she held onto a box of rubber bands.

Kaori got up, walked over to Michael, and stared at Yuki. "Just what were you two doing in here?"

"Massaging her shoulders," Michael said, still rubbing Yuki's shoulders.

"They really hurt," Yuki said to Jamal.

Jamal turned to Dōm Coquí. "I thought you said they were…"

Dōm Coquí waved his hands, signaling innocence.

"Ut ie weh am qa," he said, and Michael's eyes lowered halfway.

"No, we weren't you porn freak."

Yuki connected the dots on what Michael and Dōm Coquí meant, and her face turned red.

Michael felt Yuki stand up, pulling away from his fingers, and walk outside, obviously embarrassed. "Yuki, wait!"

Michael rushed to her, but Ely stopped him and gave him a big hug. He saw Yuki exit the store, stroking her hair to cover her face. As he pushed Ely off with Angela's aid, Kaori sat down on a seat with a beet-red face.

"I feel stupid," she said.

"You better." Michael successfully freed himself from Ely's grasp. "Jeez, it's no wonder you'll never get a man. You're such an overreacting pervert, thinking like that."

Kaori stood to her feet, with an aura of anger around her.

Outside, a loud slap echoed across the store, and Kaori marched out of the storage room. Michael stepped out with a red hand mark on his face, and Jamal passed by without a care.

"Well, I better get going."

"Where?" Michael said.

"To fight that Sam guy, remember?"

"Oh yeah." Michael rubbed his face. "Should I get an ice pack ready?"

"Yeah, for when I knock you upside the head, you idiot."

"Huh?"

"Forget it. I can deal with you another time. Good night."

"Good night."

※ ※ ※

The clouds drifted under the moon. The grassy hill of the eastern district of Suburbia swayed with the wind. Jamal arrived at the intersection of Main Street and Van Kull Road where a 'To Thin Kill Riverwalk' sign directed travelers further down the state highway. He turned right onto the winding Van Kull Road, walking up the hill pass a sign that read Glory Estates. The gated mansions lined up at the summit. Some mansions had fountains spilling water, while others had rows of flowers in bloom. The scent gave the area a melancholic feel that countered the insane stench of the Metalworks District on the western side of the city. He whistled as each home became bigger and more impressive.

"I want to live here one day," he said, arriving at Ken Smith Park. It was an open park with no trees and rolling hills, only the grass, a pond, and a children's playground. Down below the highest hill was a view of Thin Kill, a wide winding river from north to south, and forming the city border. Not too far just down the hill, he noticed the stream from Blossom Park feeding to the river. Further away was the Thin Kill Bridge crossing the river to the next town over continuing State Highway 51 eastward, and the riverwalk with its lampposts lit along the boardwalk.

Jamal saw Sam standing out in the grassy open. The blades of grass tickled Jamal's legs as the wind blew them in one direction. He stood before Sam, and they stared at each other. Jamal could see the anger in Sam's eyes, though he still had never figured out why, or who Julia even was. He just wanted to get it over with and get ready for work tomorrow.

"Ready?" Sam said, raising his fists, and Jamal shook his head side to side.

"Fine." He raised his fists too. "Ready."

The two fighters stood there, each waiting for the other to attack. The clouds moved along, revealing the moon and lighting the grassy field. As the wind blew the grass to the point of touching the dirt, they both lowered their eyes.

"Ack!" Sam and Jamal said, gripping their shoulders. "It's cold here!"

They rubbed their own shoulders to warm up their bodies. They hadn't expected the nightly weather to be intense.

"Sam, couldn't we do this during the day?"

"Then our fight wouldn't be cool under a moonlit, grassy area, would it?"

"No, I suppose not."

"So you want to ring the bell?"

Jamal dashed right up to Sam and swung his fist to Sam's face.

"Ding!" he said, and hit Sam again. "Ding!"

Sam stumbled back and regained his composure. "That hurts!" he said, rubbing his cheeks like a child.

"You have got to be kidding me." Jamal hadn't expected Sam would complain about pain, let alone remain standing, after those punches.

"You'll pay for that, Jamal!"

"I thought I was paying for Julia."

"Her too!"

Jamal took a defensive stance, and Sam threw a flurry of punches, a rapid-fire blur that looked like flailing rather than an actual throw. Jamal stepped back, swinging his arm at the punches, and matching Sam's ridiculous speed. He saw an opening under Sam's arms and pushed the palm of his right hand into his opponent's stomach. The impact made Sam stumble back again. Jamal felt his arm tingle and realized that blocking was not good enough against Sam's assault. He had to rethink his strategy, but did not have enough time.

Jamal blocked a punch, but found himself swept off his

feet. He landed on his back and winced. When he opened his eyes, he saw the heel of Sam's sneaker land on his stomach. Jamal gritted his teeth; the food felt ready to explode out of his mouth. He rolled to the side and sat on his knees, coughing. Sam swung his arms around and made a wooing sound, and Jamal's eyebrows lowered halfway at how ridiculous that made Sam look.

Jamal stood up, and Sam charged at him. So Jamal thought about Kaori's move, and just as Sam threw his fist, Jamal grabbed the wrist and used the momentum to make his opponent fall face first. Jamal looked at his hands in surprise and smiled at his success, but not paying attention cost him, for Sam spun upside down like a top and his heel struck Jamal's face. Jamal stumbled down to the ground. He nursed his jaw, while watching Sam flip from his spin and stand to his feet. Jamal dashed at Sam and kneed him in the stomach.

Sam stumbled backwards, flailing his arms in a circle.

He's tough, Jamal thought. My hits knock him back, but he can take the pain.

Jamal heard heavy breathing. It was not from him, but from Sam. He saw how focused his opponent's eyes were. The steady breathing allowed Sam to concentrate on not feeling pain.

So he's using his ki to take my punches, Jamal thought. If only I could focus my ki, I can match that strength. All I'm doing is pushing him to the floor, but maybe...

Sam charged at Jamal and swung his left leg toward him. He felt Jamal's hands push his leg back and lost his balance.

Sam's leg stretched horizontally on the ground, making his legs split. He screamed, holding his crotch.

"My…pain…" He slowly stumbled to his feet, and Jamal took a defensive posture with his arms.

"You know, this is pointless," Jamal said, and Sam raised his fists again. "I don't even remember a girl named Julia."

"Girl?"

"Yeah, a girl."

"What are you talking about? Julia is my hamster."

"What?!" Jamal suddenly remembered the entire story. The memories were fuzzy at first, then cleared. He'd been at the party, and Sam was the host. The fruit punch was spiked and everyone knew it, but no one cared. Drunk as he was, Jamal saw a hamster in a cage running on a wheel. An equally drunk blonde, green-eyed woman laughed at him as he stuck his tongue out at the hamster. He turned his attention to her and froze for a moment. They locked eyes and talked. What it was, he couldn't remember, but he knew she had a pleasant voice and liked his voice as well. He did notice Sam across the room twisting a paper cup, but neither Jamal nor the young lady paid any mind.

"And that's what happened." Sam said.

"I thought that lady I talked to was Julia."

"No. Julia is my hamster, and I don't like people making faces at her."

"Wait." Jamal waved his hands. "How did I de-blossom your hamster?"

"You reached into the cage and petted her like a cat! Your filthy hands touched her!"

Jamal faced the floor, a sweatdrop hanging over his head. His hands trembled and his mind went blank. The reasoning behind it all it was so ridiculous that Michael's antics seemed rational by comparison. At least he knew what Michael was all about. He knew nothing about Sam. He just looked like an ordinary guy with martial arts skills. To hear such irrational reasoning behind the anger was a waste of time. He wanted to hurt Sam, and that was when it happened. Once Jamal opened his eyes, he saw a blue aura around his body. He felt the wind blowing around him, the grass shaking, and the dirt rising from the ground. Thoughts of the flowing stream at the park he'd practiced at resonated through his mind. He saw a green aura around Sam.

Jamal whispered. "The Flow."

Sam tilted his head and watched Jamal rotate his arms. A trail of five arms followed his right arm, and then his left. He brought his hands together, and with the image of a tree behind him, he achieved enlightenment, summoning the Flow from within his rage. He could see Sam trembling and stepping back. Jamal swung his arm back, the sparks of the Flow gathering in the palm of his right hand.

"No, don't…" Sam waved his hands. "I didn't know you knew the Flow."

"Neither did I." A ball of blue energy formed in the palm of his hand.

"What?!"

"This palm glows…from the mighty Flow!" Jamal envisioned the flowing stream of water. He took two steps forward, and his legs lifted off the ground, like a volleyball player ready to slap the ball over the net. Instead, his target was Sam. "Streaming Spike!"

The sound of a slap on the top of Sam's head sent a shockwave of enlightened energy throughout his opponent's body. Sam's legs wobbled like jelly, his ability to sense ki gone, negated by the Flow of Jamal's hand. Sam screamed out loud, but the howl of the wind drowned out his voice. The wind pushed the grass to the side in a radial blast, as though a bomb had been detonated.

When Jamal released his hand, Sam looked to the sky as he felt his back flop on the ground. With Jamal's back turned, Sam saw an image of the Japanese Kanji for stream, nagare, the symbol of the Flow, glowing on the back of Jamal's shirt. "You call that…an attack."

Without looking back, Jamal pointed his finger at Sam. "You are already blown up." Jamal walked away from Sam, and a bright light covered his opponent's body. It exploded turning night into day for a moment.

Sam lifted up his body, with torn clothes smoldering from the energy, and fell back down.

"So…much…awesome…"

※ ※ ※

The next day, Jamal saw ki all around him in the store. When he saw Michael's ki energy, it was very weird. It gave him insight to his old friend and the Rhythm, even though it made no sense.

"Kaori, does the ki energy you see in The Impossible Man always look strange?"

"Don't think about it too much. Just know that it's positive energy."

"I see."

"You want me to bring back lunch?" she asked. "I have the afternoon shift."

"Sure, Kaori. Thank you."

After Kaori left the store, Jamal stood behind the counter, reading his manga. His day just went on without any worry, and he felt peace of mind, just the way he liked it. Then the door opened, and he saw the blonde lady from the day before enter. He closed his book, and she stood before him with a smile.

"So are you a fan of manga?" Jamal said, leaning on the counter, and noticed Michael was gone from the store. He spotted him peeking from outside. Michael gave a thumbs up, then left Jamal's sight. He understood at that moment what Yuki meant about Michael's kindness.

"Yes, I am," the lady said, getting Jamal's attention. Her arms were behind her back. Her smile was pleasing, and her eyes welcoming. "I have a big collection."

"So do I, miss…"

"You can call me Julia."

"Julia?"

"From the party last Friday." She giggled, and Jamal's

eyes grew wide. "I knew you'd forget. The punch was spiked, after all, but I remembered you stuck your tongue out at the hamster. I thought that was cute."

Jamal smiled and nodded. He almost let out a hysterical laugh, but he maintained his composure.

"My name is Jamal."

Episode 15

[~ Journey and a Half ~]

Alternate worlds and realities in anime and manga are no different from most stories told here in the West. Usually, a character is teleported to a fantasy world, the future, or even an alternate Earth and goes on a long journey. They follow many basic storytelling structures, like coming of age, mecha, or comedy. A common question asked with the alternate world story is "will the main characters go back home...

...or not?"

May 17, 2002

Angela entered the store, playing her favorite portable video game before beginning her shift. She stopped before the counter as Jamal leaned over to see what she was playing. Her eyes never left the small screen, reading the game text that listed her choices: to attack, cast a spell, or use items. She made her selections and waited for the characters to play out the scenario on the screen. All she saw were flashes over the standing monsters and text telling her what type of damage she'd dealt to them. Angela never even realized that there was a customer waiting.

"Angela, could you step aside please?"

"Get the Demi Birds," Angela said, to the sound of the long drawn-out song playing, but then the screen went black. "No! I lost again."

"Angela!" Jamal tapped her head, and she turned to him. "Customers."

A young man, holding three manga and a poster, was waiting. She stepped aside with a little giggle and pressed the start button.

"Put the game away." Jamal looked at her from the corner of his eye, opening the register. "It's your turn to clean the shelves."

"Aw…"

"Hey," said Jamal, handing change to the customer. "Do you want to build up college credits or not?"

"I do."

"You have lots of time to play your game when you finish, now get started."

"This stinks!"

"This is work," said Jamal, "no different from what you do with Kaori and Sasuke at the station. It's part of grow-ing—" He heard the video game music and leaned over the counter, tapping her head, as the spoon watched them from the top shelf. It focused on the game. "Hey, are you listening?"

"Yeah," Angela said, as Jamal flipped the switch to turn the game off. "Hey!"

She turned to Jamal and saw a roll of paper towels and near-empty cleaning spray right in her face. She put the game away and took the cleaning supplies as Jamal sat on his chair, reading the newspaper.

"So are you excited for the party tonight?"

"Yeah. Michael and Yuki reserved the seats at Minét's last week. I didn't realize it was that popular. I wish you and D.C. would join us."

Jamal lowered his newspaper. "I'm sorry I won't get to join you and celebrate your adoption."

"It's okay. I heard you have a date tonight."

"Yeah…"

"I hope it goes well."

"Thank you. Besides, Angela, this is Festival Weekend. How about I treat you and Kaori to something? I'll ask Coquí if he wants in."

"Sure!" Angela smiled.

Jamal noticed the game sitting on the counter. "So what are you playing, Angela?"

"Treasure Quest." Angela sprayed the side of the glass

counter and wiped it with the towel. "It's a role-playing game."

"What's it about?"

"It's about three heroic girls who team up to save a young prince from the evil Mantis Witch."

"How far are you in the game?"

"I'm almost done." Angela stood up and sprayed the top of the counter again. "I haven't been able to put the game down one bit since I got it."

"It's that good, eh?"

"Yeah." Angela nodded with a smile and pocketed her video game system. "The story is the best part, because these three girls kept fighting over the hero trying to fulfill his destiny. It's been funny and exciting."

"How cliché." Jamal returned to reading the newspaper and flipped a page. "When you're done, I'm going to show you how to file the inventory papers, okay? Michael should be coming here soon with the paperwork."

"Okay."

Michael came into the store carrying a file box, Ely attached to his leg. He handed the box to Jamal, then saw Angela cleaning the shelves, so he dragged Ely across the floor and stood before Angela.

"Angela, could you help me get Ely off, please?"

"Ely, down!" Angela crossed her arms.

Ely whimpered with begging eyes, but Angela was not having it and reached out to her, yanking Ely off Michael's leg. Angela struggled, and Michael tried to maintain his balance. "Ely, stop being a bad girl and let him go, or I won't feed you goat tonight."

Ely stopped fighting and thought it over. She turned to Angela and received an angry look.

"That's right, I'm going to feed you cat food rations if you don't let go."

Ely looked up at Michael, and tightened her grip.

"Enough!" Angela felt Ely's hands loosen. She pulled the chupacabra to her chest and worried Michael would be mad, but he just rolled his eyes and sighed. As he walked back to the counter, Angela realized something. "Why didn't you use your Rhythm to break free, Michael?"

"The what now?" Michael turned around, and she covered her mouth.

"Which means you need to go easy, Michael," Jamal said. "We can't have you losing yourself, like you did when you went against the giant robot."

"I still can't believe you freeze up if you push yourself," Angela said, turning back to the shelf and handing Ely a paper towel.

"Yeah, well, the city was getting destroyed and Snickertime could have destroyed the apartment building with all of you in it."

"That's true." Angela looked back from the corner of her eye. "Still, you shouldn't put your health in danger like that."

"Don't worry. I'll be careful."

"Promise?" Angela clenched the towel tight by her chest, and Michael smirked.

"Sure. Promise."

Angela smiled and went back to cleaning the shelves. Michael, meanwhile, turned to Jamal to talk about the paperwork in the box.

Then Yuki, as Scarlet Sorceress, and Kaori entered the store, obviously tired and exhausted. They both rested their hands on their knees to catch their breath. Kaori set Seizon on the counter, and Yuki rested Tsubasa on the other side.

"We lost the spoon," Kaori said.

"Are you okay, Michael?" Yuki said. "You don't look crazy anymore."

"Since when has he never looked crazy?" Jamal said.

"Aey!" Michael turned to Jamal and saw him smile. Michael sighed, patted his pockets, and felt nothing but his wallet and keys. "Well, the spoon isn't here."

"Strange," said Yuki. "Did it give up on you today?"

"Maybe it got tired," said Kaori.

"I don't think so," Michael said. "Every time I try to get the spoon inside Kats' apartment, it disappears. Perhaps it's aware of his abilities, and is getting smart on how to annoy me."

Yuki leaned on the counter and crossed her arms. "I see. So we'll have to find a way to drop its guard long enough for you to get it into the apartment."

Kaori nodded. "That means no more going into Kats' apartment to throw him out, or you lose your once-a-day entry."

"Aww…"

"Michael," Yuki and Kaori said together, but they paused and stared each other down. They knew what they wanted to say to Michael, and neither wanted to be beaten to the punch. Focused only on each other, the sound of Jamal's newspaper crumpling snapped them out of their rivalry, and they turned to Michael, but he was not there.

"Chupa. Chupa."

"Ely?" Yuki and Kaori saw Ely pointing to the storage room. They both marched inside, their weapons in hand, and saw Michael opening a box up, holding an inventory sheet.

Kaori spoke. "Michael. We haven't finished talking about the spoon."

Yuki pushed her aside. "Do you really want the spoon around you every day for the rest of your life?"

Michael dropped the inventory list and planted his hands on his hips, but as he was about to speak, Angela came inside with an empty bottle of solution. "Look, why don't you two just take the day off and investigate the spoon again? Find something about it. Call your supervisor, Yuki, and find out if she discovered anything about it. Check in with Kats, Kaori. Just stop this madness you two have with each other."

Angela climbed the stepladder and took a new bottle of cleaning solution, unaware of the spoon resting behind the bottles. As she stepped off the ladder, her game system turned on by itself. She took out the device. The title screen for Treasure Quest flashed on the screen. She watched the cursor select start without touching any buttons, and on the file screen, it chose Angela's recently saved game.

"Why is my game doing this?" Angela said, and Yuki and Kaori sensed the spoon's presence.

As they raised their weapons, the screen melted and twisted like a whirlpool, then the system floated in the air, glowing red. Everyone stepped back, caught off guard. Angela turned around and saw Yuki and Kaori reach out to her. Then the storage room door closed, trapping them all. Everyone looked twisted and distorted. The storage room moved farther away from Angela; she never had a chance to scream. She felt her body stretch inside the vortex. Her hands and arms glowed red and broke apart into tiny square blocks. Angela saw the same thing happen to Yuki and Kaori, and everything went black.

Angela opened her eyes. She sat up, startled. Yuki and Kaori sat up on their beds, looking at their hands. Everything in the room was made of wood, and the bed felt soft and cushy, yet flat and sturdy. The walls alone looked as though they could fold in half. The drawer added more to the strange world, since the knobs were flat as well and unable to open. The air itself was stale, but still breathable, though they were unsure if they were breathing at all.

Yuki's mouth moved, and a flat rectangle appeared out of thin air in front of her: [Where are we?] The box typed out her statement for Kaori and Angela to read. Yuki covered her throat. [My voice? There's no sound.]

[A text box?] Angela saw her text box appear. [Whoa...]

Yuki knelt on her bed, pressing her hands on the flat window, and saw only blue outside instead of a world. She lifted her arms up and found herself in a long dress. It exposed her left thigh, covered in white knee-high boots. She picked up a large staff in her hand and saw the green jewel as the headpiece. [What happened to Tsubasa? How did we change into these clothes?]

[I don't know,] Kaori said. [But at least I can read what you're saying.]

Kaori got out of bed and looked at her skintight lavender jumpsuit, with a metal vest pressing on her chest, gloves laced with metal around the arms, a helmet that stretched over her cheeks, and metal boots clamped around the knees. She felt a shield and Seizon attached to her back. [Seizon? Wait. This outfit is ridiculous. It's making every part of my body stick out. My butt has a wedgie, my breasts are exaggerated, and my crot—]

[I'm the heroine of the game!] Angela smiled at her outfit. A short one-piece dress, covered in armor, a hooded cape draped down her back just slightly below her dress, short boots, gloves, pink hairclips, and a boomerang with a shield attached to her hips. [We're in my game!]

[Your game?] Yuki and Kaori faced each other.

Angela jumped up and down in excitement. [Yeah! Yuki, you're the sorceress, and Kaori is the warrior.]

Kaori grasped Angela's shoulders. [Wait a minute. Are you telling me we're in your video game that I bought for you?]

[Yeah! Isn't it exciting?]

[No!] Kaori's legs turned to jelly, and Yuki helped her sit down. They both watched Angela spin around and take out her boomerang, making action poses. Watching Angela having fun, they weren't sure if she understood the situation. [The spoon brought us here.]

[I know,] Yuki said, staring at the flat surface of the room. [What would happen if we die in here?]

[We should focus on getting out of this world.]

[What about Angie-chan?] Yuki watched Angela examining her weapons. [She thinks this is all a game. It could break her if reality settles in.]

[We'll just guide her through this. After all, she's played this game. She knows how the world works. Angie-chan?]

Angela turned around to Kaori. [Yes?]

Yuki breathed in relief. [At least she can respond when we're not looking at each other.]

Kaori nodded. [Angela, we are in a very dangerous situation. The spoon is involved in this. This may be a game, but we could lose our lives if we're not careful.]

Angela slid her hand over the wooden drawer; the knobs were flat, and the surface was smooth. [It's so real!]

Yuki stood before Angela. [It's not. The spoon is making it real. Please listen to what we say. Your safety is our top priority.]

Angela nodded, and Kaori spoke. [Still, you're the only one who knows this game and how it works. So we're relying on you to help us through this.]

[Yes!] Angela said with a smile.

Yuki crossed her arms. [What part of this world are we in?]

[We're at the Inn Area, where I last saved the game. Just before the final castle.] Angela took Yuki and Kaori's hands, gripping them tightly. Her face brimmed with excitement. [I'm ready to go and save the prince. Come on.]

Kaori and Yuki walked towards the door. [Angie-chan, we can't rush—whoa!]

Yuki and Kaori followed Angela against their will. They followed her in a straight line, unable to walk freely. They walked through the door, and the world faded to black.

✳ ✳ ✳

Then the world reappeared, and they walked down the flat stairs. They were surprised that they didn't slide down or fall over.

As Yuki and Kaori kept up with Angela, they saw the innkeeper behind a desk, a young man standing in front of a bookcase, and a young woman just walking back and forth in a straight line. As Angela stopped at the front desk, Yuki and Kaori bumped into each other, and Yuki looked back at the stairs. [Why are we walking in single file?]

Angela smiled. [Because that's the way the game was made.]

Kaori tapped Angela's head. [We're not video game characters. Can't you undo this so we could walk freely?]

[Sorry, but I can't. *Sigh*.]

[Sigh?] Kaori read the word in Angela's text box and turned to Yuki, who signaled her to ignore it.

Angela turned her attention to the front desk.

The innkeeper spoke with a smile frozen in place. [I hope you enjoyed your stay?]

[I most certainly did,] said Angela.

Yuki waved at the character to get his attention. [What's wrong with him?]

[Non-Player Character, or NPC. He doesn't say much. Watch...] Angela walked in a circle, with Yuki and Kaori following her lead. She stood before the innkeeper again.

[Would you like to stay for the night?]

A smaller text box appeared before Angela. [Yes. No.]

Angela's eyes moved the cursor to 'No'. It flashed and the text boxes disappeared. [Wow.]

[Then go about your business,] the innkeeper said.

[And there you have it.] Angela turned to Yuki and Kaori. They slouched in disbelief. Angela walked to the young man by the bookcase and stood before him.

[That castle up ahead has a secret entrance. I heard it's near the moat,] the young man said, and his text vanished and reappeared. [That castle up ahead has a secret entrance. I heard it's near the moat.]

Yuki and Kaori wondered what it was that Angela was doing. As they waited for Angela to hurry up and move the game along, they noticed the young woman walking up to the desk from the corners of their eyes. The game character stood there for a moment, turned left, and walked away from the desk. The strangeness of the world was getting to them. They felt their bodies follow Angela to the woman.

[I'm sorry, but that's all I know.] the woman said to Angela.

Yuki and Kaori shrugged, unsure of what the woman

was talking about. All they knew was that she went back to walking back and forth.

Angela snapped her fingers. [That's right. I already talked to her before I saved the game.]

Kaori rubbed Angela's shoulders, ready to crush them. [Angela? Sweetie…is this how you play these games? Wasting time talking to everyone?]

[Rule number one to playing RPGs. Talk to everyone, and rule number two…] Angela ran up to a treasure box next to the foot of the stairs, with Yuki and Kaori behind her and bumping into each other. Angela opened up the chest, and a small sack with the letter G on it jumped out.

It disappeared, and a text box appeared. [You found 10 Gauld.]

[Put that money back, Angie-chan!] Kaori said, and Angela turned around, smiling.

[Hee hee. It's all part of the game. Watch. I'm taking your gauld now! See, the gauld! Right here, the sack in my hand! Gauld?]

Kaori and Yuki saw no one reacting to the thievery or calling for the police. They just stood there, staring into nothing.

[See, I told you.]

Kaori spoke. [Way too creepy.]

Yuki smiled. [Not really.]

[This is Tuesday for you.]

Angela walked toward a white sphere, pulling Yuki and Kaori along in a straight line. Angela stood before the orb. [Now to save.]

The text box appeared before Angela. [Save game? Yes. No.]

Angela moved the cursor next to 'Yes,' and it flashed. Suddenly the game paused; nobody was moving, not even the heroes. Everyone heard a soft and melancholic melody that was soothing to the ears. The song imprinted itself in their memories, repeating like a broken record.

[How virtual,] said Angela.

Yuki smiled. [That was such a sweet melody.]

Kaori nodded. [Yeah, it was. So now can we find a way out of this world, please? I'm already freaked out over these people.]

[Okay, okay,] Angela said, and looked out at the front door. [Maybe if we beat the final boss, we'll get out of this world?]

Yuki nodded. [No reason why it couldn't undo what the spoon did.]

She turned to Kaori, and received a nod. [Fine. Lead the way, Angie-chan.]

[Yay!] Angela ran out the door, forcing Yuki and Kaori to run behind her in a straight line. The world faded to black for a second.

✳ ✳ ✳

The world faded back to the outside, where the ladies stepped past the door. The Inn Area was three-dimensional. There were no natural sounds, no birds chirping or winds blowing, and they couldn't feel the heat of the flat sun in the blue sky beating down on them. The flat-looking trees never swayed, and the inn itself looked flatter than the inside, despite its three-dimensional look. The dirt never picked up with each step they took, nor was there a single blade of grass in the painted patch of green on the ground.

After Angela walked three steps, the world went blurry. Against their will, the ladies drew their weapons, and two giant birds swooped in, floating before them. They had large black feathers, razor-sharp teeth, and spiral eyes.

A text box popped up: [Demi Bird A and Demi Bird B appeared before your party.]

The only problem was that Yuki and Kaori could not move to attack or cast spells. Another text box appeared before Angela. [Fight. Flee. Misc.]

Angela selected Fight.

[All right, let's beat them…up?] Kaori saw a text box appear before Angela. [What?]

[Attack. Spell. Ability. Item. Defend.]

As Angela selected Attack for herself, Yuki and Kaori watched in disbelief. Sweatdrops appeared over their heads. Angela repeated this process for Yuki and Kaori, selecting Attack for both, and choosing which Demi Bird they could attack.

Kaori spoke. [Why can't we do this ourselves?]

She was the only one to move and swing her sword at Demi Bird B. Upon impact, the number 35 appeared over its head.

[Because this is the way the game was programmed,] said Angela.

She threw her boomerang. It struck both birds, and the numbers 20 and 15 appeared above each of them. Demi Bird B fell on its back, and a pillar of light made it disappear. Angela cheered. Demi Bird A flew right at Angela and rammed its beak into her.

[Aaahh!] she screamed, as the number 15 appeared over her head. She felt the pain from the attack, even though she was still standing on her feet, and it was unlike anything she'd felt before. Her eyes trembled, and she pressed her hand to her chest. She saw Yuki and Kaori standing there, struggling to come to her. It was all real now. It was no longer a game. She understood what Yuki and Kaori were saying. She felt death all around her. If she ran out of Hit Points, she would die. Angela just stood there, and the text box of choices appeared before her.

[Angela, we have to finish this fight,] said Yuki.

[No!] Angela clutched her hair and dropped to her knees. [This is a game. This isn't real. This isn't supposed to happen.]

[Angela!] Kaori said, struggling to move.

[I can't do this! We're all going to die!]

[Angela. Look at me,] said Yuki.

Angela turned to her.

[You'll be fine. We're not going to leave you. Never.]

[Remember what I taught you, Angie-chan,] said Kaori. [I'm here for you. You can do it. You can lead us.]

Angela nodded.

[Now let's beat this game and go home.]

She read the text box and saw the Demi Bird beyond it. She stood up and made her selections.

Kaori ran up to it and swung. The bird fell on its back and disappeared. The battle ended.

[Your party gained 40 experience points and 50 gauld,] said the text box. Yuki and Kaori didn't know how they got all that, but it did not matter when Angela pounced on them.

[Waaah!] Angela cried in their arms, her eyes shut tight. [I want to leave this world!]

[It's okay, Angie-chan,] Kaori said, and she and Yuki tightened their grips on Angela. [We're going to beat this game together. Okay?]

Angela wiped away her tears and nodded. The battlezone faded to black, and they were back to the road. Everyone took only two steps, and they found themselves right back in the battlezone with the Demi Birds.

[I can't believe this!] Kaori said, and Yuki clenched her hair to hold her sanity together.

[The programmers overdid the encounter rate in this game,] Angela said, entering in the commands.

From this point, if it were not one step before entering a battle, it would be ten. Either way, they were always fighting, gaining experience points and gauld. This went on for quite a while, until they arrived at the end of the three-dimensional plane of the Inn Area and exited onto the world map.

The shape of the flat map that had converted them restricted their most basic movements, and so they found themselves just twiddling their feet with each step, like opening and closing a pair of scissors. Flat as it was, and as flat as they were, they literally found themselves stepping over trees as big as they were, bumping into white triangles that were the snow-capped mountains, and trekking over green surfaces that were the grass.

During each fight on the world map, Yuki and Kaori saw the determination in Angela's eyes to beat the creatures. It frightened them, because Angela showed no signs of exhaustion from combat and running across the game world. It was as though she were on a mission. She looked heroic with each battle, yet there was a feeling that a piece of her had gone away.

Kaori stopped Angela from walking. [Angie-chan? We need to get to the castle and beat this game.]

[I know.]

[So why are we doing nothing but fighting?]

[Level grinding.]

[Level grinding?] Yuki and Kaori said together.

[We need to gain a few levels before we enter the castle, or the enemies will overpower us.]

✳ ✳ ✳

After spending two hours fighting, they'd gained only one level. Everyone arrived at the castle on the map. The game faded to black and changed to a more three-dimensional world, like the Inn Area. They split away from their single line formation. Yuki and Kaori dropped to their knees in relief, happy to move freely again. They saw Angela standing in front of the moat, looking out at the castle. They saw strange white lines flying past her, spinning into little loops, and brushing her cape to the side.

[The wind?] said Yuki.

Kaori pointed up at the tower window. [Look!] Michael was there, looking down at them.

[Michael!] Yuki ran up to the edge of the moat and stood next to Angela. She saw Angela clasp her hands together. Her eyes looked lost, watching Michael above.

[My prince,] Angela said.

Kaori turned Angela to face her. With Kaori's hands on her cheeks, Angela tilted her head slightly and blinked her eyes.

[What happened?]

[Are you okay, Angie-chan?] said Kaori.

[I don't know.] Angela realized she had clasped her hands together. [What did I do?]

[Is there some way that we can take over the game so you can rest?]

Angela looked at her hands and felt strange. For a moment, she felt like she was someone else, even though she knew who she was. She was ready to grip her shoulders, but instead, she took Kaori's hands. [I'm fine, Kaori. Really I am. Come on.]

Kaori watched Angela walk along the edge of the moat. Then Yuki set her hand on her shoulder, startling her. Before Yuki could say anything, the world faded to black and changed scenes again.

Now Yuki and Kaori found themselves standing behind Angela, walking around the castle, which was built with flat, stone white walls and a dark cloud above it. The water in the moat looked flat and unmoving. Not even the sound of a splash made them feel comfortable. They stopped and saw Angela standing before a rock.

[Press the Switch? Yes. No,] the text box said to Angela, and she selected Yes.

[You flipped the switch,] the text box said at the sound of a click.

Even though there was no switch or device physically on the rock, it slid to the side, exposing a grey, flat square. The shape of the steps led down, revealing the secret entrance to the castle. Angela stepped onto the square and the world faded to black.

✳ ✳ ✳

The scene changed into a tunnel, with flat stones for walls and flat drops of water falling to the floor.

Angela spoke. [This is it. From here on, we're going to fight our way to the top of the tower.] She led her party through the tunnel, but suddenly they just stopped for no reason. Angela tried to move her legs as Kaori and Yuki broke out of the line, but found themselves in the same situation. Their bodies floated in the air, and everything around them looked blurry. They did not know how or when this happened, but what they did know was that they saw a large smile and pair of eyes floating in the air before them: a giant smiling bubble.

[Wohohoho!] said the text box, and a woman's face appeared before the heroes, wearing a tiara with a jewel.

Angela's eyes widened. [It's the Mantis Witch!]

She had no pupils in her eyes. The image was holographic and blue. She was not physically there, but she was watching over them with a smile. [So you have fallen for the Viscous Sphere. Feel your life drain away and your body melt in a puddle of goo. Soon, your beloved prince will be mine, Sera. Wohohoho!]

A text box pushed the Mantis Witch's text box aside. [Witch, I wouldn't marry you if you had a total body make-over, complete with bulimia.]

[That text reads like Michael,] Yuki said, as the Mantis Witch stumbled aside and Michael's head floated over the girls.

[The hell you all floating in there for? Hurry up and get me out of here!]

[The Impossible Man!] Kaori and Angela said, and they watched Michael and the Mantis Witch try to push each other aside, fighting for the image. Without thought, Yuki, Kaori, and Angela grabbed each other's hands and surrounded themselves in a rainbow of colors. The Viscous Sphere wobbled and bounced off the walls, inflating like a balloon.

[Pop!]

Everyone fell to the floor, and a splash of slime spread out all over the area, dripping down the ceiling and sliding down the wall. They looked at each other, covered in ooze, and saw they still held each other's hands.

Yuki spoke. [Amazing.]

Kaori shook the slime off her arm. [Try gross!]

Angela smiled. [We could do this. We could beat the Mantis Witch. We have the power.]

With a nod, they got to their feet and looked out to the end of the tunnel. Standing heroic, hand in hand, ready to take on whatever the Mantis Witch threw at them. It was going to be a long fight, yet they felt nervous about what other creatures they were going to find in this castle. Michael's holographic head floated right behind them.

[Get moving!] Michael said.

They jumped and watched his angry face disappear.

[Let's go!] the ladies said, raising their fists in the air.

✳ ✳ ✳

Yuki, Kaori, and Angela raced through the hallway, defeating Squishy Rabid Rats and Tiny Vampire Bats in the stone hallway. They reached the end and went up through the stairs into the courtyard. It looked like nighttime, thanks to the dark clouds in the sky.

They ran past the well toward the throne room, where Kaori had a swordfight with a Dark Knight on Horseback. He had a purple cape, red eyes, and a large sword. Angela selected her commands and Yuki provided Kaori with Strength Spells, increasing damage to the armored soldier. Angela succeeded in knocking the knight's helmet off, and Kaori bashed the sword over his head. Although she never struck the horse, it somehow just flopped over, with the soldier still sitting on it, and they both disappeared.

[Wow,] Angela said, running through the main door. Inside, they walked on the red carpet and stood before the throne. There was no one around except for a couple of Gizzard Wizards.

With the commands set, Yuki cast magical barriers to protect Angela and Kaori from the wizard's confusion spells. She then spun her staff in the air, creating a circle of fire, and threw it at the spellcasters. Angela took her turn, activating a team-up ability with Kaori. Their combined attacks created an 'x' over their opponents. The magicians fell over and disappeared.

[Do you know where we have to go, Angie-chan?] said Yuki.

[I don't have a map of the castle. We'll just have to keep going upstairs.]

Everything was trial and error now. Each staircase they chose would send them back to the throne room. They tried every set of stairs that went up until they got the right pattern to advance.

On the second floor, Yuki cast an Ice Spell on a Walking Skeleton, while Kaori slashed a Vampire Bat. Angela threw her boomerang through a pair of Stumbling Trolls, knocking them over.

The text box appeared. [The Stumbling Trolls dropped a treasure box. You opened it and got a key.]

They ran to the nearby locked door and opened it. Inside, Angela touched the treasure chest, only for it to open up on its own with teeth and a tongue: a Mimic. When they entered the battle, they found each of their attacks dealing only one point of damage. It felt like forever, but finally, they were successful in killing the monster off, yet they received only a medicinal herb for all their trouble.

Kaori stomped the ground. [We wasted so much time and energy on this. We need to recover.]

Angela approached the door. [There may be more chests ahead. Keep moving.]

The third floor. The party found themselves doing nothing but running past spike traps shooting out from the ground. Parts of the ceiling tried to crush them. Despite the floor shaking with each impact of the stone ceiling, it never affected their running speed. As the shaking became more violent, everything slowed down. Yuki and Kaori struggled to advance forward. It felt like walking through knee-deep mud.

Yuki spoke. [What's going on?]

Angela turned around. [Frame rate! There are too many characters and moving objects in the area at once. This happens all the time when I play.]

She reached the door at the end and opened it. The scene changed, and the slow movement ended. Before them was a bridge, and below was the courtyard. They ran across. A trap activated and the bridge collapsed. The courtyard below transformed into a field of spikes. Angela picked up speed, forcing Yuki and Kaori to keep pace, and they made it to the other side. Looking below, Yuki sensed something strange.

[I just sensed magic that changed the scenery.]

Kaori kept Angela back from looking below. [The spoon may have done that. Angie-chan, get the door!]

Once Angela opened the door, everyone ran up the stairs.

The fourth floor. There, Kaori used her sword to block the jagged blade of the Slaying Mantis. Its mouth snapped open and shut, trying to bite her.

A text box appeared: [The attack missed.]

After the Slaying Mantis stepped back, Yuki held her staff to the giant bug, and flames dealt double damage to the monster. With a smile, Kaori used one of her abilities to swing the sword seven times, and defeated the mantis.

[The Slaying Mantis dropped a treasure box. You opened it and got an empty bottle.]

[Really?] Kaori watched Angela smile.

[This is great. If we're lucky, this bottle will save us.]

[How?] Kaori said, but Yuki pushed her forward.

[We'll get the answers later. Let's move.]

The fifth floor. The ladies felt exhausted, yet they looked physically healthy; not even one bruise was on their body, nor a single tear on their clothes. Angela's text box showed they were low on hit points and magic points. She saw an open door with a white light and a magical door to the right.

So she stepped inside the magical door, and everyone broke free from the single line. The ladies gasped with awe. In this stone room rested a pool surrounded by flat flowers. Angela stood before the water, and a tall woman appeared before them, wearing a pink and white dress, with large, clear wings sprouting from her back. Her blue hair was long and covered her back. Her beauty made Angela, Yuki, and Kaori blush.

Angela spoke. [It's the Grand Fairy.]

[Rest, weary warriors, as I heal you,] the Grand Fairy said. She threw her arms into the air, and a band of light surrounded the party. A text box of their Hit Points and Magic Points appeared before Angela. The numbers instantly changed from being in the 10s to the minimum 500 points. When the Grand Fairy left, smaller fairies stayed behind, floating around aimlessly. Some bumped off the walls, like they were drunk.

Angela took the empty bottle she got from the Slaying Mantis and swung it at one of the fairies, then closed the lid. With a smile, she lifted the bottle over her head with one hand. As the bottle spun around like a showcase, the fairy inside pounded on the glass, wanting to be free.

[Why did you do that? And why are you posing like that?] Yuki asked.

[Insurance... and to look good.]

Once outside the fairy room, they stood by the open door. Angela saw a small sphere save point at the corner of her vision, glowing bright. She breathed a sigh of relief and approached it, then saved the game one more time, and the soothing melody brought a smile to their faces.

Yuki spoke. [I'll never get over that cute melody.]

[Yeah.] Kaori said.

[Are you ready?] Angela said. Yuki and Kaori nodded.

Angela led them through the door, which faded the world to white, and changed scenes.

※　※　※

They stood before a very wide stone walkway leading to the tower. In front of them was a young woman, no older than Kaori.

Angela stepped back. [That's the Boss.]

The young woman had shoulder-length red hair and lightly tanned skin. She wore the game boss' black and purple dress, and held a black, spiky staff. The only catch was that her eyes were red and pupil-less.

The spoon was attached at the neck of the staff. Its eyes glowed red, remembering that this was the armored woman she had control over and understood the situation.

[Aey!] Michael's text box appeared before the party. He waved to them, getting their attention, and they looked up. [She's working for the spoon!]

[What?!] The party's text boxes appeared at the same time. They watched the red eyes of the young woman cry out to them. Her text box appeared.

[help…me…] A tear dropped down her cheek. […spoon…using…me…ah…]

Black smoke surrounded her body and the staff. Her body stretched out in different directions. A faint scream from the woman echoed in everyone's minds, rattling their nerves.

Angela stepped forward. [She's real. The spoon is hurting her.]

The woman's body took the shape of claws and a tail. Her face and head became a large snout, and black wings shot out of her back. She was no longer a human being, but a large Black Dragon. Its red eyes glowed at them.

Angela stepped back from the dragon. [She's not supposed to change into a dragon until we've beaten her human form.]

Yuki stood beside Angela. [The spoon is not playing by the game's rules. Be on guard.]

[Look.] Kaori pointed to the spoon, attached to the belly of the beast, and glowing red. [It must have taken over the boss of the game and merged it with that woman.]

[If we aim for the spoon, we could damage it.] Angela entered the combat commands and saw 'Spoon' as an option. [Lucky.]

Angela pointed the cursor at the spoon. When she chose to attack it, the dragon struck first. She watched the flames engulf Kaori, dealing 90 damage to her. [Kaori, are you okay?]

[I'm alright, Angie-chan.] Kaori ran up to the dragon. She jumped up with the sword over her head and struck the spoon. Instead of a damage number appearing over the dragon, the spoon glowed red. Kaori jumped back to the party, and Yuki cast a fire spell next. Angela followed her by throwing an ice covered boomerang at the spoon. Each strike made the spoon glow red.

[We did it!] The party said together.

[Aey!] Michael said. [It's not over yet!]

[Roar!] The dragon lifted its head up, mouth wide

open. It looked at the heroes and waited for Angela to make her selection.

[Um...] Angela stood beside Yuki and Kaori. [I think the dragon has a very high HP count.]

[Well...] Kaori raised Seizon. [This game is not going to win itself.]

The battle continued. It felt like forever. Spell after spell. Attack after attack. Item after item, but there was no progress. Everyone wondered when this would all be over. Even the spoon looked tired.

Michael stood by the window, leaning on his arms. [Yawn!]

Everyone stood still for a moment and just stared at each other. Kaori shook her sword. [This is crazy.] She pointed at Michael. [Why don't you try to do something, I-Man?!]

[I have been, but I keep falling on my face. The best I could do is this.] Michael raised his hand up and threw a little flat wooden cup toward the dragon. It spun downward until it became a tiny square block next to the beast and bounced off its head. [See?]

[Just get out of there!] Kaori pointed her sword at him.

From out of nowhere, Michael slumped over the window. He took a long, deep breath, leaning his back on the side of the wall with sweat on his face.

A text box appeared. [Huff. Huff. Huff.]

[He's struggling to use the Rhythm... and the spoon...] said Kaori.

The party finally connected the dots. [The spoon!]

Everyone looked at the utensil, and Kaori slapped her forehead. [All this time, the spoon has found a way to shut down the Rhythm.]

Angela spoke. [But why?]

[I don't know, but something is wrong.]

[I understand what you mean,] said Yuki.

[What?] said Angela. [I'm lost, Yuki.]

[That spoon sent the three of us down here to trap us. It could just leave at any time. Instead, it's trapped in here with us, and it brought Michael. In fact, why would it bring him down here when its purpose is to get us out of the way to have him all to itself?]

[Ah!] Angela said. [Maybe it sent I-Man down here by accident and followed him in?]

Kaori kept her eyes on the dragon. [If that's the case, then it could have left with I-Man at any time, and we would never have known.]

[You don't think ...] Yuki said, looking at Michael's text box continue to read

[Huff. Huff.]

Kaori nodded. [Maybe his Rhythm and the spoon's power activated at the same time when they came down here and bound their powers together.]

[No doubt Michael would have gotten us out of here faster.]

[Yeah.]

Angela pointed to the dragon. [What's it doing?]

The spoon glowed red and broke the game rules again. The ladies watched a strange rainbow of colors gather at the dragon's mouth. Angela brought up the text box to give out commands before it struck, but she was too late. The rainbow beam engulfed their bodies, and the number 1,000,000 appeared over each of their heads.

[No!] Michael cried out. [My employees and intern!]

With zero hit points remaining, the world surrounding Angela, Yuki, and Kaori went dark. They all spun around a couple of times, and fell flat on their faces. The screen faded out and Angela appeared in a teal spotlight surrounded by darkness—wide awake—and a text box appeared before her.

[Sera, it appears you got your head on the platter again. So how about another chance? Yes. No.]

Angela selected, [Yes].

[Are you certain? The next time you fail, you will be sent back to your last save point. Okay? No. Yes.]

Angela selected, [Yes].

[It was all just a nightmare. Do your best, Sera...and crack that bottle open.] The spotlight turned off, then turned on in the distance with Angela still standing there. It repeated the action one more time, only further away. The screen finally went black and there was Angela, Yuki and Kaori lying on the ground dead, but the fairy in the bottle appeared and burst out to float over their carcasses. It flew to Kaori and Yuki and tapped them gently with her wand, then flew right into Angela, kicking her in the face. It crossed its arms in anger, watching the text box with their Hit Points appear. It scrolled up to the maximum points they had. The world appeared again; they were completely healed. As Angela looked up, the fairy pulled its lower eye-lid, stuck its tongue out, and flew away.

Kaori lifted herself up. [What happened?]

Yuki held her head. [Weren't we dead?]

Angela stood to her feet. [The fairy revived us. Kaori?]

Kaori pointed to the tower. [I see him.]

Yuki looked at the tower. She saw Michael pressing his hands against the side of the window frame, as though he were pushing the opening apart. A strange wave came from his body, and suddenly her mind trailed off again. Yuki shook her head and saw Michael just standing there, waiting for them. She felt déjà vu.

Angela smiled. [The Impossible Man broke the rules.]

While the Black Dragon rocked its head back and forth from the strain of casting such a spell, Angela, Yuki, and Kaori created a duplicate of the rainbow of light, as they had done before inside the Viscous Ooze. They summoned the rainbow beam to their hands, clasping them hand in hand, fingers crossing each other. Suddenly the beam shot out and struck the Black Dragon.

After roaring, the dragon turned into black smoke.

Angela watched the spoon's hostage levitate with it. She ran for her, and saw the woman's eyes open and look at her. They reached out to each other, but the black smoke pushed Angela back to the ground.

[No!] Angela stood to her feet. She watched the woman and the black smoke disappear in the air. The spoon fell to the ground and sat there. Angela grabbed the spoon and talked right into it. [Where is she?! Did you kill her?!]

Angela looked at Yuki, and handed the spoon to her. [I failed. I'm sorry.]

[It's not your fault, Angela.] Yuki examined the spoon. [If she's alive, you'll get another chance. This spoon is a threat to the world. Once I get this to Katsuragi-san, we'll have our answers.]

[Get me out of here!] Michael said above.

Angela turned to Kaori. [Kissing the prince will end the game. That might free us.]

[Kiss?] Kaori and Yuki said together and turned to each other, unaware of Angela walking past them in a trance.

[Hurry!] Angela said, and Kaori followed.

Yuki waved to Michael. [We're coming, Michael!]

As Angela and Kaori ran toward the door, Yuki realized she was no longer in a line formation, free to move around. With a short spin to celebrate her freedom of movement, she ran after her friends, who waited by the door. They opened it, and the game took them to the top floor.

※ ※ ※

Inside, a Little Mushroom with Feet approached them with a smile. [I'm sorry, but the prince is in another tower.]

[What?!] Kaori picked up the Little Mushroom with Feet, her eyes lit aflame. Yuki and Angela had the same aura of anger.

The Little Mushroom with Feet howled as Kaori hurled him out the window, past Michael. [Aaahh!] The little creature fell into the chasm below, its body breaking up into little squares until it was no more.

Michael shivered in fear, watching the creature's sudden death. He knew never to play such a joke like that on them. He turned to the party and saw the softness of their eyes staring at him. He stood before them, dressed like a prince, in white and blue with a cape. Michael was worried about their next move; he braced himself for a catfight.

[My prince…] Yuki and Kaori said. They turned to each other with cold eyes.

[Your prince?] Kaori said. [He's mine!]

[No way, Kaori. Who said you could have him?]

[My prince,] Angela said, ending the argument. [I have fought so hard to be with you.]

[What?] Michael stepped back, unsure whether Angela was joking or not, since her voice couldn't make an actual sound.

Yuki and Kaori spoke. [Angela?]

[Finally, we can be together forever.]

[Angie-chan,] Kaori said. [What's gotten into you?]

[Angie-chan?] Angela turned around to Yuki and Kaori. [My name is Sera, and this is my beloved prince.]

[Whoa!] Michael said. He stumbled back as Angela rested her head on his chest. [What's wrong with you?]

[The game's gotten to her,] Yuki said. [We have to stop her from kissing him.]

[Don't do it!] Kaori reached out to Angela and watched her stand on her toes.

Michael pushed Angela's head back. [Wait, Angela, you're only—]

Angela stared into his eyes and kissed him on the lips. Her legs turned to jelly. She enjoyed the kiss, and her cheeks blushed, but for some reason, it wasn't right. It was the game character controlling her body, and she knew it. She felt conflicted … his lips felt good on hers, yet she could tell he didn't like it. This was her dream come true, and as much as she told herself it wasn't genuine, she enjoyed it for what it was worth. Angela knew she would not get this chance again, so she allowed the Sera persona to wrap her arms around his shoulders, standing on one leg, and ignored his flailing, noodle-like arms. After a heart flew up in the air and disappeared, Angela stepped back and placed her fingers on her lips. She blushed. [I have control over my body again. Michael? I'm …]

Yuki and Kaori tackled Michael and stomped his back.

[How could you kiss her like that?!] Yuki said.

[Angela is fourteen, you pervert!] Kaori said.

[I didn't ask for this!] Michael struggled to break free. [It's not my fault!]

Angela smiled. [I got to steal a kiss from The Impossible Man before Yuki and Kaori got a chance. That is so awesome. Huh?]

Suddenly, a group of words appeared out of thin air. Angela waved for everyone to see them and stepped aside, revealing the text rising from the floor.

Staff Credits.
Director Kenichi Matsumoto.
Producer Yumiko Murata.

Angela hurried up next to Kaori. [It's the end of the game! The kiss worked. If we don't find the exit before the credits finish, we'll have to start the game over from the beginning...and it took me forty hours to complete this game!]

[Nooo!] Everyone screamed and quickly ran all around the room, pushing the flat walls, opening and closing the doors to see if another world would come out, stepping on the floor to find a trapdoor.

Character Sketches by the All Nippon Crew
Animation by ZAP
Music by Maria Obata

Angela read the credits. [Wow. I didn't know Maria Obata did the music.]

[Angie-chan!] Kaori said, trying to move the flat bed by the wall. [This is not the time!]

[Sorry!]

[Hey! Look!] Yuki said, pointing at the mirror. [Listen!]

Everyone gathered around the mirror and heard Jamal and Dōm Coquí on the other side. They could see the storage room through the glass and smiled with joy, ignoring the scrolling credits.

Michael reached out to everyone. [Hold hands.]

He felt Yuki holding his left arm and Kaori holding his right.

[Grrr...] they both said as Angela took Kaori's hand.

Michael rolled his eyes and turned to the mirror. [Keep quiet! I have to concentrate.]

✳ ✳ ✳

"Where are Michael and Angela?" Jamal said, standing outside the storage room door. "We were supposed to teach Angela how to take care of inventory."

"Tu wa un ji," said Dōm Coquí, looking inside Michael's apartment from the door.

"I have no idea what you just said."

Ely entered the storage room and heard the game music playing. She picked up the video game system and looked at the screen, where she saw pixel drawings of Michael, Yuki, Kaori, and Angela screaming through the text box to put the game down. Ely remembered Kaori warning Angela about leaving the game on: "It's wasting energy on the batteries, and the batteries aren't cheap."

So Ely emulated Angela and placed her hand on the on/off switch. As she looked at the computer versions of her friends, one last text box appeared.

[NOOOOOOOOOOOOOOOOOOOOOOOOOOOOO—]

And the batteries were saved.

Game Over.

Episode 16

[~ Puerto Rican Day Parade ~]

F estivals. There are all kinds of festivals around the world. Some celebrate a town's history, some are run by schools, and some celebrate a nation's pride. The Puerto Rican Day Parade is no exception. Started in 1952 in Denfair City, the parade marched its way through Grove Street northbound in the Downtown District from Van Vorst Plaza at San Juan Avenue until reaching City Hall at Trenton Boulevard. It features business floats, marching bands, and community groups. Many Puerto Rican communities from other parts of New Jersey gather here to celebrate our heritage. Then after the parade, we go to a street festival with games, rides, flag waving, and music.

Have fun!

May 18, 2002

"My date was a failure," said Jamal, as his watch clicked to midnight. He was covered in dried noodles. He entered the apartment building and climbed the stairs. "It's Festival Weekend. It would have been the perfect time to take Julia to the Puerto Rican Day Parade and the Cherry Blossom Festival. Instead, I have to stay with these idiots…because that's what they are going to be all weekend! Well, except Angela…and Yuki…and Kaori…and Ely…and yes, even Coquí. Just him."

Jamal took out his keys. "Damn him," he muttered. "Left me with the frog all night. I had no idea what he was saying. Made me late. Such a bad first impression."

He unlocked his apartment door, and when he opened it, he heard a familiar sound. It was the video game that Angela played, coming from upstairs. He climbed up to see what was going on. When the third floor came into sight, there was Ely, sitting on the floor, holding the portable video game system.

"Ely?" Jamal said, and Ely turned to him, looking like a little kid in costume with the game in hand. Jamal shuddered. He stood before Kaori's door and knocked. "Angela? Kaori? Are you both home?"

There was no response.

"Chupa. Chupa." Ely held the game system up, but Jamal waved her away.

"I'm not interested in playing games, Ely," he said. He knocked on the door again and got no response again. "Where are they?"

"Chupa. Chupa." Ely waved the machine at Jamal.

"Why are you talking like a Kaijuzoid?"

Ely growled and grabbed Jamal's shirt. She pulled him down and showed him the screen.

"It says Treasure Quest. So?"

Ely saw the game title on the screen, asking to start or continue. She screamed and stomped around in circles, pulling her fur.

"Are you even an animal?" Jamal said, and she nodded. He sighed. "I'm going to sleep."

Ely pressed continue and selected the save file. As Jamal took the first step down the stairs, she pounced on his back. Ely pulled Jamal onto the floor, and they wrestled each other past the game.

On the screen, there was a pixel drawing of Michael, Yuki, Kaori, and Angela, all were sleeping on the floor from the game being turned off. While lying on the floor, the adult bodies were as long as the two squares that make up the sections of the wooden floor while Angela occupied one square, their arms to the hip as though they were squeezed—they looked like statues that fell over in place, and their faces only had eyes.

Michael opened his eyes and saw out of the screen. Without hesitation, he woke everyone up. He scooped Yuki and Kaori under each of his arms as Angela ran across the screen to them. Michael knelt down and Angela hopped on his back. He closed his eyes, surrounded in a pixelated glow, but Yuki and Kaori started reaching around Michael, slapping each other out of jealousy. As Angela tried to get them to stop, Michael's concentration broke. Angered, he took a deep breath, closed his eyes, and then walked to the side of the left screen. He threw Yuki off the screen, then Kaori, and he grabbed Angela by the waist and tossed her as well.

Angela landed next to Yuki and Kaori—still dressed in their game costumes—lying on the apartment floor struggling to move their near paralyzed bodies as Jamal and Ely rolled past them, wrestling.

They lifted themselves up and felt the pain throughout their worn bodies, tired and exhausted from the ordeal. Seizon was back to being a wooden sword, and Tsubasa had turned back to a brooch, attached to Yuki's game outfit. As Yuki held her head and felt déjà vu, Kaori hurried to Angela to check on her. They noticed Jamal and Ely pulling each other's cheeks.

"What are you doing to Ely, Jamal?" said Angela.

As Angela placed her hands on her head, Jamal and Ely stopped.

"Angela." Kaori turned Angela around. "Is it you?"

"Yes," Angela said, looking at her body. "I'm not Sera anymore."

They hugged each other. Yuki jumped in and they all moaned. "Ow…"

"Chupa. Chupa." Ely also jumped in and hugged Angela.

"I miss you, Ely."

"Hey," Jamal said. "Where were you guys? And where's Michael?"

A large block slammed on the ground behind them and shook the floor. They turned around and gasped. Michael was frozen in a solid block of ice.

"The Impossible Man!" Kaori, Angela, and Jamal said. Everyone gathered around. Inside, his teeth chattered and his fingers twitched. Everyone was so busy trying to figure out how to get Michael out of the ice that no one noticed the spoon, leaning on the railing like a human being, using it to maintain balance and wobbling its way down the stairs.

Jamal turned to Yuki. "What happened?!"

"The spoon trapped us inside Angela's game. I'll get you out, Michael. Hang on."

As Yuki raised her brooch in the air, Kaori looked around.

"It's gone."

"What's gone?" Angela said, hugging Ely.

"The spoon." Kaori pounded the wall. "Damn! It must have escaped while we weren't watching." Kaori turned to Michael and placed her hands on the block. "We'll worry about it later. Right now, we have to get The Impossible Man out. Yuki?"

As Kaori held Seizon, Yuki raised her brooch over her head. "Forever…Heart…Rave!"

✳ ✳ ✳

Moments later, Yuki and Kaori pulled a fifth layer of blankets over Michael's body. His teeth chattered, so he could barely talk. With Yuki and Kaori staring at each other, he was afraid that they were about to fight. Instead, they just walked out without saying a word. He watched Angela by the door, Ely in hand, trying to keep her eyes open. Michael knew she was tired from this latest adventure.

"Come, Angie-chan," said Kaori, leading Angela away from the room. "Let's get out of these clothes."

"Will he be okay?"

"He's The Impossible Man," Kaori replied, and Yuki stood in shock. "If this takes him down, it's all over."

Yuki turned to Jamal as he grabbed the doorknob. She stared into the room, thinking about what it meant to be The Impossible Man. Once again, she suffered déjà vu around him, and could not remember what he'd done to get them out of that world. For now, she had to put that question aside and focus on his health. She heard Michael try to talk.

"Jajaja … mama … llll …"

"Yeah?" Jamal turned to him.

"Rere … dada … memem … ahah … stst ooo ryry."

Jamal slammed the door. "Read your own damn story!"

Yuki giggled. "It seems Michael still has a sense of humor, Jamal."

"It may seem that way, but he's hurting inside."

"He is?" Yuki looked back at the bedroom, but Jamal led her out of Michael's apartment. She'd never thought about how he felt. Since his behavior was random at times, especially with his feelings, it never occurred to her how he truly felt inside. She wished there was more she could do for Michael.

"I'm off to bed," Jamal said, and they walked up the stairs. "Good night."

Yuki opened the door to her apartment. "Good night, Jamal."

She stood at the top step of the stairs, with Michael's apartment in view. She felt scared for him. Her failure, having not protected him from the spoon, was getting to her. To make things even worse, she'd lost the spoon when she had it in her hand. When she walked through the door, her Scarlet Sorceress outfit changed back to the game costume she wore. She leaned on the door to close it, and her body slid down to the ground. Yuki hugged her knees, thinking about Michael in that block of ice. Her tears would not stop. "I'm sorry, Michael."

Yuki's brooch blinked; she wiped away her tears and regained her composure. She tapped on the jewel. "Supervisor?"

"What happened, Scarlet Sorceress? You failed to report."

"It was the spoon. It's more powerful than we thought."

After explaining what just happened Yuki received her orders. "You have permission to use lethal force."

"Negative," said Yuki. "It still has the hostage. I'll give you her description so we can find out who she is."

"Understood."

"I'll have the brooch transmit my memories."

"This is dangerous with your condition."

"Lives are at stake." Yuki thought of Michael and crossed her arms. "Please."

"Okay, but I'll handle it from my end. I don't want you taking risks with your psyche."

"Understood, Supervisor." Yuki tapped her brooch and made it float. The jewel pointed at her forehead, blinking.

"I have remote control now. Close your eyes and relax."

Yuki closed her eyes and took a deep breath, her hands shivering a little. "Ready."

"I'm proceeding with memory copy now."

It was lunchtime, and Michael stepped out of his apartment, wearing a shirt with "Puerto Rico" written on it and carrying the Puerto Rican flag. He locked his door, and then saw Yuki at the top of the stairs. With her hand over her heart, her eyes were watering. He wondered if she was okay, so with a big smile, he waved.

"How ya doing?"

Yuki stood there, unable to move. She couldn't believe he was standing there so cheerfully. Was he hiding any pain? She thought, Yuki opened her mouth to say something, but the sound of footsteps trampling down the stairs made her stop. Angela arrived first, dressed in a white t-shirt with the Puerto Rican flag emblazoned on it, and Ely stood beside her, holding the Puerto Rican flag. Kaori arrived just shortly afterwards.

"Michael?" Kaori said, and she and Angela looked at Yuki.

"Hi, Kaori, Angela."

As Michael waved at them and opened the door, ready to leave, they remained quiet. They saw him standing there, wondering if he was truly all right. They wanted to know what was on his mind, if he wanted to put an end to the spoon antics once and for all.

"I'm hungry," Michael said, laughing out loud. He didn't get a response from them. Not even a giggle. With a sigh, he turned his back on them. "One more day."

"Thank goodness," Kaori said.

"Yay!" Angela ran down the stairs and hugged Michael, he jerked his head back and his arms rose high.

Yuki tried to understand what he meant. It felt so secretive that she felt left out. As Michael stepped outside from out of nowhere, Yuki turned to Kaori. "What did he mean by that?"

"His Rhythm will return by Monday. I hope the spoon won't make a move until then."

"I hope so too." As Angela walked outside, Yuki called out, "Why won't anyone tell me...who is The Impossible Man?"

Kaori stopped at the bottom of the step. She was quiet. She knew that Yuki had to learn the truth. The problem was explaining it to her. It was something that only Michael could tell her.

"You're not ready."

"Why? Because you said so?"

"Because Michael said so."

"He doesn't trust me?"

"No, in fact, he trusts you more than you could imagine. The problem is...you're in denial."

"Denial? Don't tell me Michael said that too."

"Believe me, Jamal and I had talked to him about this."

"You all don't get to decide for me what I should and shouldn't know. Denial? Jamal goes into denial when something strange like a chupacabra, or alligators in the sewers, occurs. How come he knows who The Impossible Man is if he's in denial?"

"Damn it, Yuki!" Kaori turned around, her fists shaking. She looked back to make sure Michael wasn't at the door, and took a deep breath. "Look, there's a reason why Jamal is always skeptical when Michael catches wind of such things. When Michael is ready to tell you, he will, but you're still in denial."

"I faced all kinds of crazy things. How can I be in denial of The Impossible Man?" She realized that something was far bigger than she could imagine. That Kaori was even talking to her about this, knowing that Kaori could lose Michael to her, showed the situation wasn't all about them. "Please, Kaori. I don't want to be shut out."

"If I tell you…" Kaori looked back from the corner of her eyes. "You'll lose Michael."

Yuki's eyes froze in place as Kaori left the building. To lose Michael sounded so heartbreaking. Yuki clenched her hand to her brooch, hearing Michael call out to her.

"Are you coming to the parade?!" he said, standing in front of the door outside.

"I…I don't know," Yuki said in a low voice, so Michael wouldn't hear her.

"Yuki!" Michael looked at her and saw she was upset. He tilted his head, trying to figure out what was wrong.

He thought about saying something, but he felt a strange pulse in his heart and wondered if it might upset her more. Michael felt sad for her. "Is this concern?"

He looked at his hands and caught Yuki's attention.

"What do you mean?" Yuki stared at Michael, and he smiled at her.

"Come on, Jamal and Coquí are holding our spots at Grove Street. It won't be fun without you."

"Denial…" Yuki's eyes welled with tears. She cracked a little smile and ran downstairs. As she walked through the door and saw him reach out to her, she knew all it would take to know who he was is to stop being in denial. Whatever that was, she felt determined to end it, so she could be with him.

✳ ✳ ✳

Downtown Denfair City. It was live and bustling. The stores along Grove Street sold all things related to Puerto Rico: t-shirts and caps, sculptures of Coquí frogs sitting on rocking chairs, music from the island itself. Vendors sold piraguas to help beat the spring heat. Cars drove by, blasting loud music. Flags were tied to the car doors, flapping in the wind, and horns were blaring.

"Boricua!" called the driver from the window.

Yuki looked like a little girl seeing all these wonder-ful things. It reminded her of the community parade back home, with the shrine carried on the street and taiko drums beaten to celebrate the kami of her hometown. The drumbeats got loud, and it felt real. She shook her head and saw a man beating an upside-down, empty plastic can with drumsticks. His bandmate played a long, hollow wood cylinder with ridges on its side, rubbing it with a scraper. It was set to the tune of salsa, and she saw the band's friends dancing to the beat. Yuki swayed along. "I've never seen this instrument before."

Angela smiled. "It's called the güiro, Yuki."

"When was that made?" said Yuki, walking along with her pass a 'To Route 80' highway sign pointing south toward the city border where the freeway was at.

"We believe we made these and the maracas first because of our Taíno ancestors, but others say that their own countries in South America invented them," said Michael.

Yuki faced Michael. "Taíno?"

"Time for an abridged history lesson, Yuki."

Kaori smiled at Yuki. "Oh…uh, the professor is going to give you a test."

"Before the Spaniards came to Puerto Rico, there were natives called the Taíno, a subgroup of the Arawaks. The island itself was originally called Borinquén. They dominated the island and other Caribbean islands until the Spaniards arrived. Then it was all over."

"Why? What happened when the Spaniards arrived?"

"We were colonized by them."

Yuki stopped in her tracks, looking around at everyone having a good time. "How could your country be colonized? You're part of America."

"There was no United States around that time."

"Oh. That's right," Yuki said. "But you're part of America now, so you're all free."

"True, but we were handed over to America after the Spanish-American War in the late 1800s, so we never had sovereignty like other nations...say, Mexico or England. We may be free, but not a free country or a state of the Union, only a commonwealth—all the rights of the U.S. Constitution, but no Congressmen to vote on our behalf in Washington. Either way, this is way better than what the Spaniards did to our ancestors."

"Yeah!" Angela said, holding Ely's hand and crossing the street with everyone.

"I never thought of it like that."

"Don't sweat it, Yuki." Michael smiled and Angela nodded. "We still know who we are, and our history. We have a sense of national pride and identity. Some of us just happen to have added a little American pride as well. After all, we're still here, aren't we?"

"Yeah," said Yuki, following Michael into the crowd. She felt Kaori push her, and everyone slipped and dodged their way around. Yuki felt lost in the sea of people. Children climbed up porches for a better view of the street on both sides. The crowd got so thick that she lost sight of Michael. She wished he could use the Rhythm to avoid this crowd. Instead, she felt his hand pulling her through. She smiled. Yuki saw Kaori following her with Angela and Ely in tow, too. That was when she heard Jamal calling out.

"We're over here!"

Yuki saw Jamal behind them, standing over the crowd.

They turned and worked their way back in his direction. She wondered how he'd gotten tall all of a sudden. When they arrived, Yuki saw Jamal standing on Dōm Coquí's back, shaking and wobbling. They had made room on the edge of the sidewalk to use as seats for everyone.

"You guys finally made it," Jamal said.

"Gu op min fack," Dōm Coquí said.

"Did he say back?"

"Yeah," Michael said. "The frog said that this is the best action he ever had on his back."

"Qwani?" Dōm Coquí stood up and made Jamal fall. As Coquí and Michael prepared to fight, Jamal got up and bashed their heads together, so they stumbled in a circle.

Kaori crossed her arms. "I hope you two will behave today. Especially you, Michael. You have to take it easy as you recover."

"Yes, Kaori…"

Dōm Coquí shook his head and regained his senses. He stepped aside and presented a seat to Kaori on the sidewalk, right next to where he was sitting. "Wo bu mi tu ze beh re Poime?"

"Oh look, the parade is coming," Kaori said, sitting at the far end of their spot, and Dōm Coquí lost his balance.

As everyone sat down, Yuki heard the wailing of sirens. She looked down the street and saw motorcycle police driving by. The crowd roared. The first float to arrive was the Grand Marshall, led by a group of teenage girls twirling batons into the air. Following them was a fire truck lead by Puerto Rican firemen, carrying a banner that read 'Ladder

Company 12,' and all wore lapel pins that read 'Remember Always.' The crowd waved their American and Puerto Rican flags at the firemen with a loud cheer.

Yuki heard the crowd cheer for the floats. Angela snapped a few pictures while Ely waved the flag. The next float to arrive was the local radio station, WPRB 107.9 FM. They played the latest songs from Puerto Rico, and got the crowd to wave to the beats. It was the first time she'd ever heard this music, and it brought a smile to her face. She tried to emulate the crowd, but Angela laughed at her.

"You're doing it wrong, Yuki." Angela took Yuki's picture.

"I am?"

"Just follow my lead." Angela waved her hands and guided Yuki. They both followed the crowd, and Ely joined in, laughing together.

The next group to arrive had no float. Instead, two men walked by carrying a banner with dominoes on the corners and a frog character that read the El Coquí Club. They were followed by a group of ten men, and they saw Dōm Coquí waving at them. They waved back.

"Dōm Coquí!" they called.

"Blaya!"

"So those are your playing buddies?" Jamal asked the frog.

"Syi. Neb la meh ba zek et na nomuty denter."

"When are you going to speak with one language?"

"Hee hee." Dōm Coquí smiled as a large float arrived. Standing on this float were Miss Puerto Rico, Miss Teen

Puerto Rico, and Little Miss Puerto Rico. All were dressed in elegant gowns with shiny tiaras. They waved to the cheering crowd.

Angela stared at the winners, imagining herself on that float as Miss Teen Puerto Rico, waving to the crowd and holding flowers. "I guess I'll have to wait until next year to try to win a chance to ride the float."

"Angie-chan," Kaori said, placing her hand on Angela's head as they watched the back of the float. "You might not be allowed to, since you work for me and Sasuke on TV."

"I know." Angela turned to Kaori. "But it would be awesome if we had a float in the parade at least."

Michael sighed. "Unfortunately, Angela, our store deals with Japanese culture. Even with the type of popularity that we have in Japan, I doubt the Parade Committee would grant us a spot in the parade."

"It's not fair! We should try."

"She's right, Michael," Kaori said. "We could have all kinds of publicity if we could get a float. The number of customers could increase."

"Come on, Michael, you know that anime alone is quite popular in Latin America," Jamal said. "We should expand our brand. We're concentrating our Coquí trademark in Japan too much. We don't even have Coquí doing Spanish commercials here. We got Bergen County and Hudson County alone to draw the Hispanic communities to our store."

"Right, and how do we convince them to drive all the way out here to Morris County?"

"There's always establishing a jitney route to here. We have Root 80 to our advantage." Kaori crossed her arms. "Besides, nobody would understand what Coquí's saying anyway."

"He doesn't have to say anything. Just have him do something and scream 'Coquí' to the audience. Well, Michael?"

Michael sat there, watching a high school marching band walk by. "We'll hold a meeting and discuss this, okay, Jamal?"

"Alright, Michael, we could do that."

"Hmm…" Yuki turned to Kaori. "Shouldn't the word be pronounced route, not root?"

Kaori waved passively. "You'll develop the accent in no time."

"Accent?" Yuki tilted her head as Michael smirked.

"You'll be pronouncing your t's like d's in no time Yuki."

"Just don't say Joisey." Kaori leaned into Yuki with serious eyes. "No one says that here."

"Okay. Okay." As Yuki shivered at the thought of mispronouncing words, Ely slipped behind her towards Michael.

"Chupa. Chupa." Ely gave Michael a big hug. The impact pushed him down, and he used his hand to keep from falling.

Michael felt something soft and squished it. He heard a growl while looking at Yuki, and she covered her mouth. Michael knew it wasn't her, so he figured it was Kaori. He took his hand off, sat up, and turned around.

"Sorry, Kaori, I was just—" Michael saw Kaori behind

him, and his reflection in her eyes. His forehead turned blue, and sweat poured out from his face. To the side, Angela sat herself up with crossed arms and blushing cheeks.

"She doesn't have Seizon."

"Michael!"

"Get up…"

"You pervert!"

"…And run!" Michael ran, with Ely wrapped around his waist and hearts for her eyes.

"I'll kill you!"

"I was only trying to keep from falling down!"

As Angela giggled, Yuki, Jamal, and Dōm Coquí watched Michael and Kaori run down the street, passing by a float from a local community center.

Without a care, Jamal heard a vendor calling out to the crowd offering drinks, and so he got up from the sidewalk. "Anybody thirsty?"

"Yes," everyone said, and handed him money to buy their drinks. As Jamal stood up, the sound of a siren drowned out the crowd of the parade. Everyone saw Michael, Kaori, and Ely walking alongside the community center float. They waved batons like a marching band in the parade. The trio looked back and ran away screaming, while a policeman on a motorcycle chased them. With a collective sigh, everyone got up off the sidewalk and left the parade before those three returned.

Jamal spoke. "We'll go to the fair before those idiots bring the police back with them."

"Okay," Yuki and Angela said, and they disappeared into the crowd.

"Help!" Michael, Kaori, and Ely screamed for their friends as they ran past their sidewalk spot, with the motorcycle cop following them.

Later in the afternoon, they arrived at the street fair. It covered two city blocks, the street closed off to vehicular traffic. At the entrance, people were making donations at a stand. The sign read 'New York City Relief Fund' and Yuki stood in line with a twenty-dollar bill in hand. There were food stands, booths that sold Puerto Rican merchandise like sculptures and toys, and at the far end of the street, a large stage where music played and people danced. Yuki stood wide-eyed before everyone. It was similar to the student festival her school held back home, but out in the open street. She didn't know where to begin. "This is so amazing."

She looked at Michael, nursing the three lumps on his head stacked like a snowman. "What should we do first?"

Kaori grabbed his arm and smirked at Yuki. "Yes, Michael. What should we do first?"

"I just wanted to go and eat food," he said glumly.

Yuki grabbed Michael's other arm. "That's a great idea! I've never had Puerto Rican food. I'd love to try it."

As Yuki and Kaori pulled Michael away, Jamal rolled his eyes and turned to Angela and Dōm Coquí. "You guys want to try to win prizes?"

"Yeah! Come on, Ely." Angela tugged Ely away, and Dōm Coquí followed. She arrived at a game stand: a pop the balloon race. Angela reached in for a dollar, but Jamal paid for her game, as well as himself. "Oh…thank you."

"I told you, Coquí and I are taking you and Kaori out this weekend to celebrate your adoption."

"If only Kaori was with us."

"Poime de fro, Michael."

Angela nodded. "True, she's still determined to win a first date with him."

"First date?" Jamal said, and that got Angela's attention. "They already had a first date…it did not go well."

"What?" said Angela. "But she and Yuki agreed—"

Jamal sighed. "Ooh…"

Dōm Coquí shook his head side to side. "Poime de fro The Impossible Man."

"Really?" Angela turned to Jamal. "It's not Michael Kaori is infatuated with?"

"Yeah. She is into The Impossible Man." Jamal nodded. "Angela, I just want to make sure…so, how do you feel about Michael? Not The Impossible Man."

"He's a good friend." Angela covered her lips with her fingers and giggled. Then she laughed, realizing why Kaori was concerned about her infatuation with The Impossible Man. As Jamal and Dōm Coquí shook their heads, Angela turned to the game. "I beat Yuki and Kaori to the punch!"

After Angela stopped laughing, Jamal reached out to her. "Angela…"

Dōm Coquí clutched Jamal's arm, getting his attention. He shook his head, signaling Jamal not to say anything. Looking at Angela, her eyes showed sadness, and she turned to the game with a smile. Not fully understanding the situation, they let it go. Dōm Coquí sat down on the seat, and Jamal joined them.

Michael, meanwhile, stood before the booth and pulled his arms away from Yuki and Kaori. He read the menu above, and Yuki watched some of the food as it was prepared. A large pork shoulder seasoned with sofrito and adobo, called pernil. Chicken served with rice and fried plantains. In the fryers there were the following: a large, round fritter made of ground beef covered in taro and green plaintains called an alcapurria, a salt cod pancake called the bacalaítos, and a folded dough pastry filled with meat called by Puerto Ricans the pastelillo—to non-Puerto Ricans, the empanada.

"I want to try that one," said Yuki, pointing to a woman scooping a tied wrapping out of a boiling pot of water. "What is that?"

The woman spoke. "Pasteles. It's usually meat and vegetables stuffed inside mashed green bananas, green plantains, yautía, and a russet potato called masa. It's wrapped and then boiled."

"Wow." Yuki watched as the woman unwrapped the pasteles. It did not look like food to her, and she felt nervous about trying it out. She turned to Michael and saw Kaori looking smug, as though daring her to eat it.

As Michael ordered his food, Kaori spoke. "What's the matter, Yuki? You don't like how pasteles look?"

"I … ah …" Yuki stepped back for a moment. She felt like she was being rude, but she clenched her fists and pointed at Michael. "I want pasteles now!"

"What's gotten into you?" said Michael.

Kaori pointed at the menu. "And I'll have the chicken with arroz and tostones."

Michael stepped back and pushed Yuki and Kaori before the cashier. "Knock yourselves out. You all got the money to pay for your food."

As Michael took his plate and ate, Yuki and Kaori's shoulders felt cold.

"What would you like to order?" said the cashier in Spanish, and Yuki and Kaori faced each other, each hoping the other could translate.

After they finished their meals, Michael, Yuki, and Kaori stood before the stage and watched the band play. The crowd stood in the middle of the intersection, dancing away to the beat. Michael waved to Jamal, Ely in hand. They saw Angela and Dōm Coquí dancing together. The crowd watched in disbelief as the two had fun. For Michael and the others, it was perfectly normal. Michael felt his hand tugged. He saw Yuki's hand holding his, hiding it from Kaori's sight.

Yuki's hand was warm, gentle, and soft. "So this is what your hand feels like," he said.

"Huh?"

"What?" Michael blinked his eyes twice at her.

"Uh … say, could you teach me how to dance?" Yuki said, catching Kaori's attention.

"Why not?" Michael escorted Yuki to Angela and Dōm Coquí.

Kaori reached out for him, but he never noticed. With Ely in her arms, Kaori watched him teach Yuki, alongside Angela and Dōm Coquí, how to dance to the music. She felt left out, and a hand appeared before her. There was Jamal with a smile, wiggling his fingers for her to take his hand.

"Don't spoil the fun, Kaori."

"Hmph. She wins this round."

Jamal and Kaori ran to their friends, and they all reached out, bringing the newcomers into the circle. Everybody danced the night away, happy that no strange incidents with any outsiders occurred.

Episode 17

[~ Cherry Blossom Festival ~]

The matsuri. In Japanese, it means "festival." Historically—every year around the spring—the Japanese celebrate the start of the harvest. Most Shinto shrines, towns, and villages would honor their kami and celebrate new beginnings. Today, the matsuri continues to celebrate Japan under a more modern setting, with days off during Golden Week. Here in America, though, the matsuri also celebrates relations between our two countries. Americans interested in Japan have an opportunity to participate in Japanese culture and customs, hands on. For Denfair City, we celebrate our Shinto shrine's fortieth anniversary, since it was built in 1962, and the late-May blooming of our beautiful and uniquely rare sakura trees.

May 19, 2002

Michael placed an empty bowl in the new sink. As he slid his hand over the sink, he felt glad that he didn't have to fight this one. He went back to his bedroom to change, but then heard a knock on the door. While pulling his shirt down, he opened the door a little. There was no one to the left or to the right. Then he looked down; there was the lion-headed spoon, floating before him. Michael closed the door, but was too late, and the spoon came inside and laid itself down on the table. It lay face down, looking as though it was trying to catch its breath, regaining some lost energy. Michael shook his fist and scooped it into his hands, his eyes twitching.

"Just what is it you want?" Michael said, and received no response. He felt a strange energy from the spoon. "You mocking me? You think it's funny following me around and hurting my friends? You don't know who you're messing with. You watch…have fun now, but when the time comes…oh, yes…when that time come, you'll learn why I…am…The…Impossible…Man!"

He laughed loudly and maniacally, and the sound rattled the hallways. Michael sounded like a villain.

Jamal and Yuki opened their doors. Yuki looked downstairs, and Jamal ran past her. Kaori peered down from upstairs. As Yuki left her apartment and headed for Michael's, Jamal stepped aside, and Michael came out with delirious eyes. Yuki covered her mouth, watching Michael squeeze the utensil, struggling to bend it.

"Michael," Yuki said, as Kaori came down the stairs with Seizon. "Let go of the spoon!"

"I can't hit it with Michael in the way," said Kaori.

"Don't hit it," Yuki replied, "it might retaliate and hurt the hostage she imprisoned."

"Damn." Kaori lowered Seizon.

Michael held the spoon up. "Soon, Yuki, Jamal, Kaori… soon this spoon will learn who I am."

He collapsed and curled up with a giggle, but Yuki's hand touched his shoulder, and he stopped. Strange energy vanished from the spoon. Like a statue, he just lay there. Michael saw Yuki's hand reach for the spoon, but it disappeared, and her hand touched Michael's hand instead. His eyes blinked once, and he sat up. He patted his body down and found himself normal again.

"What happened, Jamal?"

"You went insane."

Yuki spoke. "It was the spoon."

Michael felt Yuki's hand, warm and soft in his. He looked into her eyes and got up. Then he entered his apartment, everyone following behind him.

"We need to get rid of it," said Yuki.

"How?" Michael said, facing everyone. "It disappears every time we try to trap it."

"Can't you use the Rhythm to stop it?" Yuki said.

"The what?"

Yuki punched Michael's shoulder and crossed her arms. As Jamal and Kaori tried to move her aside, she pushed them away and stood before Michael. "Stop this game! You know what I'm talking about! The Rhythm! You know, the very powers you use to get yourself out of all the predicaments you fall into!"

Michael tilted his head.

"Your life is in danger! Don't you care?! How can I protect you if you shut me out about yourself?!" Yuki's chest heaved up and down with each breath she took. Everyone was silent. She could see Angela, Ely, and Dōm Coquí outside the apartment from the corner of her eyes. They looked scared. Yuki turned to Michael and saw his head looking down, his forehead veiled in shadow.

"It's just…I don't want you in this world." Michael saw Yuki's eyes. Tears were building up. "No, that's not what I… meant."

He turned away and leaned his hands on the chair. "Damn."

Michael's watch buzzed. It was time to leave.

"Excuse me," he said. "I have a scheduled call to make." He walked off to the store.

Yuki stood there, watching his door slam shut. Her hands were shivering, and Kaori placed her own hands on Yuki's shoulders, but she jerked her body to the side, away from Kaori, and stood there staring at the store door. Her heart skipped, her eyes widened, her thoughts screamed; You are more than just a friend, why don't you see it!?

Jamal and Kaori led everyone away, but Yuki never moved a muscle. Tears fell down her cheeks. She felt alone. Scared that she'd worsened her friendship with Michael, she left the apartment. When she arrived at her home, Jamal was leaning by his door with his arms crossed.

"Yuki," Jamal said, and Yuki stood there, shivering like a leaf. "I'm glad you told him off, but, consider his feelings, he—"

"Why?" Yuki wiped her tears, staring at the door. "I don't know him. What is so dangerous about his powers that I can't learn who he is?"

"That's exactly why he can't tell you. You call him reckless about the spoon, but you're being reckless about The Impossible Man."

"He could tell Angela but not me." More tears fell down. "How is that fair?"

"That's because Angela has Ely. She understands there's more to the world than reality and logic."

"I cast spells! I've seen it all!" Yuki stared Jamal in the eyes, and he backed down. "And what about you?"

As Jamal's eyes lowered, Yuki stepped back. "I'm sorry."

"It's okay," said Jamal, pacing around with his hands on his hips. "Look, I try to keep him grounded in reality. His powers require suspension of disbelief no matter how insane or illogical it may be, but it can get messy if he pushes himself too much."

"When he gets cold…"

"Yes." Jamal approached her with his fist curled, and Yuki was ready for a fight, but he only tapped her forehead with his knuckle.

"That's my Yuki version of knocking you upside the head when you say something stupid. Hmph…in a way, you two are a perfect match. Always pushing yourselves to your limits." Jamal turned around and headed for his apartment. "We're all still going to the Cherry Blossom Festival together in one hour. If you don't want to join us, I understand."

Yuki watched Jamal enter his apartment. She thought

of what Kaori said, about being in denial. Of what, she couldn't figure it out. She thought to herself; does it have to do with the déjà vu attacks I've had? Is his power so beyond my comprehension that my mind truly can't handle what my eyes see? That I can't accept the fact that there are things in this world beyond my experiences? Is he guiding me? Or is he…protecting me?

Yuki stared at Michael's door, unaware of Kaori watching her from above. She took off her brooch, raising it above her head, aiming at the ground.

"Don't," Kaori said, and Yuki looked up. "That is how you will lose Michael."

Yuki's face was now red from tears as she watched Kaori enter her apartment without another word spoken. She held her brooch gently, unsure why Kaori would say that to her knowing she also had feelings for Michael. Then it hit her. Kaori said Michael, not The Impossible Man. Looking back at Michael's apartment once more, Yuki closed her eyes and took a deep breath. Focused in thought, she saw two men, one she knew and the other she didn't. The difference became night and day. She followed what she knew. Yuki opened her eyes, and she understood the man more than the myth. Her disapproval of his attitude just now remained, but her heart smiled at knowing where his intentions lay.

He cared.

And if that was the truth, she knew it was time for him to earn hers.

One hour later, Yuki stepped out of her apartment in a pink kimono with a pattern of cherry blossom petals. She closed the door, and Angela came down dressed in a green and white kimono. Yuki smiled, watching Angela spin around to show off her outfit with Ely beside her.

"You look beautiful, Angie-chan, and I like your purse too."

"Thank you," said Angela, taking Yuki's hand. "You look beautiful too."

"She better," Kaori said, walking down the stairs dressed in a blue kimono with a flower design. "After all, it's as close to beautiful as she'll ever get."

"Close?" Yuki clenched her fist. "Don't get ahead of yourself, Kaori."

Jamal came out in a kimono, and stood there looking at Yuki, Kaori, and Angela. "Wow."

"Thank you," they all said, and Dōm Coquí came out dressed like a samurai. Everyone looked at him, a sweat drop hanging over their heads.

"Poime?" Dōm Coquí stood beside Kaori, acting like a hero. Kaori stepped back, and the frog reached out to her, but she punched the top of his head, and his knees bent from the impact.

"We're not in feudal Japan, frog," Kaori said, watching Dōm Coquí spin around in a circle and fall to the ground.

Yuki positioned herself to stand before everyone. She looked them all in the eyes and bowed. She stayed in that posture to everyone's shock. "I'm sorry for the way I acted."

Everyone was confused.

"I didn't understand." Yuki brought her hands to her chest. "I never considered your feelings about Michael. You were right, Kaori."

"Yuki."

"I am in denial. I stood here telling all of you I saw it all, but in truth…I didn't accept the fact that I was in shock from The Impossible Man's powers. His Rhythm."

Jamal raised his hand out to her. "Yuki, this is unnecessary."

"I'm sorry, Jamal." Yuki lifted herself up and looked him in the eyes. "I had no right lecturing you about your concerns about The Impossible Man when I couldn't even face his powers. Yes, I saw horrible things growing up as a magical girl, but I never realized that my mind had had enough of the insanity that I had seen."

Kaori clutched Yuki's shoulders, and they faced each other. "Stop this now. It's okay. We are not mad at you. You had a valid point. We should be apologizing to you."

"I keep having déjà vu when I see the Rhythm. My mind, I feel it, the pain. I never realized it because I blocked it out."

As Yuki's eyes wandered off, Kaori planted her hands on her face. "Look at me. It's okay. We've all been there. We know."

Yuki's eyes tracked her friends and saw it in their eyes. She could see they'd been where she was at. She was not alone.

"We have our share of powers and horrors," said Kaori, and Yuki turned to her. "And when Michael…The

Impossible Man came into our lives, it was overwhelming to comprehend. It was scary."

"How?" Yuki felt Kaori's hands slide off her cheeks and watched her step back with a smile. "How did you manage?"

"I don't know." Kaori let out a light breath. "I just stopped thinking about it and did what I wanted."

Yuki felt light. Her thoughts were calm, and her heart paced itself. She realized tears had welled up, and as she wiped them off, Jamal patted her shoulders. "Come, Yuki. Let's go have fun."

His smile opened her eyes, and she scanned everyone and saw smiles as well. She smiled in return. "Yeah."

Michael stepped out of his apartment, dressed in a long-sleeve shirt and jeans, and saw everyone walking down the stairs toward him. First he focused on Yuki in her kimono. She looked beautiful, and her appearance etched itself into his memory. Michael wanted to say something, anything, but she turned her head away. He felt her cold shoulder and dared not say anything to her. Everyone felt the intensity of the atmosphere.

"Let's go," Jamal said, walking down the stairs.

Outside, Angela took a camera out of her purse and made everyone stop. "I want a picture of us in front of the store."

Michael held his hand up. "Hold on. Before you start…"

He took out his keys and unlocked the gate. Then he raised it up, exposing the storefront window with the store emblem on it.

"Awesome," said Angela, waving her hand to get

everyone closer for the picture, but Michael raised his hand again.

"You need to get in here, Angela!"

"Yeah," Kaori said, and saw a woman with her children passing by. "Excuse me. Would you please take a picture of us?"

"Of course," said the woman.

"Thank you," Angela said, and she hurried to Kaori's side.

Everyone smiled and the camera flashed. As Angela received her camera back and Michael closed the gate, everyone headed for the shrine, and never noticed the lion-headed spoon inside the store watching them leave.

※ ※ ※

The Kasumimori Shinto Shrine, home to the kami, Inari and Ame-no-Uzume-no-Mikoto. It sat atop Bergenside Hill at Cherry Blossom Park, with a panoramic view of Denfair City's four surrounding districts. The shrine's name derives from both the locals' name for the woods, Misty Forest, and the eleven-year-old girl Kasumi Hanashida—her first name meaning 'misty' in Japanese—who wrote a letter to Japan and Denfair City officials to bring a shrine to the city when Little Edo was first established.

Visitors walked under a Tori gate, two tall pillars bridged by a board, marking the shrine's entrance. The pathway led everyone to the main grounds, where to the right, a small dedication shrine to Kasumi Hanashida—wrapped with prayer charms to protect her spirit—welcomed guests.

As guests read her history plaque, with her last picture in life when she was twelve, other guests, mostly Japanese residents, stood before the shrine and bowed to her. From this section, Kasumi could see clearly how far her wish had come true.

As Michael and his friends walked under the gate, the sakura trees greeted them with raining petals made by the gentle wind. They looked like snowflakes on a winter day. Angela and Ely ran ahead of them with arms raised up, enjoying the petals.

Yuki lifted her head as the petal rained down. "I'm surprised they're still in bloom this late in the season."

Michael stood next to her. "Botanists come here every year to analyze this anomaly to figure out why the trees do that? All the cherry blossoms here originated from Kasumi Hanashida's hometown which normally blooms in early April. It was discovered that the soil here is similar to the acidic soil in the Pinelands down in South Jersey, so it made it difficult to bloom here. They were dying. However, legend has it that during this time in May, Kasumi sat under one of the trees and prayed. She was found alive but not moving, and the first petals hanged above her. The locals believed her spirit left her body to make the trees blossom at this time rather than earlier."

"Amazing." Angela said.

Yuki walked forward without saying a word. Michael cringed.

Kaori smiled at Angela. "Angie-chan, Sasuke and the crew are waiting for us."

"Okay."

As Angela took pictures, everyone arrived at an open area just before a stairway leading up a hill. There were directory signs guiding the visitors to the events held around the shrine. They saw Kaori's camera crew setting up in the area. Sasuke had finished speaking with the cinematographer on camera placement.

"Good morning, Sasuke," Kaori and Angela said.

"Good morning," Sasuke replied, and he shook hands with Michael, Jamal, and Dōm Coquí. He and Yuki bowed to each other. "Kaori, are you ready for the big evening?"

"I'm nervous," said Kaori. She and Angela sat on their actor's chairs to receive makeup, and Ely sat next to them. "It's been a couple of years since I sang."

"You'll do fine. Just give it your best." Sasuke handed Kaori and Angela notes and instructions for filming.

"You will do great!" Hino said, approaching the crew. He stood before Kaori and Angela with a big smile.

"Good morning, Hino-san." Kaori and Angela bowed to him.

"Good morning. How are you girls doing today?" Before they could answer, Hino continued talking. "Tonight you're going to be back big in Japan … and you, Tangerine …"

"Angela." She crossed her arms and lowered her eyes.

"…are going to become an international sensation when we put you on stage as tonight's host for the music festival. We got the twin sensations ReRe here while on tour. They say they're your fans, Kaori."

"I doubt I have any at this point," said Kaori, looking away.

"Confidence! Confidence!" Hino took one step forward, removing his smile, getting Kaori's attention. "And keep that temper under control."

Sasuke stood before Hino, his eyes piercing the agent. "We're ready to film. I want you off the set." His tone of voice made Hino smile sheepishly and step back. Sasuke then approached Michael and pointed at an 'x' on the floor. "I just want everyone to stand here. We're going to kill two birds with one stone."

Michael nodded. "Okay."

Michael, Jamal, Dōm Coquí, and Yuki stood at their spot. After Kaori and Angela received their microphones, the light shined on them, and the cameraman got in position. The director gave the signal to begin. "Action!"

"Good morning, Japan," Kaori and Angela said together, and bowed.

"I'm Kaori Saito."

"I'm Tangerine."

"We're here at the Sakura Matsuri, celebrating the shrine's fortieth anniversary here in Denfair City, New Jersey. As you can see, it's a beautiful day, and everyone is out here to celebrate…even the staff of The Impossible Man's Anime and Manga Shop."

The camera shifted over and everyone waved. After a few takes, the filming ended. Angela ran over to her friends and Ely hugged her.

"Angie-chan, don't go too far," said Kaori. "We're going to film you playing some of the games."

"Okay." Angela turned to Jamal and lifted up Ely. "Could you watch her for me? I don't want her chasing Michael around and ruining the filming."

"Sure." Jamal took Ely and held her in his arms. Ely crawled to his back, acting like a backpack.

"Chupa. Chupa."

Michael smiled. "I see your master is ready to take you to a swamp planet and train you in the ways of the Flow."

"Screw you, Michael!" Jamal leaned into his face, making him run off in a giggle.

Everyone followed the camera crew, walking past a sign that read Goldfish Game. They stood behind the director and watched Angela pick up a paper paddle with other, smaller children. She was so out of place next to them that everyone smiled awkwardly.

Goldfish swam around in the pool by the game. Angela and the kids all struggled to scoop the fish up with the paddles. Michael knelt beside her and took a paddle, twiddling his fingers.

"A little trick I learned," he said, and Angela smiled. "When I was twelve."

"The Impossi—" She slouched. "Oh."

Angela watched Michael lean the paddle on the side, pushing it underwater to trap the fish in the corner. In one swift motion, he flipped the side of the paddles over and pulled it up before the fish could react. He caught two at once. "Thank you, Michael."

She looked at the camera and gave a victory sign, then gave the fish to two of the kids. "Thanks, Tangerine!" they said.

As the director stopped filming, Yuki turned to Michael. As she watched his little trick, she realized from Angela's reaction who he was.

"Michael. Just…Michael." Yuki stared at his smile, her heart skipping. "He never used the Rhythm and still did that trick."

Yuki placed her hands over her brooch. "Wow."

At noon, Kaori and Angela finished filming and rejoined everyone. They passed by a sign that read 'Chanoyu Demonstration Participants Welcomed' and entered a tent. With the crowd watching, they removed their shoes and sat next to Jamal and Yuki on a mat. They waved to Michael and Dōm Coquí across the way. This was a makeshift room emulating a teahouse, where visitors watched and listened to the lecturer talk about the history of green tea in Japan.

"Now, many people have mistranslated Chanoyu as 'tea ceremony,' but the correct translation is 'hot water for tea.'" The lecturer noticed how everyone was kneeling on their legs, and took the moment to address it. "It is not necessary to sit in the seiza position, where you sit on the back of your legs, as these guests have shown. It can be very uncomfortable at times, so it is okay not to sit in the seiza position."

While the lecturer walked the crowd through the

demonstration, the hostess used the wooden tea ladle to collect the hot water in the pot and poured it into a cup, where green powder rested on the bottom. She took a small wooden whisk and stirred the tea gently. After stirring, she turned the cup to the right twice and presented it to Michael. Then the hostess repeated the motion for everyone else.

After setting the ladle aside—upside down, so the scoop part would not touch the ground—everyone bowed to their hostess. They picked up their cups and turned them to the right twice, then sipped their tea. Everyone turned to Ely and watched her sip her tea. Strange as it was, Ely looked at everyone and rubbed the back of her head, smiling.

"Chupa. Chupa." Ely took another sip, and Yuki, Kaori, and Angela giggled while Michael and Jamal made painful faces, their bodies squirming and shivering. Both of them fell over on the matting.

"I got cramps," Michael said.

"I can't feel my legs," Jamal said, and everyone took a sip of tea, ignoring them.

The lecturer waved his hand, presenting Michael and Jamal. "As you can see, ladies and gentlemen, this is why it is okay to not sit in the seiza position during Chanoyu."

✳ ✳ ✳

Their next stop before lunch was the origami booth. They split into two groups before sitting down at the tables, where paper was piled up for folding. The male and female hosts helped guide Michael and Dōm Coquí through the process. Michael looked at the other table and saw Yuki smiling while talking to Kaori. Her smile distracted him. As the female host leaned over Michael, pointing out his mistakes, Yuki watched him struggling to make an origami and saw his determination to learn. She smiled.

After everyone had finished but Michael, they gathered at the main table with their creations. Starting with Yuki, everyone shared their origami.

"I made a cat." Yuki held up the white paper sculpture with a long tail and large ears. Then she placed it on the table, and Angela stepped forward.

"I made a new crane," said Angela, approaching her along with Kaori.

"You're always making cranes. Now I...made a dragon." Kaori planted her origami on the table, larger than the other; its claws and open snout looked as though it was ready to eat the cat and the crane. "I beat you, Yuki."

"Does everything have to be a competition?" Yuki said, and Jamal held his origami up.

"I made a frog." The sculpture was in a crouched position. He planted it on top of the dragon, as though it was riding it.

"Hey!" Yuki and Angela realized Jamal and Kaori's origami were teaming up against theirs.

"Yoi," Dōm Coquí said, staring at the funny-looking sculpture. He then held his up: a ghostly figure. Everyone tilted their heads. "Kaori..."

"Stupid frog!" Kaori slammed her fist over the back of his head. "I am not a shikigami spirit!"

Ely hopped up and down in front of everyone. She lifted her origami. It had spikes along its back, long arms with claws, and was hunched over with a long dog-like snout, standing on two legs like a kangaroo. Angela smiled.

"It's a chupacabra!"

As Michael continued working on his origami, Jamal, Dōm Coquí, Yuki, and Kaori's foreheads turned blue watching Ely plant the sculpture next to theirs. Jamal turned to Kaori, shivering. "Be sure not to feed Ely after midnight."

Kaori replied, "Yes."

"Chupa. Chupa." Ely nodded to everyone, and they applauded out of fear that if they didn't, she might eat them in anger.

Michael was still sitting by the table, unaware of Ely's sculpture, continuing to fold his paper.

Everyone gathered around and watched over his shoulders. As the paper sculpture took shape, everyone slouched. Michael stood up and faced his friends, making a victory sign with his thumb extended. He presented them with an origami in the shape of the letter 'I.' Sweat drops appeared over everyone's heads, and Michael laughed.

"Idiot," they all said.

✳ ✳ ✳

During lunch, Michael and Jamal stood by a sushi bento box stand, waiting for their orders. Jamal turned to Yuki, Kaori, and Angela, sitting on a bench and waiting for them to return. Kaori seemed to be picking on Yuki, which made Jamal chuckle a little.

Michael turned to his friend. "What's so funny?"

"Nothing." Jamal turned to Michael. "When will you apologize to Yuki?"

"What?"

"Idiot. You haven't apologized for what you said to her this morning?"

"I don't know what to say to her."

"Just say you're sorry."

"I know, but it feels hollow."

"How?" Jamal saw Michael's eyes aimed at Yuki, and he nodded. "I see. You feel you can't make it up to her."

"Yeah." Michael received the bento boxes from the cashier and took them. "Thank you."

Jamal took three boxes, leaving Michael with only two. He shifted his head, signaling Michael to go to Yuki, and received a nod in return. Jamal led Michael back to the bench, and Dōm Coquí showed up with a bowl of beef over rice, with broccoli and carrot slices. As Jamal handed Kaori and Angela their lunches, Michael stood before Yuki and presented her lunch.

"Here," Michael said. "I got you lunch."

Yuki turned her head away from him and took the lunch. "Thank you."

Michael looked at her. So much to say, but he didn't know where to begin. He closed his eyes and walked away.

Kaori reached out to him, but Jamal pulled her hand down, shaking his head side to side. She looked at Michael and Yuki apart from each other, and resisted her thoughts admitting the truth.

"Michael," Yuki called out, and he stopped. "I arranged a meeting with a fire reader. The energy level of this shrine is very high. Perhaps they would help us learn more about the spoon. Since you seem to be having a hard time getting the spoon to Katsuragi-san, I figured this may help clear the situation."

"I see," Michael said without looking back. "Thank you. Let's do our best to stop the spoon."

As Michael walked away, Yuki closed her eyes and took a deep breath. She smiled a bit, despite trying to stay angry at him. She feared she may be pushing too hard to get him to see her anger. As she stared at the bento box, she remembered the day she made lunch for him. He was oblivious then, as he was right now, but she did not want Michael any other way. "Idiot."

Kaori looked into Yuki's conflicted eyes, and she turned to her own bento box, tightening her grip with a nod.

After lunch, everyone walked up the stairs. At the top, they stood before a well, where they cleaned their hands and took a sip of cold water. They walked through an open entrance. It was an enclosed area, with two side entrances to other parts of the shrine. At the corner, there was a large tree with a rope around it and paper tied to it. People lined up at the main hall, where the shrine of Ame-no-Umuze-no-Mikoto stayed. Visitors offered their prayers to the kami, with the help of the shrine maidens of Shinto, called miko.

Yuki led everyone to the booth, where a few miko were accepting donations and handing paper-wrapped talismans to the visitors. She presented an envelope to one of the miko, who opened it and read the letter inside. The miko then came out of the booth and stood before everyone.

"I am Hitomi Hamasaki. Who's getting a reading?"

Everyone pointed at Michael.

"I will be performing the reading for you," she said. "Please come this way."

Hitomi raised her hand as a guide, and everyone followed her out of the side entrance. She led them up a hill, where the trees swayed with the wind. Hitomi sensed something in the air, then looked at Michael. "Interesting."

Everyone passed by the shrine of Inari. There was a gate surrounding a small house, statues of two foxes sitting upright by the entrance. Coins sat atop their heads. Jamal took out two quarters and planted one on top of the head of each fox.

"A little luck wouldn't hurt."

At the end of the path, they entered a building with a wide opening. Two other miko knelt before the licking flames of a little bonfire, praying. They stopped and bowed to her, then the guests. Hitomi knelt between them.

"Please sit before the fire," she said to Michael. "Everyone else, sit behind him."

"We shall begin." Hitomi clasped her hands together, and the miko closed their eyes. The flames jumped out and roared. They waved and curled, intensifying the heat. The miko sensed a strange aura. In fact, they could not make out what it was exactly, but knew it was dangerous and powerful.

Michael spoke. "One of our…customers is captured by this spoon, can you sense her?"

Hitomi nodded. "I do sense a soul within, but I cannot visualize her. That soul is strong, fighting this energy. This is very strange. It's as if something has been hovering over all of you."

"It must be the spoon," said Yuki.

"It's more than just the…spoon?" Hitomi looked up for a moment and paused. "Anyway, you're all close to facing something stranger. It's getting cloudy…I'm losing it."

"Can you hold on?" said Michael.

"We're trying, but…" The heat of the flames knocked the miko over. Michael and Jamal were ready to help, but Hitomi raised her hand, signaling she was okay.

Michael looked at the miko. "Is everyone all right?"

"We're fine," Hitomi said, and the miko nodded when Kaori and Yuki helped them up. "There's something more ominous than what you're dealing with right now. It's as though something greater is going to happen."

Michael lowered his head. "Great."

"Whatever this…strangeness is…" Hitomi pointed her finger. "It's going to shape your destiny."

Everyone followed Hitomi's finger and saw it aimed at Ely. She flailed her arms in a panic and didn't want to get involved.

"No, the one next to the creature."

Everyone turned to Michael, staring blankly at nothing. He had no idea what she meant by that.

Back at the main hall, Yuki bowed to Hitomi and they parted ways. Then Yuki approached Michael, Jamal, and Dōm Coquí. She noticed that they were looking at Kaori and Angela, who were both swaying a red and white rope to ring a bell. After clapping their hands twice, they prayed to Ame-no-Uzume-no-Mikoto.

"Please watch over our friends. Help protect the lady the spoon captured," Angela said. "Protect them from all the crazy weirdos that bother them. Also, could you watch over Kaori? Tonight is her big night, and I want her to be back on top in Japan."

"Angie-chan…" Kaori smiled at Angela. They clapped their hands twice and turned to a miko. They bowed before her, and the miko swayed a branch with leaves to give them a blessing. Kaori and Angela then took paper strips with prayers and tied them to a bamboo branch with other paper strips. Even Ely tied one up, and they giggled. Kaori, Angela, and Ely returned to their friends.

"That was so cute," Yuki said.

"It was my first time praying at a shrine," Angela said. "It was amazing."

Kaori placed her arm around Angela. "You did good, Angie-chan."

"So do you think we prayed enough to help Michael?"

"I don't know, Angela," said Jamal. "He wasn't too thrilled with the fire reading."

"He looks stressed," said Yuki.

Kaori crossed her arms. "So talk to him. He'll listen to you."

"I thought you were my rival."

"What good is a rival if she can't push back?" Kaori pushed Yuki forward, toward Michael, but he wasn't with them.

Everyone looked around at the shrine, and suddenly the bell rang wildly. Over at the main hall, they saw Michael shaking the rope violently, and a miko raising her hand out to stop him.

"I beg you. Please keep that spoon away from me! Damn that spoon! Please, damn the spoon."

Jamal, Yuki, and Kaori tackled Michael and stomped on his back.

"Don't disrespect the shrine!" they said over his mangled body.

"But I need my freedom!" Michael said, and his friends dragged him out of the shrine. Angela, Ely, and Dōm Coquí bowed to the miko and the crowd before running away.

❋ ❋ ❋

Late afternoon, in a dressing trailer, Kaori and Angela sat before a mirror, where hairdressers were making a ponytail. Entering inside were twin teenage girls, one year younger than Angela, accompanied by a young woman. They stood before Kaori and Angela, and they all bowed to each other.

The woman spoke. "I am Sora Kinomoto. I represent ReRe. Reya and Rena Urashima." She presented the twins, Reya in a blouse and shorts with long black hair, and Rena in a blouse and skirt with short black hair.

The twins bowed again. "Pleased to meet you."

Kaori and Angela bowed back. "Pleased to meet you."

"Take your seats, girls. The hairdressers will take care of you. I have to make calls outside. I'll be back in a moment."

"Yes," the twins said together, and took their seats. As they faced the mirror, watching the hairdresser's brush, Reya turned her eyes to Kaori. "Thank you for opening for us tonight."

Rena smiled. "Yeah, I love your songs."

"Oh," said Kaori, as the hairdresser made a tail. "I didn't know I was still popular at home."

"You are." Reya paused to watch her words. "Well, I haven't forgotten you."

"I blame The Impossible Man guy." Rena shook her fist. "He ruined your career."

"It's not like that, there was more to the stor—wait, everyone blames I-Man?"

The twins nodded, and Kaori realized so much time had passed that, despite keeping up with what was happening in Japan, she never thought of what was going on behind the scenes. "How?"

Hino opened the door without knocking, catching everyone off guard. "Kinomoto-san said you haven't dressed yet, so let me take this opportunity to wish you both the best of luck. Now, Tangerine…"

"Angela." Her hands started to shiver, getting the attention of Kaori and ReRe.

"This will be your big Japan debut. Once we get an outlook on everyone's reactions there, we'll begin making arrangements for photo shoots and a recording contract."

"I can't sing." She shivered at the thought of singing. "I only do stunts with Ely."

"Well, I will have singing lessons arranged for you, Tangerine."

"Angela," she growled, but remembering what had happened to Kaori, she kept her temper under control.

"Hey," Kaori said, but was ignored.

"Once we go to Japan, you will start with a television interview, where you can introduce yourself to all of Japan, and smile. Always smile. Even if you don't mean it. People love smiles."

As Kaori watched Angela lower her head, making an inauthentic smile, she saw herself sitting there, with her mother and previous agent hovering over her. They barraged her with appointments and schedules. Her smile disappearing with each second, her lips moved, asking for her friends. They smiled and nodded.

There she was, surrounded by other girls. Only they were not her school friends, they were other singers and performers, all talking to each other, but not her. She felt the distance between herself and them. It was like another world, as they showed no care for Kaori. Her watch showed thirty minutes had passed, and not a single word from the girls.

When they finally decided to talk to her, a fire ignited within Kaori, and her first temper flare silenced the girls. Kaori's mother was angry, but Kaori pointed out they were not her friends, the ones in school were. She got up and walked away. The shadows of the girls, her mother, and her agent, all stood behind her child-self. As each shadow vanished, whatever smile she once had also vanished with those shadows. Flames surrounded her body. As she aged year by year, she did not smile one time. No joy, just anger. Now a light in absolute darkness, it was that day those flames struck a man, and her temper subsided when his hand reached out to her.

"The Impossible Man," she said upon taking his hand. She smiled, and from that point forward, she started her path of controlling her temper and making her career come back from her mistakes. As the voice of Hino echoed in her ears, pressuring Angela, she saw the teen's anger reach its peak, and her mouth opened, ready to scream. Kaori stood up. "Hey!"

Hino stopped and turned to Kaori. As she looked at Angela and Hino at the same time, she felt the flames of her temper take shape. It became Seizon. "Don't you see Angela is under stress?!"

He saw the anger in Angela's eyes. "Oh…" He noticed everyone, even the hairdressers, staring at him. He covered his mouth and turned away. "I'm sorry Tanger—"

"Angela!"

"Angela. I'm sorry. Let's focus on tonight. We'll talk about the rest tomorrow."

Kaori crossed her arms. "Tuesday."

"Tuesday."

Kaori got in his face, making him step back into the wall. "And if you ever tell me to watch my temper again, even in front of people, I will fire you. You're not the only agent in this world, and this is a professional business."

Hino's eyes trembled. "Right. Excuse me." He exited the dressing room. "Do your best out there, girls."

As the door closed, Kaori saw ReRe looking at her with widened eyes. "I'm sorry you had to see that," she said with a bow.

"That was awesome," Reya said with a smile.

Rena nodded. "I never thought we could do that."

Upon Reya's statement, Kaori observed her hands. She felt the inner ki resting on the palm. The flames of her experience were now under her control. "If you ever feel pressured, stressed, or tired, it's okay to put your foot down and assert yourselves. You're still young, and have plenty of time for all of this when you become adults. Don't let the pressure and stress turn into anger, though. This is still a business, and we have to give it everything we've got. Don't forget to have fun while doing so."

"Yes," the girls said, and Kaori returned to her seat, unaware of ReRe's agent, Sora, watching on.

Kaori saw Angela smiling at her. "You don't have to smile because Hino-san said so."

"I'm smiling for you."

Kaori smiled in return. "Thank you."

Night fell. Michael, Yuki, Jamal, and Dōm Coquí gathered on a grassy hill overlooking the stage, but Michael walked away from everyone and stood alone by a cherry blossom tree on another hill at the far end of the field. He was looking out at the festival below, where two teenagers—a boy and a girl—teased each other while heading to the stage, parents with children in hand, and an elderly couple sitting on a bench looking up at the sakura trees, hand in hand. He heard footsteps. He turned in its direction, his eyes widened, and spoke under his breath. "You're beautiful."

"Thank you." Kaori approached him, dressed in a blue one-piece skirt with a pink shrug jacket, stockings, and mini-boots. Her hair was in a tail, with a blue flower attached. She stood before him, her arms crossed.

Michael nodded. "I know, I know. I have to apologize to Yuki."

"That's not what I wanted to talk to you about. What you said to Yuki this morning. Not wanting her to be in your world. Is that how you feel about all of us?"

"No."

"Then why did you say that?"

"I don't know. I feel like …" Michael looked Kaori in her eyes. "I feel like I dragged Yuki into my life's problems for no reason. I don't want her caught up in this. She deserves better."

"How do you know she deserves better?"

Michael shrugged. "I don't know. I just have this feeling. I can't describe it."

"Oh, geez …" Kaori rubbed her forehead. "You really

are an idiot. You're not protecting Yuki. You're pushing her away, and you don't realize it." She clenched her arms tight. She remembered the first time she'd arrived in America, standing before Michael at the store, but it wasn't Michael she was looking at, she saw a different person in him.

"She wants to be a part of your life."

Kaori's memory flashed back to her first date with him, dressed nice in a skirt and blouse, but when she opened the door she saw Michael, despite his nice pants and shirt. He escorted her to a movie. As Kaori sat next to Michael, she was disappointed and uninterested in him, as she watched him laugh with the rest of the audience.

"She wants to be a part of your world."

When their date ended, Michael reached out to Kaori, offering to take her to a café. With her head lowered, she gave her answer, "I wanted to date The Impossible Man," and left Michael standing there in silence as she closed the door on him. Her thoughts returned to the present, and she kept her composure despite her pounding heart.

"No, Kaori. I want to be a part of her world. That normal world she is living in. This is not normal."

Kaori's eyes grew wide. She saw the sincerity in his eyes, and she laughed. Then she turned around, her back facing Michael. "She's exactly the type of woman you need in your world…The Impossible Man…Michael…"

Kaori choked up, but regained her composure.

"Kaori?" Michael said, and Kaori looked back at him with twitching eyes and a little smile.

"Yuki has the potential to be the best part of your world,"

she said. "The best part of you." Then she left Michael alone, with the wind brushing the leaves of the sakura tree. She kept her head down, passing by Yuki, who was heading for Michael. "Don't lose him."

Yuki stopped and looked back at Kaori. She could have sworn she saw tears in Kaori's eyes, so she figured Michael had hurt Kaori's feelings and wanted to put him in his place. She marched toward Michael, his hands held out at the petals of the cherry blossom tree raining down on him. The full moonlight, veiled around him, created an aura that she had never seen before. He was looking at the sky, as though he was trying to reach out and grab the stars. His smile made her heart skip. She wanted to forgive him.

"Such a special feeling these petals give to the human heart," said Michael. "Where one story ends, another begins. Such is the way of the sakura tree. A tale spoken with each bloom."

Yuki just stood there, outside the raining petals, and listened.

"I'm sorry. I shouldn't have said that this morning. I care about you. I like you."

Yuki stepped inside the raining petals and took his hand. "I'm sorry... I should respect your reasons for not telling me. Still..."

She tightened her grip on Michael's hand. "You're an idiot!" she continued. "You're oblivious! You're stubborn! You're arrogant! You put yourself in dangerous situations without thinking about me... I mean us... I mean, our friends..."

Yuki calmed herself and took a deep breath. "But you're also nice. You're respectful. You're brave. You're…mine."

"Whoa there. How about we go on a first date?"

Yuki's eyes grew wide, and she laughed. When she finished, she saw Michael focused on the sky. She stood beside him, gazing out at the full moon beyond the falling petals. It made the petals glow. It was so beautiful that Yuki wondered what Michael thought of it, but instead of asking, she just looked at his eyes and saw them twitch as he enjoyed the moment. That was when it hit her. This was who her heart was falling for. This was not The Impossible Man she was standing by. "This is what I want to see. This is the world I want. You…Michael."

Yuki stood in front of Michael and placed her hands on his cheeks. She tilted his head downward and looked deep into his eyes. "I don't care who The Impossible Man is."

Michael said nothing. Fireworks shot out to the sky. He wanted to tell her. Without his powers active, he could not even show her, but he knew if he didn't answer her now, he would lose her.

"Michael?"

"Tomorrow."

"You will tell me about the Rhythm?"

"Yes," Michael said, and she nodded, walking away with her hands behind her back. He watched her stop and turn around. Her smile released the tension within him.

"I'll be ready," said Yuki, and winked.

Michael smiled and followed her, his hands in his pockets. "Who came up with the Rhythm anyway, Yuki?"

"I don't know. You'll have to ask Kaori after her concert."

And the branches of the Sakura tree swayed gently with the wind.

✳ ✳ ✳

At the concert stage, Sasuke had the cameraman lined up in the center. The cinematographer then checked on the camera's positioning. The crowd surrounded the setup. His crew handed pamphlets to concertgoers, and they handed one each to Michael and his friends.

Yuki read the pamphlet. "Oh wow, this is all about Kaori."

The front page was a photo of Kaori in the same concert outfit she was wearing tonight. When Michael opened it, there was a short biography about her career in Japan and then America. The next page had music lyrics for tonight's song, written by Kaori herself. Yuki read it out loud:

"Hometown Hero"

> When I first laid my eyes on you
> You were not the person I met, or wanted to see
> Then the next day I was mad at everyone
> And I lost everything, but there you were right
>   there with me
> No one gave me a second chance
> And you showed me another way
> I worked hard to be where I want
> And it was all thanks to you

You're the greatest friend I'll ever have!

> 'Cause you'll always be my hometown hero
> You're like the rays of the shining sun
> So no matter where we go
> You'll always be my inspiration
> Whoa, I'll never forget you
> You are my lasting memory, yeah

> The day I opened my eyes to you
> I saw an ocean of lights, where ideas had came true
> It was a fantastic world to see
> I never wanted to leave, but I knew what I had to do
> So I reached out to my new idea
> And seized it in my hands
> I succeeded at what I want
> And it was you who believed in me

Thank you for being my friend!

> 'Cause you'll always be my hometown hero
> Who will always be there for me
> No matter where the time goes
> We know where we will be
> Whoa, I'll always be there
> Whenever you call for me, yeah

> I'll rise up when I'm down
> I'll reach out to the stars

I'll never let the light fall
I'll always find that third way!

'Cause you'll always be my hometown hero
And know that the light is within my heart
We will grab the flames that we hold
And never break that bond apart

You will always be my hometown hero
Like the rays of the shining sun
So no matter where we go
You'll always be my inspiration
Whoa, I'll never forget you
You are my lasting memory, yeah

Yuki closed the pamphlet. "That is beautiful."

The lights went dark, and Angela, dressed in a lavender skirt, white blouse, and corsage, stepped on stage with her microphone. "Good evening, ladies and gentlemen! I'm Tangerine, your host for the evening. Before we start, please be sure to donate to the New York City Relief Fund by the promenade. Your donations are deeply appreciated. Now, singing her American debut single, 'Hometown Hero'... Kaori Saito!"

The crowd cheered and raised glow sticks over their heads. Kaori approached center stage, waving to everyone. She looked out at the crowd and had a hard time spotting her friends. A single hand went up: a victory sign, with a thumb extended. She focused and saw Michael. Yuki, Jamal, and Dōm Coquí also raised their hands with the same sign. Kaori smiled and addressed the crowd.

"Hello, Denfair City!" The crowd cheered. "This song is dedicated to a friend … my friend, who taught me that even if people tell me something is impossible, I should do the impossible anyway."

Yuki's eyes grew wide, and she wondered what Kaori meant by that. She turned to Michael, but he was gone. "Michael?"

Michael, meanwhile, had slipped to the front, navigating out of the crowd, and was looking up at Kaori on the stage, listening to her sing. She looked down from the corner of her eye and saw him nod with a smile. Then she focused back on the crowd and he walked away, with hands in his pockets; just like the fateful day he'd bailed her out of trouble back home. Kaori noticed him slip further into the crowd. She smiled, her heart beating, and a thought flashed.

Thank you, The Impossible Man.

After the main concert, everyone except Michael sat on the hill overlooking the stage, where the next phase of the show was setting up. Sasuke was directing his crew to pack up. Kaori and Angela below were talking with ReRe. Each of them carried a bouquet of flowers. Sora arrived and spoke briefly. Kaori and Angela received business cards from her, and they all bowed to each other. Kaori and Angela joined their friends and sat on a picnic blanket. After placing their flowers on the blanket, they received glasses of drinking juice. Dōm Coquí took a bottle of sake. They clinked their glasses together. "Congratulations, Kaori and Angela!"

"These gifts are for your home," Jamal said, and everyone handed Kaori and Angela gifts and the tag read 'Mother and daughter.'

"Uh…" Angela rubbed the back of her head. "We agreed to see each other as sisters. Our age difference is still a little close."

Jamal smiled. "Oh, well, I'll take this back then, Angela."

"No, wait!" Angela took the gift with a smile. She looked at Kaori, and tears fell down her cheeks. "Kaori…"

"Angie-chan, what's wrong?"

"I'm happy." Angela wrapped her arms around Kaori. "I wanted a mom again…and I didn't get one. I thought it was impossible, and then I got you. I don't want you to ever go away."

Kaori hugged Angela, and Ely jumped in.

Dōm Coquí followed. "Poime! Et tu hah ne!"

Kaori pushed Dōm Coquí back without letting Angela go.

As Angela opened each gift, Michael arrived and sat down. "That was a lovely song, Kaori."

"Thank you."

"Where did you go?" said Yuki.

"The bathroom."

"Oh." Yuki faced Michael. "Wait a minute…"

"Okay, I lost you guys in the crowd."

Yuki sighed, and everyone laughed. She turned to the

stage and gasped. Two drums stood perched on towers, laid sideways. It was time for Taiko drumming and folk dancing to conclude the evening.

Michael and his friends made their way and stood with the crowd. They watched women in kimonos form a circle. The drummer pounded away on the drums, and paused as a young woman with a flute arrived. Then the drummers kicked in again, and the atmosphere became serene and poetic. More people gathered, forming the outer circles, and danced. Michael took Yuki's hand and led her into the circle, with Angela and Ely following them.

Kaori watched them smile at each other, and with a nod, she came to terms with her defeat. She felt a hand and thought it was Dōm Coquí. When she raised her fist, she saw it was Jamal. Without saying a word, he took her into the circle. Now only Dōm Coquí watched on, but Kaori grabbed him and pulled him in, bringing a smile to his face. Everyone held hands.

The dance, the final event of the night, marked the end of Festival Weekend.

Until next year.

Episode 18

[~ Spoonful ~]

So the day has come. I'll finally share the truth about myself with Yuki. You can call me a fool all you want, but I cared about her enough that I wanted more for her than what I ever had...after one month of knowing her... okay, okay, I have an idea for a first date. Pizza. She loves pizza. All right, seriously, I believed I was making a right choice for her...for us. We are of different worlds beyond our own imaginations, and I made a critical error. Hmph... and yet, Yuki held my hand and smiled.

I owe her.

She's worth everything.

May 20, 2002

Yuki exited her bathroom and finished tying her robe. Festival Weekend was still fresh in her mind. She was filled with excitement, knowing that Michael would tell her how he got to use the Rhythm. She paused for a second and realized what she'd said under the sakura tree. That she did not care who The Impossible Man was. Looking at the brooch, she had forgotten that he was her first case.

"How do I explain to Supervisor that I want to close the case?" Yuki picked up the brooch, and its jewel blinked. As her finger was going to tap it, she hesitated. Different types of excuses ran through her mind, but she was taking too much time. She tapped the jewel. "Supervisor?"

"Is everything all right, Scarlet Sorceress? You took a while to answer."

"Sorry. I just got out of the shower."

"I regret inconveniencing you. I have finished investigating the hostage you requested."

Yuki hurried to her desk and took a notepad and paper. "I'm ready."

"Her name is Naomi Steel. Age nineteen."

Yuki wrote down the information and waited, and waited. "Is that it?"

"Yes. None of her personal information, including birth date, are on any international records. All we can find is her name and age. No specific country of origin. It's like she disappeared from Earth."

"Maybe she works for an agency and her records have been purged."

"Perhaps, or she's working for the enemy."

"No. I was there…she pleaded for help and had absolutely no control over herself. Her will was bent by the spoon's power."

"Okay, we'll keep that under consideration. As soon as the hostage is cleared, you are to eliminate the spoon immediately."

"Yes, Supervisor. Signing out." Yuki's finger was about to touch the jewel.

"About your primary case, The Impossible Man. Any new developments?"

Yuki stared at the jewel. She could tell the supervisor that Michael was going to reveal himself, but she could not. Then an idea popped into her head. "I will send a formal request to place The Impossible Man case as classified and closed."

"Why?"

Yuki's hands trembled. "Information on The Impossible Man's powers is inconclusive. Unless we take him into custody and physically examine him, which would be a direct violation of our human rights policies."

"I understand. Some of your early reports did not make sense. However, the case will remain suspended until new evidence is presented or he becomes a threat to the world."

"Yes, Supervisor."

"Dismissed."

Yuki tapped the jewel and slumped back in her seat. She took a long, deep breath. Clenching the brooch, she smiled. Knowing that she'd bought Michael time from being investigated by the Order would make it easy for her to tell him the truth about the case.

Michael took a deep breath. The moment had arrived. His apartment was silent and calm. He closed his eyes and focused his mind. He curled his hands into fists and raised them up, feeling rejuvenated. His energy came back to him. He felt ready to make his move and reached out to a card on the table. When he flipped it over, he revealed…

…an ace of hearts.

"Yes!" Michael raised the card over his head. "I did it!"

He moved the ace of hearts aside, on top of a small pile, and moved the ace of spades over a row of cards to an empty spot.

"I can't believe I'm going to win solitaire," Michael said, flipping the card over to reveal the two of diamonds. He moved the cards around, and they fell into place perfectly until he'd created four separate piles, with four aces on top, and won the game. "Yes. I finally won, after twenty-one times."

There was a knock on the door, and Michael stopped for a moment. He turned his head, worried it might be the spoon. So he took a bat leaning against the wall and held it behind his back. "Who is it?"

There was no response. Michael figured it was the spoon and tapped the bat on the heel of his feet, as though he was ready to swing at a pitched ball. He opened the door all the way and swung. "Die, spoon!"

"Michael!" Yuki said, and Michael stopped the bat in mid-air. He stood by the table, the bat behind his back.

"Aey," he said, smiling and waving innocently.

Yuki's heart raced as she watched Michael toss the bat to the living room, pretending she didn't notice. After taking off her sneakers, she marched up to him with her fist raised. "Are you crazy!?" Then she stopped and realized what he had done. "The Rhythm?"

"Almost there." Michael sat down, scanning Yuki in her blouse and skirt, then faced the cards with a smile. "Just have to do a double check before I open the store."

"Solitaire?" Yuki watched Michael flip the cards over again.

"Yeah," Michael said. "It's basic. It took me twenty-one tries to get my first win."

"Really?"

"This is where it all began. Just watch. I'll guide you."

Yuki watched him play, and noticed he started with the king on the bottom of the pile, rather than the ace. She didn't understand, but she watched him get every card order right, unaware of the light bulbs brightening up the room. As she focused on Michael, the spoon floated by the store's door watching the apartment glow bright. Suddenly, Yuki sensed something weird, and envisioned him observing the pack of cards' box. It was like two forces of nature clashing with each other. She felt her memories slowly fading and her fear building up.

Yuki took a deep breath, resisting the pain, keeping her eyes on Michael. Using him as a guide through the struggle, she watched him reach for the box. With the childhood pain and trauma pushed aside but not gone, she could see something in her mind, a world coming into focus through the box. She was reaching for a door, until a force of energy distracted her. Yuki looked at the door where the spoon was, taking a step toward it. "Michael…"

"Get Tsubasa!"

"What?" Yuki turned to Michael's seat, and he wasn't there. The game was over. Four piles lay on the table, with the aces on top, and the box rested before them. Yuki stepped back. Her vision blurred, and her memories of Michael and the box were wiped out. She never saw him finish the game. Realizing the spoon had interfered with her chance of knowing Michael, she turned to the apartment door with shaking fists. "Damn spoon."

"Katsuragi!" yelled Michael from the hallway. A loud thud and tumble blared outside. "You're not…going anywhere spoon!"

Yuki ran outside, and heard a loud thud again from above. She realized the spoon was disrupting Michael's Rhythm. He was falling on his face. When she reached the fourth floor, she saw the door closing with Michael holding the spoon, with a few bruises on his face. She noticed a red light around his body, his arm shaking with the spoon in hand. Yuki reached for the doorknob so she could get inside, but was too late. When she grabbed the knob, electricity surrounded her body. With a scream, she stumbled back. Her feet slipped on the top step. As Yuki fell back, she felt a pair of arms catch her and push her back up. When Yuki opened her eyes, she saw Dōm Coquí looking at her.

"Daiben?"

Everyone gathered around on the fourth floor.

"Okay? Y—yes. I'm okay." Yuki realized that she was in the arms of a frog, and was not scared. "Thank you, Coquí."

"What happened, Yuki?" said Kaori.

"I think Michael got the spoon and brought it to Katsuragi-san. He was glowing red."

Kaori turned to the door. "So he got his Rhythm back?"

"I...think so? He was falling on the floor a lot."

"Well, what did he do before he got the spoon?" said Jamal.

"He played solitaire."

"How many times did he win?"

"Once, I think. He said it took him twenty-one times to win his first game."

"Then he's still not back at full strength."

Kaori turned to Jamal. "But his Rhythm is working."

"You may be right. He wouldn't have gotten this far with that spoon."

"So is he safe, Jamal?" said Yuki. "Katsuragi-san locked me out."

"It's okay, Yuki," Jamal said. "Now that he got the spoon to Katsuragi, there's nothing more we can do. Let's get ready to open the store. I'm going to get dressed."

Kaori waved Angela to move on. "Come, Angela, we have to get ready for the show this morning."

"Okay." Angela walked downstairs alongside Dōm Coquí.

As everyone left, Yuki stood before the door, clenching her brooch, ready to change if necessary. Jamal reached out to get her, but Kaori pulled him away to leave her alone.

❋ ❋ ❋

Meanwhile, inside Shinichiro's apartment, Michael stood inside the spotlight, struggling to keep the spoon in his hand. Frost built up around his arm, resisting the red glow of the spoon. As the song of the humming choir got their attention, they watched Shinichiro land before them. He took out his favorite pipe to smoke. "I am glad you both have arrived…finally."

"Excuse me." Michael presented the spoon. "I had traffic problems."

"I don't have time to play," said Shinichiro, and lit his pipe. "The spoon, please…"

Michael handed Shinichiro the spoon and dropped to the ground, nursing his cold arm. His spotlight warmed up, melting the frost from his arm. Michael was able to move his fingers. "The fire readers at the shrine told us yesterday that there was something more to the spoon and it could shape my destiny."

"Interesting," Shinichiro said, struggling to keep the spoon from escaping.

"The spoon has a hostage; can you get her out now?"

"I see. First an analysis on what this is. I don't want to

risk harming the victim." He saw the Japanese inscription on the utensil: "spoon." He spread his hands apart, creating an orb of light around it. The spoon glowed red and the reader concentrated. He heard a faint voice, female, with a slow moan. He dropped the spoon, his face flushed with sweat.

"Well?" Michael said, and Shinichiro took a rag and wiped his forehead.

"This spoon is horny."

Michael stood there with a blank face, which transformed slowly into an angry frown. He raised his fists.

"I'm afraid this spoon is jealous," said Shinichiro.

"What?" Michael stood over Shinichiro, his fist short of striking the old man's forehead. "Jealous? Of who?"

"I don't know." Shinichiro took a puff and blew smoke in Michael's face. The rancid scent pushed Michael back into his own spotlight. "That spoon is too strange…and horny. You must get rid of it."

"How?" Michael said, sitting on the floor. "It always comes back. Just like that episode title said before."

"Focus, The Impossible Man." Shinichiro pointed out into the darkness. "Fortunately, I have no walls in my apartment."

"Really?" Michael said, looking around in the darkness. "I thought you were a vampire."

"This is no time to joke around. The bones tell me…"

"I thought the bones tell you nothing."

"They always tell me something."

"Did they tell you this?" Michael stuck his middle finger

into Shinichiro's face. Suddenly, from outside, Yuki saw the door open, and Michael flew by screaming. He rolled down the stairs and slammed into the wall, upside down. His eyes spun in a spiral, and Yuki ran downstairs.

Angela exited her apartment to see what had happened. "Are you okay?"

Yuki knelt next to Michael and laid him on the floor. They all looked at the fourth floor. The door closed slowly.

"I'll see what I can do to free the hostage and get rid of the spoon for you, shrimp. Until then, keep your guard up." The door closed.

"Damn you, Kats." Michael's head bumped the floor. He looked at the ceiling, and Angela and Yuki giggled.

They helped him to his feet, and Yuki spoke. "So what did Katsuragi-san say?"

Kaori and Ely exited the apartment and listened to Michael.

"He said the spoon was weird, horny, and jealous."

Kaori spoke. "Is he serious?"

"He was," Michael said, walking past Kaori, as Jamal and Dōm Coquí arrived. "It doesn't matter. He's got the spoon, and he's dealing with it now."

"Everyone," Yuki announced, "I spoke with my supervisor this morning, and she said the hostage's name is Naomi Steel and she's age nineteen. That's all the information they have."

Jamal spoke. "Are you sure?"

"Yes." Yuki nodded. "Sorry."

Michael nodded. "Well, it's something. Thanks, Yuki."

Shinichiro finished analyzing the spoon in the spotlight. His eyes grew wide and looked up. "It can't be. That is where the spoon came from? This spirit beyond the stars?"

He lowered his head and focused his energy. Pressing his index fingers together, he created a sphere of light around the spoon. It glowed red, resisting his power. He stretched his fingers outward, forcing the spoon to fire two beams of light from its eyes. A portal opened and he saw Naomi Steel floating in a fetal position. "You will be free."

Shinichiro pressed his palms together creating a beam of white light. It shot into the portal surrounding Naomi inside. He gently moved her towards him when red electricity grabbed the white light. "What?"

A tug of war began. His hands smoldered, and his energy was pushed to its limits.

Walking downstairs, Michael told everyone what Shinichiro had said from the beginning. They reached the front door and Michael took out the store keys, ready to open for the day. When he grabbed the doorknob, a flash of red light pushed him back. He stumbled into Kaori, and they both fell over. Michael felt his hand squishing her body, and his forehead turned blue. His hand was on her belly and nowhere else.

"You got lucky this time," Kaori said, and pushed Michael off.

Jamal tapped his finger on the door, feeling the shock of the red flash bouncing his hand back.

"I feel a strange power," Yuki said.

Ely growled, and Dōm Coquí shivered out of animal instinct.

Jamal spoke. "This is some crazy power I'm sensing."

Kaori nodded. "I agree."

Michael entered his apartment, with everyone following him, and tried to open the door to the store. Again he bounced back and slammed into the wall. Michael nursed his head, and Yuki checked on him.

Jamal crossed his arms. "What's going on here?"

"It's the spoon."

"What does it want with you, I-Man?"

"I don't know!"

"Katsuragi-san said that it was jealous," said Kaori. "Jealous of who?"

Michael pointed at Yuki, Kaori, and Angela. "Maybe all three of you. All you've done is fight over me, and … and that pet too."

Yuki, Kaori, and Angela went silent, even Ely. They all looked at each other and blushed.

As Michael stood up and opened his mouth to say something, the apartment vibrated, and dust fell from the ceiling. "Kats!"

Everyone ran to the fourth floor and found Michael in front of the door, lying face down. He lifted his body up and pounded the floor. "This is getting annoying!"

Then he stood up and reached for the door, but Yuki wrapped her arms around his waist. She buried her face in his back. "Don't! You're hurting yourself. The spoon is trying to get you to use up your energy."

Kaori, meanwhile, sat on the stairs, catching her breath. "Yeah. Well, the spoon is making us waste energy running up and down the stairs."

Michael took a deep breath and calmed down. He took Yuki's arms and moved them off his body. He turned around and nodded to her. "Okay, Yuki."

Angela hugged Ely. "The spoon is still shutting down your Rhythm."

"Exactly how is it doing that?" said Jamal, leaning on the wall.

"It's not ki energy," said Kaori.

"Or magic," said Yuki.

Jamal tapped the doorknob to Shinichiro's apartment to see if it bounced him back. "So the spoon creates some kind of… Anti-Rhythm Field to shut Michael down?"

Angela lifted up Michael's hand. "An A.R. Field."

Jamal opened the door as Dōm Coquí said, "Reng. Op fro un Yuki, Kaori, ta Jamal?"

Angela nodded. "That's true. Why don't your ki energy and magical powers shut down like his?"

No one had an answer.

"We'll ask Kats." Jamal peeked inside Shinichiro's apartment. "Hey! Are you okay?"

"Barely," Shinichiro said, lifting himself from the ground, rubbing his arm, and shaking his head. "I had the hostage in my sights, I was pulling her out but the spoon pushed back and escaped. It was more powerful than I realized. Come in. Except the shrimp."

"Why not?" Michael said.

"Because…"

"Katsuragi-san, this is serious," said Yuki.

"Hmph…there's this field of energy the spoon left behind that will shut the shrimp down."

Yuki placed her hand gently on Michael's shoulder. "Wait here and save your energy."

"Fine." Michael watched the door close.

✳ ✳ ✳

Inside the apartment, Shinichiro took a puff of his pipe, and everyone sat in their own spotlight. The old monk revealed his hands, charred and blistered from his fight with the spoon. Everyone jerked their heads back, grossed out by the injury, but Shinichiro showed no pain.

Yuki stood up, but Shinichiro waved her to sit. "Are you sure you're okay? I can use my spell." she said.

"Thank you, but I'm fine," he said, "though I'm now out of the battle. All of my energy drained out and I won't recover in time. As for the hostage…"

Yuki interrupted. "Her name is Naomi Steel."

"Naomi Steel…she appears to be safe, but from what I could tell she's in some sort of stasis created by the spoon's energy."

Yuki gripped her skirt. "Why won't you let Michael inside? He's not safe out there."

"He'll be fine." Shinichiro took another puff. "The spoon has set up some kind of field to trap us in this building."

"The A.R. Field," said Angela.

"A.R. Field?" Shinichiro said, taking out his cup and dice.

"It's some strange energy that is stopping him from using his powers."

"Interesting. Then this new force of energy shall be called Anti-Rhythm."

Angela smiled. "I've already made that word up."

"Oh."

Yuki waved to Shinichiro to refocus the conversation. "Katsuragi-san, what did you mean by the spoon being jealous?"

"Ah," Shinichiro said, slapping the dice into the cup and slamming it onto the ground. "Well, I heard a woman moan from within the spoon. At first I thought it was the hostage, but actually it's some kind of imprisoned spirit, tethered within the spoon."

Shinichiro pulled the cup up and revealed a pair of sixes. He sensed a positive glow and looked up to everyone. "The bones say that you all must be true to Michael. Be honest about your feelings toward him. That's how he'll beat the spoon."

Angela raised her hand. "With the power of love and justice?"

"No, with the power of the strange and surreal." Shinichiro faced Yuki. "Your heart for Michael will be tested."

"My heart?"

"Yes. Your magical powers will help guide the way." Shinichiro turned to Jamal. "Master of the Flow, do not hesitate to act. Your ability will prove invaluable."

"Oh, the drama," Jamal said, rolling his eyes.

"Kaori, your samurai and pop idol skills will be an asset."

"Seriously?"

"Angela, your friendship will press him forward."

"I'm ready." Angela raised her fists, brimming with confidence.

Kaori turned to Angela. "You're not coming!"

"Oh, come on!"

Shinichiro cleared his throat to quiet them. "She goes. There is no way to avoid it."

"Hooray!" cried Angela.

Shinichiro turned his attention to Ely. "You eat animals."

Ely nodded. "Chupa. Chupa."

"I see." Shinichiro turned to Dōm Coquí, who shivered in fright.

"Dōm Coquí, you're…you're…" Shinichiro tilted his head, and Dōm Coquí leaned closer, absorbing his advice. "Well, you're a frog."

Dōm Coquí fell over, and Shinichiro floated into the air.

"Well, I must go now." The sound of a humming choir cued his exit. Shinichiro floated into the darkness, leaving everyone behind. "Thank you for coming to have yourselves read…read…read…"

"Wait!" said Yuki. "Aren't you going to help us in some way?"

"No…no…no…"

✳ ✳ ✳

Outside, Michael—sitting on the stairs—turned around and saw the confused faces of his friends. He got up to his feet, waiting to hear what Shinichiro had told them, but they were just silent. Michael crossed his arms. "Useless info?"

"Yes," everyone said together, and walked down the stairs.

Kaori approached Michael. "Actually he said there is some kind of imprisoned spirit with the hostage. It is tethered within the spoon."

Jamal spoke. "Maybe a possession? A curse?"

Kaori nodded. "It is a possibility."

"Did the spoon show up, Michael?" asked Yuki.

"No. It's been quiet out here." Michael led everyone downstairs. "We have to figure out what this spoon is, or we'll be trapped here forever."

Angela stopped. "The game."

Kaori stopped at the bottom step. "Angie-chan, what is it?"

"The game. Treasure Quest. Naomi Steel was with the spoon. Did you sense any strange energy from her?"

Kaori rubbed her chin. "Come to think of it, Naomi's energy was not like ours."

"Probably the spoon's energy? Angela said.

Yuki spoke. "No, it would have been obvious."

Kaori turned to Yuki and Angela. "This was unique."

"She could be part of a secret agency," Yuki said, and everyone turned to her.

"Does she know you Michael?" Kaori crossed her arms and turned to him.

"I've never heard that name before."

"Someone has to know you."

Jamal placed his hand under his chin. "Hide the spoon."

Yuki turned to Jamal. "That message."

"Er weh li toh dest?"

"You have a theory, D.C.?"

Dōm Coquí nodded. "Sa che Naomi Steel du op weh."

"You think Naomi Steel might have been investigating the spoon?"

"Syi."

Kaori spoke. "Who would send you guys the spoon and leave a message?"

"Wolfgang, maybe?" said Michael.

Yuki shook her head. "That makes no sense."

"Right, he was hunting that spoon." Kaori sat down on the stairs. "That spoon has something he wants."

Michael leaned on the wall. "Maybe Naomi Steel?"

Yuki turned to Michael. "If that was the case, he could have told us he was rescuing her and we could have helped."

Kaori crossed her arms. "Unless she's his partner and had information."

Jamal rubbed his head. "Theories. That's all we have. There's no evidence or clues about this."

Michael looked at Yuki. "Did your supervisor or the Order have any other information on the spoon itself?"

"No." Yuki shook her head. "And my orders are to destroy it after freeing Naomi Steel."

Michael sighed. "The spoon is waiting for something, and we don't know what it is. I'm going back to my apartment to relax."

"Michael!" said Yuki and Kaori.

They faced each other, and stepped back from each other.

Michael walked downstairs, leaving everyone behind. "It's best if you all get ready for the spoon. We're not exactly prepared."

✳ ✳ ✳

Michael entered his apartment, glad to at least have a few moments of rest. Lying on the couch, he saw his pile of unopened mail. He shuffled them around and noticed the unopened letter from his mom, dating back to March 25th. "Oh, I mixed this up by accident, or was I annoyed? Hmm, this was two weeks before Yuki arrived. Heh…"

Michael thought about Yuki over the past two months. He smiled. He chuckled. He laughed. Then he stood up. "If I'm waiting for the spoon's next move, I may as well see Yuki."

There was an explosion, and his ceiling shook. "The spoon…"

Outside his apartment, from out of nowhere, Michael fell on his face. He could hear Yuki reciting her speech through the closed door above. "The Scarlet Sorceress."

He picked himself up, and the apartment's front door opened. He felt the breeze from outside, and the sun blinded his eyes. When the door closed, Michael's forehead turned blue. Standing before him was Wolfgang.

"I've come for my spoon."

"You can have it." Michael heard Jamal and Dōm Coquí knocking on Yuki's door. "After Scarlet Sorceress frees the hostage inside it."

"Hostage?"

"Naomi Steel." Michael raised his fists up. "You know her?"

"No. Now stop playing games with me…and dance!" Wolfgang threw a punch, but Michael was not there to receive it. Instead he appeared flat on his face, sliding down the stairs. Yuki's scream got Michael to lift his head and crawl up, but Wolfgang caught his leg and pulled him back down.

"Michael! Help! The spoon is too powerful!"

Michael turned around, rammed his foot into Wolfgang's stomach, and watched Wolfgang stumble back. Michael ran up the stairs, and Kaori jumped down the stairs with Seizon in hand. Michael rammed his shoulder into the door, but the red barrier bounced him back.

"The Impossible Man!" Wolfgang charged up the stairs, and Dōm Coquí leapt at him. Wolfgang stopped. He braced himself, and Dōm Coquí's legs bounced off his muscles. He barely felt anything and watched Dōm Coquí fly backwards, over Kaori and Jamal landing on his back. He smiled. "Next."

Jamal approached Wolfgang. As he did, Kaori struck the door with her sword, but she bounced back. "Are you kidding me? Seizon should have ripped the spell out of existence."

As Michael bounced off the door, Jamal opened the palm of his right hand and gathered the Flow.

"This palm glows...from the mighty Flow!" Jamal took two steps forward and his legs lifted off the ground. He looked like a volleyball player, ready to slap the ball over the net. Instead, his target was Wolfgang. "Streaming—"

Wolfgang palmed Jamal's face and held him up in the air, breaking Jamal's concentration. "Tell me what you think about the name of my attack..."

He turned to the wall and rammed Jamal's head into it. "Head Slam!"

A crater formed on the wall, and Jamal slid down the stairs, holding his head.

"Jamal!" Kaori watched him rolling to the bottom and aimed Seizon at Wolfgang.

"Well, the name doesn't sound good," Wolfgang said, walking up the stairs toward Kaori. "Oh well."

"Electric Mayhem!" Yuki yelled behind the door.

Wolfgang's eyes shifted to the door, behind which he heard crashes and explosions. From the corner of his eye, he saw Kaori swinging Seizon at him. He slapped his hands on the wooden blade of the sword, stopping Kaori's attack. Wolfgang rammed his fist into Kaori's stomach, creating a bulge in her back. As she lurched over to her knees, Wolfgang turned to Michael and watched him lying facedown on the floor. Wolfgang smiled at his victory, but Michael lifted himself up and raised his fists, ready to fight back. As they stepped forward, ready to punch, Yuki screamed out loud and a green light shined through the crack of the door.

Everything stopped, and the apartment became silent. The door opened on its own and Michael, out of nowhere, kicked his way through. He saw Yuki lying on the ground with Tsubasa on top of her. "Yuki!"

Michael moved Tsubasa and rolled Yuki on her back. Her eyes were red and pupil-less, her skin pale. He heard Wolfgang's footsteps approaching, but Michael didn't care what Wolfgang did to him. He just focused on waking Yuki out of her trance. He saw the spoon floating before him. It flew next to him and nuzzled his arm. Michael saw it scooped up by Wolfgang, only to disappear from Wolfgang's hand and return to Michael.

"I get it now," said Wolfgang. "It likes you."

"It likes me?" Michael brought the utensil to his face. "I hate you! Stupid spoon!"

Michael threw the spoon into the wall. It clanged onto the floor. He embraced Yuki and rubbed her soft, silver and black hair, hoping she would snap out of the trance. Then he planted one foot on the floor and used his legs as an incline for Yuki. He spread out his fingers and aimed for her heart. As frost built up over his hair, he rammed his palm to Yuki's chest. A red barrier bounced his hand back. He saw the spoon glowing red, floating before him. He growled and prepared to ram his palm into her again, but Yuki's body, and Tsubasa, floated into the air and disappeared. They reappeared before Wolfgang, and he held his arms out to carry her and the staff.

The spoon floated above Wolfgang and Yuki. It created a pillar of light, and Michael fell on his face. Wolfgang smiled at Michael. He saw the despair in his eyes, reaching out for them.

"Give me Yuki," Michael said. "And free Naomi Steel!"

"Only if you find us," Wolfgang said, kicking Michael's hand aside. "And this time, I won't tell you where we're going."

Michael tried again, but he fell flat on his face once more. He looked up, and Wolfgang disappeared with Yuki and Tsubasa. The spoon looked down.

"If you want her," the spoon said with a mature adult female voice, "come and get her."

"You can talk?"

"Of course I can talk, The Idiot Man."

"But how?"

"Internet." The spoon vanished, and the pillar of light disappeared.

Michael stood up, and as he did, felt his bones snap back in place. The pain did not faze him. As he watched everyone stand up, nursing their injuries, Michael stood before Shinichiro's door from out of nowhere and heard the footsteps of his friends coming up.

"I may have used up my one entry per day, but I'm getting in whether you like it or not." Michael grabbed the doorknob and soon felt electricity flow through his body.

As everyone arrived, he gritted his teeth and turned the

knob. A strange wave glazed over the door, and his feet slid back. Michael pulled the door open and laughed like a maniac. "Katsuragi!"

The world turned black.

When Michael opened his eyes, he found himself floating in a spotlight. He flailed his frozen arms and legs in a panic, thinking he was going to fall down, but he was okay. He saw his friends floating in spotlights, too, except for Angela and Ely, who were updating Shinichiro on the situation. He noticed most of his injuries were gone, and the same thing had happened to Kaori, Jamal, and Dōm Coquí.

"So you're finally awake, shrimp," Shinichiro said, and smoked his pipe. "Good. Now I can tell you where to find Yuki and Naomi."

Episode 19

[~ Man and Myth ~]

Big battles. Lots of stories have them. Sometimes they are one on one fights. Other times, a group against another group. It can even be bigger with war scenes. These are the moments that people wait for. Man to man. Mano a mano. Cajones contra cajones. Big explosions. Cool stunt fighting. The hero takes on the villain. When a mortal man meets an immortal myth. We scream. We cheer. We ooh and aah when someone does something awesome.

Fight on!

May 20, 2002

Kaori, Jamal, and Dōm Coquí's feet touched the ground in their spotlights, and Angela hugged Ely. Their injuries were healed, but Michael stayed afloat in his spotlight. The ice covering his arms and legs continued to melt. They paid attention to Shinichiro slapping his dice into the cup and slamming it into the ground. Everyone leaned forward. The dice had rolled a seven.

"You're all going to win," Shinichiro said, and everyone lost their balance.

"Nice way to ruin the story," Michael said.

"Well, it's quite obvious." Shinichiro took a puff of his pipe. "What makes it compelling is how you're going to win. Each of you is going to be tested."

"With what?" Michael said, as his arms were freed from the ice. "Math? Spelling?"

"A driver's test." Shinichiro picked up his dice and cup. "You'll all be tested by this spoon. Your friendship, love, and courage."

"Sounds like a magical girl anime, Kats." Michael stretched his shirt, emulating a skirt. "Look at me, I'm the all-powerful magical girl, looking to conquer love and vanquish evil."

Jamal punched Michael in the back of his head. He crossed his arms and watched Michael spin around in the spotlight.

Shinichiro smoked the pipe. "Can we be serious for a moment?"

"Yes!" Everyone covered Michael's mouth before he said another word.

Shinichiro spoke. "The spoon has some sort of spirit inside that is in love with Michael. It obviously was jealous of Yuki."

Jamal spoke. "Who's spirit?"

"I don't know, but it definitely was imprisoned there for a reason." Shinichiro puffed his pipe. "This spoon is very powerful. It has been with all of you long enough to know your weaknesses. The spoon is dangerous, and you may get hurt very badly. Maybe even die...horribly. Even unimaginably. Help Michael if you must, but if you all choose not to, there is no shame. You'll just deserve a spanking. Go now and save your friend."

Everyone just stared at Shinichiro. They turned to Michael, expecting a snappy comeback to counter what they'd just heard, but even he did not have anything to say.

Dōm Coquí spoke. "Eban Michael, sa ku Kats zeh na."

Angela nodded. "Yeah, D.C., we're in trouble."

"Let's go," said Jamal.

As everyone got up and left the apartment, Michael stayed behind, floating in the spotlight. His legs were finally freed from the ice, so he was face to face with Shinichiro. He saw only Shinichiro's straight face, and he let out a big, cheesy smile. Then Michael screamed, flying out of the door and down the stairs. He landed on the third floor, bouncing on his back. The door closed slowly.

"The spotlight is not an amusement ride."

Michael sat up and found himself surrounded by his friends. They smiled at him, but he could not return it. For a moment, he thought he saw Yuki standing amongst them.

Michael stood up, and everyone stepped back. He smirked. With a nod, he walked down the stairs. Everyone followed him out of the apartment building to rescue Yuki. Out of nowhere, Michael was at Shinichiro's door, and pounded on it. "You forgot to tell us where they are!"

"Oops…"

✳ ✳ ✳

Jamal, Kaori, Angela, and Ely all waited outside the Metalworks District as Michael and Dōm Coquí arrived. Dōm Coquí carried a bookbag. The side of the bag bulged a bit, making everyone step back.

Jamal pointed at the bag. "What's in the bag?"

Michael smiled. "A plan."

"Are you going to share it with us?"

"No. It's a precaution." He twiddled his fingers feeling the tense muscles to make sure they can move. "What I did to get this, I don't want the spoon to extract that info from us."

"Coquí?"

Dōm Coquí shrugged. "Ih nah ney."

"He doesn't know," said Angela.

Kaori rested Seizon on her shoulder. "We're wasting time. Move."

They entered the junkyard and walked past Clipperstein, sitting in its makeshift throne made out of garbage. Everyone was awed at the giant robot's size.

Angela and Ely placed their hands on its metal foot. "I can't believe that the Woobles actually piloted this machine."

Michael walked past her. "Believe me, Angela, it's a miracle they didn't destroy the city."

"We'll admire it later," said Jamal. "We should hurry. The energy is off the charts here."

Kaori closed her eyes. "I sense a high power energy nearby." She led everyone around a mountain of twisted metal and broken parts. They saw five buildings marked by numbers from one to five. Everyone looked at the buildings.

Michael crossed his arms. "Great, we'll have to search each one."

"Michael, it's—" Kaori turned to him, and he and Dōm Coquí were gone.

"The end is here, Wolfgang!" Michael said through an open door in building number one with Dōm Coquí. He got no response. He looked; there was no one inside. Michael and Dōm Coquí ran past everyone and entered building number two. "You're going down, Wolfgang!"

Dōm Coquí posed. "Ya haa!"

Kaori rolled her eyes, led the others to building number four, and ignored Michael and Dōm Coquí opening the door to building three. "Your license to hunt is revoked!"

It was quiet inside. Michael and Dōm Coquí returned to their friends and saw them enter building number four, marked 'Smelting Area.'

"We haven't tried this building yet. Let's go."

"Syi."

✳ ✳ ✳

Inside the Smelting Area, Wolfgang stood before Yuki in her Scarlet Sorceress costume, floating in the air in a deep sleep. Tsubasa was above her body, and the spoon floated above them, shining a white light. It looked like a fountain of water flowing to the floor.

Wolfgang reached out to the light, and with a touch, it rippled like water. He pulled his fingers back and felt the pain. "When will I get my wish, spoon?! My benefactors have already sent assassins after me for failing to retrieve you."

"Soon."

"No. Now! I went out of my way to catch you. Now I want you to do as I say." Wolfgang got no response from the spoon. He curled his hand into a fist and raised it up. "Do you hear me!? I suffered to get you into my hands. I am owed a reward."

There was nothing but silence. His teeth tightened with a growl. He turned around and walked away.

"Yes, I know," said the spoon in her booming voice. "You want what I can give you."

"Yes." Wolfgang looked back from the corner of his eye. "I want my wish, you little genie."

"Genie? Hmph… all you have to do to make your wish come true is to sacrifice a human."

"Sacrifice?" Wolfgang jerked his head back. "You mean, sacrifice kill?"

"No. I mean a sacrifice fly ball."

"You sound like The Impossible Man."

"Don't say that name!" The spoon glowed red. "When

I convert this girl's positive magical energy to negative energy, all you have to do is kiss her. You will complete us, and we will grant your wish. Her soul will be sacrificed, and I will become her."

"Ah, excellent. First I will ensure my life is saved from the assassins, then—"

"I ran out of awesome heroic entrance quotes to say!" Michael said from out of nowhere, standing in front of the crates with his fist aimed at Wolfgang.

"The Impossible Man!" Wolfgang said, and Michael's friends stepped out of the shadows of the crates and gathered behind him. "And the Anime and Manga Shop employees!"

Dōm Coquí dropped his bookbag, took out a remote control, and pressed a red button. A small explosion burst out from behind the crates, creating a moment for their heroic arrival. The explosion went out of control and collapsed the wall behind them, exposing the outside. As the plume of dust rose in the air, everyone but Michael and Dōm Coquí rolled their eyes.

"You used too much, Coquí," said Michael.

"Bomen ne." Dōm Coquí smiled.

"Impressive entrance, gaijin," said a familiar voice from behind a pair of crates near Wolfgang. "But we have one better."

Mr. Tanaka stepped out of the shadows with Sam, Barry, and the giant alligator, who now looked human, like Dōm Coquí. The alligator took out its own remote control and pressed a red button, creating a moment for their own villainous arrival. The background exploded, and Wolfgang and his new allies took a pose as the explosion collapsed the wall behind them, just as Michael and his friends had done.

As the plume of dust rose in the air, Michael shook his fist. "It's the same thing! What's the difference?!"

"We're posing," Mr. Tanaka said, and Michael and his friends lost their balance.

The spoon spoke. "Idiots!"

Everyone looked at the spoon and saw Yuki in the air asleep.

"Yuki!" Michael said, taking a few steps forward, but Wolfgang stood in front of him.

"You thought I would be all alone, eh?" Wolfgang waved his arm over to his allies and introduced them. "Say hello to our benevolent team."

"Barry." He stood before Angela and Ely, his Trap-a-zoid in hand.

"I know who you are," said Angela.

"Sam." He stood before Jamal, with glowing ki around his body.

"No, really?" replied Jamal.

"Al." The gator spoke with a child-like female voice to Dōm Coquí, towering over his tiny body.

"Ronto?"

"Tanaka," he said to Kaori.

"Should I care?" she said.

"Wolfgang," he said to Michael.

"And?" said Michael.

"We are—" Wolfgang and his allies posed again. "The Amalgamated Union of Malicious Malcontents!"

"A.U.M.M.!" said the team together.

Michael smirked. "How much do you guys pay each other at night?"

His friends giggled.

Wolfgang growled. "You think this is funny!?" He pointed at Yuki and the spoon behind him. "Soon your precious girlfriend will be consumed by the spoon's energy, and I will have my wish!"

"I've been telling you this for the past two months," Michael said, taking a deep breath to control his anger. "You can have the damn spoon! Just give me Yuki back, free Naomi Steel, and take the damn spoon! Damn it!"

The spoon spoke. "You will have Yuki back. Only it will be me in her body."

"Why?" said Michael, looking up.

"I have my reasons." The spoon levitated all of the crates surrounding everyone, then threw the crates away, creating a large circular space.

Mr. Tanaka spoke. "Watch the crates spoon! The yakuza will cut my fingers if you break those crates!"

"You'll live?" The spoon looked at Michael. "Rough him up, boys. He can't use his Rhythm."

"Be careful, Michael," said Angela, "the A.R. Field is up."

Michael smirked and looked back at his friends, making the victory sign with his thumb extended. He stared at the spoon's eyes, and everyone remained quiet. Then he approached Yuki, who was sleeping in the beam of light. He thought she looked pretty with that restful face. As the spoon looked back, he realized the situation right now was not in his control. With a deep breath, he curled his hands into fists and closed his eyes. Out of nowhere, he laid face down on the floor and groaned in pain. "Ref…"

The referee from the wrestling match arrived from the collapsed wall. "Coming." He approached the center of the circular area, and Michael stood up to his feet. He walked back to his friends.

"Are you okay, I-Man?" said Angela.

"Yeah," Michael said, and Kaori lifted his head and checked on his nose.

"I don't know what you have planned, I-Man," Kaori said, "but we got your back."

Michael turned to Jamal and Dōm Coquí, and they both nodded. "Keep that bookbag close."

Wolfgang marched toward the referee. "What's the meaning of this, The Impossible Man?"

Michael appeared out of nowhere walking alongside Wolfgang toward the referee. "I overheard the spoon say all you had to do was kiss Yuki. Right?"

Wolfgang raised his left eyebrow. "R…right?"

"So it makes no difference if we save Yuki now, or after she absorbs the manipulated energy." Michael and Wolfgang stood before the referee. "Therefore, I propose we battle each other in a non-messy tournament-style combat."

"Wait! Are you crazy?!" said Jamal.

"It worked in anime."

Jamal approached Michael and pulled his collar. "This isn't anime! This is real life! Yuki and Naomi are up there. We have to save them from the spoon."

The spoon spoke. "Naomi Steel?"

Everyone listened to the spoon.

"Yeah, she's out of my way. You will all be, too." The spoon glowed red. "I won't be going back into that box unit on Containment Station 9 in Andromeda."

Angela covered her mouth, Kaori raised Seizon, and Dōm Coquí spoke to Michael. "Et nah vo berty sabisode."

"I know! The fighting won't last thirty episodes, though." Michael smirked at Jamal, looking at his pulled collar.

Staring into Michael's eyes, Jamal understood why he kept quiet. He hated that Michael was doing this again. Twisting the world around—but this time it was different. Two lives were at stake, and the spoon had control of the situation. Now that Michael had set up this crazy plan of his, he realized he had to trust The Impossible Man. Jamal's eyes widened, and he removed his hands from Michael's shirt. "Okay. Let's do this."

Jamal patted Michael's shoulder, and they turned to Wolfgang. "Here are the rules". Michael said. "Each person fights once and only once. Not twice, not zero times. One time and one time only. The outcome does not matter. The first to three wins claims Yuki."

Kaori spoke. "I-Man, are you sure about this rule?"

"Yeah, I finally read my mother's letter about Yuki before we left. It turned out that I had it since March 25th, two weeks before Yuki arrived, explaining everything that happened there. My mother couldn't explain it over the phone because she didn't want to rack up a phone bill in the hotel. It was an exhaustive letter."

As the bookbag shook, Wolfgang nodded. "I agree to your terms, The Impossible Man."

The spoon floated to the edge of the light. "You fool!"

Michael fell on his face, just short of reaching Yuki. The spoon moved back into its original position. "I almost lost her," it growled. "He made me lose my temper and my concentration."

The spoon watched Michael return to his friends.

"I see. He wanted me to be angry and lose my concentration. This charade is to buy time so I could finish possessing her body. Once I'm finished, he could jump in and kiss her. If I move away from her, he would free her, and if I teleport somewhere else, he'll have access to his Rhythm and find us easily. I have no choice but to stay put and shut down his Rhythm. He can't beat Wolfgang without it. Which means I have to rely on these fools for victory, just like he is relying on his friends to win, but I don't have to honor it in the end, or perhaps that's what he is expecting, but then again, he could risk everything and just take her right now. I don't get it."

The spoon vibrated. "Oh my… he really is impossible. I can't figure him out."

Wolfgang pointed at Michael. "The Impossible Man, as captains we'll go last."

"Save the best for last, eh?"

"Indeed." Wolfgang stood before his comrades and crossed his arms. "So which one of you will go first?"

✳ ✳ ✳

Al stepped forward. She did not say a single word. She walked past the referee and pointed to Dōm Coquí. With her mutant finger, Al twitched it to call him over. She waited with her arms crossed.

Michael whistled and kicked Dōm Coquí in the butt to move forward.

"Nio!" Dōm Coquí said struggling to stay away.

"You'll be fine," Michael said. "Just jump on her head."

Dōm Coquí faced Michael, and Al's hand clamped down on his head. His feet left the ground, and he flailed his arms. Dōm Coquí cried for help, and he was planted at the center of the circle. He perched like a frog, and the referee raised his hand up.

"Al, teh chu reter wari?"

Al replied in her child-like voice, "Lu weh bi po qwe."

Everyone turned to Michael and Angela, and as Dōm Coquí and Al kept talking, the two humans translated what they said.

Angela spoke for Dōm Coquí: "Al, you're the gator from the sewers?"

Then Michael spoke for Al: "Yes. I am the one who fell in the chasm."

"How did you survive? I saw you fall down with The Impossible Man."

"I landed in a river of toxic sludge that spilled outside the city and emerged like this. It shrunk me down to this size. Strange, normally you grow big when you jump in."

"How did you learn to talk?"

"Internet."

"Why do you want to hurt me?" Angela and Dōm Coquí pointed at Michael. "It's The Impossible Man that sent you down there."

"Because I'm hungry and I want to eat you and your children."

"I don't have any children."

"Then I'll let you live to make children with Kaori, so that I may eat them before I eat you."

Dōm Coquí and Al faced Michael and his large smile. They watched Kaori punch Michael to the floor.

The spoon glowed red. "Enough! Get on with it!"

The referee raised his hand, and Dōm Coquí made a fist. "Ready…fight!"

Dōm Coquí felt a fist to the top of his head slam him, like a hammer on a nail. His knees bent and vibrated. He swayed side to side and fell on his back. His legs twitched like a dying roach.

Al placed her foot on his chest and raised her arms up in the air.

The referee raised his arm. "Winner…Al!"

Dōm Coquí's tongue wrapped around Al's snout and caught her off guard. He retracted his tongue, pulling her down. The momentum tripped Al up, and Dōm Coquí threw his fist up, ramming it into her nose. The impact broke his knuckles and Al's nose. His tongue returned to his mouth; the taste was salty and bitter. Dōm Coquí slid his body back and saw Al covering her bloody nose. It was so sensitive Al could not get up. Dōm Coquí crawled away from her and lifted himself to his feet. He limped back to his friends.

"You're a little late, Coquí," Michael said, placing his hands on Dōm Coquí's shoulders. "But good job on messing her up. It may pay off in the endgame."

Al crawled back to her comrades in shame and fell over, knocked out. Her eyes turned to spirals.

✳ ✳ ✳

Sam stepped forward, cracking his knuckles. He arrived at the center of the circle with his finger pointed at Jamal. The fighter used his thumb and slid it across his neck.

"Pathetic," said Jamal, approaching Sam with his hands in his pockets. He stood before Sam with eyes half closed, watching him stretch and crack his back. He sighed.

The referee raised his hand. "Ready…fight!"

Sam threw a punch, but Jamal shifted his shoulder to the side. He threw a flurry of punches, and Jamal dodged each one, his hands still in his pockets. Then Sam left an opening, and Jamal lunged forward, ramming his forehead into his opponent. Sam fell to the ground and rubbed the bruise.

Jamal stepped back and took his hands out of his pockets. He opened the palm of his right hand and gathered ki. "This palm glows…from the mighty Flow!"

Jamal's eyes lit up, and he saw Sam channel the Flow as well. Jamal's green ki energy clashed with Sam's blue ki energy: sparks flew, and heat waves bent the air. There was a mutual sense that this was going to decide the fate of their match.

The fighters took two steps toward each other and lifted off the ground. They looked like volleyball players reaching to slap the ball over the net. Instead, they targeted each other with a collective shout. "Streaming…Spike!"

In midair, their energies collided. Their hands pushed into the ki barrier that separated them from each other. The struggle sent a blast of wind outward. The force of the air knocked crates over. They could see the hatred reflected from their eyes. Their shirts ripped apart and exposed their muscular bodies.

With sweat trickling down his face, Jamal realized that he hadn't known how strong Sam had gotten. His opponent trained hard. Yet there was no sense of enlightenment coming from Sam. It was like yin to yang. As ridiculous as it was that Sam still held a grudge against him, Jamal was not going to take him lightly. He pushed his hand forward. Goosebumps raised on his skin from Sam's ki energy. Jamal felt his feet touch the ground. "How?"

"I'm stronger than you…more powerful than you… and soon, with you defeated, Julia will have her honor."

"Again with the hamster?!" In a flash, the thought of that terrible date with Julia drove Jamal mad. That lapse of emotion brought Sam's fingers close to his face. With Sam's strike within inches of him, Jamal grew tired of this madness and raised both hands at Sam's fingers, just before they connected with his face. He channeled the Flow and felt a tingling sensation in his fingers. Jamal's ki pushed Sam back to the ground.

"This can't be!" Sam said, and his body leaned back with the force of the energy. "I should be the one mastering the Flow!"

"Nobody's perfect," Jamal said. He slapped Sam in the face with both hands and he recited his setup move in Japanese. "Enlightened Flow Style!"

A ball of light formed between his palms and Sam's forehead and called out his attack in Japanese. "Dual Flash!"

A beam of light fired over Sam's head and shockwave of ki energy flowed throughout his body, this time with double the enlightenment.

Sam's legs wobbled like jelly. His ability to sense the Flow was gone, negated by the Flow of Jamal's two hands. The wind pushed the dust to the side in a radial blast. Sam's eyes stared at the ceiling when Jamal released his hands. With Jamal's back turned to him, Sam saw the Japanese Kanji for stream again, in flames.

"You are already blown up…twice." Jamal walked away from Sam.

A bright light from Sam's body exploded once, flipping his body over toward Wolfgang. When he landed on his face, he exploded again, right on top of Al, forming a pile of defeated losers. Sam lifted up his body with torn, smoldering clothes. "Too…much…awesome…ness…uh…"

Sam slumped over and the referee raised his hand. "Winner…Jamal!"

Jamal returned and Kaori helped him sit on the floor.

His hands trembled. His body was drained of energy. He saw Kaori's eyes tremble, too. Jamal let out a smile, and noticed Angela and Ely walking out to the circle.

"Angela," Jamal said, and Kaori turned around.

"Get back here, Angie-chan!"

"We have to do this, Kaori."

"Chupa. Chupa."

Angela saw Barry step forward. Ely growled at the Kaijuzoid summoner and his Trap-a-zoid. They hadn't forgotten what Barry did. Before they began, Angela turned to the spoon and glared at the utensil. What the spoon said earlier about the station gave her doubts. "Why did you imprison Naomi Steel?"

"She's not your concern."

"So you're not lying about that station in Andromeda. You and her are not the same?" Angela did not receive a response from the spoon, and she nodded. "I see. If you can hear me in there, Naomi, my friends and I will save you as well! If you can fight the spoon from inside, we'll be able to beat it together."

"Angela," Kaori said, and she called out to Naomi. "Angela is right, Steel-san! We'll do everything we can to rescue you as well, so if you can fight back, give it all you've got!"

The spoon glowed red. "Silence! And fight already!"

The referee raised his hand. "Ready… fight!"

"Time for revenge," Barry said, and aimed his Trap-a-zoid into the center of the circle. "Ironex! I want you!"

Barry pressed the button on his Trap-a-zoid, and a purple light struck the floor. A large turtle shell with spikes all around its body appeared before Angela and Ely. It was metal, and as big as a car. Fleshy gray legs stuck out and lifted the shell off the floor. An iron ball popped out at the end of its tail. When its snapping turtle head stuck out, it wore an official Kaijuzoid baseball cap.

"Ironex!"

"How do you like my new Kaijuzoid? It's Rank SS+++. There's no way your No Rank Kaijuzoid can beat my buddy."

"Ironex!" nodded the Kaijuzoid.

"How many times do I have to tell you?" Angela said, crossing her arms. "Ely is not a Kaijuzoid."

"Chupa. Chupa." Ely nodded, pounding her fist into her palm.

"We'll see." Barry pointed at Ely and gave his orders. "Ironex! First Step!"

Ironex took a step forward. That made the ground shake, but it had no effect on Ely. Ironex jerked its head back. It watched Ely jump towards it, her teeth exposed. The Kaijuzoid stood there, waiting for its next order.

"Shell Duck!" Barry said, and Ironex tucked its head into its shell, just as Ely's teeth bit nothing but air. "Head Crash!"

Ironex's skull rammed into Ely's face at high speed. The attack knocked her senseless, and she stumbled around for a bit. Ironex watched Ely shake her head and growled.

"See?" Barry said. "If you had your Kaijuzoid in a Trap-a-zoid, it would obey everything you say."

"She's my friend. She doesn't obey me, she listens. Something you wouldn't understand."

"How silly of you." Barry's eyes lit up. "Hey?"

Ely planted her hand on Ironex's neck and bit into it. Her teeth vibrated and went numb. She stepped back, rubbing her cheeks.

"Oh yeah. I forgot to mention. It's an Iron Class Kaijuzoid. Its soft skin is as tough as iron. I hope your Kaijuzoid didn't lose its teeth."

"Come here, Ely." Angela knelt down and Ely ran to her. She checked Ely's teeth and saw a chip on one tooth. Angela gave her friend a tender hug and glared at Barry, already calling out his attack.

"Ironex! Iron Blast!"

Ironex opened its mouth, and a blast of grey light flew right at them. The blast consumed their bodies. When the light disappeared, they were bruised and burned. Ely lay unconscious in Angela's hands. She heard Barry laugh, and Kaori knelt beside her.

"Angie-chan…" Tears trickled down Angela's face. Kaori raised Seizon, but Angela grabbed Kaori's wrist and stood to her feet.

"Your defeat is a great gift for my eighteenth birthday," Barry said, and everyone took a step back in shock except Michael.

"You…" Angela said, her forehead veiled in shadow.

"You're eighteen years old and you're playing with Kaijuzoid?!"

"A lot of us adults play with Kaijuzoid," said Michael.

Angela's eyes shifted to Michael, and he hid behind Jamal. "I like Kaijuzoid, Jamal."

"That's nice, I-Man."

"Well, yeah," Barry said, and pressed the Trap-a-zoid to return Ironex. He turned to the referee. "Did I win or not?"

Angela ran up to Barry like a track runner. She was so fast that nobody could keep up with her. She left behind a trail of tears floating across the circle. Her fist rose up in the air and smashed into Barry's face. Then she grabbed his arm and spun him around until he slid on the ground. She stomped on his back and twisted his arm, turning his wrist in the opposite direction. Kaori smiled in pride. He screamed and tapped the floor with his other hand. Her trail of floating tears splashed on the ground. She released Barry and he passed out from shock. Angela walked past the referee; her eyes warned him to watch what he said next.

"Since this was a two-on-two fight and Ironex is not out to fight," he said, "this match is a draw."

Wolfgang roared. "Damn!"

The Union moaned at the fact that the tournament remained tied. Wolfgang saw Michael staring him down with a smirk. He noticed that Michael's friends were still on their feet, and he watched Mr. Tanaka toss Barry on top of Al and Sam, adding to the pile of losers.

Angela took Ely from Kaori's hands and hugged her.

She heard Ely breathe and felt Kaori move her hair aside. Angela took a deep breath and smiled, staring at Seizon.

"Thank you for teaching me those moves, Kaori."

"What?!" Wolfgang said.

✳ ✳ ✳

Mr. Tanaka walked toward the circle. Kaori approached the landlord, resting his hands on his cane. Whoever won this next match would give an edge to either Michael or Wolfgang.

She tapped Seizon on her shoulder. "Hello, pervert."

"How dare you?!" Mr. Tanaka aimed his cane at her face. "If you hadn't interfered with the yakuza, I would have won my apartment."

"Then my friends would not have a place to live." Kaori looked back at everyone. "And I refuse to let my friends live in the streets."

Kaori saw Mr. Tanaka hold his wooden cane up like a sword. She jerked her head back, and the landlord made practice swings. Kaori held Seizon up, waiting for the match to begin.

The referee raised his hand. "Ready…fight!"

The wooden sword and the wooden cane clashed. Each swing was fast. The snaps echoed around the high ceiling. Kaori and Mr. Tanaka ran around in a circle. Mr. Tanaka's cane was so strong that when it struck the crates, they exploded on impact, and Ohayō Kitten dolls burst out like a volcanic eruption. Kaori's Seizon sliced through a crate and it burst into droplets of light, erased from existence, leaving behind a pile of Ohayō Kitten dolls. They both stopped for a moment to catch their breath.

Mr. Tanaka watched the dolls land on the ground. His arms shivered. "The yakuza warned me not to destroy their smuggled shipments. I may have to pay them off for this."

Kaori spoke to Michael, without taking her eyes off Mr. Tanaka. "Why isn't his sword disappearing? Is his cane made from something powerful?"

"Maybe…don't drag it out too long, Kaori."

"Actually," said Mr. Tanaka, "this was owned by Yagyu Munenori."

Kaori stepped back. "Miyamoto Musashi's great rival? The one awarded the post of official sword teacher to the shoguns? A post Musashi wanted. That Munenori?"

"Yes, that Munenori." Mr. Tanaka raised his cane up. "Perhaps we should make this a final strike."

"Fine." Kaori raised her sword up. "We don't have time for this."

Kaori and Mr. Tanaka slid their feet toward each other. They stared each other down, reading each other's faces, reading their eyes, reading their body movements. This was a big moment. In one step, they launched their bodies toward each other. Step by step, the image of Musashi and Munenori appeared. Two of Japan's greatest samurai charged and ran past each other. Swords swung, and the sound of a clang shook the crates. With backs to each other, Kaori and Mr. Tanaka smiled.

Mr. Tanaka's sword burst into droplets of light, as well

as his belt buckle, and his pants fell, exposing his white underwear with a smiling cat face. His body lurched back in
shock, the power of her strike drained him of energy, and
Kaori dropped to her knees, collapsing to the floor.

Jamal and Angela ran up to her. "Kaori!"

They stood over her, and Kaori winced from the pain,
but she smiled at them.

"Winner… Mr. Tanaka!"

As Jamal and Angela held Kaori up and escorted her
back to the group, Mr. Tanaka walked past them, holding
his pants up. With little energy left, he flopped on the pile of
losers and fainted.

✳ ✳ ✳

The score was now two wins for the Amalgamated
Union of Malicious Malcontents, one win for The
Impossible Man's Anime and Manga Shop, and one
tie. So the lead favored Wolfgang, though Michael still
smirked. As Wolfgang entered the circle, Michael waved
Dōm Coquí over. Dōm Coquí presented the bookbag,
and Michael stood in front of it, blocking Wolfgang's
view. He unzipped it.

"Scared, The Impossible Man?"

Michael approached Wolfgang without the book-
bag. It appeared out of nowhere at the far end of the circle
near Yuki. The referee held his hand up, and Wolfgang and
Michael just stared at each other, neither making a single
move. Everything was tense. Michael's eyes trembled. He

wanted to look at Yuki, but he kept his focus on his opponent. There was a clang on the floor.

Michael and Wolfgang shifted their eyes, and there was the spoon, bouncing on the ground. Yuki's body was covered in a red aura, and the A.R. Field vanished. The Impossible Man looked at his hands, smirked, and raised up two fingers with a thumb extended. His friends took one step back. The referee raised his hand. "Figh—"

Suddenly, Michael stood before Yuki from out of nowhere, and Wolfgang ran with a sonic burst past the referee. Michael felt a punch to the face and flew into a pile of broken crates. He appeared out of nowhere again, beside Wolfgang, and swung his leg into Wolfgang's face. The impact sent Wolfgang sliding to the ground. Michael watched, reaching for Yuki, but Wolfgang tackled Michael and pinned him to the ground.

"I will have my wish."

"Over my dead body."

"So shall it be."

"What does that even mean?" Michael tried to make sense of Wolfgang's comment, and he felt Wolfgang's elbow rammed into his stomach. Michael lost air for a moment, and with a deep breath, he had Yuki in his arms. Before he could kiss her, Wolfgang pulled Michael's hair back and dragged him away. Michael stood behind Wolfgang from out of nowhere. Wolfgang saw Mr. Tanaka in Michael's place.

Michael appeared before Jamal to hand Yuki over, but when Jamal touched her body, a burst of red light repelled him back. Michael felt his back punched by Wolfgang and growled. Michael dropped to his knees, and Yuki's body rolled away. As he nursed his wound, Wolfgang walked past him and knelt before Yuki. Michael's friends jumped on top of Wolfgang to stop him from kissing her, but his muscles pushed them away. Michael stood to his feet, and the book-bag shook.

Before Wolfgang kissed Yuki, he felt the cold floor on his feet. He saw that his shoes and socks were gone. When he turned around, Michael was not behind him. He turned back and Yuki was gone. Suddenly, Michael appeared, hold-ing Yuki up, and his lips came close to hers. Charging like a bull, Wolfgang roared. The bookbag rolled between him and Michael. When his left foot stepped beside the opened bookbag, he screamed out loud. He slipped on the floor and slid into Michael and Yuki, separating them.

Wolfgang lifted his foot up, and emerging from the bookbag was a giant Japanese spider crab, takaashigani, gripping his toe—orange with white spots, its legs stretched out and its hard shelled body emerging. Its outstretched legs, from end to end, were as long as Wolfgang was tall. Its claw snapped at the toe as though it were cutting paper. As Michael rolled Yuki over to him, Wolfgang removed the crab and threw it at Michael's face, knocking his head back. Wolfgang lunged forward, punched Michael away from Yuki, and sent him flying into the crates. Then he pulled Yuki over and drew his lips close to hers, but the crab re-turned and clipped Wolfgang's other foot. He ignored the pain, closed his eyes, and kissed her.

"I wish to be like The Impossible Man," he said. "I want his powers. It will help me beat my former employers." When Wolfgang opened his eyes, he jerked his head back. There was Dōm Coquí, smiling at him.

"My hero…" Dōm Coquí said.

Wolfgang roared, wiping his lips, stumbling backwards.

As the spider crab stood guard, The Impossible Man gently lifted Yuki's head up. He gripped her right hand tight and pressed his lips into hers. The red aura around Yuki shattered like glass and rained down. Yuki's fingers crossed his fingers, her left hand caressed his cheek, and she returned his kiss. It lasted. As a white light consumed Michael and Yuki, they looked into each other's eyes.

"So this is what it's like to be a hero."

Episode 20

[~ Who is The Impossible Man? ~]

Well, that's it. This is the end. As our story comes to a close, you will now know who The Impossible Man is. I know. I know. Why not just tell you all from the start? Well, by now, you got a handle on the life of The Impossible Man. You seem ready to handle the truth. After all, we wouldn't want you to lose your mind and suffer déjà vu, like Yuki. So in conclusion, I hope you all enjoyed this little tale. When you come again to Denfair City, remember to ask for I-Man's, and people will point the way. In the words of The Impossible Man...

Oyasumi Nasai ... Buenas Noches ... Good Night.

May 20, 2002

"Who is The Impossible Man?" said a mysterious female voice in the air to Yuki, still in her costume within the white light.

"That's what I'd like to know," Yuki said, floating in the world of white. There was no end in sight. No ground to stand on.

"Who is The Impossible Man?"

"Is it Michael?"

"Who is The Impossible Man?"

"Tell me already! I can handle it!" Yuki blinked once and found herself in darkness. There was an aura of familiarity around her. "Am I in the store?"

A single white lightbulb above her turned on. She was inside the store, but within that light, and beyond it was darkness. Piece by piece, Yuki saw the place filled with customers of all ages. It was a busy day. A couple of children ran by her, laughing. They purchased the latest giant robot models from Michael. A couple of teenagers entered the store and peered through the latest anime DVDs on the shelves. Businessmen picked up the manga books and approached Michael as he smiled, scanning the barcodes. "I don't understand."

"What you see," the female voice said, and the store disappeared, "…was not his dream."

"It's not?" Yuki saw one red lightbulb shine in the darkness.

A boy's voice spoke from it. "Are you crazy, Michael? You think you can make an anime series?"

Another red light shined, and a girl's voice spoke. "Nobody in Japan is going to watch that. They stick with their own kind and never use outsiders."

Mr. Tanaka's voice echoed. "Gaijin!"

It came from another red lightbulb, and Yuki turned around, covering her mouth.

A bedroom appeared around her. It was not Michael's apartment, but somewhere else. She saw Michael sitting before a computer on a desk. He was a teenager, at least thirteen. Yuki walked past his bed and stood behind him. She leaned over, and when she saw how young he looked, she smiled. Next to him lay an essay called 'Anime and Manga Culture,' dated around the 1990s. It had received a grade of C, and had this note from the teacher:

'It will never happen.'

Yuki tried to pick it up to read it, but her hand went through it like a ghost. "Why?"

"Ha ha ha!" The laughter caught Yuki's attention. She turned around and saw each red light shine for each student, laughing at Michael.

"You don't even draw," said a boy in a red lightbulb. "So how are you going to make a manga?"

"What's a MAN-ga?" said a girl from the adjacent lightbulb.

"Whoever heard of a Puerto Rican making an anime in Japan?"

"You'll never have any of your games picked up by a Japanese company either. It's impossible."

Yuki watched red lights shine bright, leaving behind a dying white lightbulb. The laughter drifted into silence. As Michael picked up his creations, Yuki's tears fell. She choked up and wanted to reach out, to say to him that it could be done. She wanted to encourage him and tell him there was a way. "Please, don't give up."

She wiped away her tears and found herself in Michael's dorm, playing solitaire. He was in college now. She watched him play the game by the original rules, and he lost.

Michael took a deep breath and played it again backwards. He started from King to Ace, rather than the traditional Ace to King. This time he won. He repeated it over and over, and had an idea. The white lightbulb above slowly built up energy. He borrowed his mother's camera recorder and invited Jamal to his home.

Yuki was shocked to see how young Jamal looked, taking the camera and standing over Michael. She watched them record this feat, and after a long day, they registered it on the Internet.

"Hmm, let's see," Michael said, as Yuki looked at the screen. He was on the Internet, a website called 'Anime and Manga World.' A text box asked for a screen name to enter for the message boards. "A lot of people sure use the same name. Octopus17. Oil39. Cement890. Fire10903? I need a name that's original, one no one uses."

Michael opened his notepad. There was a list of plans, from creating video games to drawing manga. Included in that list was creating an anime and manga store with a checkmark next to it. It was at the bottom of the list, newly added in fresh ink. He stared into it for a while and curled his fist, looking at the teacher's note.

"It can't be done, he says." Michael turned to the screen. "I'll show him that it's possible."

Michael's eyes lit up, and he smirked.

Yuki tilted her head and leaned close to the monitor. She saw what he typed; she stood there for a moment.

Michael leaned back with a smile, his hands resting on the back of his head. "Yeah…"

Welcome, The Impossible Man. You will receive confirmation in your e-mail soon.

Yuki turned her head slowly to Michael. She looked like she was ready to strangle him. She had a lot on her mind, she knew what she wanted to say, but it did not come out the way she wanted.

"That's where he got the name from?! That's why he calls himself The Impossible Man?! A screen name?!!" Yuki stepped back, shaking her head side to side.

The female voice spoke. "At first, it was just a fun name for the Internet. Something he never took seriously until…"

The white lightbulb behind Yuki shined bright and got her attention.

"…they got it on the Internet."

Yuki turned back to the monitor, and there was a video of Michael playing solitaire backwards, receiving praise and criticism. The views increased enough that one person asked a simple question.

'Where is your store?'

Yuki's eyes grew wide, as Michael smiled.

As Michael and his desk disappeared, the female voice spoke. "It starts with discouragement."

"What starts with discouragement?"

"External disbelief. Internal failure."

"Failure?" Yuki found herself back in the store. She saw Michael and Jamal surrounded by "going out of business" signs hanging on the walls. She watched the duo finish packing up the boxes, ready to carry them outside, when suddenly a four-foot-tall naked frog walked past them. "Dōm Coquí?"

Yuki noticed that the storefront window did not have the frog emblem. She followed Michael and Jamal inside Michael's apartment, and there they watched Dōm Coquí slip on a muumuu. As Michael and Jamal turned to each other, Michael smirked, raising his hand up with a victory sign. She noticed him looking at his thumb for moment, and then he extended it with a nod.

"The third way, Jamal." Michael presented his three fingers.

"I don't understand." Yuki found herself floating under the white lightbulb, surrounded by the darkness.

"That's because the odds are against him. Many people tell him it can't be done. That it's impossible."

"Then what needs to be done?"

"The impossible," the female said aloud. Her voice echoed throughout.

"What is impossible?" Yuki turned her body around, trying to find the person.

"Everything in life."

"Nothing in life is impossible."

As her feet touched the ground, a red light shined above Yuki. A girl's voice spoke. "You will never be a magical detective, Yuki."

Yuki stepped back, and another red light shined over her head. "Ever since your fight with that frog, you hesitate to act due to shock."

"No."

Another red light shined. "I'm sorry…you failed your test. I can't recommend you for magical detective."

"It's not fair!" Yuki watched more red lightbulbs turn on within the darkness. At first her tears welled up, but instead she curled her fist and growled. "I found…I found a way to be a magical detective! I found…a way. It's just…impossible…but I know I can do it!"

A red lightbulb shined over a door. Yuki approached it and found herself before a door drawn in pencil on a wall. Then she had a flash of memory; it was when she told her supervisor that she wanted to take the detective-level case about the spoon. It was at that moment that she knew she had a chance to get that promotion by solving that case.

"I can do it." Yuki grabbed the flat doorknob. The lightbulb turned white. She opened the door, and stepped outside.

Yuki saw an endless field of hanging white lightbulbs. Each one shined brighter than the next. She took a couple of steps and turned around. The building she'd stepped out of was a large brown cardboard cube, and had a sign reading

'THIS END UP' with the arrow pointing at the door she'd exited from. She turned around to the field and heard different voices.

"I want to be a baseball star." Yuki saw inside a lightbulb, a boy looking out to the field.

"I want to be an astronaut," a girl said in another lightbulb, looking to the sky.

"I want to climb Mount Everest," an old man said in one more, looking at the picture of a mountain in a magazine.

Yuki stepped back and stumbled on a row of lightbulbs.

"No way." She saw Jamal, Kaori, Dōm Coquí, and Angela in their own bulbs. Her eyes grew wide, and she saw their dreams inside. She stepped back, turning around at all the lightbulbs, seeing the dreams of every person who aspired to success in their lives. She saw Michael's lightbulb, and her heart skipped. He stood in front of the storefront window with the frog emblem on it and a line of people waiting to go inside. "This is why he calls himself The Impossible Man?"

"More to it ..." Michael said with a female voice, behind Yuki from out of nowhere. His voice returned to normal. "... for I believe I can do anything."

Yuki turned around and stumbled back. She slapped Michael's shoulder out of reflex. "That was a pretty dumb voiceover."

"Yeah, well, it had to be done." Michael let out a cheesy smile. He felt Yuki's hands caress his face and shifted his head toward her. As Yuki showed frustration and exhaustion, Michael looked into her eyes.

"Please, tell me the truth," she said. "Who is The Impossible Man?"

"After my success in Japan," Michael said, holding one lightbulb in his hand, "I stumbled into this area out of nowhere. I didn't understand at first." He released that lightbulb, walked past Yuki, and gently held another. "Then I realized what The Impossible Man was all about."

Michael lifted his head up. "It is a state of mind."

"How?"

"It is ambition formed into a persona to achieve success." Michael released the lightbulb and turned to Yuki.

"Okay," she said, "but impossible is a contradiction."

"Impossible is a limitation. Patience and endurance… tenacity and drive…these are the applications of human perseverance. It allows us to realize our fullest potential to work hard and accomplish anything."

"Goals." Yuki had a flash of memory and realized something. "You never used the Rhythm to beat Mr. Tanaka for the apartment's title deed. The Impossible Man is not really about the powers. It's…us?"

"Yes. Flying to space…a simple job promotion…learning how to read a book after your mother read it to you in your bed. When people tell you 'it can't be done,' it's like they're telling you 'it's impossible.' So you go out, do the impossible, and make it a reality."

Yuki broke into a smile. Looking to the side, she processed his words, and nodded with a chuckle. A couple of cherry blossom petals fell past the lightbulbs and rained over her. A few petals planted themselves on her hair and shoulders. "So is it true what you said before? About life being impossible?"

Michael removed the petals from Yuki and held them gently in the palm of his hand. "Yes. Unless you want to live in that building." He pointed at the cardboard building.

Yuki took a couple of steps towards it. She looked around at the field and reflected on the differences between both worlds. She shook her head side to side and turned back to Michael. "Or I could just live out here."

Michael nodded, and Yuki saw the lightbulbs above her. "So is this how you use the Rhythm?"

"Oh, that … well, since I believe I can do the impossible, I just don't think about it and do the impossible."

"That's it?" Yuki blinked.

"Yeah." Michael nodded. He looked up, thought it over, nodded, and looked back at Yuki. "Yeah."

Yuki took his hand and placed it on her cheek. "I understand, Michael. I'll be here for you."

"Heh … I like you."

Yuki's eyes twitched.

"You're smart. You made me money, and unlike the others, you call me by my name."

"The Impossible Man?" Yuki looked him in the eyes and lightly gasped. "Michael."

He smiled. "Hearing your voice say my name makes me smile more than the store itself does. Like a star falling to my arms."

"I'm sorry for not consider—" Yuki felt Michael's

arm around her waist, and his hand interlocking with her fingers. "Oh…"

As Michael rocked Yuki back and forth, her smile grew wider. A lightbulb now appeared above them, and she saw an image of Michael watching her in the store. She recognized it as the day she'd suggested selling imports. His praise for her idea made her happy, because she'd helped him in a different way. Now she saw Michael had a dream of being with her. He struggled to say something to her. He looked at his shaking hands and walked away without saying anything. Seeing that image made her heart pulse and her chest heave. Michael never ignored her, all this time. He just didn't know how to approach her. She tightened her grip and pressed herself onto his chest, enjoying this moment.

As they danced away, the lightbulb above brightened and enveloped them. "Now about that first date, Yuki?"

Yuki opened her eyes and found herself in Michael's arms. Looking into his eyes, she smiled. She noticed the roof of the smelting factory, and broken crates around her. On reflex, she lifted herself up, and found Tsubasa in her hand. She saw her friends smiling in relief of her recovery. It was a peaceful moment until she saw the spider crab standing guard. She tracked its legs from point to point, her whole head turning from side to side. "That crab looks familiar."

Yuki noticed Wolfgang on his knees, his eyes widened at his defeat. The referee had yet to declare a winner.

Michael helped Yuki to her feet. "Yeah, I read the letter my mom sent me before you arrived. It's the one that distracted your mom in their fight. He calls himself Kahn."

Kahn snipped his claws, and Yuki tilted her head. "Oh, it knows Morse code."

"You understand it?"

"It was part of my training." Yuki listened. "Kahn said he hopes we finally settled our issues."

Michael waved. "Yeah, Kahn. Thanks for your help."

Kahn waved and Wolfgang screamed. "It's not fair!" He pointed at Michael and Yuki. "You cheated! Heroes don't cheat!"

"Hero?" Michael said. "I just own a store."

"You are a hero," said Yuki.

Michael saw it in Yuki's eyes, a person who saw more of him than he saw in himself. He processed the idea of being a hero, like her, holding Tsubasa in her hands, showing resolve despite what she'd gone through, standing tall. He nodded and faced Wolfgang with fists tightening.

Wolfgang stood to his feet with fists raised. "Our match isn't over, and the score is still two wins to one win to one tie. We have the lead."

"Oh…well, yeah." Appeared before Wolfgang from out of nowhere. "Okay then, Wolfgang. You want your wish. You got it."

Michael's friends pulled out their sunglasses, and handed an extra pair to Kahn. As the referee saw what they did, he closed his eyes. A strange wave rippled through the air, and Wolfgang screamed in horror.

Watching what was happening, Yuki took short breaths. She could not believe that Wolfgang had screamed for help. Learning who The Impossible Man was had overwhelmed him. Even Angela hugged Kaori, just to hide in her arms and not watch. Dõm Coquí took the referee by the hand and led him to a nearby box to get farther away. When the wave left, the referee opened his eyes and saw Wolfgang lying on top of the pile of his fellow Union members.

"Well, ref?" Michael said, standing before the pile.

The referee held his hand up. "Winner…The Impossible Man!"

Everyone cheered, and Yuki still could not figure what they were doing and why everyone looked beaten and bruised. Instead, she smiled, and suddenly found herself standing before the pile of losers.

Michael put on his sunglasses. "Scarlet Sorceress, would you do the honors? It's your turn to fight."

Yuki saw her friends ready to see her finish this conflict off. She understood what Michael was expecting, and nodded. Then she turned to Wolfgang and his allies, aiming her staff at them. She heard Wolfgang laugh hysterically, his face contorted in disbelief. He had no shoes and a swollen toe. Remembering how her mother lost—laying in the infirmary with a swollen toe as Michael's mother stood in disbelief, Yuki's mother silent on the defeat due to embarrassment—she laughed for a moment. With a deep breath, she cast her spell. "Shining Light!"

An explosion sent all five members of the Union into the air. One by one, each busted through the roof. They flew high into the sky until five stars flashed, one after another. Yuki found herself surrounded by her friends, cheering and congratulating her, but Michael stood quiet until the celebration ended.

The referee raised his hand up. "Winner by virtue of tiebreaker, The Impossible Man's Anime and Manga Shop."

As confetti fell from the sky, the referee left the scene, walking over the debris as if they were hills with the sun in the sky, and exited the building through the collapsed wall.

✳ ✳ ✳

The spoon, disoriented, floated into the air, and Michael swept the utensil into his hands from out of nowhere. "No!"

"Yes!" Michael smiled like a monster ready to feast on its victim. He felt the spoon pull his arm in the air, struggling to break free. So he tightened his grip, and the spoon felt weak.

The spoon was shocked. "My energy! What happened to my energy?!"

Out of nowhere, Michael pounded his fist into the start button by the conveyor belt. He saw his friends, as the scrap metal rolled along the moving platform. The metal entered a furnace that led to another room. "No, they'll stop me from finishing you off, spoon. Let's go somewhere private."

"Let me go!" the spoon said. It glowed a little, but not enough to stop Michael. It found itself in another room, staring at an inclined spigot leading to an empty vat. It was the other side of the furnace, and molten metal spilled out, intense and red with heat. The spoon pulled Michael's hand, trying to escape. It glowed red again, but was faint. The spoon realized all its energy was used on possessing Yuki. It needed to recover.

"Real smart, choosing a metal recycling plant as your hideout." Michael thrust his hand over the liquid metal. The frost around his arm melted and evaporated. The heat swelled and blistered his hand.

"Are you crazy!?" the spoon said, and Michael brought the utensil close to his face.

"You can die... die a horrible, horrible death."

"Wait, you don't understand," the spoon said.

"Don't understand?" Michael giggled like a lunatic. "You couldn't leave me alone. You tried to kill my friends. You wouldn't leave me alone. You hurt Yuki. You didn't leave me alone. Oh, and did I forget to mention... you never left me alone! Why?! Why?!"

"I need a body to be free." The spoon looked at the molten steel and sighed. "Fine, I'll confess. The woman that I imprisoned, she tried to apprehend me when I broke out of my cell, so I trapped her in my pocket dimension. I hid in the warden's personal ship and used the escape pod. I ended up here. At first, I was found by some auctioneers. They discovered my power and put me on sale. Before I was sold, someone took me away and hid me in a pizza box."

"Who hid you?" Michael stared at the spoon, unaware of Yuki slipping through the door alone, staying hidden for a surprise attack.

"I don't know. I just saw a hand. It was like a shadow from a mist."

Yuki lifted her head up, and a still memory of the file Michael handed over flashed in her mind. Her memories fought the childhood trauma it was inflicting on her. She punched a panel and took a deep breath. As the spoon continued talking, Yuki regained her focus.

"Then you came into my life. Your energy was so amazing, but it as too intense to possess. Then that day of the storm, I ended up possessing the woman you call Naomi Steel after being struck by lightning. Her cyber energy was incompatible with my own. Yuki however…"

Michael straightened his back. "I see."

"Right? Her magical energy was perfectly compatible. If I had Yuki's body, I would have freed Naomi Steel, and I would have been freed from that cursed spoon." Michael's left eyebrow raised, Yuki lifted her head up with the idea of two spells popping up in her mind like a light switch, and the spoon continued. "She would just have my energy merged with hers, and my memories. With our energies, we would be together, The Impossible Man."

Michael lowered his eyebrows. "Who are you, really?" He moved his hand close to the liquid metal. "Tell me!"

"No." The spoon shook in a panic. It tried one more time to break free, but failed. "You wanted Yuki, right? Her body?"

Yuki hesitated to make her move and listened.

"She isn't just a body." Michael pulled the spoon right to his face, and Yuki's eyes lit up. The lamps above brightened the area. "She's smart, nice, gentle, happy, caring. She's there when you need her. What good is Yuki if she's just a body without those feelings I care about? No…those wouldn't be her feelings. They would be yours, and I…don't…like…you."

"Come on, you know you like her figure. Remember the hot springs? How you fell for her so easily when I took the shape of her body?"

Michael growled. "You've forgotten how I kept running away from you in the springs."

"Come on! You're a man. Men love a woman's body."

Yuki stepped out from hiding. "Some woman you are, spoon!"

Her presence startled Michael, and he almost lost his grip on the spoon.

"Yuki?" Michael said, holding the spoon over the river of metal.

"Don't listen to her, Michael. She would never understand how you feel about me." Yuki took a step, but Michael held his hand up.

"Don't come any closer." He turned his attention to the spoon.

Yuki saw it and tightened her grip on Tsubasa. "I felt you, spoon. Your cold heart. Using me to hurt the one I care about more than I ever felt about my own career."

"Yuki," Michael said, and Yuki closed her eyes, taking a deep breath.

"You don't understand, Michael! You don't understand his feelings at all!" She relaxed, lifted her head up with gentle eyes, and smiled. "Go for it, The Impossible Man."

Michael lifted his head. He looked Yuki in the eyes, and she presented Tsubasa. The way she said The Impossible Man was different from how others had said it. He nodded, and turned to the spoon. Together, Michael raised the spoon over his head and Yuki raised Tsubasa over her head.

"Shield…and Gentle Bless." She chanted. As Tsubasa glowed blue, so did Michael's hand, and Yuki felt the Rhythm guiding her energy to cast two different spells at the same time. She felt her heart expand and she made it pour her trust onto Michael's energy when she heard his next words.

"This is why…I AM…THE IMPOSSIBLE MAN!"

Michael dunked his hand into the molten river. He felt the spoon shaking and heard it screaming. It suffered in ways unlike any other. Michael screamed with the utensil, and it lifted its lion head out of the river, bending back with a gurgling sound. A beam of light shot out from its red eyes into the air. A portal opened. Michael saw a body in the fetal position inside the portal. "Naomi's coming out!"

"I can't get her!" Yuki stood helpless to keep Naomi from falling into the molten river. Then she saw it. A ghostly image of Michael reaching over the river with one hand, while keeping the other submerged in the liquid metal. Michael pulled Naomi away from the molten river with one arm. It looked so natural that her mind handled what she saw; she never forgot the sight.

Michael's ghostly image placed Naomi's body on the floor, and he felt the spoon break apart inside the river. Frost covered his free arm and turned into a block of ice. The image pulled itself back into Michael's body, and he turned around, facing Yuki. His legs now covered in a block of ice, he took one step and slid across the ground, past Yuki. As Yuki's eyes grew wide at Michael passing by her, he merged with another ghostly image of his body. Standing before a tub of water nearby, he submerged the liquid metal covering his hand, and Yuki turned around, keeping Tsubasa aimed at Michael.

"Ergh…" Michael lurched over the tub, his legs covered in ice. He gasped for air, with the steam rise over his face. He saw Yuki losing strength, keeping her spell up. "Yuki, I can still feel the heat!"

"I can't hold on!" Yuki's knees buckled, but held up, and Michael screamed. She saw his eyes trembling. Scared that Michael had lost his hand, Yuki approached him, and he pulled his hand out, screaming.

"My hand!"

"Noooo!"

Michael smiled and pointed at her. "Gotcha…"

As Yuki raised Tsubasa over her head, ready to strike Michael, he slipped from his ice-covered legs, and his head hit the ground. He sat up in a reclined position, acting like nothing had happened.

Yuki sat on her knees and helped him sit properly. She saw him lift his hardened metal arm up. They laughed.

"Could you get this off, Yuki?"

"I'm too weak to get it off."

"I'm too weak to get it off, also."

They laughed out loud, and Michael lifted the metal

glove. There was an imprint of the lion's head welded tight onto it. They became silent, and he held the metal glove up.

Beyond the glove, he noticed a distinct energy surrounding the beam of light above the molten metal. "Yuki? Is that a spell?"

"Yes, it's Gentle Bless." Yuki faced Michael. "You can see it?"

He nodded. "It's amazing." They watched the spell take the form of a female body. The portal pulled her in.

"No! Don't send me back!" Her body was completely inside, struggling to break free. "Its dark and col—" The portal closed and only the sound of the machinery was left.

Michael spoke in Spanish. "Goodbye, spoon."

He took a deep breath, flicked his hand, and the metal glove landed on the floor with a thud. He lurched over Yuki's arm, and she lifted his head up, checking on him. Michael cracked a smile with a nod. They heard a moan near the molten metal river.

"Where am I?" Naomi said in Japanese.

"Naomi Steel!" Yuki and Michael said, watching Naomi struggle to her feet. Yuki dragged Michael across the floor, the ice on his legs leaving a trail of melted water. They approached Naomi, and Yuki released Michael. His body flopped to the ground with a thud.

"Are you okay, Steel-san?"

"You're…Yuki?" Naomi said.

"Yes. It's me."

"I felt your presence in the spoon." Naomi stroked her shoulder-length red hair and pressed her fingers on her tanned face. She examined her one-piece blue suit, now armor-less. There were silver sockets on her suit around her ankles and elbows. There was a plug on the back of her white vest and a yellow jewel on the front, just below her neck. It flashed on and off like a lightbulb. She tapped it with her fingers, and a holographic screen appeared before them. There was a picture of her face; it read "classified." Her name and age appeared under the photo. "Naomi Steel? Age nineteen? Is that my name?"

"You don't remember?"

"Everything is a blank." Naomi stood up as the screen turned off. She read the badge on her shoulder with the initials A.C.E. Then she took another look at her outfit. It was like a second skin on her. "What happened to me? And why am I wearing this tight outfit?"

Michael pinched his nose to keep from bleeding as he looked at Naomi. He opened his mouth to answer, but Yuki aimed Tsubasa right in his face. He let out a smile and raised his hands up for mercy.

"I'm looking up you." Michael's eyes were aimed up at Yuki's skirt. "I'm looking up you!"

"You better look up me, Michael." Yuki nudged his forehead with Tsubasa.

"Wait..." Naomi took her time and her eyes grew wide. "I'm a Lieutenant for the Artifact Corp of Engineers, a division of the Intergalactic Defense Force. The spoon?"

Michael pointed at the metal glove. "Over there, Ace."

"Ace?" Naomi turned to Michael, but Yuki waved at her to not worry about it. As Naomi approached the metal arm, Jamal and the others showed up.

"Is everybody okay?" said Jamal.

Michael sat up. "Yeah."

"Fire Claw!" Yuki cast, and flames in the shape of a claw swiped at Michael's legs melting the ice.

Kaori swung Seizon at the block of ice around Michael's arm, and it shattered into sparkles. "Where's the spoon?"

"With Naomi." Michael pointed to the metal block and watched her hold it in her right hand.

"Spun wo fa met."

"Yeah," Michael said, and Naomi tapped her right hand to make a scanner materialize over her right arm to analyze it. "I turned it into scrap metal. Thankfully, the spoon freed Naomi before it got destroyed."

Angela smiled and ran up to Naomi with Ely in her arms. "My name is Angela Rodriguez. This is my pet chupacabra, Ely."

"Chupa. Chupa." Ely reached out to shake Naomi's hand.

Naomi's eyes rolled back, and she fell over.

"Oh no!" Angela heard the sound of sirens outside growing louder.

Michael, from out of nowhere, propped Naomi on his back, holding Kahn in his hand. His legs buckled under him a little, but he regained his footing.

"Take it easy Michael." Yuki said. "You need to recover."

Michael smirked and tossed the bookbag to Dōm Coquí. He led everyone out of the building.

Yuki ran alongside Michael out the door. "Michael, you should tell her who The Impossible Man is so we don't have to go through this mess again."

"It's not as easy as you think," Michael said, turning the corner with the exit to the street up ahead.

Everyone spoke. "Just do it!"

They ran past Clipperstein and out of the junkyard. The police arrived once Michael and his friends were out of sight.

Two days later…

Inside Yuki's apartment, her brooch blinked on the coffee table in the living room next to the newspaper, reporting on her latest crime-fighting task near a school. She tapped it and her supervisor spoke.

"We've read your report." Suddenly, a horn outside blared beyond the windows. "Excellent job, Scarlet Sorceress."

"Thank you, supervisor," Yuki said, and sat on her couch. The horn got Yuki's attention.

"We've added this to your record and noted your new ability to cast two different spells at the same time. With these accomplishments, I have put in the recommendation to promote you to magical agent."

"Magical agent?" Yuki growled under her breath.

"Yes. You will remain assigned in America and continue to remain undercover as their store security guard."

The horn blared one more time. "Excuse me, supervisor." Yuki marched over to the window, opened it, and stuck her head out. "Would you stop honking the horn?! I'm having a phone conference right now!"

The man outside spoke. "I'm trying to pick up my date!"

"She's not going to jump out the window for you!"

One of the neighbors yelled, "Would you two stop yelling? I have to work at midnight again!"

"Buy some damn earplugs!" Yuki slammed the window and returned to the couch.

"Yuki," Supervisor said, her voice stunned at what she'd heard.

"Sorry, supervisor." Yuki sat down, crossed her legs, and leaned back. "So I have to be a magical agent?"

"Yes."

"And observe The Impossible Man?"

"Yes."

Yuki stared at the floor and closed her eyes. "But my report—"

"Still needs more information. 'Mostly harmless' is not good enough for the report."

"Yes, supervisor."

"Also, see if you can work together with Lieutenant Steele while we try and figure out how to contact this Intergalactic Defense Force she works for. We would like to discuss with their Artifact Corp of Engineers division. If they are involved with dangerous magical items, we would like to provide them assistance here on Earth."

"Yes, supervisor." Yuki looked down. "Hmm…"

"What's the matter?"

"Well," said Yuki, clenching her brooch tighter. "I had hoped for the magical detective promotion."

"Your scores are just too low. You need more

experience, especially out in the field. Being a magical agent is a good start. Keep up the good work and you'll get that promotion."

"I understand. Thank you."

"Good luck, Magical Agent Scarlet Sorceress." The brooch stopped blinking.

Yuki leaned back, staring at the ceiling. "As long as I have the case, I can stall them. They just want to make sure you're not a … threat." She turned her head towards Michael, standing across the room with arms crossed.

He lowered his arm and sat on a chair across from her. "I'm not worried, Yuki. Just keep doing your job and get your dream. As far as I'm concerned, they're on probation. If they don't mess with me, I won't mess with them. If they want my help, I'll think it over."

"Thank you." Yuki looked down. "And I'm sorry again."

"I'm not mad at you, so don't worry about it." Michael stood by the front door out of nowhere, ready to open it.

Yuki spoke. "So is our first date still on tonight?"

Michael turned his head slightly and let out that smile she liked. "Tonight. Pizza."

Yuki's eyes lit up like a little kid when she heard the word pizza. After Michael left, she reflected on everything that had happened since she got here, and the world Michael had showed her. She smiled, knowing she had a chance to become a magical detective.

Michael marched up the stairs and stood before Shinichiro's apartment. He opened the door and walked into the spotlight. Shinichiro appeared to the sound of the humming choir, the sputtering noise drowning out the melody. Michael crossed his arms.

Shinichiro lit his pipe and blew the rancid smoke at Michael. "You didn't show up yesterday, shrimp. I thought you'd given up."

"Since when have I ever given up a challenge?"

"Good to hear that. Now live up to your name, for today will be the last day of this challenge. You lose and it's game over."

"Sure," Michael said with a smirk. "But perhaps you could give me a reading first."

"Very well." Shinichiro pulled out his cup and dice. He slapped the dice into the cup and slammed it on the ground. When he pulled up the cup, the dice revealed two sixes. "The bones say you will win."

Shinichiro gasped at the stairs before him. He turned around, and Michael was facing the apartment door, showing the victory sign with his thumb extended. "I lost?"

"That's right." Michael turned around, his finger pointed at Shinichiro's face, trying to look cool.

"I admit defeat." Shinichiro stood to his feet and bowed. "I shall vacate the apartment."

"Do what you want with the apartment," Michael said, rubbing the back of his head. "You already paid your rent, so there's no point in throwing you out."

"Thank you." Shinichiro walked past Michael, entering his apartment. He stopped and looked back. "Curious. All this time, you rarely used your gift to throw me out. You could have won easily anytime. Why now?"

"It was fun." Michael shook his head 'no.' He sat down inside and looked up at Shinichiro, watching the old man's energy wave in the air like a gentle wind. "I was disrespecting you for not using the Rhythm, given your abilities. I'm sorry. Truth is, I didn't show up yesterday because, after everything that happened with the spoon, it got me thinking about my powers. I felt like I had abused this power and took everything around me for granted."

"Oh?" Shinichiro sat down in front of Michael. "So you were worried about abusing it when taking on my challenge?"

"Yeah…I never even knew everyone had a name for it. The Rhythm. What a name."

"It is a remarkable gift."

Michael chuckled, and then lowered his head. "I wasn't paying attention to these things. I wasn't paying attention to everyone…to Yuki. I was so focused on accomplishing the impossible with my store that I…" Michael nodded. "Whether for game or for gain, I have to take a moment to look back at where I came, because everything forward will never be the same."

"I see." Shinichiro lit up his pipe. "I appreciate your honesty. Thank you."

He blew smoke and smirked.

Michael screamed, flying down the stairs, and landed in

front of Naomi, dressed in a t-shirt and shorts. He bounced past her and slammed face first, upside down, on the wall. His body peeled back and rolled along the wall until he laid across on the floor like a bear rug.

Shinichiro looked from the top of the stairs. "It will be my pleasure living here. It's so lively."

"Me and my big mouth," Michael said, and his body twitched. He turned his body over to Naomi, resting his head on his hand in a reclined state. "Hi, Naomi."

"Does this happen every day, sir?"

"Sir?" Michael eyebrow twitched and spoke under breath. "I work for a living." He shook his head and answered her question. "Depends. Maybe. I don't know."

Naomi presented him with her application.

"I followed your mother's instructions, sir. Everything should be in order."

"My mother?" Michael took the application, and Naomi stood straight like a soldier. He read it and saw his mother's signature. His head slipped off his hand, bumping the floor. "Mother—"

Yuki climbed the stairs behind them. "Yes," she said. "Your mother. I called her and my mother and told them everything that happened. She helped arrange Naomi's hiring, and she gets one of the apartments. Also, she said she left you a message three weeks ago. You never returned her call."

"Sir, I need funds to create a communications device to contact my captain," said Naomi. "Your technology is underwhelming, which means I'm stuck here on Earth. So I need a place to stay undercover."

"Are you an alien?"

"No. Just a scavenger hired to work in your store … as far as the public is concerned."

"Great." Michael walked down the stairs from out of nowhere, leaving Yuki and Naomi behind. "Fine. Pick an apartment Naomi, and Yuki will show you around the store."

"Roger!" Naomi said, giving Michael a salute to her forehead. As Yuki waved her to follow downstairs, Naomi saw something on the floor where Michael rested: a business card. She picked it up and read it aloud. "Shinichiro Katsuragi. Party Magician and Reader. Birthdays, Bar Mitzvahs, and Quinceañeras. Call Today."

Naomi looked up at the door for a moment and walked away.

✳ ✳ ✳

Michael entered his apartment and took out a box that read 'employee files.' He flipped the lid and scrolled through the files of his friends. Michael took an empty file and marked it Naomi Steel. He read her information and took out the standard forms for her to fill out. He stepped into the store, and Dōm Coquí headed outside, wearing his muumuu and sandwich advertising board, carrying a broom.

"Wait a minute, Coquí, we need you here."

"Syi."

Michael saw Kahn walking down the aisle writing on a clipboard, minding his own business. He turned to Jamal and placed the file before him.

After reading, Jamal dropped his head in disbelief. "Your mother?"

"Aey! No insults."

"I meant, your mom hired Naomi without your knowledge again."

"Oh." Michael shifted his eyes to the side and comprehended what Jamal meant. "Yeah."

"Before we get into this," said Jamal, shifting the computer monitor. "Look at what Naomi did."

Michael and Dōm Coquí leaned close to the screen and saw nothing different. When Jamal clicked on the mouse, pointing at a folder marked monitor, the scanner gun fired a holographic screen out of thin air, with a holographic keyboard.

"Codenwa?" Dōm Coquí leaned close to the hologram.

"She modified the computer." Jamal slid his hand over the hologram, moving the pointer and tapping it. The screen showed their entire inventory, up to date and in order.

Michael growled. "She organized my disorganization!"

"Idiot. She's used some insane high-tech on our computer. I've never seen anything like this."

"Ow kin?" Dōm Coquí touched the screen and it rippled like water.

Michael slapped Dōm Coquí's hand to make him stop. "That must be what she learned from the Intergalactic Defense Force."

"Maybe." Jamal tapped on the hologram, scrolling through the list. "Well, she made our files better. The loading time is like turning on a light switch, and it's virus free."

"Gentlemen, she can rebuild it. She has the technology. She has the capability to make the world's first bionic register." As Michael nodded, a sweatdrop appeared behind the backs of Jamal and Dōm Coquí's heads.

"Hibentori?"

Jamal nodded. "Good idea. We could let her handle orders, shipping, and inventory, since she could keep things well organized."

"Syi." Dōm Coquí and Jamal looked at Michael.

"Do it."

A courier truck parked outside. It caught Jamal off guard, though Michael smiled. As Dōm Coquí opened the door for the deliveryman, Michael hurried over to the corner of the store and made space.

As the deliveryman pushed the large crate inside, Jamal approached Michael. "What is that? Deliveries aren't until another two hours."

"A very special package I've been waiting for." Michael signed the clipboard as Kahn raised its legs over the aisle to observe. "Something to add to the store."

Michael took a crowbar from out of nowhere, and with one pull, the crate fell apart. He stood before Dōm Coquí and Jamal, their mouths wide open. Before them was a statue of a giant white carrot-looking vegetable with the roman numeral IV etched on it.

"Qwani?"

"Daikon Statue Number 4." Michael pushed the statue into the corner. "Limited Edition."

Jamal's left eye twitched. "How much are we selling it for?"

"We're not selling it." Michael brushed it with a rag, wiping his fingerprints off, and Jamal crushed the order form. "It's going to be for display only."

"Michael…" Jamal towered behind Michael, enveloping him in a shadow of darkness. The anger in his eyes projected onto him.

Kaori walked Naomi into the store with Angela, Ely, and Yuki. "You're going to like working here, Steel-san. This is a very peaceful store and—"

They saw Michael trapped in Jamal's headlock, receiving punches from Dōm Coquí.

"We're selling that statue, Michael, and we're making back the seven thousand dollars you spent on this!"

"Waka!"

"Okay, okay!" Michael smiled at Kaori, though Dōm Coquí's punches kept striking his face. "Hello."

"Put Michael down, boys," Kaori said, walking past them approaching the statue. "You don't know where he's been."

"Fine." Jamal released Michael.

Michael fell to the ground, and Kahn stood before him. He watched the spider crab clack his claws a couple of times, and Naomi translated. "He's says you're an idiot for screwing with the budget."

Kaori turned to Naomi. "I know, right? It's like nature to him."

"Aey!" Michael got up and stood at the counter out of nowhere. "Naomi…"

"Yes sir!" Naomi stood straight like a good soldier, and sweatdrops hung over everyone's heads.

"Uh…at ease?"

Naomi moved her feet apart and placed her hands behind her back. She saw Michael signal her to relax. She tilted her head in confusion.

"It's time for a meeting."

As Michael prepared to hold the meeting, Jamal whispered into Kaori's ear, "Let's talk after this."

Kaori turned to Jamal with a snap. Staring eye to eye, she nodded. Then she turned back to the counter and lowered her head. Her face lightly blushed as Michael spoke.

"It's a tradition, Naomi, that we all introduce ourselves to the new employee, and you introduce yourself."

"Oh…" Naomi said. She stood before everyone. "I am the Artifact Corp of Engineers' Lieutenant Naomi Steel of the Intergalactic Defense Force! You may call me Ace! I will be…I will be…what?"

"Inventory," Michael said.

"Inventory! I hope we all work hard and do our best!" Naomi stood straight, bowed in a perfect angle, and saw everyone overwhelmed with her introduction.

Angela raised her hand. "My turn. I'm Angela Rodriguez. I'm the intern."

"Yuki Shimizu. I deal with security."

"I'm Kaori Saito. I handle public relations."

"Jamal Jones. Store partner and management."

Kahn snapped his fingers, and Yuki translated. "Kahn, accounting."

Kaori turned to Michael. "Seriously!?"

"He's good at tapping numbers. Just let him have his dream."

"Dōm Coquí. Ri re pe na ta wescut."

"What did he say, sir?" Naomi turned to Michael.

"He said he's the resident fool."

"Waka!"

"Loco!" Michael leaned his head on Dōm Coquí's forehead and they both pushed at each other, like a pair of rams. Dōm Coquí stepped back, making Michael stumble forward. The frog stuck out his long tongue, slapping him in the face twice, as if it were a hand. Michael chased Dōm Coquí out of the store, passing by the window. The frog jumped out of the sandwich board and taunted him until they were out of everyone's sight. "Get back here, you stupid frog!"

Yuki crossed her arms. "Idiots."

Kaori placed her hands on her hips. "They never learn."

As Angela smiled, Ely broke free and ran outside, waiting at the door. Naomi just stood there, watching Michael chase Dōm Coquí across the street. She could not believe what she just saw. A pen appeared before her face. Naomi turned to Jamal, who presented her employee tax form.

"Welcome to I-Man's. We'll help you out with the rest of the forms if you need us...and don't worry about those two fools. This is routine."

"Thank you," Naomi said, hearing the loud noise outside. She looked out the window, watching the two run by the front of the store again. Ely, with hearts for eyes, jumped on Michael's back. She heard Michael's scream. "Heh… they're funny."

It was another typical day at The Impossible Man's Anime and Manga Shop. Everyone inside watched Michael and Dōm Coquí run along Grove Street, with the people outside passing by minding their business. The first customers of the day parked their cars and entered the store.

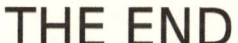
THE END